HAVE LOVE WILL TRAVEL

ELAINE REED

ISBN: 978-1-7342959-4-8

Published by Fabulist
Released in the United States of America
Developmental Editor: Patricia S. Cook, lastword.biz
Line Editor: Jessica Cale
Cover Art and Formatting: Suzanna Chriscoe,
ElefontBooks.com

Disclaimers

Dedication

For all the career girls/gays/non-binary baes.

Contents

Chapter 1 1
Chapter 2 11
Chapter 3 21
Chapter 4 27
Chapter 5 39
Chapter 6 57
Chapter 7 65
Chapter 8 83
Chapter 9 97
Chapter 10 103
Chapter 11 109
Chapter 12 113
Chapter 13 121
Chapter 14 129
Chapter 15 135
Chapter 16 151
Chapter 17 163
Chapter 18 177
Chapter 19 187
Chapter 20 195
Chapter 21 203
Chapter 22 211
Chapter 23 223
Chapter 24 235
Chapter 25 239
Chapter 26 243
Chapter 27 249
Chapter 28 257
Chapter 29 263
Chapter 30 277
Chapter 31 289
Chapter 32 299
Chapter 33 309
Chapter 34 317
Chapter 35 325
Chapter 36 331
Chapter 37 337
Chapter 38 349
Chapter 39 355
Chapter 40 359
Chapter 41 371
Chapter 42 379
Chapter 43 391
Chapter 44 403
Chapter 45 407
Chapter 46 415
Chapter 47 421
Chapter 48 429
Chapter 49 433
Chapter 50 447
Chapter 51 461
Chapter 52 471
Acknowledgements 479
About the Author 481
Also by Elaine Reed 483

CHAPTER 1

I-95 North Jacksonville to Savannah

Sue tapped her fingers discordantly against her car's gear shifter, her thoughts racing at light speed. Her to-do list was miles long, but instead of tackling those things, she had to drive. Jacksonville to Savannah was only about two hours, but this last hour crawled, even though Sue drove a good fifteen miles over the speed limit.

"Suse!" Darryl nudged her hand. "You're way off the beat. You okay?"

"Huh?"

"You've been on the road with us for a few months. You should be able to keep a rhythm by now," the keyboardist said. "What's going on?"

"Oh." Sue moved her hand from the shifter to the steering wheel, flexing her fingers along the way. When she'd joined the Words Fail Me tour as their publicist, she knew she'd face intense situations. She figured it would be along the lines of lost luggage, bad photos, and quotes attributed to the wrong band member. Not accusations of someone spreading a sexually transmitted infection and secret love children. "Yeah. Just thinking."

"About Adam?"

She smiled. Adam had been on her mind. The man had been putting himself in her path ever since they'd met by accident in a taco bar in Texas. It hadn't taken much for her to agree to a date, then another. And another. In fact, they had a date planned in Atlanta in a few days. She'd been thinking about how to get to the city before the band and maybe stay a little while after to give her more time with Adam.

Until she and Darryl stopped for gas and Sue had gotten a call from that reporter. Julie, the one who'd been a thorn in her side since Words Fail Me had their run of shows in Texas a few weeks ago. Julie had it out for Chris, the band's bass player and womanizer, and apparently was willing to plumb the oceans to find dirt on him.

"Maybe," Sue said.

"Maybe, probably." Darryl turned down the music. "Kinda cool that he's gonna be in Atlanta when we are."

Sue nodded. It was cool. For now. She was touring with Words Fail Me straight through the summer leg in Europe. She'd best make the most of Atlanta; she'd likely be too busy after that. And if her relationship history—if it could even be called that—was any indication, Adam wouldn't wait around. She didn't expect him to, since her focus was entirely on her new PR business.

Her phone chimed, making her flinch, and the text alert flashed across the screen in her car.

TEXT FROM ADAM

Relief washed over Sue. Julie's accusations had been so wild that Sue didn't want anyone knowing about them until she spoke with Chris. If only he'd answered his phone when she called him after talking to Julie. That this text wasn't from him—or Julie—at least kept things quiet. For now.

"Speak of the devil," Darryl said. He reached toward the screen. "Do you mind?"

"Mmm," Sue hummed. The text might be flirty, but it wouldn't be intimate. At least his messages hadn't been so far. Adam knew she might be surrounded by people at any given moment, just like him. Still, she had fun titillating Darryl. It was a nice break from the anxiety she'd been stewing in.

"Ope! I should mind my own business."

"Yep."

Darryl pulled out his own phone. "I'm gonna text the guys and take bets on how dirty the text is."

Sue gave his leg a light punch. "Don't you dare." Then she hit the 'read text aloud' button.

Adam: Landed in Atlanta. You sure you want to see sportsball? We could go to the zoo instead. Make zoos our thing.

"Aww," Darryl crooned. "He wants a thing with you."

Sue rolled her eyes and tapped the button for talk-to-text. "I spend too much time with animals. Let's watch sportsball." She tapped send.

Darryl laughed. "The bus does sometimes smell like a zoo."

"It definitely feels like someone gave all the chimpan-zees energy drinks."

Adam: At least at the zoo you aren't trapped in the enclosure.

"Oof." Darryl clutched his chest. "Direct hit."

Sue smiled. "And that's why he gets another date."

She let Darryl play DJ for the rest of the drive, while she built more mental lists. Who to contact, how to respond, whether any of this even warranted a response. How to best protect Chris. Her lists kept growing, but she kept adding to them, trying to examine all the possibilities. She needed to be prepared so if the shit hit the fan, they would get as little on them as possible.

Not for the first time, she wondered why Chris had to fuck his way across the country. Couldn't he hit pause for a few stops?

They weren't on a tour. They were in a maze twisting from one mess to the next.

Savannah, Georgia

Sue and Darryl made it to the hotel first. As soon as Sue was alone in her room, she started texting Chris.

> *Sue: We need to talk as soon as you get to the hotel*
> *Chris: Call me now*
> *S: You'll want privacy*
> *C: These guys know all my shit*
> *S: Not this*
> *C: Doubt it*
> *S: Would you tell them if you had herpes?*
> *C: Prolly. Cept I don't*
> *S: A reporter says you do*
> *C: Im-fucking-possible*
> *S: You sure, fuckboi?*
> *C: Fuck you*
> *S: Meet me at the hotel.*

She sent him her room number along with a gory threat to meet her as soon as he stepped off the bus.

When he finally showed up, a good thirty minutes after the bus had arrived, Sue ended her call with Emily, her friend and attorney. She'd enlisted Emily to help figure out how the hell this reporter had pieced together this story.

"What do you want?" Chris stormed over the threshold as soon as Sue opened the door.

"The reporter from Austin who wrote the smear piece has something new." Sue closed the door and moved to the window, closing the drapes.

"I don't fucking have herpes."

Sue faced Chris and noted his set jaw and the vein throbbing at his temple. "Right. She has evidence of other things."

Chris contorted his face in aggravation. "What things?"

Better to rip off the bandage fast. "She said you got a woman pregnant."

"Untrue. I have the condom receipts to prove it." Chris balled his hands into fists, his face growing red.

"And the woman is pregnant again."

He threw his hands up. "What woman? In Texas? This was my first fucking trip to Texas. We got a few weeks before anyone pops a positive pregnancy test."

Sue winced, wishing she had better news to give him. "There's more."

"Of fucking course." Chris leaned against the dresser, arms crossed, a lethal glare aimed at her.

"According to Julie, the woman contacted the record label to find you. When she told them she's pregnant, they offered her money for an abortion."

"Was she looking for an abortion?"

"I don't know. All Julie said was that the woman wanted to reach you."

"What kind of asshole offers a random woman money for an abortion?" He kicked over a chair, his body vibrating, the furious look on his face a sign that it took a monumental control for him not to do more. "What kind of asshole?"

At a loss for words over his reaction, Sue shrugged.

"Gimme her number."

"Why do you want Julie's number?"

"Not the bitch reporter. The mother. Give me the mother's phone number."

"I don't have it."

Chris ripped the phone out of the wall, threw it across the room, walked over to it, and repeatedly stomped on it. Plastic pieces flew up around him. "Why the fuck not!" Chris stomped on the phone again.

Sue held perfectly still, hoping her calm would anchor him. She hadn't expected such vehemence, but in a way, she understood his reaction. As far as she was aware, no one in the band or on tour knew that someone had been looking for Chris. And instead of the record label passing along a message, they offered to pay the woman off and shooed her away. Sue couldn't fathom the logic. "The reporter told me this. Not the label. The label would contact Tom."

"Tom wouldn't keep this from me."

"No, he wouldn't." Tom, the band's manager, would've come to Sue with this information and they would've approached Chris together. Sue held her elbows. She hadn't been prepared for Chris to be this angry. It concerned her. Not for her safety. Chris wouldn't physically hurt her, but even when they'd argued, Chris had never been so... full of rage.

He gave the bits of phone another savage stomp. "How the fuck did the bitch find her?"

"I don't know."

"Fucking find out, Sue!" Anger radiated off Chris in waves.

She took a big step away. "I asked Emily to hire an investigator. I gave her all the information Julie gave me."

"Have you given me all the fucking information?"

Sue unlocked her phone, pulling up the photo from Julie. "Everything but this." She held out the image of the little boy.

Chris stalked across the room and snatched the phone from her. He paced the length of the space, then slammed the phone onto the bed. "This is not my child. I did not *abandon* a child!" He gripped his skull, his fingertips turning white, his eyes glassy. "I wouldn't." His voice cracked on the last word.

Rooted to the spot, Sue kept a neutral expression. Chris was a raw nerve, and the last word Sue had expected him to use was abandon. "Okay."

"I didn't do this. Not on purpose. Not by accident. Not at all." He pointed at her phone. "That is not my child." Hands on his hips, he looked away before focusing on Sue again, his rage simmering rather than roaring. "Stop this story. Whoever the kid is, he doesn't deserve it." Chris stepped closer. "Kill it."

"I'll do my best."

His jaw ticked again. "Don't do your best, Sue. Fucking stop it!"

"I don't know if I can." She twisted her hands together. "We can tell them it's a lie, but if the woman corroborates the story, even part of it, Julie can run it."

Chris paced the room, stopped at the dresser, and pressed his fists against it, his head hanging between his shoulders. "I can prove I don't have herpes."

"You have recent test results?"

"From the start of the tour. I'll get tested again. Where can I get tested?"

"I'll figure it out." Sue pushed a shaky hand through her hair.

"Soon. Figure it out soon. And a DNA test."

"Only if the mother agrees."

Chris snarled at her. "I'll take a fucking DNA test."

"Okay."

Chris stalked to the vanity, washed his face, and gargled with the hotel mouthwash. He rubbed a small towel across his face and over his head. He tossed the towel on the floor and caught Sue's eyes in the mirror. "I'll take all the tests. It'll be fine. Then I'll sue that bitch for invasion of privacy or some shit. Emily'll help, right?"

"We can ask."

"Good. Do that." Chris gave a sinister smile. "This is all gonna be fine. You got this, right?"

Stunned, Sue nodded. "Yeah. It's...it's gonna be fine."

"Cool." Chris walked across the room. "Sorry about the phone. Let me know what they want to do about it."

"Yeah."

He stopped just shy of the door and faced her. "You talk to the label yet?"

"No."

"Probably better if you handle that instead of me."

"Yeah."

Chris rubbed a hand over his head, similar to how he'd rubbed the towel over it. "I need some air. Call me when I can get tested." He walked out of the room perfectly calm, as though nothing had happened.

CHAPTER 1

Brad cut through the water of the hotel pool with steady strokes. He pulled his body forward, flipped at the end of the empty pool, pushed off the wall and did it all again, swimming lap after delicious lap in the late afternoon sun. Most people came to Savannah for the culture— food, music, art. He'd focus on culture later. Right now, he wanted the pool.

When the familiar burn lit the muscles in his shoulders, Brad flipped over and floated. A rhythm from the lapping water slowly shaped itself into a melody. Lost in composition, Brad played his guitar in the air.

"Got your key, Shamu."

He turned his head toward Tom's voice to find the man standing next to the lounge chair where Brad had tossed his shirt. When he'd seen the pool through the lobby doors, Brad had abandoned Tom and the rest of the band while they all checked into the hotel.

"Thanks, man. Leave it. I'll get out soon."

"No interviews tonight. Sue scheduled one tomorrow, though. Before soundcheck."

Brad held up a thumb. "Cool, mostly free day."

"Yep." Tom tossed the key onto Brad's shirt. "Enjoy the city."

Brad waved and disappeared back into his song. He flipped again and swam to the beat in his head, working out the shape of it. Even when other people came to the pool, he continued swimming laps in a tighter space until he had the whole song formed in his head. When he eventually climbed out, he went to the room he'd share with Justin, his best friend and the drummer in their band.

Brad scribbled the primary melody on hotel stationary then jumped in the shower, continuing to hum the song. Once dressed, he sat at the desk, softly thrumming the beat against the furniture while Justin napped.

He'd finished writing out all the chords and quietly jammed on his air guitar when Justin finally woke. Justin read the notes over Brad's shoulder, along with the snippets of lyrics.

"I like that." Justin hummed some of the melody. "Yeah, that's gonna be good."

"Thanks." Brad knew the song still had a way to go; it was only an outline until the whole band tinkered with it together, but it was a solid start.

"I'm gonna get a shower. Then food?"

Brad sat back and ran a hand through his damp hair. "Yeah."

He dug a notebook out of his overnight bag and pressed it open to a set of blank pages and re-wrote the song, filling in the gaps between the bridge and the chorus. He needed to play it to hear the notes working together. After dinner he'd grab a guitar from the bus.

A discordant *tap-tap-tap* on the door pulled Brad out of his music.

"Hey," Sue said. "I'm gonna walk some squares. You guys wanna come?"

Brad moved aside to let her into the room and wrinkled his forehead. Of course he'd go anywhere his delectable press manager asked him to, but he had no idea what she meant. "Walk some squares?"

"Yeah, Savannah has squares all over the city, almost like mini parks. Most of them have some kind of fountain or statue or something. They're cool. *Forrest Gump* filmed in a square."

"Okay." Brad banged on the bathroom door. "Just, you wanna walk some squares?"

"Sure, when?"

"Now!" Sue called back.

Justin came out of the bathroom, wearing only jeans and still toweling off. He squeezed the water out of his hair and tossed the towel back toward the tub.

How he could walk around like Sue was one of the guys escaped Brad. The few times Brad had been shirtless around her, he wanted to know if she noticed—really noticed—how he looked. Did she like what she saw? Meanwhile, Justin might as well have been burping and picking his ass in front of her. None of it seemed to faze him—or her.

Justin finally finished dressing and faced her. "You okay?"

She blinked. "Ready to stretch my legs."

Justin walked toward the door. "Let's go."

Brad grabbed his room key and trailed after Sue, only berating himself a tiny bit for checking out her ass.

After a few blocks, Sue led them into a manicured area. "Welcome to Columbia Square." She lay on a shady patch of grass near the fountain.

Justin lay beside her like it was no big thing.

Brad seized the opportunity to do the same. It'd be weird if he didn't. As he lay on Sue's other side, he quietly patted the beat of his new song against his stomach.

Sue sighed. "I could live here."

"In Savannah?" Brad asked.

"Yeah, why not?"

"I don't know. I never pictured you in a city like this." Brad gestured wide at the sky. This city seemed too laid back for a woman like Sue.

"Where have you pictured me?"

Justin snorted and Sue smacked him in the stomach with the back of her hand. "Don't ruin my relaxation."

Justin coughed before mumbling "Sorry."

"Seriously, Brad. Where do you see me living?"

"I don't know. Someplace busier than this."

"Why?"

"You're always in motion. Maybe Austin."

"Austin would be cool," Justin said.

"Yeah, but I can relax here." Sue stretched her arms over her head.

"You can relax with tourists craning around us to take pictures?" Brad asked.

"Yeah. There are tourists in every city. *We're* usually the tourists. I'd live around them."

"You're actually relaxed." Justin sounded skeptical.

"Yep."

"Laying here in the middle of a square?" Brad wanted to roll onto his stomach to look at her. Study her expression, understand what about this city drew her.

"Yep."

"You wouldn't be more relaxed if say, you were here with someone you wanted to make out with?" Justin asked.

Brad balled his hands into fists. Why did Justin insist on torturing him with this shit?

Sue chuckled. "I would enjoy that, but I wouldn't be this relaxed."

Brad's pulse picked up. Maybe her connection with Adam didn't run as deep as he feared. "Adam doesn't relax you?"

"He does, but it's different."

"How?" Justin asked.

Brad had no desire to know how Adam "relaxed" Sue. He needed to know if the guy had finally been sidelined.

"Do we have to talk about this?" Sue sat up and rested her arms on her knees. "You guys have nothing else to talk about?"

"Well, sure, but you aren't gonna tell us anything about Darryl and Lena," Justin said.

Sue glanced back at Justin. "You got that right."

"What's the deal? Did you dump him?" Brad shifted to sit behind Sue. If Justin could treat her like one of the guys, Brad could treat her like his sister. And his sister liked shoulder rubs. Sure, odds were Sue'd push him away again, but he needed to be near her. Especially if she'd ditched the sports guy.

"No, but I should." Sue rolled her head and stretched her neck.

Brad continued his massage, glad she didn't see him smile. Plus, she let him continue, even moving her head to give him more room to work.

"Why?" Justin raised himself on his elbows.

"Because." Sue shrugged. "All this traveling? I suck at giving relationships time when I'm working. And I'm always working. Touring takes it to a whole new level."

Touring was the main reason they were all single. But Sue was touring with *Brad*. They were together all the time. That had to be an advantage.

"He's a road warrior, too," Justin said. "This might be the perfect relationship for both of you."

Brad resisted the urge to sneer at Justin. Encouraging the woman you knew your best friend wanted to pursue some *other* guy had to be near the top of the list of things not to do in the guy code.

"Dating only works for me when there's no long-term expectations," Sue said.

Justin winced. "Guys are stupid."

Justin needed to shut the fuck up. Sue's long-term option sat right *here* with her now. Brad squeezed her shoulders and leaned a little closer for a moment before resuming his massage. He needed to find a way to make his intentions clear.

"No comment." She rubbed her forehead. "I can't shake the feeling it's wrong for me to start something when I'm in the middle of all this. And it's not fair to you guys to split my attention."

"You've gotta get Chris out of your head," Justin said.

"Amen." Brad rubbed his thumbs along her neck. Chris had been giving Sue shit since the moment she'd joined the tour. After a massive fight in New Orleans, the kid had finally backed down, but the tension between them lingered.

"Chris isn't in my head. That's the logical part of me trying to build a successful business." Sue swatted Brad's fingers. "I should end it when I see him in Atlanta."

"Relationships aren't logical, Sexy Sue." Brad scooted closer to her, one hand on her shoulder and the other massaging down her back. "Besides, this could work with the *right* relationship."

Justin sat up and hit Brad's arm, the expression on his face asking *What the hell do you think you're doing?*

Brad scowled and returned his focus to Sue. She needed to know she had options.

"It's *because* relationships aren't logical that I should end it." Sue stretched and shifted away.

Brad dropped his hands, disappointed to have lost the physical connection but determined to find another.

"Sue," Justin protested.

She held up a hand. "Let's not talk about this."

"Okay." Justin drew out the word.

"Come on." She stood and left the square.

Brad and Justin followed her through the city.

Eventually, she ducked into a convenience store on her own.

"Stop trying to convince her to end it with Adam. You're not *that* big of an asshole," Justin said.

Brad raked his fingers through his hair. "I know. I'm trying to move on. I figured if I knew she's into him, the harsh reality would propel me forward."

"But now that you smell blood in the water, it changes things?"

"I know it shouldn't."

"Damn straight." Justin crossed his arms. "It probably wouldn't change anything for *you* anyway."

"I have to know where I stand."

"She was never into you. She *is* into Adam. Let it go."

Brad sighed and paced, his attention on the trees. "I know."

"Will you at least stop encouraging her to dump the guy?"

Brad rolled his eyes but acquiesced. "If she tells me she's going to, I'm not talking her out of it, either."

"Fine." Justin glared.

Sue walked out of the convenience store with three bottles of water and waved her phone. "Tom's trying to get everyone together for dinner. Wanna go?"

—■————————————————————■—

Brad looked around the table, impressed. Tom, Sue, the entire band, and even their bus driver were in the same place at the same time and no one was about to go onstage or pump gas. Usually they all tried to take little breaks from each other when they were on the road. It helped them stay sane and kept fights to a minimum. But Brad had to admit, Tom had the right idea with this dinner. For once they all hung out, not talking about work.

A second round of margaritas hit the table and Sue pulled her phone out of her pocket, smiling at something on the screen. Normally if she got messages or alerts when they were eating, she silenced the phone and responded later. This time she didn't hesitate, nor did she put the phone away after she finished typing.

When she got another alert a minute or so later, she giggled.

Brad's hopes sunk. Girls didn't giggle like that when they were about to dump someone.

Justin leaned over. "What's going on there, Sexy Sue?" He whispered.

She blushed and sipped her margarita. Finally, she lifted her gaze and shook the phone. "Adam."

Justin bumped his shoulder to hers. "Nice."

Another message came in and Sue jumped on it. A few seconds later her phone rang. She left the table, barely excusing herself as she all but ran for the exit.

Brad fought not to react, but he desperately wanted to call her back. Accuse her of being rude, even though she wasn't. Anything to keep her in the chair next to him.

Once the door closed behind her, Justin nudged Brad. "A hundred dollars says she doesn't dump him."

Everything had to be a fucking game. "You want to bet against me?"

"I know the odds. Did you see her smile when he texted? And she bolted out of here when he called. She's not leaving him. At least not before Europe."

Brad gazed at the door. "A hundred bucks?" Didn't Justin know Brad well enough by now to see he'd given Brad a fresh reason to pursue her?

Justin offered his hand. "Yeah."

Brad shook. "You're on." Hell, getting Sue would be more than enough. He wouldn't even ask Justin to pay up when he won.

CHAPTER 3

"Hey, Adam." Sue sat on the stairs outside the restaurant.

"Hi. I didn't pull you away from anything important, did I?" After her encounter with Chris and the awkward pep talk from Justin, Adam's voice calmed her stress.

"Just dinner with the guys. Dinner hasn't arrived yet, though."

"Cool," Adam said. "We can plan."

"Okay."

"The Braves' early game's on Sunday, not Saturday."

"Damn," Sue said. "No baseball?"

"No, sorry."

"Wait. Is this a weak ploy to get me to wear the skirt?" Sue asked.

Adam's deep chuckle sent a thrill up her spine.

"I'm not that devious. I flipped the days. They play at seven on Saturday and three on Sunday."

"Okay. I guess we can get together another time." Sue worked to keep the disappointment out of her voice.

"Whoa, we're still going out Saturday. There's plenty to do besides the game."

"Okay," Sue said, surprised by his determined tone. "You sound unsure."

She took a few seconds to weigh her options. This would be the perfect time to end things. She knew she should, especially with the new shitstorm coming for Chris, but her disappointment when he told her there wasn't a game had nothing to do with baseball. "I'm on my second margarita and a mostly empty stomach. I'm a little slow on the uptake."

"Then listen closely." Adam's voice dropped an octave and hit her straight in the gut. "I want to see you. Texts and phone calls aren't enough. I need you in person. As soon as possible."

Any alcoholic haze in Sue's brain immediately lifted. Her pulse quickened as she sat straight. "Good. When will you be in Atlanta?"

"My flight lands at eight tomorrow morning."

She panicked; the next day had a schedule jam packed with things she couldn't—and wouldn't—put off, not the least of which involved Chris and the tests he wanted. "I can't be there in the morning. I have interviews in Savannah at eleven, and doors open for the show at seven."

"It's okay. I have meetings until at least five. Can you meet me after the show?"

"Yeah, but I probably wouldn't get to Atlanta until after two in the morning." She knew what joining him at

2 a.m. implied and she embraced it, even if they did only have Saturday before their relationship crashed and burned.

"Can you be there by lunch on Saturday?" Adam asked.

"Yes."

"What time do we need to be back for the guys?"

"Fiveish," Sue said.

"When do you leave again?"

"Sunday around noon."

"I can work with that," Adam said. "Will you wear the skirt?"

"Is this plan contingent on it?"

"You're the only drunk person I know who can use the word 'contingent' in a sentence."

Sue giggled. "I'm not totally drunk. And I'm about to eat, so the window on my drunkenness is waning."

"Go eat. I'll call you tomorrow."

"Have a safe flight."

"Think about wearing the skirt," Adam said.

"You're incorrigible."

Adam laughed. "I wonder how big your vocabulary gets when you're good and sauced."

"You'd be amazed."

"I already am. See you Saturday."

"Yeah." Sue pushed the disconnect button and stayed on the stairs, leaning back to take in the cityscape. Getting wrapped up any further with Adam didn't make sense. She knew it could lead to heartache. But she wanted to see him. She'd never been more thrilled than when he said he needed her in person. She still questioned her decision. Chris needed her even more now, and in a few weeks the likelihood that she and Adam would be able to get together before Labor Day would be slim to none. How long before he got tired of her career being her first priority? Would she get back from Europe to find she'd been replaced? Ugh, another list of questions to tackle.

Darryl poked his head out the door. "Hey, Suse, they brought out the grub and it smells good."

"Thanks, D." Sue smiled, accepting the hand he offered and stood.

"Hey, before we go back in there, I gotta ask you something." Darryl let the door close behind him.

"Sure. All set for your trips?"

"Yeah, it's not about that." Darryl pushed his fingers into his pockets. "Justin and Brad were talking about you breaking up with Adam."

"Okay." Sue glanced at her feet for a second before looking back at Darryl.

"Are you going to?"

"I don't know. Maybe."

"Has he done something?"

"No. He's great." Sue pushed her hair off her face. "I need to focus on the tour and press. Worrying about him's a distraction."

"That's complete bullshit." Darryl's eyes flared.

"I'm sorry?"

"If you wanna end things, you need a better reason."

Sue raised her eyebrows. "Funny, my job was a perfectly good reason for the last two guys to dump me."

"Don't let stupid assholes set the bar for you."

"Thanks for your opinion, but I'm pretty sure I get to decide."

He nodded. "I went a little too hard there. Let me try again."

Fists on her hips, Sue tilted her head, waiting.

Darryl shook out his arms and rolled his head back and forth like a boxer. "Okay. You know how you said you could tell the night I met Lena that she's the love of my life?"

"Yeah."

"You and Adam can make this work. I can see it."

Sue opened her mouth to protest, but Darryl held up a hand, stopping her.

"Give the guy a fair chance before you call it a day. That's all I'm saying. Get to know him, figure out what you want. If it still seems like a dead end, it is. But don't kill it before you've given it a real shot."

Sue studied Darryl for a moment before she said, "Okay."

"Really?"

"Yeah." Sue dropped her arms to mirror his posture. "You're right. Adam deserves a chance. And I like him."

"So you deserve a chance, too." Darryl gave her a wide grin and held the door open.

"I guess I do."

Sue's phone shook with a text as she resumed her seat at the table.

A: Listening to your playlist again. Did the guy from Phantom Planet memorize every note Paul McCartney has written?
S: Why do you ask?

A: His songs build the same way
McCartney's do
S: There isn't any McCartney on that list
A: And?

Sue looked up and caught Darryl's eye. She already grinned from Adam's texts, the perfect respite from the mess that waited for her, but her smile broadened for her friend. She liked Adam, but him listening to the music she loved? Talking to her about it? Yeah, he gave her exactly the kind of escape she needed.

S: You talking rock and roll is dead sexy
A: Miniskirt sexy?
S: Maybe. Keep talking.

CHAPTER 4

Sue stretched and rolled over, reaching for her phone on the nightstand. It had only been a week since New Orleans, but she appreciated sleeping in a real bed instead of one of the bunks on the bus. She'd slept on the bus twice so far and it'd made an impression. Even though the guys had sprung for real mattresses, the sleeping spaces were small. Being able to stretch out upon waking had become a luxury, especially since the room didn't smell like sweaty T-shirts or corn chips.

She opened her calendar for the day and scrolled through the list. Standard stuff filled the page. The "media training" that afternoon with Chris had her stressed, though. She'd set aside three hours and had no idea if it would be enough.

Emily had put Sue in touch with a private doctor who'd come to them in Savannah to administer the tests. She would send Chris the results no matter where they were. It would cost a fortune, but he said he didn't care. The proof was worth the price.

With the doctor in place, Sue waited for the background check on the reporter. She needed to know more about what drove this woman to look for horrible stories. Plus, learning more about Julie might lead them to the little boy's mother. Were the women friends, scheming together? Sue needed to know exactly what they were facing so she could protect Chris and the band. They weren't famous enough for a secret baby to be a scandal. But framed the right way, a story about an *abandoned* baby could limit their potential.

Sue knew Chris didn't care about other people's opinions of him. But the idea that he'd abandoned someone had almost burned him down. If he showed the press the same level of anger she'd seen last night, that would be the story: *Dangerous Rocker Abandons Child*. Chris wasn't dangerous, and the guy who chipped in money for a friend's college fund didn't seem the type to abandon. Until Sue had more facts, her best course was to deny the story and work to keep it from seeing the light of day.

Worried and dreading more fights with Chris, she flipped to her text messages. Adam had taken to sending her daily random factoids from his travels and his own interviews. The night before he'd regaled her with information about the Atlanta airport. She smiled as she reread the messages, grateful to have him giving her an escape. Sue needed some levity, so she focused her response on their upcoming date.

*S: While you're warming up Hotlanta for me,
I'll be considering my wardrobe. xoxo*

After showering and dressing, she checked her phone again.

A: I'll talk the Hawks into a demo game if it means you'll wear The Skirt.

She grinned at the idea of him desperate to see her in a miniskirt, her satisfaction almost primal.

S: Basketball arena is too cold. But I look great in a parka.

She smirked and called Tom to invite him to breakfast. As a nod to his role as official planner and scheduler of the tour, Sue tried to talk with him daily to make sure they stayed in sync, though today she wouldn't share much about the scheduled media training.

Her phone buzzed with a text as they were shown to their table at a local diner.

*A: Basketball's out. You like beach volleyball?
S: Can't wear the skirt for volleyball, interferes w/my spike.*

"That's an interesting look," Tom said as he slid into the booth.

"Excuse me?" Sue sat across from him and put her phone facedown to focus.

"The expression on your face. It was interesting."

"Okay." Sue flipped open her menu. She already had Darryl, Justin, and Brad weighing in on her love life. She didn't need Tom's opinion, too.

"You planning something?"

"No."

"Huh. I figured you were plotting your revenge against Darryl."

"I totally forgot!" Sue entered a reminder into her phone. *Darryl. Revenge. Must be big.*

Tom scratched his head. "You forgot?"

"Yeah. New Orleans, Chris—I've been busy. It's back on my radar now. I'll get him good."

"I have no doubt."

The waitress brought drinks and took their orders.

Tom added sugar to his coffee. "D's going to Brazil. I guess you win that bet."

When Darryl had explained the trip to Tom the night before, D expressed surprise that Tom's reaction had more to do with logistics than the reason for the trip. But like Sue, Tom—and the rest of the band—had an instinct about D and Lena.

Sue wiggled her eyebrows. "It's not official yet."

"It's close. The guys all thought I'd get married first."

"Why?" As far as Sue knew, Tom hadn't actively pursued anyone since his last breakup about a year before.

Tom slouched in the booth. "I'm the responsible one."

"True, but not bet worthy."

"Exactly."

Sue drummed her fingers against the table. "I'm a little surprised you're unattached, though."

"Why?"

Sue considered her words before answering. The last year had been a huge anomaly. Tom had never been known to be openly passionate, but he did usually have a girlfriend. They seemed like the kind of relationships that checked a box. Have someone to call every day. Done. Netflix and chill partner: acquired.

When it came to his life and the things he loved doing, Tom rarely included the women he dated, which meant his relationships never lasted long. Six to nine months, tops. As soon as the woman realized he wasn't going to invite her on a road trip, meet her family, or even purposely introduce her to his friends, she left.

Sue understood and it made her cringe. She didn't hold people at arm's length quite the way he did, but she knew she made it difficult. On purpose. She had goals. Men who couldn't handle that were better off leaving sooner rather than later. She shuddered. Adam was hanging in there, though.

Tom waved a hand in front of her face. "Hey-o, you gonna tell me why I'm not supposed to be single?"

Sue blinked. "You like taking care of people."

"Not all people."

"Of course not. We have standards. Look at the family we come from. Not a divorce in the batch. Nan loved Gramps desperately until the day she died. My parents flirt with each other right in front of me. Yours are no better, even with your dad in the Middle East for all those years." Sue rubbed her thumb along the handle of her fork. "Your parents made long distance relationships look easy."

"They could've at least faked a fight to help us feel normal." Tom fidgeted in his seat, propping an elbow along the edge.

Sue sipped her orange juice. "It's not easy to find that, and it's clear you want the same thing. Who can blame you?"

"So my trouble with women is that I want the unicorn of a relationship both our parents have?"

"Your trouble is hormonal. You date women who turn you on, but you don't care about an actual relationship," Sue said. "If you did, you'd at least let them visit you on tour."

Tom furrowed his brow. He opened his mouth as though to talk but drank his coffee instead.

Sue drummed her fingers on the table. "Well?"

"I work on a rock tour. My options are limited."

"Cop out."

"Most chicks are interested in the band. And the women who *are* interested in me usually hate the fact that I'm a professional wanderer."

"Point taken. What about back in Michigan? Any prospects there?"

Tom squirmed.

"Ahhh, nice."

"It's more like an extremely vague possibility. It's nothing like you and Adam."

It was Sue's turn to squirm. "There's not much to me and Adam."

"Isn't there?"

The waitress appeared with their food at the perfect time. Hopefully this would get Tom onto a new subject. The mere mention of the happy marriages she'd grown up around reminded her that maybe she *should* break up with Adam. Her parents were each other's biggest cheerleaders. None of her previous boyfriends had been comfortable with her ambition.

Tom unrolled his silverware. "Well?"

"Well what?"

"What's going on with you and Adam?"

Sue shoved a forkful of pancakes into her mouth and surveyed the table. She needed something to derail the conversation since it raised things she didn't know how to process. She'd intended for Adam to be a fun escape. An oasis in the mayhem of her job. Feelings had no business there.

"You can play your avoidance game with the guys, but I know you better."

Sue finally looked Tom in the eye. "I'm not avoiding."

"Then what's the deal?"

Sue put her fork down and sat back, glaring. She shouldn't be surprised. Forcing uncomfortable conversations was their MO. "Why do you all want to talk about him so much? You guys are the *worst* gossips."

Tom cut into his omelet. "Sue, we all more or less live with each other."

"Yeah. And you guys hover around me constantly." Sue's climbing pitch gave away her aggravation. She paused to regain control of her voice. "Everybody knows everything."

"You know better than that." He could've smirked or looked smug. Instead, Tom's gaze showed compassion. Damn it.

Sue rolled her eyes and picked up her fork. She stared at Tom for a long moment before she dug into her breakfast again. "One question. Then we talk shop."

"Would he go to Brazil for you?"

Sue stilled, not wanting Tom to see her choke on her food. "I don't know." She should break up with Adam, but she didn't want to. She figured him meeting her on tour would be cumbersome, but she didn't ask him to stay away. She could've slept with him in New Orleans and gotten him out of her system, but she hadn't. What the *hell* was she doing? She sawed her knife across her pancakes. "Part of me hopes he would."

A: *No basketball, no volleyball, will the skirt interfere w/your golf swing?*

Adam hit send, checked the time, and consulted the meeting itinerary. So far everything had been on schedule. Normally he'd be happy with that, but today he wanted to speed it up.

"Adam! Good meeting this morning." Keith, a partner in Adam's newest venture and one of the few friends he kept in contact with from college, jogged over.

"Yeah, looks like the next round of funding is on lock."

"Yup and the team'll have the project done on time."

"Even better." Adam's phone vibrated. "Hang on a second."

S: *Only if I can wear heels on the course. Golf shoes don't go w/the skirt.*

Adam smiled and slipped the phone into his pocket. "We're ready to roll out the marketing plan?"

"Yeah, but we may need to borrow a body or two from Sports Mecca to get it out the door," Keith said. "Speaking of, everything okay back at the office?"

"Running like clockwork. Why?"

"You're checking your phone more than usual."

"I'm staying in the city for the weekend and trying to coordinate some plans."

"I thought Lauren did that for you."

Adam shook his head. "Lauren manages my work schedule."

"Ah, so you're here for business but staying for pleasure." Keith gave a leering smile.

"Something like that." If he hadn't known Keith for so long, the lewd suggestion would bother Adam. Sue couldn't be boiled down to "pleasure."

"Please tell me it doesn't involve your family or a sports event."

Adam rolled his eyes. "What's wrong with staying in town for a soccer match or two?"

"I knew it!" Keith clapped a hand on Adam's back. "I'd criticize, but my wife's threatening divorce if I miss the baby's birth over sports."

Adam smirked. "Most people celebrate their team winning the NBA finals with wild sex. But you guys had to celebrate LeBron snagging a cherry deal."

"Don't lie. If you had a woman, you'd celebrate that gift of stories the same way."

Adam lifted an eyebrow in response.

"Anyway, I keep telling her as long as she doesn't go past the due date, we'll be fine. She still threatens me."

"Weren't you late for your wedding rehearsal because of a Braves game?"

Keith adjusted his watch. "She shouldn't have been surprised. I gave her the schedule."

Adam studied his friend as he laughed. "You're excited about the baby, aren't you?"

Keith blushed. "Yeah. Lacey has no idea, but I've sold my Braves seats for most of the season."

"That should more than make up for your wedding rehearsal."

Keith smiled before snapping to attention. "Want me to pick you up for the Saturday game?"

"Not this time. But thanks."

"Got a hot date?"

"Yes," Adam said.

Keith's eyebrows shot up. "You do?"

"Yeah. Any chance we can wrap this a little earlier than what the agenda says? Like around four?" Adam held out the schedule, grateful he didn't have to explain how badly he wanted to get to Sue.

"You don't need to be here for the last meeting. It's announcing the budget we went over last week," Keith said.

"You sure?"

"Positive. The board approved it this morning. Nothing's changing. We're telling the teams what they can spend next quarter. Skip it."

Adam tapped the page. "I think I will."

"They're heading back in."

"I'll be right there." Adam pulled his phone out and sent Sue a quick text.

> **A: Heels, golf spikes, not much difference. Go for it.**

CHAPTER 5

"When does the doc get here?" Chris stormed into Sue's room and walked straight to the back of the space. He leaned against the vanity, not looking at her.

"About fifteen minutes?"

"Why didn't you tell me to be here in fifteen minutes?"

"So we could talk." Sue opened the picture of the little boy on her phone. His resemblance to Chris was striking. They had the same face, but the boy had darker hair.

"What's there to talk about? Not my kid. I'm taking a fucking DNA test to prove it." Chris knocked against the counter. "Then I'll lay a massive lawsuit on that bitch so she'll think twice before dragging innocent people down."

"She doesn't see you as innocent, Chris."

"I meant the kid."

Few things shook Sue, but his glare gave her a chill. "I'm sorry."

Chris turned and faced the mirror.

"I hired one of Emily's investigators to find the boy and his mother. See if she's actually talking to the record label."

"The kid isn't mine."

"I believe you. But if we find them, we take away Julie's power. And Chris, he looks just like you."

"He looks like me." Chris shook his head, his back still to Sue. "You won't get mad if I ask every redheaded kid I meet if you're their mom?"

Sue dropped her phone on the dresser. "Point taken." She bit back the apology on her tongue. She didn't like this line of conversation any more than he did, but she needed as much information as possible to protect him. He was right, though; the little boy was innocent. If she learned more, she might be able to protect the child.

"He's too old to be mine, anyway."

Sue wrinkled her brow. "Julie said he's three. You could have a three-year-old."

"I was capable of fathering a child three years and nine months ago." Chris stepped away from the window and looked her in the eye. "But my child wouldn't be older than two. At the most."

Sue held his gaze for a moment until what he said sank in. A knock at the door stopped her from speaking.

Chris pushed past her to answer it. "You the doctor?"

"Yes."

Chris held the door wide and gestured for the woman to come in.

The doctor introduced herself, set a case on the dresser and explained the exam and testing process before taking out a stack of papers. "You'll need to sign consent forms for the tests. Are we doing a full panel of STIs?"

"Yeah," Chris said.

"On both of you?"

"No," Chris said. "Just me. You can share results with her, though. I'll sign whatever saying as much."

"There's no release for that. You can disclose your results to whomever you want once you have them."

Chris nodded as he filled out the paperwork.

"You'll want some privacy for this," the doctor said.

Sue snapped to attention. "Right. I'll go...somewhere."

Chris held a card out to her. "Go to my room. Darryl's eating his way through the city." Before he let her take it, Chris pulled it, and Sue, toward himself. "Everything we discussed stays right here." He gestured between them. "No one knows any of this shit and if they find out, I'll know it's you."

"You can trust me."

"You better fucking hope so." Chris let go and turned toward the doctor.

■━━━━━━━━━━━━━■

While Chris got his tests, Sue called Emily again to confirm the private investigator had been put on the case. She needed to hear the woman's story firsthand, not filtered through a reporter with an axe to grind.

She kept busy so she wouldn't obsess over the situation, at least not until she had more information. After she'd wrapped things up with the local reporter and sent the band off to soundcheck, Sue rearranged the merch table for the third time. She focused on a challenge she had a better chance of overcoming—selling more T-shirts. They moved a surprising number of CDs on show nights, but aside from the new designs they'd produced in New Orleans, they hadn't sold many shirts. She needed to change that, and fast, so they could order more of the new designs and not have to take the older shirts to Europe. After rehanging all the signs, she noticed the stickers were low, so she crouched down for a quick inventory before she made a run to the bus. Her phone vibrated with a message as she stood.

A: Heels and golf tomorrow. But what are you wearing right now?

Sue's lips curled into a little smile. Adam was always an excellent distraction. Their back and forth had her legitimately considering wearing the skirt, simply for his reaction. "Well, he's getting saucy now, isn't he?"

"Am I?" Adam spoke right in her ear, his breath tickling her skin and sending a bolt of desire through her.

She jumped and almost knocked over the merch table.

"I'm sorry, I didn't mean to scare you." Adam pulled her to him, steadying her against his side as he kept the table from tipping over.

Hand pressed to her heart, Sue steadied herself. She'd been startled, but she wasn't scared. She wanted more. "What are you doing here?"

"I told you I needed to see you as soon as possible." The words were low, and his hand on her waist might as well have been electricity pulsing through her.

Sue wrapped herself around him, unfathomably happy to see him and annoyed that she had to work. "I still have to put in a few hours."

"I can be patient."

"You sure?"

"Waiting for you is much easier when I'm near you." Adam leaned in, brushing his mouth over hers.

"Not here." Sue twined their fingers. After a week of thinking about him and dodging prying questions and comments from the band, she wanted a minute alone with him. She wanted to react without worrying about an audience or judgement or anything but his hands and lips on her. "Come with me."

She led him out to the alley behind the club to the bus. She went into the attached trailer and retrieved a small box. She gestured for Adam to follow her to the other side of the bus. Once she couldn't see the club, she stood on her toes and wrapped her arms around his neck, kissing him deeply. She melted against him, happy and relieved to have a minute where he was the only thing on her mind.

He skimmed a hand up her back and pulled her tighter against him.

She squeezed his body against hers until she thought she might lose her balance. Sue pulled back. "Welcome to Savannah."

"If I knew *that* was waiting for me, I would've been here hours ago."

"Then I never would've gotten any work done." If what she'd said hadn't given away her desires, the low pitch of her voice probably did. Damn, it was good to see him. Sue stepped away, grabbed his hand, and reluctantly led him back into the club.

She dropped the stickers at the merch table and made sure not to touch Adam as a reporter asked her about Words Fail Me tour dates. She forced a T-shirt on him with the excuse that it had the schedule printed on it. She silently willed him to wear it, even though she knew he wouldn't. Not tonight, anyway. Not at their show.

When the band finally hit the stage, Sue left the merch booth in Tom's hands and mixed in with other concert-goers. Adam wrapped his arms around her from behind, holding her close. His chest rumbled against her when he sang along, which only endeared him to her more.

She surveyed the audience several times, always disappointed when she found each of the three reporters who'd interviewed Words Fail Me before the show. Normally this would thrill her. They liked the band enough to stay. Tonight, their interest was torture. Sue wouldn't leave until the reporters did—it helped her to ensure they had what they needed for their articles. She needed their stories and she needed them to be good enough to generate buzz the record label would notice, even though she made sure the suits saw every bit of media she got for the guys.

As the set wound down, Sue slowly untangled herself from Adam. It had been a great hour, but she had to make sure the guys mingled and didn't piss off the reporters. And she needed to sell some fucking T-shirts. When the house lights went dark after the final song, Adam pulled Sue back against him, lifted her chin toward him, and kissed the hell out of her.

"I'll be at the bar." He set her loose on wobbly legs.

That he seemed to understand her priorities was as big of a turn on as his kiss had been. How long would it last, though? Eventually he'd tire of waiting.

Sue plastered on a fake smile as she helped Tom sell CDs, took pictures for fans, and all but begged people to buy T-shirts.

The time between Words Fail Me's set and Skein's was both lightning fast and agonizingly slow. CDs, stickers, and pins flew off the table, and social media mentions had Sue's phone pinging almost nonstop. Still, each time she looked up and caught Adam's gaze on her, she wanted to abandon her post and go to him. He didn't look impatient or bored or annoyed. He seemed interested. At one point, she caught him staring as she bent over. He looked hungry. Skein couldn't get on stage fast enough.

Brad, Justin, and Darryl came out as soon as they got their gear off the stage and immediately got the attention of their fans. Sue loved it, knowing that even if she didn't move the damn shirts, the guys were selling music and earning loyalty. It wouldn't win her many points with the record label in the near term, but she played the long game. Fan loyalty would serve them well.

When the house lights dimmed for Skein, most people moved toward the stage, but Sue stayed at the merch table while Tom got more CDs from the trailer. Darryl and Justin hung out at the bar with Adam. She joined them when Tom returned.

About halfway through the set, Darryl leaned toward Sue and encouraged her to leave early with Adam. Although grateful for the suggestion, Sue declined. When the show finally ended, she sold CDs and stickers for the thirty minutes it took for the place to clear out. She even took a quick walk around the building to make sure the reporters were gone before helping to load the trailer. Adam waited at the bar again, his patience becoming more and more impressive, while Sue grew more anxious to be done for the night. She got a pleasant surprise when she found Chris and Brad had done most of the work during Skein's show.

On her way to the front of the house, she bumped into Darryl, who carried a box of shirts.

"They're almost done back there. Can you believe it?" Sue asked.

"Brad must be hot to get to the hotel or else he would've waited for the rest of us to help."

"Anything left?"

"The actual table," Darryl said.

"I'll get it and meet you at the trailer." She hustled to the front of the club, folded the table, and carried it toward the back door. She met Darryl backstage again.

He reached for the table. "I got this. You and Adam get out of here."

"I got it. It'll take two seconds."

"Nah." Darryl took the folding table from her. "Go have fun."

"Thanks, D." She gave him a fist bump.

"Hey, before you go." He leaned the table against his leg and fished in his pocket. "I'm not using these. Someone might as well." He gave her two condoms from his wallet.

"D?"

"You know the deal with Lena. I don't know what's up with you guys, but just in case."

Sue pressed her lips together. She loved that this seemed so nonchalant for him, like they'd truly accepted her as part of the group. But she purposefully kept certain details to herself. She shoved them back at him. "It's okay. I'm good."

Darryl held up a hand, stopping her. "I don't want to know if they get used, and I won't tell the fellas in case there's any outstanding bets."

"This is weird." Yes, Darryl had to tell her about Lena, but aside from Chris's bragging, the rest of them kept their sex lives to themselves.

"Remind me to show you where the stash is on the bus. Then it won't be weird." D grinned and picked up the table again. "Get outta here." He took a few steps backward.

Sue shouldn't have been surprised they had a condom stash on the bus, but it still amused her. "Thanks, D."

"Go!" He shooed her away.

Sue tucked the condoms into her pocket and headed to the front of the house. Adam still sat at the bar where she'd left him. Patience had never looked sexier. She grabbed his hand and motioned toward the door. "Let's go."

Adam absently threw some bills next to his half-empty glass and let her pull him out of the club. "Where are we going?"

"To a square."

"Any one in particular?"

"The closest one. I want to test a theory."

Sue made a beeline for one of the benches in Telfair Square. Adam put an arm around her, and she turned halfway to face him, finally letting all her giddy joy over his surprise come to the surface. "I can't believe you drove out here. I'll be in Atlanta in less than twelve hours."

"Your texts made me anxious." He slid close.

"That was the idea."

"And you're wearing a skirt. Not *the* skirt, but I'm glad I didn't miss this one." Adam played with the wisps of hair that had fallen out of her clip. He rubbed the edge of her skirt against her knee with his other hand.

Sue shifted her head toward his palm. As much as the running commentary on her wardrobe annoyed her—she sure as hell hadn't put the skirt on for anyone but herself— she finally felt normal. Adam liking her more when she was authentic was a prize she cherished. "It's getting too warm to wear jeans all the time."

"One more reason to love the spring," Adam said, his lips against her shoulder.

"Spring Training and skirts?" Sue shivered as he worked his way from her shoulder to behind her ear.

"And the Champions League final."

"Can't forget the Champions League." Sue settled into his arms, enjoying his light touches and the fact that even though he'd spent the evening with her in a sweaty club, he still smelled like grass warm from the summer sun.

"What's the theory you're testing?" Adam kept his mouth by her ear when he spoke.

Sue moved to face him, but his lips were so close that she had to have them. She pulled him closer as they kissed, her hand resting at his nape, her thumb against his quickening pulse.

Adam's fingers trailed up her spine, making her want to crawl under his skin. She arched her back, pressing her chest into his. He shifted on the bench, pulling her into his lap. The look in his eyes when they broke their kiss was pure fire.

"This is not relaxing," Sue whispered.

Adam kissed his way down her neck. "No?"

"Not even close."

"Wanna go somewhere?"

"Yes." Sue kissed him again.

"Walk or drive?"

"Drive."

Adam kept his hands on her as he led her a few short blocks to his rental car. He opened the door for her, kissing her before she got in. They pulled away from the curb before he asked where they were going.

"The Hyatt." He probably hadn't booked his own room. He'd come to Savannah to stay with her. She hoped he'd been thinking about it all day.

After the longest three-block drive in history, Sue pushed opened her hotel room, wrapping her arms around Adam before the door closed behind them. He skimmed his hands down her sides, grabbed her legs and lifted her, wrapping her legs around him. She tightened her legs, impressed and turned on that he never broke their kiss as he put her where he wanted her and carried her to the bed. He sat on the edge, Sue straddling him. He kissed her mouth, her jaw, her neck, her shoulders. All the while his fingers teased her waist and back. When he cupped her breasts, she untied the neck of her halter and let it fall forward, desperate for his hands on her bare skin.

The look he gave her knocked the wind out of her. She mentally berated herself for waiting so long. This man was a refuge. She leaned over to kiss him and pulled his shirt out of his waistband. He worked his way back down from her mouth, taking extra time to kiss her skin on either side of the pendant he'd given her. She smoothed her hands over his shoulders, appreciating the shape of his toned body and wondering how to keep his mouth on her while she removed his shirt, when his phone vibrated against her thigh. He grunted and shifted, pulling the phone out of his pocket. He tossed it behind him and refocused on her breasts, pulling at her nipples through the thin fabric of her bra. The phone lit with another call a few seconds later.

"Adam." Sue's skin tingled, and she ached to get him out of his clothes, but the phone distracted her. "Can you turn it off?"

"Yeah." He kissed her then leaned back, his gaze fixed firmly on her.

She pulled his shirt off and tossed it in the same direction as the phone as it illuminated again. That she saw anything other than the solid chest below her annoyed her. "The guys don't even call me this late."

Adam pushed the phone off the bed and danced his fingers down her back until they hit the edge of her clothes.

"Maybe they're pranking us." Adam pulled her top over her head, dropped it, and felt around her waist.

She used the opportunity to press their bodies together again. The way his fingers barely touched her seared. She wanted more. More pressure. More grip. More teasing. More him.

His fingers found her zipper and he yanked. "Finally."

Sue stood and stepped out of the skirt and her shoes. She climbed onto him again, tugging his zipper. He flipped her over and balanced above her, teasing her with his body, so close but not touching her. She felt his breath, his pulse, and wanted his weight. She unzipped his pants as he pulled her bra down and kissed her chest.

His phone let out a loud alert tone that froze them both.

"Fuck." Adam reached for the phone. "911 page." He kept a hand on Sue as he scrolled to the message on the phone. "I'm sorry, I have to call my sister."

Sue sat up and readjusted her bra while he placed the call. Should she get dressed? Should she curl herself around him like she wanted to? The questions left her uncomfortably vulnerable. She found her blouse and held it against her chest.

"Claire, what's going on?" The hard lines of aggravation fell from his face as he listened.

Sue touched his shoulder. The swift change in his body language told her this wasn't a nuisance call. He sat up straight and tense.

He leaned into her while his sister talked. "I'm in Savannah. I'll get a flight." He pulled Sue closer to him, gripping her waist. "Yeah, sit tight with the kids. I'll get there. Don't worry… Bye." Adam sighed and faced Sue. "My grandmother fell down the stairs. She's in bad shape. They're taking her into surgery."

"Oh no!"

"They're worried about her hip and maybe a spinal injury. She's eighty-five. She shouldn't be on the stairs."

Sue didn't hesitate. "You have to go." If it had been her grandmother, she'd be on her way, no questions asked. Hell, if it had been anyone she loved, she'd be on the next flight.

"I do. I'm sorry." Adam had a sad, pleading look in his eyes.

"It's family."

Adam pulled her in close and hugged her.

Sue laid her head on his shoulder. She closed her eyes, overwhelmed with the urge to kiss his neck. She wanted to comfort him but also feel his whole body against hers. She held her breath instead, trying to focus on letting him go.

"I'm sorry," he repeated, still holding her. "My parents can't get there until sometime tomorrow night. My brother-in-law is on the road. Claire wants to load the kids in the car and drive there now."

"Even if they could all get there before you, I'd still tell you to go." As much as she wanted him to stay, she knew if he did, it would change the way she saw him. He truly would be a fling. A quick token of fun, not a reward to savor. She silently willed him to be the reward.

Adam kissed her forehead. "Most women would be pissed."

"Pissed is not the word I'd use right now." In desperate need of an orgasm, preferably from him, was more accurate.

"But it doesn't matter. Call the airlines and figure out when you can get there." Sue slid off the bed and handed Adam his shirt.

He shook his head as he took it. "Look at you."

"What?" Sue glanced down. Heat flushed her chest and her face when she realized she only wore her bra and panties. She'd gotten so wrapped up in her thoughts, she'd forgotten she hadn't put her clothes back on. She considered teasing him but figured it would only frustrate her more. And she wanted a reward, not a fling.

"This timing sucks."

She pointed to his phone. "Make your calls."

Sue got dressed and sat with Adam while he arranged a charter flight to Maine. He called his sister with the details and cursed after Claire hung up.

"What?"

Adam rubbed his forehead. "I summoned a pilot in the middle of the night."

"That's kind of badass."

"Not when I can't ask him to wait so I can have my way with my girlfriend."

Thrown by his use of the word "girlfriend," Sue had no idea what to say. She'd convinced herself long ago that she wouldn't have a boyfriend until things were more stable in her life. When she could be reliable and offer something solid. She squeezed Adam into the margins of her life, and he called her his girlfriend. She should correct him. But how? She hunched her shoulders.

Adam pulled her into another hug. "I'm sorry."

"Please believe me, I am, too." Sue kissed him before walking him to his car. With so much on her mind and a lot of lust still swirling through her, she needed to get him on his way. Otherwise she might say something emotional she'd regret. "Call me when you have an update."

"I will." Adam gave her one more kiss before he climbed into the car.

She leaned down when he closed the door. He lowered the window and she said, "Adam, I truly hope she's okay."

He frowned, putting his hand over hers on the door. "I do, too."

After he pulled away, she trudged back toward her room. Digging in her pockets she found the condoms but no room key. She swore and went to the lobby.

"Suse!"

She froze in her tracks and turned. When she saw Darryl, she relaxed.

"What are you doing out here?" he asked.

"Locked myself out." Sue held up the new key.

"Where's Adam?"

"He had to go." Of course D asked. They all would. *Shit.*

"Everything okay?"

"His grandmother fell down the stairs, and they rushed her into surgery."

"Shit!"

"Yeah." At a loss for what to do, Sue looked away and frowned.

"Let's sit." He steered Sue to a couch. "What's wrong?"

"What's he gonna find when he gets there?" Sue choked on her words. She hoped Adam wouldn't face the worst on this trip, as she had a few years before when she'd gotten a similar call. Not a fall, a stroke. The one that prompted the call had been minor, but the second one a few days later hadn't been. She'd never regret dropping everything to see to her grandmother one last time.

"I'm sorry."

Sue pushed her hands into her pockets and sighed when she found the condoms again. "Part of me is worried about his flight and his grandmother, and part of me is deeply frustrated. Which makes me feel like an asshole."

"Frustrated?" Darryl asked.

Sue gave him a significant look. Normally she wouldn't even hint at this kind of detail. But she and D had moved past that when he'd given her the condoms. Plus, she trusted him to keep it to himself.

"Oh! If it's any consolation, I've been frustrated for a couple weeks myself."

"Good. You're part of the problem," Sue said.

"What?"

"Victor made me *swear* that Lena and I would stay in our room in New Orleans all night, with no one else. All night, Darryl. All night. Do you know what I could've done with just a sliver of the night?"

"Oh, believe me. I do."

"And we had so much time the night of the benefit and I blew it." Sue flopped back on the couch and sniffled. "What the hell is wrong with me?"

Darryl glanced away before he answered. "Victor is a terrible influence."

"Yeah!" Sue rubbed her temples. All the talk of Lena's virtue had Sue putting much more thought into sex. She'd wanted Adam since Vegas. Maybe even since the taco bar in Austin. But Lena's abstinence had given her a lot to consider. Damn it! Couldn't an orgasm just be an orgasm?

"What about when he pulled you out of the mosh pit? You didn't *thank* him after that?"

Sue pushed her hair behind her ear. "No. It was the last day of my period. I wasn't ready."

"Aw, shit."

"Yep. All green lights on benefit night, though, and I blew it. Tonight I was almost naked when his *sister* called." Sue threw her hands in the air. Why couldn't she stop talking? She'd be better off finding the local adult book-store and getting herself a power tool.

"Suse, of everyone on tour, I can truly sympathize."

"Lemme tell you what you can do with your sympathy." She wiped away a tear, her frustration reaching new heights.

D pressed his lips together and fidgeted. After a few seconds his shoulders shook.

"You're laughing at me? Laughing?" Sue looked at him in disbelief before she also broke into laughter.

CHAPTER 6

Adam sat at his grandmother's bedside, waiting for her to wake. She had the strength to sail through the surgery. Her pre-op appointment for the long-planned hip replacement earlier in the week had confirmed it. The doctors issued a good prognosis, but Adam needed to see for himself that she was recovering. Once he had that assurance, he'd go to her house and check the banister. Had it been loose? There were conflicting stories from the paramedics and Mrs. Thurston, the nearest neighbor, about exactly what shape the stairs had been left in.

A nurse padded in and gingerly slipped a blood pressure cuff on one of his grandmother's bruised arms. "Has Miss Shirley opened her eyes again?"

"No." Adam sat up in his chair.

"Don't worry. All the medication has her groggy." The nurse clicked a pen, wrote on a notepad, and slipped pen and pad back into her pocket. "Her vitals are good. She'll be awake soon."

"Thank you."

The nurse nodded as she gently removed the cuff and left as quietly as she'd entered.

Deep into a daytime talk show, Adam almost fell off his chair when his older sister burst into the private room.

"Claire! How did you get here so soon?"

"Bullet train." Claire pushed a hank of light brown hair behind her ear.

Adam crossed the room and hugged her.

Claire studied Shirley. "How is she?"

"Stable. No internal bleeding. No spinal injury. Since she had her pre-op appointment a few days ago, they went ahead and did the hip replacement. The break was severe enough that they would've had to operate anyway. She's bruised, but the doctor says she's doing well." Adam touched his face in the same spot where his grandmother had a small cut.

"Best news all day." Claire kissed Shirley on the forehead, then collapsed into a nearby chair. "Steve called right after we talked last night. He got a red-eye home, so I booked an early flight this morning."

"Steve's a trooper."

"Gram belongs to him as much as she belongs to us," Claire said.

"I know. It's hard to believe he wasn't born into the family."

While Claire fussed with Gram's blankets, Adam quietly switched the television to a sports channel. They were broadcasting news he'd already seen or had reported himself, but he didn't want to defend his choice in daytime television to his sister. No matter what, he'd lose that battle.

Claire moved the chairs so they were side by side. "Maybe I got my dates wrong, but weren't you supposed to be in Atlanta this weekend? Did I miss something?"

"I was in Atlanta during the day, but I drove to Savannah after work."

"Bar hopping with old college buddies?"

Adam rubbed his forehead. "I kind of had a date."

"A date?"

"Yeah." Adam crossed his arms. "You don't have to be so shocked."

"I'm not shocked, I'm sorry. I ruined a date!"

Seizing the opportunity to give his sister a guilt trip, he decided to lay it on thick. "Yeah, it was a good one, too." He grimaced. "Who knows if she'll see me again."

"What do you mean *if*? What kind of harpy is she? If she can'—"

Adam interrupted with a laugh. "Harpy? Calm down, Granny Claire. She was actually incredibly cool about it. As soon as I said Gram needed surgery, she told me to go. She didn't even think twice."

"Seriously?"

"Yeah. And she texted me this morning asking how Gram's doing."

Claire's eyebrows lifted. "She did?"

"Yes. She's been great about the whole thing. Especially—" Adam paused, trying to keep his frustration about how they'd parted at bay. "She's *not* a harpy. She's amazing."

Claire smiled, but the longer she looked at him, the more impish her grin became. "She's been great especially because why?"

"I didn't expect her to be so understanding. Wouldn't you be pissed if Steve's sister ended one of your dates early?"

Claire tapped a finger to her lips. "If memory serves, I called around one in the morning. Not exactly early."

"Claire, come on."

"You come on." Claire smiled and gave him a light shove.

"It was closer to midnight."

Claire put her chin on her hand. "What were you doing?"

"We went to a concert."

"It wasn't noisy when you called me back, not even street noise."

Adam glared at her for a long moment. He knew she'd continue to needle until she got what she wanted or they got into a fight. Gram wouldn't wake to an argument. "Fine. I may never forgive you for interrupting."

Claire let out a low chuckle. She rested her head on the back of the chair and looked toward him. "Did you ever tell her how Gram's doing?"

"No." Adam scratched his ear. "I didn't want to leave the room in case Gram woke."

"Go call her." Claire pointed her chin toward the door. "I won't leave. I'll get you if Gram wakes up."

Adam hesitated, then smiled and slipped out of the room. He walked the corridor in search of a quiet place.

Sue answered immediately. "Good news?"

"Yes. How is Atlanta?" Adam pushed abandoned magazines down a bench in an empty alcove and sat.

"It's missing you. How is your grandmother?"

He couldn't remember a time in his adult life when anyone had ever sounded so happy to hear from him. It made him grateful he'd gone to Savannah, despite how the night ended.

"The surgery went well. She should be fine."

"What a relief." A door clicked into place, and all the background noise around Sue vanished.

"Yeah. Thank you."

"Were you able to convince your sister to stay home?"

"Not entirely." Adam stifled a yawn. "She waited until her husband got there. Our parents should be here by four with our younger sister, Jessica."

"It's good you guys rally like that." Sue's warm voice wrapped around him.

"Gram'll be annoyed we dropped everything, but she'll be happy to see us."

"My dad used to tease my grandmother that she'd fake an illness to get the family together," Sue said.

Adam rested his elbows on his knees. "Would she?"

"No. We're all pretty tight."

"Sue, I'm sorry I ran out last night," Adam said.

"I would've done the same thing."

"It's the timing I regret the most."

"Yeah, I'm right there with you."

"I'll catch a flight to Atlanta once my parents get here."

Sue stayed quiet for a beat. "I would love that, but you shouldn't even consider leaving until your gram's settled.

No matter when your parents arrive. Plus, there isn't enough time."

"I'll meet you tomorrow in Myrtle Beach."

"For twenty minutes? Adam, we're in a new place every day until Charlottesville."

"I can make this work." Adam squeezed his forehead, hoping his desperation didn't bleed through his words.

"Listen to me." Sue's voice changed to a stern business tone.

He blew out a breath. "What?"

"I've worked up a good head of steam here. Even if you got on a plane *right now,* it would not leave us enough time to work through it all."

Adam couldn't speak for a full minute. He stood and walked in a wide circle. "Fuck. Why did I call you from a waiting room?"

Sue's laugh sounded devious. "Are you parked nearby?"

"I have no idea. My brain is too busy calculating how much time we need to work through *my*...steam."

"I hope it's a long, *long* time." Sue's voice dropped.

"You'd better not be teasing me, woman."

"Teasing is for texting. I don't waste breath on teasing."

Adam took another minute to collect his thoughts. "We're still on for Fox Field?"

"As long as you can still make the trip."

"If all goes as expected, Gram should be home in a few days."

"Then we're still on," Sue said.

"Thank God." Adam glanced around at the waiting area. "Sue, I think I have to go."

"You *think* you have to go?"

"I don't want to." Adam walked to the end of the hallway. "But I can't keep talking to you out here, and I can't concentrate enough to find someplace where I could *really* talk to you."

"Ah. And knowing our luck, the guys will show up any moment now and carry on our streak."

"At least we can get them back."

Sue laughed. "Good point."

"I'll call you as soon as I'm in a private place. Later tonight?"

"We have the show, but I'll make sure I'm free by midnight," Sue said.

"I'll call you then," Adam said.

"Looking forward to it."

CHAPTER 7

Sue handed Darryl the lock for the equipment trailer. "You had us packed in record time, man."

"Yeah, D." Justin grabbed Darryl's shoulder. "Now I'm gonna use Lena as my excuse whenever I need something from you."

"Whatever, dickhead." Darryl tugged on the lock and faced Sue. "You ready? I wanna make sure you get some sleep tonight. Want me to drive?" Darryl had a flight booked the next morning to visit Lena during their long weekend off. Sue had agreed to drive him so the rest of the band could spend the night in the college town, but she insisted on splitting the drive so they could sleep. Her house was on the way to the airport.

"I'm good."

"Please, can I drive?"

The anxious, lovesick side of Darryl tickled her. She gave him the keys and he jogged toward her car. Agreeing to take Darryl to the airport had been as much for Sue as for him. He was eager to get to Lena; she wanted to see Adam. Fortunately, D's emotions provided cover for her own excitement. She didn't want more questions about Adam.

"I'm surprised he didn't try to get an earlier flight," Justin said.

"Right? And he didn't push to drive straight through." Sue refocused her attention. "Can you make sure Chris stays away from the reporter? This is a college town. Gossip. I'm nervous." The situation with the mystery child seemed to have had an impact. Chris still hooked up with women but less often, and he waited for them to make the proposition. If it weren't for the fact that he'd become even more rude to her, she would've been concerned.

Justin nodded. "He called someone he met last time we came through."

"Wow." Sue squinted. "He keeps their numbers?"

"She must've been special."

Darryl honked the horn.

Sue smirked. "See ya tomorrow, Just."

"Yep."

Sue fell asleep almost as soon as they got on the highway and didn't wake until Darryl turned on her street. She directed him to where he should park, climbed out of the car, and took in her townhouse. Her heart swelled at the sight.

They entered a small foyer with a terra cotta tile floor, facing a staircase of dark, glossy wood. Sue put down her bags and fiddled with her keys, sliding one into an all but hidden lock on a pair of ornate Moroccan doors next to the stairs. When she pushed the doors open and stepped into her living room, she took a deep breath and smiled. She was finally home, back in the space she'd designed for herself, with her art. She flipped the light switch and moved in to give Darryl room. He gathered the things she'd stacked in the hallway, along with his duffel bag.

"You can leave them, Darryl. Both floors are mine."

"Cool." Darryl lined everything neatly against the wall and followed Sue into a large, mostly empty room.

"You want a drink?" she asked.

"Water would be good, and the bathroom."

"Bathroom is through there, to the right." Sue pointed to a hallway on the opposite side of the room. "I'll be in the kitchen."

She stepped out of her shoes and padded to the kitchen. She turned the lights on and fixed two glasses of water then leaned against the counter and drained one.

Darryl walked in a circle in the kitchen. "Suse, where's all your stuff?"

"In the hallway." She gave Darryl the other glass of water.

"No, I mean, there's nothing in this kitchen." Darryl turned toward the living room. "Or anywhere."

"I have a pretty big pantry, so most of the kitchen stuff goes in there. Makes it easier to keep the place clean." Sue gestured for him to follow and opened a door tucked away at the far end of the room. Her oversized pantry/laundry room ran the length of the kitchen with an entire wall of shelves.

"Nice," Darryl said. "But where do you eat?"

Sue stepped away from the pantry and flipped a switch next to one of the French doors that made the alcove at the back of her kitchen. Floodlights illuminated a small but lush garden. She unlocked and opened the center door and stepped outside onto a tiled patio with a bistro table and a hammock. Azaleas and jasmine lined the sides. The second-floor deck formed a ceiling. Vines grew along it and hung down, framing the view. A few feet out in the yard, a cherry blossom tree stood in full blossom.

"Wow." Darryl stepped out and admired the flora thriving around him.

"I like to garden."

"Nice."

"Thanks. Before this I had roommates, so I never had a lot of furniture." Sue went back into the kitchen and refilled her glass.

"We need to talk about your toilet paper holder." Darryl scratched his temple.

"Does it need a refill?"

Darryl shook his head and winced. "Suse. Is it a dick?"

Sue widened her eyes, hoping to hide her smirk. "I don't know. I hope not."

"Okay, if it might be a dick and you hope it isn't, what the fuck is it doing in your place?"

Sue set down her glass. "Robin made it for me. It was a housewarming gift."

"Is it…is it him?" Darryl looked like he wanted to hide behind something.

"I refuse to ask."

"Smart."

When Sue bought the house, Robin had painted tiny concert scenes on a dozen tiles that she proudly grouted into her shower. Then he decided the bathroom also needed a sculpture. He cast his own foot and leg, slimmed it down, and added detail on the toes. An appendage stood out from the thigh at a ninety-degree angle. It was the right shape but pointed in the wrong direction and lacked key identifying details. She didn't ask the obvious question, just slid a roll of toilet paper on it and went on with her remodel. Robin had considered it an honor.

Sue decided to change the subject. "Do you want the bed or the futon?"

"Futon's cool."

"I'll get sheets and stuff. Take your laundry out. You shouldn't go to Lena with dirty clothes."

"Aw, Mom!" Darryl grinned and put his glass in the sink.

"That was a very mom thing to say, wasn't it?"

"Or a Tom thing."

"Ha! True."

Despite her nap in the car, Sue stayed awake long enough to give Darryl sheets and show him where to find the laundry detergent. She crashed hard in her bed. She woke at seven-thirty—the time they had originally planned to leave.

"Darryl!" Sue shook his shoulder. "Darryl, it's seven-thirty, we have to go!"

Darryl snorted as he woke. "What?" He grabbed his watch from the floor next to the futon. "Shit. My clothes!"

"Are they in the dryer?"

"Yeah." Darryl sat, pulling the sheets off the futon.

"Leave the sheets. Get in the shower. I'll get your clothes."

"Cool." Darryl pulled a shirt out of his mostly empty duffel and sniffed. "Thanks, Suse." He grabbed a pair of shorts and socks and ran to the bathroom.

Sue pulled the rest of the linens off the futon and waited until the shower turned on. She grabbed the sheets and Darryl's duffel and dashed into the pantry where her washer and dryer sat. After checking that there were at least a few pieces of clothes packed, she shoved the sheets into his duffel bag, lay a shirt on top and zipped the bag closed. She ran to the front door and dropped the bag near it, then went back to her room to dress and calm her nerves before Darryl finished his shower.

She left Darryl at the Departures curb at the airport with enough time for him to clear security and hustle to his gate. She headed home, stopping at the grocery store. Tom had asked her to make marina sauce from his mom's recipe. Tired of road food, Sue had agreed. That got everyone talking about home cooking. The guys asked Sue if they could use her kitchen. She agreed and managed to get them down to one dish each, plus her veggie dip. She wasn't into all the cooking, but the guys had promised to pitch in, and the foods they'd chosen would keep long enough for them to eat on the bus during the next week.

When she got home, she unloaded the groceries and put together the ingredients for the sauce. Once she could set it to simmer, Sue walked through her house with a damp cloth and a duster. She didn't have much furniture, but she had tons of art. She went from room to room, wiping each frame and the glass as she admired the prints and photos. She used the duster on Robin's sculpture and the few paintings she had, each a souvenir from a trip. When she got to the oil painting she'd bought years ago in New Orleans, she took extra care dusting it. The scene of Jackson Square reminded her of her first trip there and now, of Adam.

She climbed the stairs to the second floor—the space she used as her office—and sighed. Wide open, save for the bathroom at the top of the stairs, the space also had hardwood floors and barely any furniture. Sue immediately walked to the French doors next to the kitchenette at the back of the room, opened them, and stepped onto the deck to survey her tiny yard.

Since she lived in the end unit, she only had a fence on one side to separate her from the neighbors. Ivy all but obscured it, giving the yard a more intimate quality. The vines she'd wrapped along the railing bloomed in little tufts. Sue stretched to take in the sun. After a few more minutes of simply enjoying her space she walked back inside and opened the rest of the windows. She went downstairs to check the sauce and retrieve her laptop, then came back and set it up on her desk. She spent the next hour going through email, reading music publications, and making a list of things she needed to do and arrange before she left for Europe in a few weeks.

After she got caught up and a little ahead, Sue went downstairs to chop vegetables. She'd decided on veggie dip specifically to slice and dice. Her father had taught her how to use kitchen knives, and she loved it. It was a catharsis, not work—how she viewed the rest of the cooking process.

The spare key rattled in the lock as Sue peeled an eggplant.

"I brought you a sandwich," Emily called from the door. "I figured you bought all kinds of stuff for dinner and nothing for right now."

"You're right! How are you?" Sue rinsed her hands and met Emily in the living room, hugging her around the food.

Emily wore a crisp blouse tucked into a houndstooth pencil skirt, pantyhose and purple heels. "I'm good." Emily smirked. "You know, even though you're cooking, you look like you're in your element."

Sue gave her a brilliant smile and gestured around. "Oh, but I am."

"Turkey or roast beef?"

"Roast beef." Sue grabbed the sandwich.

"I have to eat and run, I've got an appointment this afternoon," Emily said. "But I've had a rough week. Can we listen to some girl power music?"

"Absolutely. Put on whatever you want." Sue left Emily to play with the stereo while she got out drinks and arranged lunch outside. She laughed at the song Emily queued up.

"What's so funny?" Emily asked when she joined Sue on the patio.

"Susan Tedeschi," Sue said. "I played this song for Justin, and he decided I like it because it's about oral sex."

"Ha!" Emily sat across from Sue. "Oral sex does make it more fun."

Sue and Emily chatted over their sandwiches, filling each other in on some of the aspects of each other's lives they didn't have time to discuss on the phone or through text, including the reporter coming after Chris. Her background check revealed that the woman had a difficult time holding a job, which explained some of her desperation. Emily's investigator had also found the pregnant woman.

"Have you called her?" Sue asked.

"No. The P.I. posed as a car warranty telemarketer when he made contact. Confirmed her name, address, and old car. That was it." Emily handed Sue a paper with the woman's name, address and phone number. "Didn't want to text this in case the reporter's hacking you."

"Smart, thank you."

Emily crumpled the wrappings from her sandwich and stood. "Hey, before I forget, call Axel."

"Why?"

"The intern you trained to replace you at the radio station fell for some guy who's touring with *Metalfest* and she decided to become a, uh, *band aid*, if you know what I mean."

Sue shook her head. "I thought she'd be more reliable."

"Axel needs help. Give him a call."

———————————

Two hours later, Sue had impressed herself with all the cooking she'd done: spaghetti sauce, eggplant parmesan, and veggie dip, as well as starts on some of the food the guys planned to make. She'd also managed to do a few loads of laundry and play in her garden.

The bus pulled up and parked across the street. When the knock came, Sue called out, "It's open!" She'd put a cold case of beer on the counter when Tom came in and gave her a half hug.

"The house smells great."

"Thanks, I've been freaking cooking all afternoon." Sue blew a piece of hair off her face.

"I will owe you until the end of time."

"Yep."

Tom rinsed off the spoon sitting on the stove and dipped it into the simmering sauce. He closed his eyes as he took a taste. "You will never know how grateful I am that you put aside your hatred of cooking long enough to learn how to make this."

"Everyone should know how to make a good marinara, right?" Sue peered around, seeking out the rest of the guys.

Justin and Brad studied the art on her walls.

"You guys want a beer?" she asked and turned back to Tom. "Where's Chris and Luther?"

"Luther stayed in Baltimore, visiting family. God knows where Chris is. He was on the bus when we got here. Where's Emily?"

"Work." Sue took a beer out of the case. "She'll be here in an hour or two."

Justin sauntered into the kitchen, giving her a nod as she passed him a bottle. "Nice place, Sexy Sue."

"Where's the stuff for the meatballs?" Tom rubbed his hands together.

Sue showed Tom where the spices, bowls and pans were, then grabbed another beer and took it to Brad.

He stood in her living room, staring at a photo.

"That's my mom." Sue handed him a bottle and took a pull off her own. "My dad took the picture. He said the first time he saw her, she was dancing, and he instantly fell in love."

Brad smirked and took a sip. "I can see how that would happen."

Chris thundered down the stairs. "You guys! You have to check this out! It's the perfect recording space!"

"An empty room is the perfect recording space?" Sue asked.

"Yeah. Come on!" Chris gestured to the guys to follow and took off up the stairs again.

Sue led the rest of the men to the second floor.

Justin let out a low whistle. "It *is* perfect!"

Chris beamed.

"What is this?" Brad asked.

"It used to be a townhouse, and at some point it was two condos," Sue explained. "When I bought it, I planned to rent or sell half of it. Lofts are a big draw out here, so I didn't put any walls back when I renovated. For now, it's my office. Wouldn't it have too much echo to record in?"

For the second time that day, Sue considered the room. She'd painted the far wall crimson red. A floor to ceiling shelving unit held a stereo, including a record player. Hundreds of CDs and records filled the rest of the unit. There were a few photos and small canvases on either side of the shelves, but it all filled a space about eight feet wide, leaving the rest of the wall blank on either side. Sue's desk sat in the middle of the room. An electrical outlet in the floor powered her computer and a small task lamp. A black leather sofa sat on an ancient Oriental rug at the back of the space.

"Wicked chandelier." Brad pointed to the ornate crystal fixture hanging over her desk.

"It came with the place. It's half the reason I bought it."

"Nice," Justin said.

"You're missing the best part." Chris grabbed Justin's arm and pulled him into the bathroom.

Justin laughed and walked out of the bathroom, shaking his head. "I knew you were naughty."

Sue did her best to seem innocent over the racy print. Scintillating or not, it was a classic piece of American art. "What?"

"A pin-up in the bathroom?"

"It's a Gil Elvgren masterpiece."

Justin gave her a long look and Sue laughed. She'd never explained her love of art to the guys; watching them learn this tickled her. That she'd had an interesting life before they came into it seemed scandalous to them.

Brad walked into the bathroom, made a slow circle, and came back out. "That is one hot woman on your wall. And those tiles are awesome. Can we record in here? Please?"

"Sure. But not all night. Someone lives next door."

The guys ran to get their gear while Sue and Tom went back to the kitchen. Sue brought one of the patio chairs inside and sat while Tom rolled meatballs.

"I take it you still aren't gonna rent the place while we're gone," Tom said.

"Nah, it's only two months. I haven't been able to find someone who would want it for such a short period of time."

"Would you do a longer lease?"

"Yeah. A guy transferring to Emily's office might take upstairs, but I'd have to put in a wall or two and a door. I don't want to rush it before we leave."

"You would build rooms for a tenant?" Tom asked.

"Yeah. The plan has always been to turn the townhouse into two separate spaces. Before you offered me this job, I was studying the market. I have to get the unit reclassified from one space to two if I want to get the best price, and that takes time. For now, I'm happy to rent. I'll put a wall by the stairs and a door with a lock so people can't just run up there if someone lives there when the tour is over."

"Like Chris did."

"Exactly." Sue tilted her beer bottle to take a sip.

"You've lived here for like two years and it's still empty. You're out of college. You're allowed to have more than a futon and a footlocker."

Sue shrugged. "I like futons and footlockers."

Tom rolled his eyes and passed her a fork with a freshly fried meatball on it.

Sue blew on the food and took a bite. "Mmm, I don't need to cook when you're capable of this, Tommy." She popped the rest into her mouth and gave back the fork.

Tom stabbed another meatball, dipped it in the sauce, and handed it to her. "But you still need furniture. What happened to the guy you were seeing when you bought the place? He couldn't talk you into buying a couch?"

Sue shifted, uncomfortable with the question. The guy had nudged her to buy a couch. Had offered to buy one for her since she wouldn't let him contribute to the down payment or even apply for the loan with her. She'd been thoughtless with him, cold. Focused only on her own goals. Their breakup had left a mark. She never considered that she could be unkind until he'd confronted her. It made her consider whether she'd been unkind to all her boyfriends. The idea that she might be treating Adam poorly made her stomach turn.

"We were over before closing."

Tom glanced at her as he cooked. "Sorry."

Sue desperately needed to shift away from her ex. "Remember the money from Nan?"

"How can I forget?"

She winced, realizing she'd shifted from one hot topic to another when she remembered the argument they'd gotten into about her contract, and Tom confessing that his inheritance was their safety net. "Mine is in this house. I used about two-thirds of it on the down payment, and the rest went into the renovations. The floors had to be redone, and the bookcase under the stairs is custom," Sue gestured toward the living room. "I needed new appliances. I took out all the walls upstairs, so I needed electrical and had to refinish the floor. I totally re-did the bathrooms. All the money is in this house."

"All of it?"

"Every penny. And when I'd saved enough again, you showed up with an offer. Why buy furniture when I wasn't gonna be here?" Sue didn't add that ever since learning Tom had planned to bankrupt himself if she failed, she only spent money on essentials. She wouldn't let him risk poverty, no matter how much confidence he had in her.

"Makes sense." Tom tasted his cooking.

"But I do have Nan's bedroom set. Mom and Dad brought it out once the major renovations were done."

"I remember how you used to pretend Nan and Gramps's bedroom was your entire house."

Sue stood and took another meatball. "That lake house was something special."

"Yeah." Tom dropped more meat into the frying pan.

"Anyway, if I rent out the second floor, the desk, rug, and couch come down here and it'll look more normal."

"Personal question." Tom lowered the flame on the frying pan and faced Sue. "Do you have any money?"

"Yeah." Of course he would ask that, even after he'd put his entire savings on the line for her.

"We only pay you once a month."

Sue mirrored Tom's posture before she answered. "I have money. I had enough saved when I left the radio station to pay the mortgage for a year. My car is paid off, and the insurance is paid until next spring. I canceled cable before I left for the tour, and before we go to Europe, I'm shutting off everything but the electricity to keep the air circulating. Aside from the mortgage, I don't have any debt. I'm on a sustainable budget."

"Are you sure?"

"Yes."

"If you need money between paydays, you know I'll give it to you." Tom moved meatballs from the frying pan to a plate.

Give. Not loan. He offered this knowing she could wipe him out anyway if she failed at her job. "I know. Dad says the same thing, but I'm fine. In fact, Bloody Maggots will improve my cash flow when they finish their album next month and I can line stuff up for them." Sue took a long drink from her beer and set the bottle on the counter. "Plus, something came up today that we should talk about."

"Yeah?"

"Axel and the big boss at the radio station basically offered me my old job back, on a consulting basis. Hardly anyone attended their last two events, and my replacement quit."

"Ouch."

"Yeah. The shutdown threat is looming. We've worked it out so the station's street team will do the in-person work at shows and stuff since I'll be with you guys. But I'll create and run the strategy and bill by the hour. They want a weekly call for progress reports, but they're gonna let me do what I want, as long as people come to the events again."

"How often will you get paid?"

"Monthly," Sue said.

"Seriously?"

"I negotiated a mid-month payment since you guys pay me at the end. It'll make budgeting a lot easier."

"Will you make more than before?"

"The hourly rate is more than double." Sue grinned.

Tom clinked his beer bottle against hers. "Nice!"

"It's billable hours, so when all is said and done, I'll likely be making about the same but having way more fun."

"That makes me feel better."

"You're okay with me taking another job?"

"Yeah. Why wouldn't I be?" Tom asked.

"Because I work for you with high stakes, and Chris is obsessed with how I should be focused exclusively on making him famous." She silently added the minefield she and Chris were currently wading through and wondered for the millionth time if taking on more work was wise.

"You're a consultant. Most consultants have multiple clients and don't ask permission to take on new projects." Tom dumped a plate full of fried meatballs into the marinara sauce.

"Yeah, but—"

"But nothing. Do it. It's none of Chris's business."

"Wow." Sue went into the refrigerator for more beer. "That was much easier than I expected."

"I'm not *always* high strung."

"True." Sue passed Tom a fresh bottle. "The beer helps, though."

CHAPTER 8

Running through the airport like his hair was on fire and driving his rental at top speeds for the eightyish miles from the airport to Sue's house had been worth it. When she opened the door, her smile lit Adam up. He gripped the doorframe to finally pace himself. He didn't want her to regret this invitation. As much as he needed her in his arms, he had to play the long game. Get the next date. And the next and the next.

He glanced down and noticed her bare feet. He should've called to tell her he'd be early. But as he lifted his gaze and took in her pretty dress and that smile, he cursed himself for not flying in the night before.

"Come in!" She stepped aside.

Adam crossed the threshold and finally gave into his impulses and gently pulled her into his arms, almost lifting her off the floor. He needed to feel her against him. "Hi."

"Hi."

"I missed you," he said.

Her lips curved into a smile against his neck, making his heart beat faster. What wouldn't he do for those lips?

"Me, too," she said.

Adam reluctantly pulled out of the hug but kept his hands on her waist. He didn't want to seem too eager or pushy, but he also had no idea how to behave. He'd never missed someone like this. "Sorry I didn't call. I got here faster than I expected."

"I don't mind. I'm just about ready anyway." Sue took one of his hands and led him into a large room. "It's sparse, but I'm hardly here these days. Do you want something to drink?"

"No, thanks." Adam took in the space. The lack of furniture paired with the professionally framed prints and paintings almost gave the room a museum quality.

"Give me one minute and I'll be ready." Sue kissed him lightly on the cheek and disappeared down a hallway.

He looked away so he wouldn't stalk after her. A bookcase with a few photos and knickknacks drew his eye. A framed photo of Sue, Amy, and Robin sat front and center.

"Emily invited us to her alumni tailgate." Sue walked back into what he now thought of as her gallery. "I told her maybe since I didn't know your plans."

Adam turned toward her and forgot what he'd been about to say. "How do you do that?"

"What?"

Adam skimmed his thumb along Sue's bare shoulder and down her arm. He tugged on the full skirt of her lavender sundress. "The clothes you wear make you glow. How do you do *that*?"

She flushed and smiled. "Practice."

Oh, how he wished he'd made her cheeks color from sex. Unable to resist, Adam kissed her. An electric charge coursed through him. "We don't have to go to the race," he said, his voice low.

"You have to report on it."

"I can re-run last year's article." He kissed her neck and lingered. Her scent both sweet and warm like a rose or cinnamon intoxicated him.

Sue moved closer, almost pressing against him. "But I want to wear this hat."

She taunted him by being so close, yet not close enough. He reluctantly pulled his gaze from her face down her body and noticed the floppy straw hat and small purse she held. "You wear hats?"

"To horse races."

Adam straightened. He wouldn't push. He'd show her a good time and get the next date. "I guess we have to go."

■————————————■

Adam gently pulled to a stop at the curb in front of Sue's townhouse. Using his left hand, he put the car in park and shut off the engine. When they'd gotten on the road a few hours before, Sue had threaded her fingers through his and settled his right hand into her lap. It had been the only time in his life when he'd been happy the rental car place didn't have manual transmissions.

Now he stared at her sleeping form and both thanked his lucky stars and cursed himself. He recounted all the best moments of the day, from discovering Sue had a long list of concerts she wanted to take him to, to her having read the article he wrote that day—the moment it went live on *Sports Mecca*—and grilling him on it while her friends milled around, to when she'd clearly opened the door for sex.

They'd stopped for dinner outside of Charlottesville. As they were leaving, Sue ducked into the bathroom. He brought the car around and stood outside of it, waiting for her. When she exited the restaurant, she made a beeline for him, wrapping herself around him as she kissed him. He took the kiss deeper, not caring that they were in public or that they were taking their time or anything else. He reveled in having this woman pliant in his arms and responding to his touch.

They only untangled when brash laughter from a group of people nearby interrupted them. Adam helped her into the car and noticed her hand trembling as she reached for the seatbelt. Yeah. He needed to get her to a bed as fast as possible.

And now…here they were. The end of the date. No band members nearby, Adam's entire family and even his staff accounted for and quiet. His desperation for her building more and more. And she was sleeping.

He didn't blame her. They'd spent most of the day on their feet in the sun. When they'd planned this date, he'd considered booking a room in Charlottesville, but it seemed presumptuous. Plus, with so many people in town for the race it would only invite interruption. He *had* gotten a room near Sue's place, though. Even if she wanted to be alone tonight, Adam wanted—needed—to see her again tomorrow.

Slowly, he lifted their hands out of her lap. He brought her knuckles to his lips and kissed them while rubbing his fingers down her arm. When she stirred, he leaned over and kissed her cheek. She turned toward him, and he kissed her lips. He pulled away, but she moved with him, so he kissed her again. Then deeper.

She hummed. "You're even a good kisser in my dreams."

His chuckle curled her lips into a small smile.

"Am I?"

"Oh yes." She pulled him toward her. "Do it again."

Adam obliged, giving her hand a small squeeze. "We're here," he whispered.

"Huh?" She furrowed her brow before opening her eyes and looking around. "How did that happen?"

"You fell asleep before we got to the interstate."

Sue's eyes widened. "I'm so sorry."

Adam gave her a patient smile and shook his head. "Don't be."

"Were you talking when I fell asleep?"

"No."

"Of course not," Sue said. "You set my brain on fire when we talk. I wouldn't sleep through that."

Adam raised an eyebrow. Did he imagine her words? "I set your brain on fire?"

"Constantly. It's amazing."

He all but climbed over the console to kiss her. Once again, he didn't care where they were or who was around. This woman blew him away. He loved talking with her, loved figuring out how her mind worked. After all the delays and interruptions and excuses, he figured she must think something was wrong with him. They'd been so close so many times and never sealed the deal. And then she admits she liked the talk as much as he did? Their next conversation needed to be a naked one. He poured all of that into his kiss.

"Wow," she whispered.

He unbuckled her seatbelt and helped her out of the car, grabbing her hat, and followed her to her front door.

"You're sure you weren't talking?"

Since he walked behind her, Adam let the shit-eating grin take over his face. The prizes this woman gave him were unparalleled. "Positive."

Sue exhaled as she unlocked the door. "Good."

She walked into the house, leaving the door open behind her. Despite his conviction a moment ago that he needed her naked, Adam stopped. He ached for her, but he also wanted more dates, more of her time, more of her. If he messed it up now, that would never happen. He paused, looking for the words to let her know she'd decide their next step.

She'd pushed open the interior door when she turned back to him. "You're coming in, right?"

Adam blinked before answering. "Unless you'd rather be alone. It was a long day."

Sue stepped over the threshold and grabbed his hand, pulling him into the house. "I like long days with you."

Adam closed the door behind him, and Sue reached past him, locking the bolt. Only their hands touched, but the heat from her body seared him anyway. He kept still, waiting for her to take the lead, hoping their intentions matched. She swayed closer, almost brushing her chest against him.

"I hid some wine from everyone last night. Want to open it?" Sue asked, her voice low.

"Sure."

He prowled behind her, watching her hips swing as she went to the kitchen, opened the fridge and bent toward a lower drawer. He stifled a groan but stayed close to her. Close enough that if she didn't pay attention, or maybe if she did, she'd bump into him.

"I hope you're okay with white. I wanted to save a red, but it was harder to hide."

Adam dropped her hat on the counter and took the bottle from her. He swept her hair off her shoulder, laying a kiss below her ear. "I drink both."

She leaned into him, letting him drag his lips down her throat. She held up a wine key but didn't move again until he shifted to open the bottle.

She put two glasses on the counter and slipped around him. "I'm going to put my hat away."

She retreated as Adam pulled the cork out of the bottle. He filled each glass, fervently hoping she'd come back naked.

"We need some music," she called out.

Adam recorked the bottle and put it into the fridge, waiting to hear what she selected. Hopefully something slow. Maybe a little bass heavy. Something to get her hips moving in that almost obscene roll she did when she'd danced at the Echo Chamber concert.

As he joined her in the main room, he recognized the soft tones of a singer-songwriter on the playlist she'd made for him. Love songs. He could work with that.

"Thank you." She accepted a glass of wine and sipped. "Should we go to the patio?"

When had she taken off her shoes? How had she gotten them off so fast? They had ribbons that wrapped around her ankles and had remained tied the entire day. He hadn't seen her touch them once. Surely those things took more than a few seconds to undo.

Adam took her hand. "Let's dance." He circled his arms around her waist and kissed her.

She twined her arms behind his neck and swayed with him, eventually resting her cheek on his shoulder.

He didn't even try to resist the skin she laid near his mouth. As he skimmed his lips along her neck, she moved with him, giving him more access. She still smelled like the sun, her almost cinnamon-scented soap, and God, he wanted that final note to be desire.

She stretched an arm away from them, giving him better access to trace the chain he'd given her. It thrilled him that she always wore it when they were together. As the blunt *clink* of her glass being set down registered through his lust haze, Sue glided her hand up his arm and into the short strands of hair at his neck. She tugged, lifting his head and pressing her mouth against his, taking him in a white-hot kiss. He'd grow his hair out if it meant she'd always use it to put his mouth right where she wanted it.

She kissed him deeper and he held her tighter, pressing the bulb of his wine glass against the curve of her waist. She broke their kiss, taking his drink.

He squeezed her ass with his newly free hand and followed her movements as she leaned away from him, still gripping his shoulder with her other hand. After a moment, she spun in his arms and took him with her as she stepped forward, depositing his glass on a shelf next to hers.

Adam hooked an arm around her waist and held her back to his front. He moved her hair away from her neck again, a movement he was coming to truly enjoy, and kissed her there. He trailed his lips down and across her shoulders, pushing the thin straps of her dress away. While keeping her ass pressed against him, she angled herself forward, giving him just enough room to play. He mentally congratulated himself when she sighed.

He found her zipper and pulled it down enough to undo the tiny and frustrating hook just above it, then kissed the bared skin. She shivered and grabbed fistfuls of his pants, but otherwise stayed still, as though waiting for his next touch. He opened the zipper another inch.

"Is this okay?" he whispered.

"Yeah."

Using a painfully slow pace, he opened the zipper to her waist and popped open the clasp of her bra. He gently pushed the bra and the dress away from her back. Finally, all her smooth skin, exposed only for him. He did all the things to her back that he'd thought about that night in Vegas. He ran his fingers down her spine, then his lips. He inhaled the scent at her nape, imprinting it on his brain, and pulled her fully against him in a backward hug, tightening his grip when she sunk into his arms.

Her naked back against him was a delicious tease. He wanted her skin on his, but he'd been so taken with exploring her and living out the fantasy of touching her that he'd been late to consider his own clothes. It was a minor regret. This had been long overdue.

As he held her against him, he saw that in moving her dress away from her back, he'd also moved it away from her front. One of her nipples peeked out from the rumpled fabric. He reached for it then slowed, about to ask her if he could. She put his hand on her breast, the hard nipple against his palm practically a dare.

"Adam," she whispered.

His fingers ghosted from one breast to the other, teasing her and tempting him. Deciding where he wanted to kiss her next was impossible. He loosened his grip around her waist enough to dip his hand under her dress and trail his fingers lower. When he felt the edge of her panties, he stopped, his palm pressed against her abdomen. Her chest raised and lowered in time with her quick breaths. He kissed the racing pulse in her neck.

She pushed against him again, gripping his thigh with one hand while she dragged his mouth to hers with the other.

"Adam," she said, her whisper hoarse.

Her legs quivered against him, so he scooped her up, carried her into the bedroom, and sat her on the bed.

She yanked his shirts out of his pants and sank back, bringing him with her.

He loved that she seemed as desperate as him to get them both naked. Even though he wanted to press all of himself against all of her, he hovered above, licking and sucking her nipples as he dragged her dress past her hips. When she lifted up, he slid a hand underneath her and squeezed her ass, his fingertips teasing the edge of her sex.

She worked a hand under his clothes, stoking his lust as she touched his chest, stomach, and back.

He took his hands off her long enough to haul his shirts over his head.

Sue wrapped her fingers around his belt buckle and stilled. "Where's your phone?"

"Huh?" Adam eyed her grip.

"Your phone."

He smiled as he removed her hands and opened his belt and pants. "I turned it off in the restaurant."

She purred. "Good man."

She bent forward, pushing his slacks away, but he guided her back and took off her panties, caressing her legs as the flimsy fabric fell away. He took his time exploring her from ankle to hip, hip to neck.

Sue hooked a foot in his pocket, yanked his pants down, and slipped her fingers into his underwear, dragging it away as she reached for him.

He almost lost control. Her show of wanting him was easily the sexiest thing he'd ever experienced. If he wanted any chance at satisfying her, he needed her to go slow.

Adam grabbed her hands and held them over her head. "Wait." Holding both of her hands in one, he trailed his fingers over her body, needing to touch her. "Let me get a condom."

Sue rose to kiss him even though he still held her hands. "I have some."

"I do, too." He went for his pants, but when Sue rolled over and crawled across the bed, her perfect ass in the air, he needed to touch her. He kicked off his slacks and shoes and followed her, kissing each cheek and sliding his hand over her until he reached her center.

She gasped and shivered, almost dropping the brand new box she struggled to open. Finally, she ripped off the top and grabbed a foil packet. Kneeling, she leaned back, sitting in his lap and rubbing against him. Fingers in his hair, she again brought his mouth to hers and devoured him as she gave him the condom. When he gently nudged her forward to roll it on, she faced him, running her fingers over his biceps.

He crawled over her again, settling her against the bed. He teased her nipples with his tongue and teeth while his hands lifted her hips to him.

"Adam," she said in breathless whisper, "please."

He covered her body with his and hooked one of her legs around his hip. He fought to maintain his control and eye contact with her when he entered her. She sighed and ground her hips against him, winding herself about him and touching him in all the places he wanted. He rocked against her and stopped, his eyes closed tight. His pulse beat wildly.

"Don't stop." Sue tightened her legs around his waist.

He opened his eyes and held her gaze as their rhythm built. When she came Adam kissed her, swallowing her moan, and let go.

CHAPTER 9

"You got the red for the wall from the print, didn't you?" Adam's words surprised Sue, but she was happy to hear them.

She didn't like leaving him alone in bed, but she'd been restless when she woke, despite several rounds of sex. She tried to rouse him, but Adam had been out cold. Instead, she'd gone upstairs and checked her email.

"I'm impressed. You're the only one who's ever noticed." The eight-foot tall John Singer Sargent print Adam noticed had been a gift from her father when she bought the townhouse. It hung on the wall along the stairs, even with the second floor.

"Am I?"

"Yeah." Sue drank in his appearance. Adam only wore his pants, zipped, but with the button and belt hanging open. That chest. Damn. She could look at his chest all day.

"Most people comment on the pin-up in the bathroom." Sue pointed her chin at the door near the top the stairs.

As he went into the bathroom, Sue appreciated the firm lines of his broad shoulders and back.

"Nice, but I prefer the one out here," he said as he returned to the main room.

"Ooh." Sue closed the computer, long past caring about email or anything besides the man in front of her.

"I wasn't sure how you take your coffee. This is black." Adam gave her a mug. He leaned over the desk and kissed her.

"Perfect."

"This is your office?"

"Sort of. I wanted to lease one of the floors before I joined the tour, but there wasn't time. I put the desk and couch up here so when people walk through it isn't completely empty."

"That's why you have the extra doors downstairs," Adam said.

"Yes."

"What would you do with the Sargent repro?"

Sue shrugged. "Depending on which floor I lease, it'll either go on the wall I build along the stairwell, or in the main room downstairs."

"It would be a shame to hide it down there."

Sue smiled and combed a hand through her hair. No one else seemed to appreciate the giant piece of art. Adam recognizing and admiring it gave her all kinds of butter-flies. "It wouldn't be totally hidden. I'd work from home a lot more."

"Is that what you were doing? Working?" He looked concerned. It was both endearing and unnecessary. Yes, she worked a lot. But no way in hell would her work interrupt this weekend. Especially when her most recent message had come from Chris. It included his STI test results and the note "*No herp. No nothing. Julie can fuck off.*" One less thing to worry about.

"No. I emailed my brother. He graduates from college when I'm in Europe, so we're trying to get together before I go."

"You'll miss his ceremony."

"He doesn't want to walk until his Masters is done. But he struggled to figure out what his undergrad degree should be. I want to mark the occasion."

"Neuroscience, right?"

Sue tipped her mug toward Adam, trying to stay collected even though his questions hit her in all the right places. Noticing little details, remembering others. He was exceedingly skilled at making her feel special. "Good memory."

"One more question."

Sue lifted her eyebrows and sipped her coffee.

"Are you wearing my shirt?"

Sue gave Adam a sly smile. She'd put on his shirt when she couldn't wake him so she could at least smell him while she left him to sleep. "I am." She stood and undid the one button holding it closed. "Do you need it? I can take it off."

Adam put his coffee cup on the desk and ambled around it to her. He smoothed a finger along the line of buttons.

Sue slid the shirt off each shoulder and let it fall in a puddle on the floor.

"Your skin glows even more when you're naked. How do you do that?"

He sounded reverent, and Sue fought to stay steady on her feet. This man was lethal.

"A girl can't give away all her secrets." She lowered his pants and found him without underwear and ready for her. She kissed him. "You know, I've never had sex up here."

"We have to remedy that." Adam pulled her against him and kissed her hard, then picked her up and sat her on the edge of the desk. He lingered over her, kissing down her body and sinking to his knees.

Sue gasped when he tasted her. She fell back on her elbows, pushing herself against him. This felt more intimate than anything they'd done the night before, and while she usually hated feeling vulnerable, with Adam she felt safe and cared for and so close to coming that she might lose her mind. "I need you inside me."

"Soon." He pressed his mouth to her again and slid a finger in.

She dropped her head back and moaned. "Now, Adam."

He kept his mouth on her as he dug into his pockets, then he moved away just enough to deal with a strip of condoms.

She let out a soft chuckle. "The man who offered to leave me on the doorstep last night had half a dozen condoms in his pants?"

"I didn't expect anything." Adam stood and tore open one of the wrappers. "But I had a lot of hope."

"Six times is more than a lot of hope."

Condom in place, he gripped her hips and drove into her. "We're more than halfway there."

CHAPTER 10

Baltimore, MD

"Pittsburgh, Akron, Philly, Syracuse, Brooklyn. No days off, right?" Adam hugged Sue as they talked. When they'd made their plans, it hadn't occurred to him that leaving her at the airport security checkpoint would put a damper on his afterglow from their weekend together.

"Right." Sue's chin bobbed against his shoulder as she spoke. "Rex Theater tonight."

"Did you figure out when you're going to see your brother?"

Sue sighed. "Not yet. Something came up with the band and it distracted me."

"Everything okay?" She'd been off all morning. The idea that she might end this tortured him.

"We have to make some logistical changes for a press opp. It'll be fine."

Adam gave her a light kiss and waited a moment before he spoke again. "Any chance you have time to come to Boston with me before you go to Europe?"

Sue took long enough to answer that Adam recited hockey statistics to himself to keep from begging. He wanted it clear that he wasn't done, but he didn't want to pressure her either.

"Maybe. It depends on how things go in New York and with my brother."

"I'll meet you there." Adam brushed a strand of hair over Sue's ear. He'd meet her anywhere. "New York's a commuter flight for me. We can work around the interviews."

"You're extremely generous with your time, Mr. Entrepreneur," Sue said.

"You're worth it."

Sue licked her bottom lip and smiled before she kissed him.

With things moving in his favor, he decided to make a big ask. "I'll call you when my plane lands. In the meantime, send me your itinerary. Lauren'll sync it with mine."

Sue looked like a deer caught in headlights. "I can't, Adam. That's not her job."

"Yes, it is." He kept his tone steady but rubbed the small of her back. He wanted her licking her lips again. "Lauren schedules all my travel."

"Even personal stuff?"

Adam squeezed her. "Yes. My entire family sends Lauren information."

Sue leaned back and looked Adam in the eye, her expression guarded.

"Please do this." Had he pushed too hard when he asked for her schedule? He could follow the tour dates on the Words Fail Me website, but it wouldn't tell him if she'd have time for him. He wanted to be there, but not in her way. And when he was there, he wanted Sue's attention. He racked his brain for an explanation that didn't sound stalkerish or possessive.

Sue blew out a puff of air. "Okay."

Adam hugged her tighter. If only he could take her with him.

"It may not be there right when your plane lands. I still have some holes to fill."

"Send what you have. We can update it."

Sue pursed her lips together before sighing. "Okay."

The announcement of the first boarding call for Adam's flight echoed through the check-in area. "I have to go."

Sue drug her gaze to the floor. "Yeah." Was it him? Had she slipped back into work mode? He needed to learn more of her tells.

Adam forced eye contact. "So, listen."

"Hmm?"

"Please tell Robin I said thank you from the depths of my soul for buying you *The Skirt*." When Sue had stepped out of the bathroom the night before in the super short skirt he'd missed in New Orleans, Adam's plan to take her out for dinner and live music fell right out of his head. Like the night at the boxing match when she wore the backless dress, he only saw acres of skin. But this time, he could touch her.

Sue giggled and buried her face in his shoulder. "I've never seen a man so tongue-tied over a piece of fabric."

"You haven't been paying enough attention, babe."

Sue brushed her fingers through the hair on the back of his head. There were hints of a smile playing at her lips, but she still seemed tense. "I kind of feel bad. The skirt never made it out last night."

"I don't." Adam considered the previous evening. He'd never been one to blow things off, but in this case, he had no regrets. Sue had easily bested any plans he could've made when she confessed that she'd wanted *him* the night of the fight. No one else. "In fact, I'd love another weekend with you and that skirt."

"We'd have to go out, though. Robin says fashion is meant to be seen."

"Oh, the fashion was seen. And deeply appreciated."

Sue fell into another fit of giggles.

"I'm serious. Tell Robin if he ever finds something like that again, I'll give him my credit card to secure the purchase." Adam maneuvered to see her face.

"You're terrible." Her sunshine smile came back.

"I admire Robin's gift for dressing you." He owed the guy a major favor.

"I'm not telling him about your gift for *un*dressing me."

"That stays between us." Adam leaned in to kiss her. His peck shifted into a deep, languorous kiss. He squeezed her again and pressed his lips to her forehead. "I'll see you soon."

"Good." It sounded confident coming from her lips. He liked it.

He gripped his travel bag and headed to the security gate, looking back twice. Sue stood where he left her. She still wore a smile, but her fingers twisted in the ends of her hair told another story.

"Toga! Toga!"

Sue and Adam both looked in the direction of the chant.

Darryl jogged through the airport toward Sue, duffel in tow, wearing a sheet, socks and sneakers.

Sue laughed and clapped. She waved to Adam, then followed Darryl to the exit.

Watching her leave with another man seared him.

CHAPTER II

Philadelphia, PA

Sue wound through the back of the venue to the stage entrance and stood in the doorway. She watched the guys play basketball in the parking lot while she took a minute to collect herself. She'd finally called the woman a reporter claimed Chris had gotten pregnant. Their conversation had been helpful, but still left Sue with concerns.

After a few minutes she stepped into the parking lot. "Chris!"

He took his shot and sneered when he missed. "What?" He barked.

"You get to help me set up lunch today."

Chris gave her a dirty look but before he turned away, Sue flashed the picture of the little boy.

He huffed, then chased the ball. He made a slam dunk, barely, then stomped toward her. "Make it fast." He shoved open the stage door and went inside.

She followed and directed him to the vestibule at the front of the building.

Chris pressed his forehead and fingers to the window. "Well?"

"The mother's name is Skylar. Her son is Noah."

"*Her* son?"

"She told me you aren't the father right away. You're not the father of either child."

Chris spun around his face alight. "I told you!"

Sue nodded. "I'm sorry I doubted you."

"No diseases, no kids. Julie can go fuck herself!" Chris waved his middle fingers at the people walking by outside.

"Okay, calm down before you start a brawl."

"I'd win it. Today, I'd win it." Chris crossed his arms and held his head high. "Did the record company try to keep her away?

"No. She never contacted the record company. To her, meeting Julie was a fluke."

Chris scratched his head. "You don't think so."

Sue pursed her lips. "I don't trust Julie." The reporter had told a long list of lies to both Sue and Skylar. They'd spent a few minutes trading notes about it. Some of the lies connected, but none of it made any sense.

"Do you think she sought out Skylar?"

"I don't know. Skylar wants you to call her."

"Did she tell you who the father is?"

Sue shook her head. "She said you were close to him and insisted on talking to you. I'll text you her number."

They stood in silence for a moment, Sue deep in thought. "Any idea who the father could be?"

"You worried it might be one of the fellas?"

"Maybe?" Sue paced. "If it was one of the guys, wouldn't she want to talk directly to them?"

"Probably. What do you fucking care?"

"I need to keep Julie away."

"Yeah. And while you're at it, stay the fuck off my balls." Chris opened and held the door for a pizza delivery woman.

Sue rolled her eyes, then signed the receipt as the woman took the boxes out of the heat bag.

Chris flirted as he gave a generous cash tip along with a password to get into the show later. When the pizza lady left Chris waived his phone at Sue. "I want the digits before I get the pies out back." He took the food and crossed the vestibule.

"Be nice to her." Sue pulled up Skylar's information and forwarded it to him.

"I'm plenty nice."

"Sure you are."

CHAPTER 12

Adam didn't tell Sue he planned to visit her in Philadelphia. He hadn't been entirely sure he'd make it until he got in the car to drive out there. He walked into the club, relieved that Tom had been near the door and let him in even though the place didn't open for another hour.

Sue stood arm in arm with some guy. Sure, she worked with men, but why the fuck did they have to touch her? And why did she let them?

Adam approached, ready to make an ass of himself.

The guy was tall and rangy with black curling hair and a predatory smile. He met Adam's cold stare head-on and nudged Sue.

Sue glanced at the guy then followed his gaze. Her face lit up.

"Adam!" She crossed the few feet between them and all but launched herself into his arms.

Thrown off guard by her reaction, Adam hugged her tightly. She'd given him exactly what he needed and calmed him immediately.

"What a night for you to surprise me!"

"What do you mean?"

"My brother's here." Sue led him back to the bar, directly to the man she'd been with when he walked in. "Gavin, Adam. Adam, my little brother, Gavin."

Gavin held out his hand and offered a more genuine smile. "If it's any consolation, she didn't like me this much when we were kids."

Sue rolled her eyes. "You were more annoying when we were kids."

Adam shook Gavin's hand, letting go of his jealousy. "I've heard a lot about you."

"No wonder you looked like you wanted to kill me."

Adam glanced at Sue, still firmly by his side. "Can you blame me?"

"No," Gavin said.

Sue grabbed Adam's arms and made him face her. "I thought I wouldn't see you until Friday. How were you able to get out here?"

"I'm in Manhattan all week. My day ended early."

"I'm glad you came out." Sue kissed his cheek.

"Me, too."

"I have to do some work," Sue said. "Gav, don't grill him. Tom already did. One per family is enough."

"Yes, ma'am." Gavin gave his sister a mock salute as she walked away. When she got out of earshot, he spoke again. "Tom's grilling abilities are suspect. He doesn't have a sister."

"I guess I'm due for a real third degree." Adam rolled back his shoulders, mentally bracing himself.

"Nah. Knowing I almost lost an arm for having it around her said it all."

Adam pressed his lips into a line. That hadn't been his best moment. "It's not like that."

Gavin paused, his beer halfway to his mouth. "No?"

"I don't want to control her. I just want to be with her."

"You sure about that?"

Adam nodded. "I don't play games. I want a partner."

"Smart. She doesn't put up with bullshit."

"That's why I like her."

Gavin chugged the rest of his longneck. "I bet Tom asked more than two questions."

Adam chuckled. "Way more. Want another beer?"

———————————————

"Are you actually considering UPenn or taking advantage of their interest in you?" Sue sipped her soda and waited for her brother to swallow the enormous bite he'd taken of his cheesesteak. Gavin wanted to eat, so while Tom and the band finished soundcheck, Sue, Gavin, and Adam were camped out in a nearby cheesesteak place.

"I'm probably gonna go Johns Hopkins. But UPenn is a good option. Duke, too. I had my last final when you guys were in North Carolina, so I'm visiting here first."

"They putting you up for the night?" Sue asked.

"Pssh. I'm gonna try out the rock-and-roll lifestyle. Being the band's publicist's brother will land me all kinds of pussy, right?"

Sue laughed. Gavin never had a hard time meeting people, and even if he did, Sue and Tom always had space for him. "They're not that famous yet. I'll let you know when the time is right."

Gavin offered his fist. "Good looking out, sis."

Adam sat back in the booth and put an arm around Sue. "Speaking of famous, I got your calendar update this morning. Is that—"

"Don't even speak it out loud," Sue interrupted. "I don't want to jinx it."

"It's not a spectator thing?"

"Nope. Booked. I got the call Sunday and confirmed today."

"Is that why you were weird in the airport?"

Sue nodded. This gigantic opportunity had her tied in knots all week; she didn't want to botch it, and the possibility that the reporter coming after Chris could cost them this opportunity kept Sue up at night. She spun her phone on the table, willing herself not to check her messages. It'd be fine. Nothing would get canceled. She stopped spinning the phone, forcing herself to accept that the gig was official.

Gavin swallowed another enormous bite and wiped his mouth. "What thing?"

Sue pushed another napkin at Gavin. "If you can make it to Brooklyn on Friday, we're having a big party."

"For?"

Sue threw her hands in the air. "Your graduation! Surprise!"

"You're a shitty liar, sis."

"I can't tell you before I tell the band. I just told Tom this morning. *He* wouldn't even know yet if I didn't have to change our travel times."

Gavin gestured at Adam. "But he knows."

Sue sat back and squeezed Adam's leg under the table. "He asked nicer. And we had plans together in Brooklyn. I sort of changed them." Sue caught Adam's gaze. "I'm sorry. That warranted a phone call, but I haven't been alone all day."

"It's okay. It's an awesome change to the plans."

"I'm pretty proud of it."

Adam squeezed Sue's shoulder. "You should be."

"Ugh." Gavin crumpled his napkin and shoved his empty sandwich basket at Sue. "I'm gonna go to the bathroom so you guys can finish eye fucking each other."

Sue blanched. "Crass!"

"Yep!" Gavin shouted out as he walked toward the back of the restaurant.

"I'm sorry. He likes to embarrass people. Well. Me."

Adam pulled Sue closer to him. "It's okay. If he wasn't here and you weren't working, we'd be doing a lot more than eye fucking."

Heat zipped down her spine. She raised her eyebrows. "Our marathon weekend made you bold."

Adam grinned.

"You're staying with me tonight."

"Hell yes, I am." He kissed Sue in a way that had her wishing they weren't in a public place.

Gavin made a lot of noise on his return. "Come on, let's get back before the show starts. I wanna warm up the ladies."

Sue rolled her eyes but followed, Adam on her heels.

Adam's phone trilled as they approached the club. He checked the screen. "Sorry, I have to take this. I'll be in in a minute."

Sue made sure they were a good distance from Adam before she punched Gavin's arm hard.

"Ow! What was that for?"

"Eye fucking? Really, Gavin?"

Gavin laughed as he rubbed his biceps. "Come on, I never get to meet the guys you date. You gotta let me play a little."

Sue glared. "That wasn't playing, Gav. It was obnoxious."

"I would be a shitty brother if I didn't give him some kind of grief."

"Please leave him alone."

Gavin raised his eyebrows. "Ooh, this one's special."

Sue glanced away, trying to fight the heat rising in her cheeks. "Let it go, Gav."

"Why? You let me tease the shit out of that one guy."

Sue squinted at him, trying to remember.

Gavin scratched his head. "You know, the guy at your graduation party who was wounded because you made plans to move away from college without him."

"Oh!" Sue bumped her palm against her forehead. "Yeah, he was a tool. You could've fucked with him all you wanted."

"But not Adam."

Sue froze. The excitement that had been bubbling in her all night turned to nausea. "Don't tell Mom and Dad."

Gavin wrinkled his brow. "What?"

"Don't tell Mom and Dad." Sue paused to try to get the panic out of her voice. She raked her fingers through her hair. "This thing probably won't last once I get to Europe. There's no point in putting it under their scrutiny."

"What scrutiny? When have Mom and Dad ever scrutinized any of your boyfriends?"

Sue gave Gavin a level look. "Do you not remember the stories that went around about Dad? Dating Connie Corleone would've been less stressful."

After Sue's first date, when her father wouldn't let her leave until he'd questioned the boy for more than thirty minutes and followed them in his car, she brought *no one* home.

"High school was a long time ago, sis."

Sue sighed. "Don't tell them. Please."

"I'm not gonna lie for you."

"I'm not asking you to lie, Gav. Just don't say anything to make them ask questions." Why her brother suddenly seemed clueless to a problem that had existed since her freshman year was beyond her.

"You're weird, Sue." Gavin shook his head. "But I'll keep my mouth shut."

Relief surged through her. "Thank you."

"Except for this." Gavin gripped Sue's shoulders. "Adam does not seem like someone who will let an ocean get in his way."

CHAPTER 13

Syracuse, NY

"Come on, Chris, we have to get moving." Sue swept her arm toward the door, wishing Chris would stop chatting up the busty bartender and wheel the damn amplifier outside. She held one of Darryl's keyboard cases and didn't want to risk dropping it, or she'd take the amp herself.

"Keeps your pants on. Damn." Chris sneered at her, then followed the bartender, leaving the amp.

Flagging Tom at the bottom of the ramp, Sue put her foot against the side of the amp and gave it a good push out the door. Tom caught it and directed it toward the band's trailer. She chased after Chris and flicked his ear.

"What the fuck, Sue?" Chris turned his back on the woman.

"We have to leave. Now. Get her number or don't and let's get on with it!" Ever since their earlier conversation about Skylar, Chris had gone back to his woman chasing ways with a vengeance. He was so relentless that Sue felt bad for the bartender.

"You're out of your fucking mind!" Chris stormed off, probably to catch the bartender.

Justin appeared in the doorway. Sue passed him the keyboard and stalked after Chris. She pulled him back by the shoulder and got to the bartender first. "Hey, excuse me." Sue tapped the woman's arm. "I'm so sorry about all that. We're like oil and water, but I didn't mean to be bitchy to you."

The woman tilted her head. "You weren't."

"Good. I know this may be a long shot, but he likes you. Obviously. But we have to get on the road for our next gig. If you like him, we're having a big end-of-tour party tomorrow in Brooklyn. I know it's a long drive, but if you don't have to work or whatever, please come out." Sue rifled through her pockets and found a scrap of paper and a pen. She wrote the name and address of the club and gave it to the bartender. "Give the password 'Killer Queen' at the door, and they'll let you in, no questions asked."

The woman read the paper. "This is real?"

"Yeah. Please come. Bring some friends. It'll be fun. I promise I won't pick another fight with him." Sue pointed to Chris, who stood next to her, mouth agape.

"How many friends?"

"The more the merrier." Sue elbowed Chris.

"Come on out, doll. Tomorrow I can make *you* a few drinks." Chris leered.

Sue dropped her gaze, trying not to roll her eyes.

"I'll see what I can do. Thanks." The woman gave Sue a tight smile.

"Cool." Sue grabbed Chris's arm and dragged him toward the back door.

"Dude, I can walk on my own!"

"Not fast enough. Get your scrawny ass on the bus." Sue shoved Chris out the door.

"What about the gear?"

"I got it! Bus!" She pointed to the bus and held her ground until he boarded it. She didn't miss the bird he waved as she went back inside.

"We got it all." Tom rushed toward her. The anxiety and stress on his face mirrored Sue's jangled nerves. "I did the walkthrough. Mark said they'll check again and put anything we might've missed in Skein's trailer."

"Cool, let's go."

Sue and Tom jogged to the bus.

"Everyone on board?" Tom slammed the door shut behind him.

"Yes! Jesus!" Chris yelled.

"Let's go, Luther." Sue squeezed the man's shoulder and turned back to the cabin.

"What's going on?" Justin asked.

The guys were spread throughout the main area, looking annoyed and confused.

Sue pushed her hair off her face. "You guys need to sleep. A lot. Soon."

"Why?" Brad asked.

"When we get to Brooklyn, we have to unload and set up the gear early and go to Rockefeller Center, which is about an hour from the club."

"We doing a radio thing?" Darryl asked.

"No. *The Tonight Show* had a cancellation." Sue waited for their reactions. When none came, she clarified. "The musical guest on *The Tonight Show* canceled. You guys are taking the spot. You're gonna be on *The Tonight Show* tomorrow."

Chris glared. "That's a fucking mean joke."

Tom stepped in front of her. "It's not a joke. You guys are performing on *The Tonight Show*."

"Holy. Fuckin. Shit!" Each word got louder as Darryl stood and grabbed Sue. "Holy shit!" He shook her around like a rag doll.

Brad let out a *whoop* and galloped to the bunks and back. He hugged her from behind, joining Darryl in the shaking motion.

"How did you manage this, Sexy Sue?" Justin pulled Brad, then Darryl off Sue and sat her on one of the benches. He sat next to her.

"It was a weird configuration of people connecting me with the booking agent and the booker calling the record label, and bam, you got the spot."

"No, *you* got the spot." Justin put an arm around her and squeezed. "This is amazing. Thank you."

"It is amazing, but it's gonna take a ton of work. The show tapes at five. We have to be there by one. You're on stage again at eight in Brooklyn. We have to get to Brooklyn, set up and do soundcheck, get to the studio and set up and do soundcheck there, finish the show and get back to Brooklyn before eight."

"We have to be on point tomorrow," Tom said. "No fucking around. At all."

"None," Sue agreed. "But after the show, we're having an epic end-of-tour-slash-you-were-on-*The*-fucking-*Tonight-Show* party."

Brad steepled his fingers against his mouth. "This is so fucking awesome."

"I don't want to be a buzz kill—" Justin slid forward in his seat. "But how are we gonna set up for soundcheck at the club *and* the show? I only have one drum kit."

"Excellent question, my friend. I have an excellent answer." Sue sat straighter and cleared her throat. "Annabelle is flying in with your spare kit and two more boards for Darryl."

Brad dropped to his knees. "You called my sister? She's gonna *love* this!"

"I started emailing with Annabelle in New Orleans. After you guys got on the news, she told me she's always wanted to see you on a late-night show. When we got the date, she was my first phone call."

"How did you keep her quiet? Is she on the plane already?" Brad glanced between Sue and Tom, who sat on opposite sides of the bus.

Sue shrugged. "Annabelle says she's a good secret keeper."

Justin and Darryl snickered.

"If she's a secret keeper, it's news to me." Darryl bounced a tennis ball on the floor and caught it with the opposite hand. "She spilled all kinds of shit when she was going after Justin."

Justin grinned. "She mostly stuck with embarrassing stuff about living with Brad."

"At least she didn't let anything new slip," Brad said.

"Annabelle's known about this almost as long as Sue has," Tom said. "She arranged for all the gear and didn't call me *once*, so I'd say she's pretty good with big secrets."

"You annoyed she didn't need your help, Tommy?" Darryl bounced the ball against the wall next to Tom and caught it again.

"No."

Sue covered her mouth to hide her grin. She had a lifetime of knowledge about Tom. He didn't like not being involved in all the logistical planning, but sacrifices had to be made for her superstition. Until this moment, the fewer people who knew, the better. She gave herself a moment to enjoy the excitement humming through the bus before handling all the questions the guys lobbed at her. As their questions died down and their excitement built, she noticed an odd pocket of silence.

"Chris," she said. "You have extra basses on hand. We don't need to have Annabelle carry on at the last minute, right?"

Chris sat across from her, his head between his knees. He slowly lifted his gaze, his complexion ghostly pale. "I have a bass for the club," he whispered.

"And another you can take to *The Tonight Show*?"

"I have a bass for *The Tonight Show*." His eyes grew round and large like saucers. He stood on visibly shaky legs, walked to the back, and closed the partition between the sleeping quarters and the rest of the bus, isolating himself.

"Is he okay?"

Darryl bounced his ball against the door. "He likes to freak out in private."

"Yeah." Brad sat on the floor and hugged his knees. "When he lets us see him again, he'll be good."

"It's true, Sue," Tom added. "The first time they had a sold-out gig, he disappeared after soundcheck. He resurfaced right before showtime and played one of his best sets ever."

Sue pressed a hand to her stomach to keep her own nerves in check. "I'll trust you guys. But does he really have an extra bass? Annabelle's on the first flight in the morning, there's still time to call her."

"He's good," Brad said. "Between the two of us, we have seven guitars. Only one of them is out of rotation right now. Nothing to worry about."

"Okay." Sue sat back and combed her fingers through her hair. She had less pressure now that she wasn't keeping this from them. "There's one more thing. Darryl?"

"Yeah, Suse?" Darryl caught the ball and focused on her.

"I called Lena. Her flight gets in around ten."

Darryl's face lit up like Times Square. "That's even better than *The Tonight Show*."

CHAPTER 14

New York, NY

"What do you think, Just? I can still go to Brooklyn and get the other kit." Sue stood next to Annabelle on *The Tonight Show* stage, facing Justin and his drums.

He played a muted combination. His movements were fluid, but he seemed uncomfortable. "This is so weird. Drums aren't supposed to be this quiet."

"It's standard." Annabelle mimicked his beats as he played. "It'll sound good when the whole band is here and everything is mic'ed. Otherwise it's too loud for the studio."

"This shit is mind blowing, Bells." Justin climbed down from his perch and slung an arm around her shoulder.

"Mind-blowingly *good*." Annabelle patted his cheek.

"Yeah." He turned to Sue. "Thank you."

"All I did was get you here. You still have to knock it out of the park." Sue grimaced. "No pressure."

Justin laughed. "I got your back, Sexy Sue. I'll beat these cans like I'm Muhammed Ali and they're Sonny Liston."

Tom joined them onstage. "Stage manager says we have time for one more run-through."

"Let's do it!" Justin climbed back behind the drums.

Sue led Tom and Annabelle to the first row of seats for the audience, where Lena already sat. A reporter hovered behind the line of television cameras.

Tom slouched in his seat and nudged Sue. "Who's the reporter?"

"A local guy who writes for *Sound Spectrum*."

"The magazine that ripped Chris?"

"Yeah. I figured I should make nice after I made them kill an article." Sue had always planned a "kiss and make up" opportunity with *Sound Spectrum* after the initial tussle with Julie. She had to work even harder to make sure she made more friends than enemies now with Julie specifically targeting Chris. Plus, Sue's own reputation was in the mix; she needed to be able to line up press, and not only for Words Fail Me.

Tom rubbed his temple. "What'd it cost ya?"

Sue smirked to cover her anxiety. "The guy gets to tail Brad all day. And Brad'll wear a T-shirt on the show that *Sound Spectrum* will auction for their music in schools project."

Tom sat up. "A few weeks ago, you strong-armed a national publication into changing an article that would've trashed the band. Then you called them back and negotiated a one-on-one exclusive with an extra plug for their charity?"

"Yep."

"You have *big* brass balls."

Sue shook her head. "We can't avoid them forever."

"Big. Brassy. Balls. I should give you a raise."

Sue didn't want Tom's compliment. She'd built a house of cards around this event. If the performance was bad, if Brad didn't wear the shirt, if anything was off, including Julie Griffin dropping her fucking story, the article and even their involvement in the charity would disappear. "Don't you jinx this, Tommy."

He held up his hands. "Only *you* are too superstitious to take more money when it's offered."

After the run-through they all retreated to the makeup room. Sue gave Brad a burgundy T-shirt similar to the one they'd auctioned for the zoo in New Orleans. It featured a soundwave from the song Words Fail Me would play on the show.

She expected the atmosphere to be nervous—she sure as hell was—but Lena and Annabelle went a long way toward keeping the guys calm. Chris looked like he might pass out, but everyone else relaxed and joked around.

"Calling Annabelle was genius." Tom stood near the doorway but kept his voice low.

"She definitely defuses the tension." Sue crossed her arms. "She isn't flirting with anybody, though. I figured she'd be moony-eyed with Chris."

Tom chuckled. "No, she was never into Chris."

"She wasn't?"

"No. D said she flirted with Chris because he asked her to."

"Chris asked Annabelle to flirt with him?"

Tom shook his head. "Darryl asked Annabelle to flirt with Chris. D and Annabelle are like you and Robin. Have been for years. Chris was awkward with girls for a long time, so Darryl asked Annabelle to help him loosen up."

"It worked a little too well."

"No." Tom sighed. "D wanted Chris to see women as actual people. Annabelle made him more comfortable, but there's too much damage there."

"Damage?"

"Chris's dad is abusive. He left Mrs. Lorenzo when Chris was young, but the bastard would come home over and over, and Mrs. L would bend over backward for him. Until he hit her again. Then she'd make him leave. He always comes back, though. Chris has a lot of resentment over it."

Sue turned to Tom. "Wow."

"Chris lived across the street from Brad, which is how they all met. When Darryl figured out that Mrs. L was single like his mom, he brought Chris home. D's mom pretty much adopted him. She's the only woman he treats with respect. Until Lena. Chris needs Lena's approval."

"He thinks Lena will keep Darryl away from him?"

"No. Chris *knows* D will stay away if he shows his ass around Lena."

"Huh." Sue faced the room. "Never thought I'd feel bad for Chris."

"If Chris heard you, he'd punch you. He's been clear with us. No pity."

Sue rolled her eyes. "Noted. Though acknowledging something shitty and giving people pity are two wholly different things."

"This is Chris we're talking about. He has no concept of nuance."

"So, if she was never into Chris, why isn't Annabelle back to flirting with Justin?"

Tom straightened his posture. "She told me Justin is like another brother to her. She flirted with him to learn how to do it, knowing he wouldn't cross her boundaries."

Sue stood sideways to see the room and Tom. "Interesting dynamic. Justin and Darryl are super respectful of women. Chris thinks we're beneath him. Brad is somewhere in the middle?"

Tom squirmed. "I guess?"

"What about Annabelle? Is she with anyone? Maybe another long-lost band member?"

Tom straightened his posture to board-like stiffness. "I don't know. Hair and makeup's almost done. I'm gonna find the stage manager."

CHAPTER 15

Sue slid the door of *The Tonight Show* van open to find Luther and Adam waiting outside of the club.

Adam grinned and took the keyboard case Sue dragged out with her. "The band made it here twenty minutes before show time."

"Thank God, I've been waiting for a text from Tom." Sue lifted another case out of the van.

"The club didn't have anyone to man the merch table, so he's inside moving CDs." Luther took the second keyboard case. "He asked us to wait for you with the trailer keys."

A little bit of Sue's stress slipped away. The band had made it in time, and Tom was making everything work, including providing the trailer keys she'd forgotten about. "Thanks, guys. We have to stow this stuff and get ready to break down the show ASAP so we can get to the party."

"You got it." Adam helped Annabelle, Lena, and Sue get the rest of the instruments out of the van.

Luther unlocked the trailer and pulled out the ramp.

Once Sue knew the instruments were stored and secure, she and Adam followed Lena and Annabelle into the club for the last few songs of Words Fail Me's set.

A haze of smoke hung over the stage.

"Oh my. Is this normal?" Lena asked.

"I know they were changing the lighting, but they added smoke to the show, too?" Annabelle asked.

"No." Sue took a deep breath. Assured that nothing was on fire, she shook her head. "I don't know what this is."

Adam squeezed Sue's waist. "You're not pranking Darryl?"

Sue laughed. "Nope. I stole his clothes after the Charlotte gig. It's his turn."

"Wearing the sheets in the airport wasn't a prank?" Adam asked.

Lena gasped. "He wore the sheets?"

"Yeah. Don't worry, though." Sue grinned. "He said he wore normal clothes for the flight and changed after the plane landed."

"What're you guys talking about?" Annabelle kept her eyes on the stage as she spoke.

"Sue and Darryl are in the middle of a huge prank war." Lena flung her arms out and almost hit another concertgoer.

"He threw me in a pool in Austin. When he did laundry at my house, I stuffed his bag full of sheets and kept his clothes." Sue laughed at her memory of Darryl running through the airport in her spare bedding. Before he'd put his clothes back on, he made a show of rubbing himself with the sheets. She still needed to wash them. A few times. With boiling water.

"That explains some of the questions he asked me." Annabelle threaded an arm through Lena's and moved closer to the stage.

"What questions?" Sue asked.

"I don't remember exactly." Annabelle continued to move toward the stage, shouting over her shoulder. "Something about tampons!"

Sue frowned. "That doesn't sound good."

Adam held her in a backward hug and spoke into her ear. "I'll get you a secret stash."

Sue giggled. "You still have a few more dates before you can buy me presents."

"Such a stickler."

During Words Fail Me's final song, enough smoke pumped out from the stage that a fog hung over part of the audience.

Brad's voice came through the vapor. "Zen Dave, I know you like to smoke out, but this is ludicrous."

The fans laughed and cheered as Words Fail Me continued their song. A few moments later, a blinking halo floated across the stage.

"I am the king of smoke." Zen Dave spoke into a microphone.

The audience broke into a fresh round of cheers.

"Let's hear it for Words Fail Me!" Zen Dave commanded. After the applause died down, he spoke again.

"Tonight is our last night with these guys. Tour rules say we have to mark the occasion."

Roars and whistles came from the crowd.

"If y'all love Words Fail Me as much as I do, y'all need to call home or whatever and have someone record *The Tonight Show*." Zen Dave's headband bobbed as he spoke. "They're gonna be on TV tonight!"

More cheers from the audience.

"Google it. Words Fail Me. *The Tonight Show*. Magic," Justin said.

"That's right!" Zen Dave's light halo spun around. Sue imagined him trying to make a face at Justin, with neither of them seeing each other through the smoke. "Still record that shit. Ratings, bitch."

Darryl and Brad laughed into their microphones.

"You gonna let us finish this, man? Or you got more smoke for us?" Brad asked.

"Where there's smoke, there's fire! And you boys are on fire!" Zen Dave boomed. "Now bring it home!"

As Words Fail Me finished their song, Zen Dave announced all the band members. He sang the closing line with Brad and said "Words Fail Me. *The Tonight Show*. Watch it!"

As soon as the stage lights went off, Sue directed the guys to an area with better visibility. They all waited with Annabelle and Tom for several minutes before the air cleared enough for them to move the instruments.

"Is the reporter still here?" Sue asked Tom.

"Yeah. We offered to put him in the sound booth for a good view, but he wanted to mix in the crowd."

"Dave pretty much killed the view, no matter where the guy went."

Tom laughed. "Yeah, but he made an awesome plug."

Sue fidgeted at the comment but nodded, not wanting to speak her fears where the guys might overhear. While she'd been disassembling Justin's drums one of the members of *The Tonight Show* production team remarked how odd it was that the band hadn't stuck around to record the song a second time.

"The take was great," the production guy said. "But what if sound didn't come out clear? It's the only thing we can't fix in post."

The memory of the offhand comment had Sue's stomach falling to her knees again. They had to make it to the broadcast. They'd all be devastated if they didn't.

Justin's waving arms pulled Sue out of her worry. "I can see my drums, let's go!"

Once all the gear was out of the venue, Sue stopped to catch her breath. "Did that come out of the dressing room?" She pointed to a case of toilet paper near the door.

"Yeah, leave it," Darryl said.

"I can put it in bus storage."

"No. Leave it. Please."

"I'll clear out the rest of the dressing room." Sue went back inside and jogged to the room Words Fail Me had used before their set. Only having twenty minutes before show time meant the guys didn't bring much into the room in the first place. It helped that they'd already been dressed to perform. Sue shoved the few items on the counters into a duffel bag. She checked the attached bathroom and hustled back to the bus.

"Tom!" Sue tossed him the duffel bag as she exited the building. She noticed more toilet paper stacked on the case by the door. "Why is this pile getting bigger? How much TP do you guys need?"

"Leave it!" Justin, Brad, and Darryl shouted at once.

Sue wrinkled her brow.

"Sorry, Suse," Darryl said. "We gotta get Skein back."

Chris ran through the parking lot. "This is all I found on their bus!" He added five more rolls of toilet paper to the stack. "How many songs in are they?"

"About to go into their second song." Sue put her hands on her hips. She could make the guys finish packing before executing their prank. But at this stage in the process, and with Tom and Annabelle to help, Sue knew she could have everything away and secure without the band. She dropped her hands. "Go."

"What?" Chris looked up.

"Go do whatever you're planning to do with the toilet paper." Sue gestured toward the roof. "If you want to get in the lights, the ladder is stage left."

"Yes!" Chris pulled his shirt out like a basket and filled it with rolls of toilet paper. "Come on, guys!" He gave Sue a fist bump and dashed inside.

Darryl and Justin took the rest of the loose rolls.

Before Brad took the case, Sue grabbed him by the arm.

"Please do me a favor and change your shirt before the reporter leaves."

"After this."

"I'm serious, Brad. This is the magazine that tried to take down Chris. If we don't give them what they want, they'll never print a kind word about us."

Brad nodded. "I've played nice with the guy all day."

"If he doesn't get the shirt tonight, I can't ship it until Monday. I don't want to risk it. He's gotta get it tonight."

"Sue." Brad adjusted the case of toilet paper in his arms. "He will get the shirt tonight. I promise. I know your rep is on the line as much as ours. I've got it covered."

At those words, everything Sue was responsible for hit her full force: the TV appearance, the print interview, Chris's reputation, an innocent little kid and his mother out in Texas, and Words Fail Me's next album. She closed her eyes for a second so she wouldn't freak out. "Okay. Go have fun."

Brad whooped and ran inside.

Skein finished their show a few minutes after eleven. With *The Tonight Show* airing at 11:35, Sue didn't have a lot of time to sell merchandise, secure the remaining inventory on the bus, and get to the bar down the street. It was the closest place with televisions, and where Sue had arranged a viewing of the show along with the end-of-tour celebration.

At 11:37 Sue shouted the party password "Killer Queen!" at the bouncer and rushed into the bar, pulling Adam behind her. "Did they say the name of the band? Did they say the name of the band!" Sue waved at the bartender as she asked.

"I don't know, sweetheart. Drink?"

"Damn it." Sue sighed. "McCallan, neat."

"Scotch?" Adam asked.

"Gotta steady the nerves."

He rubbed the small of her back. "They already recorded the show. You don't have to be nervous now."

Sue gripped his arm. "What if they get cut?"

"They won't get cut."

"You've seen all the shit that happens on *The Tonight Show*. They could get cut."

Adam cupped her face, forcing her to look away from the television. "They won't get cut." The bartender slid a glass next to Sue's elbow, and Adam put it in her hand. "Drink. Then let's dance until they flash the album on screen."

Sue swallowed half the scotch in one gulp, grateful for the burn grounding her for a moment. "Adam, even after all this, they may not make the broadcast. The other guests were great. The audience loved all the bits. They filmed ninety minutes for a sixty-two-minute show."

"Sue. I promise. They won't get cut."

Sue gave Adam a wary look and finished the drink. She led him onto the dancefloor.

Words Fail Me arrived about fifteen minutes and another scotch later. Brad still wore the T-shirt meant for the *Sound Spectrum* auction. When the reporter followed him to the bar, Sue relaxed her fists. Why Brad suddenly decided not to cooperate had her rattled. So much hung on this night, and if Brad didn't help her meet the obligation with the reporter, it would be a serious blow to her reputation. She'd be the bully publicist who didn't keep her word. Thankfully, the reporter hadn't left yet. She could still make sure he got the shirt.

Darryl and Lena joined Sue and Adam on the dancefloor.

"We aren't too late, are we?" Darryl asked.

"Nope." Sue checked her watch. "Still about ten minutes to go."

"Shit, I'm more nervous than when we recorded it!"

"Me, too!" Sue grabbed Darryl's elbow. "Drink?"

"Hell yes."

Adam grabbed Sue's hips and squeezed, holding her close for a moment. "Stay here. I'll get them."

Sue scanned the room again and found the reporter standing alone near the bar, beer in hand, watching the room. Where was Brad? Someone should be with the guy to make sure he didn't leave without the shirt. Shit. She needed to slow her drinking. Between her nerves and the booze, she was in no condition to host the man for the rest of the evening.

Brad materialized by her side, offering D a high five. "We're gonna be on TV tonight!"

Sue unleashed some of her ire on him. "Why didn't you change your shirt before you left the venue? I *told* you how important it is to give that one up."

He rubbed his chest. "It's comfortable."

"He needs it *tonight*."

"Stop worrying, Sexy Sue. I'll take care of it. When are we gonna be on TV?"

Brad's nonchalant attitude combined with that stupid fucking nickname had her ready to spit nails. She had to keep it together until the reporter left. "In a few minutes."

Adam returned with another scotch for Sue and beer for everyone else.

Sue tossed back the drink and pressed the empty glass into Brad's chest. "Take this to the bar and Go. Change. Your. Shirt."

Brad rolled his eyes but took the glass and walked toward the bar.

"He's nervous, too," D said.

Sue waved air at her face. "We made a commitment to the writer. I'm not gonna make him wait for us to honor our end of it."

"Brad'll give him the shirt."

Sue threaded her fingers with Adam's. She wanted to wrap herself in him, take comfort from his steadiness, but nerves had her bouncing on her feet. She kept moving on the dancefloor until the Words Fail Me album flashed on the screen. She froze and grabbed Adam's arm. "That's it. That's *it!*" She jumped and pointed at the television.

Adam glanced toward the set. "It's a commercial, Sue."

Still jumping, she shook her head. "Next. He said next." Sue stopped, gripped Adam's shoulders, and shouted. "It's coming on next!"

The entire place quieted for a moment before everyone cheered. Someone switched the house music to the television broadcast. By the time the show came back from commercial, the entire band, along with Lena, Annabelle, Tom, and the writer surrounded Sue. The members of Skein huddled around them as well. Adam stood behind her, his solid chest against her back, and his arms wrapped around her waist.

The host announced Words Fail Me a moment before they filled the screen. The bar erupted in cheers, whistles, and whooping. The reaction would've been amazing had Sue not been so intent on hearing the performance. Did they sound tinny? The band had a deep, robust sound, and if it didn't carry over, it wouldn't help sell records. It didn't quiet enough until the first chorus.

"Annabelle nailed it," Justin said, leaning toward Sue. "The drums sound right."

Sue nodded, too excited to speak. She'd been at the taping but watched from the side of the stage. She'd worried the guys would look nervous on camera and the rendition of their hit would sound thin, but they tore the house down. Justin's confirmation of what they were hearing let her finally relax.

"They killed it," Adam whispered in her ear.

Sue released her white-knuckle grip on him and gave him a light squeeze. She leaned her head on his shoulder. "I know." Of course she knew. It didn't stop her from worrying, but she'd always known the talent in Words Fail Me were worth the risks she'd taken.

She turned her gaze from the TV to Tom. He'd known it, too. It had been fucking stupid to put the band's future on the line, but she understood his decision better now. She still disagreed with him keeping it a secret, but she understood.

When the song ended, everyone in the bar broke into raucous cheers. Sue jumped and got a tackle hug from Tom, closely followed by Darryl and Justin.

Brad broke through the crowd, the writer in tow. "Best night ever, Sexy Sue!"

"I know it!" Sue's wide smile burned her cheeks.

"I wouldn't have guessed that was your first television gig." The writer addressed Brad. "Nice job."

"Thanks!" Brad threw an arm around the man's neck.

"Do you think they'll air the charity plug, Ms. Douglas?"

"No one on the production team would confirm it for me." Sue shrugged. "We have to keep watching."

At the filming, the host joined the band after the song and asked Brad about the charity auction and bantered a bit. Sue'd been proud of how Brad handled the unexpected moment, and she'd heard the guys talking about it as they left the studio. They'd been impressed with Brad, too.

Sue moved to the bar to wait out the last commercial break. Brad and the writer flanked her, and Adam stood behind her, one hand on her waist and the other on the bar beside her. His hold on her looked casual and felt amazing, but it wasn't lost on her that Adam kept her from falling over after all the scotch.

Sue kept her voice low as she spoke to Brad. "Tell me you brought a spare shirt." She didn't care if he was naked, but if she said that, she figured he *would* strip naked. She just needed the reporter to get what she'd promised.

Brad kept his eyes on the television above the bar. "The bus isn't far."

The high of Words Fail Me on *The Tonight Show* was strong enough to keep Sue from glaring, but would Brad fucking do as she asked already? She'd explained the importance of the shirt. What else did she have to do to make her point? She blew a hair off her face and fanned the hem of her top. She needed air and for Brad to cooperate.

The final commercial break ended, and the show re-opened with the host standing next to Brad. Sue held her breath until the man spoke. He asked about the charity.

Sue turned to Adam, her cheeks splitting with her smile. "I feel like I'm the underdog team that just qualified for their first World Cup."

Adam raised his eyebrows. "Did you talk sports to me?"

"I did."

"So hot." Adam squeezed her hip.

Sue chuckled and swung back to the television. Adam nuzzling under her ear helped settle her sudden bout of vertigo.

"What an awesome day!" The reporter nudged Sue's shoulder. "Hung with the band, got to see *The Tonight Show* in person, and our plug made it into the broadcast! My boss is gonna be on cloud nine!"

Sue unleashed another face-cracking smile. His words were almost as good as the band's performance. Plus, the on-camera mention meant even if the article got canceled, the shirt would still be in the auction. She elbowed Brad. "You ready to finally part ways with the T-shirt?"

Brad stood back and smirked. "Yeah." He pulled the shirt off and leaned over Sue to give it to the reporter. "I hope it doesn't smell, but I felt like I had to wear it until the bitter end. For luck."

The reporter shook out the shirt and tucked it into the rucksack he carried. "It might raise more money if it smells."

Sue blanched. "Don't lose it, smelly or not!"

"No worries." The reporter tugged the bag onto his shoulder.

Sue shook his hand. "Thank you so much. I hope this nets a lot for your charity."

"I'm sure it will." He waved and slipped into the crowd of people on the dancefloor.

Sue leaned into Adam's arms. She needed a glass of water and a private place with him.

"We did good, yeah?" Brad asked.

Sue straightened and nodded one time. "Made me proud. You guys rocked."

"Sweet." Brad pounded his chest and wiggled his eyebrows at Sue, then strutted out to the dancefloor.

The full force of all the booze Sue had drunk seemed to hit her the moment she turned from Adam back to the television. She'd hoped no one noticed, but with her obligation to the reporter fulfilled and Brad out of her hair, she wanted to *not* be drunk. She shook her head and summoned the bartender, requesting water.

Adam leaned against the edge of the bar, facing the room. "You know Brad did all that so you would check him out."

"Yeah?"

"Oh yeah. He wanted a reaction."

Sue took a deep drink of water. "Lame."

Adam scanned the dancefloor. "Yep."

Sue curled her fingers into the hair at the back of Adam's neck, pulled him toward her, and kissed him, quickly moving the kiss from chaste to R-rated. Her wooziness expanded in the best way. Adam wrapped his arms around her, both holding her up and making her knees weak. When the kiss finally ended, Sue stroked a hand up his chest. "This is the only body I want to check out. Let's get out of here."

CHAPTER 16

Even though she'd been awake for a while, Sue groaned when the alarm on her phone went off. She lay curled on Adam's chest, unwilling to move. "Can you reach that?"

He rolled on top of her, silenced the phone, and rolled back, keeping Sue in his arms. "Do you really have to get out of bed now?"

"Technically." She took a deep inhale of his scent and tucked herself further into his hold. He still smelled like grass and sun and sex, and she didn't want to leave his side. "First interview's at eleven."

"It's nine-thirty." Adam rubbed his knuckles along Sue's back and kissed her temple. "How's the hangover?"

"Much better, thank you." Sue slid her hand between his legs. "Sorry for waking you so early."

Adam groaned as she touched him. "I deserved it after I made you walk twelve blocks and drink a ton of water."

"That part was fine. Tucking me into bed with a chaste kiss is what got you in trouble."

"You were drunk, and I will suffer the consequences you doled out anytime." Adam squeezed her ass, tightening his grip as she played with him.

Sue propped herself on an elbow. "I wasn't *that* drunk."

"Babe, you were out cold two minutes after I kissed you goodnight."

"I needed to recharge."

Adam rolled on top of her. "Are you charged now?"

"Yeah, but I need to get in the shower soon."

"How soon?"

She glanced at the clock on the nightstand. "Fifteenish minutes."

"I can work with that."

When Sue finally crawled out of the bed, she made her way to the shower on shaky legs.

Adam waited for her at the vanity with a glass of orange juice when she came out of the bathroom.

"Aw, you had to get dressed?" Sue tugged on the sleeve of his undershirt.

Adam grinned and gave her the glass. "Enough to let room service in."

Sue sipped her drink. "Naked you would've been an excellent tip for them."

Adam shook his head. "Doubtful."

Sue obviously checked him out and sipped more juice. "You gotta trust me on this one."

Adam grinned.

"Is it bad that I have no guilt whatsoever for leaving everyone at the HoJo's in favor of your suite?"

"Is it bad that I have no guilt whatsoever that no one in your rowdy entourage could find or interrupt us?"

"Touché." Sue put her glass down and wrapped her arms around Adam's waist, sinking into a hug.

"So," Adam drew out the word. "Come back to Boston with me tomorrow. Spend the week with me."

Sue spoke into his chest. "Just because I have a week off the road doesn't mean I have a week off."

"I know. You can work in my office or my apartment. And when you're done for the day, I can take you out." Adam pressed his lips against her ear. "Or not."

"Or not?" She pulled back to look him in the eye.

He offered an innocent expression. "Whatever works."

"I'd like that."

"Yeah?"

She kissed him and settled back against his chest. "Definitely."

Adam leaned down and kissed her again. "I'll call the airline and get you on my flight."

"No."

"No?"

Sue stayed in Adam's embrace but moved enough to make eye contact. "I have to go home first."

"Why?"

"I have to get my luggage for Europe, pack a bag to stay with you, and take care of a few loose ends. I have an appointment Monday morning I can't miss. I need a day or two."

Adam squeezed her. "Two?"

"Okay, I need tomorrow and Monday morning," Sue said.

"I'll come with you."

"No."

Adam pulled back. "Huh?"

Sue smiled and brushed her fingers through his hair. "You *always* come to me. Let me come to you for a change."

Adam raised an eyebrow but he smiled. "I don't like missing a day, but okay."

Sue checked the bus as soon as she arrived at the band's hotel and found Justin packing stuff in the common area. She had a pang of guilt knowing Tom would likely be the only other person to pitch in. She consulted her watch and decided she had about twenty minutes to help before she and Justin had to leave to meet with Brad and an interviewer.

In that time, Sue managed to get the game systems and games organized and packed along with the basketball hoops, balls, and darts. Justin had already removed the pictures and posters in the main area and worked on peeling stickers off the window when Sue tried to call Brad.

"He's not answering. What room were you guys in?"

"Here's my key." Justin avoided looking at Sue as he passed it to her.

"Just. Did you stay in your room last night?"

He kept his focus on the window and shook his head.

"You stay on the bus?"

"Nope."

"Nice."

Justin's lips curled, but his focus remained on the task at hand.

"Meet us in the coffee shop in ten."

"You got it, Sexy Sue."

Sue jogged into the hotel and up to the room written on Justin's keycard envelope. She tried to call Brad on her way but still got no answer. She knocked lightly on the door and waited. After a minute she knocked louder and called out his name. A sleep-tousled woman answered, holding a blanket in front of her.

"I'm so sorry, I must have the wrong room. Sorry." Sue backed away from the door. She heard Brad's voice and glanced around the hallway but didn't see him.

The woman opened the door wider and looked behind her. Brad stumbled to the door, buttoning and zipping his pants.

Sue froze, surprised and a little embarrassed. She'd hate it if she opened the door to Adam's hotel room and a woman she hadn't expected was there to collect him. It wouldn't matter that the reason was strictly professional.

Brad maneuvered the woman out of the way and tried to crowd the doorway, but she stayed close and wrapped an arm around his bare chest from behind.

"Sue, hey, this is…um…" Brad hesitated, closing his eyes.

The woman dragged her claws across his chest and stepped into the bathroom, slamming the door behind her.

Sue winced, resettling her features as Brad opened his eyes.

He shook his head. "What's up?"

"Sorry. You didn't answer your phone, and we have an interview in a few minutes. I didn't know I'd be interrupting."

"You didn't…" Brad scrubbed a hand over his face. "No, I need to be there. Ten minutes?"

"Yeah."

"Where?"

"The coffee place two doors down."

Brad nodded. "I'll be right there."

"Okay. Sorry!" She offered the apology in a slightly louder voice and all but ran as Brad closed the door. She found Justin reclined in a lumpy chair in the coffee shop window, three drinks sitting on the table next to him.

"Where's Brad?"

"On his way."

Justin pushed one of the cups toward her. "You wake him up?"

"In a manner of speaking."

Justin knitted his eyebrows together.

She widened her eyes and handed Justin the room key.

"Ah, so he might be a few minutes late."

"Yeah," Sue said.

Justin shifted his glance to a person approaching them.

Sue recognized the reporter and made the introductions and an excuse for Brad. They were about three questions into the interview when he got there, shower fresh. The reporter took it in stride and kept going.

When the interview ended Sue walked the journalist to the door and went to the counter to order a coffee for Tom.

After collecting Tom's drink, she went back to their seats. "Where's Justin?"

Brad wiped invisible crumbs off the side table. "He went ahead to the bus."

"Oh. Well, let's go. We've gotta get Darryl for the next one. And we have some time to pack more."

Brad followed Sue and fell in step beside her on the sidewalk. "Sorry about all that."

"No need." Sue secured the lid of Tom's coffee cup. "The reporter was cool since Justin got things rolling. He's getting more comfortable with interviews."

"Great, but that's not all. The thing back at the room. With Dana." Brad put extra emphasis on the woman's name.

Sue glanced at Brad. "You remembered?"

"You surprised me. That's why I forgot."

Sue smirked. "Just don't turn into Chris."

"I feel like I owe you an explanation."

"You don't." Once Sue got over the surprise of an unknown woman answering Brad's door, she'd been relieved. Brad hooking up meant she didn't have to worry about him chasing her. She could officially write him off as a natural flirt and stop worrying.

He lifted his shoulders and dropped them. "I don't do that often."

"Okay."

"I don't. I—"

"Brad, you don't have to explain. It's your business, not mine."

"I'm sorry for all the awkwardness."

"Then answer your phone next time." Sue shot him a friendly grin.

"Okay." He let out a noisy breath. "I swear I don't do this a lot."

"I figured. I mean, even if you do, you're subtle about it. You get points for that."

Brad's eyebrows shot up. "You notice those things?"

"Not usually. Well, with Chris it's impossible not to. Justin is pretty lowkey, and Darryl's devoted to Lena. The only one I pay attention to is Tom because I'm rooting for him."

Brad laughed. "Yeah, we've even gone so far as to introduce him to women, but he is incredibly…restrained."

"He always has been," Sue said. "Even Gavin's tried to set him up, but he's held out. I guess he wants to find the women himself."

"Thanks for being cool about this." Brad put an arm around her.

"It's not a big deal. I don't care who you sleep with."

Brad gave her a tight smile. "Justin keeps telling me that. I know your opinion of man-whores, though. We all lost a lot of money on Owen in New Orleans."

Sue chuckled. "You guys have nothing to worry about as far as man-whoring is concerned. It's only a factor if you're trying to sleep with me. Since that's—"

Brad interrupted her with barking laughter.

"What?" Sue asked.

"Nothing."

"Didn't seem like nothing." They'd gotten to the bus and Sue stopped about halfway to the door and faced Brad.

He pushed his hair back. "You're naive if you think no one's trying to sleep with you."

"Yeah, because guys have been throwing themselves at me left and right." Sue rolled her eyes.

"I have."

"Nicknaming me Sexy Sue does not constitute—" She stopped talking when she finally looked at Brad. His head dropped and he patted his leg rapidly, as though he channeled all his energy there. "Oh."

Brad shook his head and pursed his lips.

Sue glanced away and took a gulp of Tom's coffee, the heat of the drink a stinging reminder it wasn't intended for her.

"Usually I have a pretty good poker face," Brad said.

Sue kept her gaze on the sidewalk, not sure what she should say, if anything.

"Shit. Well. As long as it's out there—" Brad took a deep breath. "After this morning, does it matter?"

"I'm with Adam," she said quietly.

"What about before?"

Sue took a moment to consider her relationship with Brad. What if she hadn't written him off the first night? She acknowledged that she found him attractive. She enjoyed his company and valued his opinion. She let herself truly consider the possibility of something other than the working relationship they had. As much as she liked Brad, it wasn't like that for her. She didn't want her answer to hurt him, but she couldn't lie.

"Not likely."

Brad put his fists in his pockets. "Did I officially kill any chance I may have had this morning?"

She squinted her eyes as she considered. She didn't mind coming face-to-face with Brad's conquest. She understood Dana's reaction when he forgot her name, and Sue also understood how he'd forgotten in the moment. None of it mattered to her, but it provided an easy out. She lifted a shoulder.

Brad combed both of his hands through his hair and let them rest on his neck as he studied her. "Was it Dana or that I forgot her name?"

"Her name."

"That would qualify as being like Chris, right?" Brad asked.

"Yep."

"I'll be better."

Sue furrowed her brow, but he ignored her questioning expression and took the coffee cup.

"I'll bring this to Tom."

"Okay." Still concerned, Sue climbed onto the bus.

Justin leaned against the refrigerator, eyes wide.

Sue flopped on one of the benches. "You heard all that?"

"Yup."

She kept her voice low. "I thought he had a crush."

"Sue, we're not twelve. Liking a woman and wanting to sleep with her go hand in hand."

"Now what?"

Justin lifted his shoulders. "No idea. He got over his fit about the horse race pretty quick. If he stays true to form, when we all get back together next week, it'll be like nothing ever happened."

Sue twisted a finger in her hair. "I hope so."

CHAPTER 17

Boston, MA

Sue swung her computer bag over her shoulder and stopped for a moment to squeeze the twinge in her arm. Only she would schedule a doctor visit for a shot on a travel day. She stacked her weekend tote on top of her suitcase and wheeled it all toward the revolving door of Adam's office building. She smiled as she approached the reception desk.

"Hello, I'm going to the Sports Mecca office."

"They have the fifth floor. Would you like to stow your luggage here in the coat check?"

Relief swept over Sue. Adam knew her flight out of Boston would be the first leg of her trip to Europe, but she still felt awkward arriving with two bags and her laptop. She wasn't moving in, but it looked like it.

The receptionist wheeled Sue's items into a closet and gave her a tag.

"Thanks." Sue pocketed the tag and went to the elevator, pushing the button to summon the car.

She rubbed her upper arm, hoping to relieve some of the soreness there. Being on the road with Words Fail Me had been hectic, and she'd forgotten to take her birth control pill often enough that she figured swallowing it had become a symbolic gesture. Her doctor advised her to get a birth control shot, which would protect her for three months. Plenty of time for her to complete the tour with Words Fail Me, begin working with Bloody Maggots, and figure out if she should switch to a form of birth control like an IUD that didn't require daily attention or quarterly medical visits.

Sue checked her reflection in the elevator and straightened her clothes. She smoothed her hair and admitted another truth to herself about the birth control: she also wanted the three months to figure out if things would work with Adam.

At first, she had enjoyed their connection as an in-the-moment pleasure. But the more time she spent with Adam, the more it grew—they were well beyond simple attraction. This week would be the closest thing to "normal" they would experience together thus far. If they didn't get on each other's nerves over the next few days, maybe this could be more than a good time on the road. She squeezed her arm again. For the first time in her life, she wanted an actual future with a man. The elevator dinged and the doors slid open before panic truly set in. She gave herself a moment, then stepped onto the fifth floor before the doors closed on her.

The Sports Mecca floor had lots of open areas, offices and conference rooms with glass walls, televisions all showing different sports, and scoreboards with standings. The atmosphere felt casual and friendly, but most people seemed busy. A six-foot tall blonde goddess with a warm smile and a firm handshake greeted her outside of Adam's office.

"You must be Sue," she said. "I'm Lauren, Adam's assistant."

"It's nice to meet you. Adam talks about you all the time." Sue returned Lauren's smile.

"He didn't expect you for another twenty minutes or so, but I can pull him out of his meeting." Lauren leaned over her keyboard.

"Please don't. I don't mind waiting."

She and Lauren talked more before Lauren ushered Sue into Adam's office. Sue sat and rubbed her sore arm as she went through some of the messages on her phone. She heard Adam before she saw him and leaned forward in her chair to watch for his approach.

He strode down the hallway with another man, both of them dressed casually and carrying tablets. It sounded as though they were discussing a change in team ownership. They stopped a few feet short of Lauren's desk, having a charged discussion about how the story should be covered.

When the man asked Adam if he'd eaten lunch, Lauren subtly interrupted them by clearing her throat.

Adam glanced at her, and she tilted her head toward his office. His gaze shifted to Sue.

She sat with her elbows on her knees and a fist under her chin. She smiled and raised her eyebrows quickly. She didn't trust herself to do much else. His confident gait had been a huge turn on, and the way his expression heated when he looked at her made her want to throw herself into his arms.

With his eyes on Sue, Adam declined the invitation. He walked into his office, dropped his tablet on the nearest chair, then pulled Sue to her feet and kissed her.

She expected a peck on the cheek or even a quick skim of the lips, but the passion in his kiss took her by surprise and delighted her at the same time.

"Adam, at work?" she asked, unable to tame her smile.

"I'm the boss. I can do what I want."

She chuckled in spite of herself.

He pulled her close, and she let herself sink into his arms for a moment before she took a step back.

"I'm sorry, the glass walls make me self-conscious." Sue nodded toward the area around his office and noticed a few people watching. One of them realized he'd been caught and shifted his focus back to whatever he'd been doing.

"It does take some getting used to," Adam acknowledged. "Where's your luggage?"

"The woman in the lobby stowed it for me."

"Lunch?"

"Yes, please."

Adam put the tablet on his desk. He checked his computer, then took Sue's hand and led her out. "Lauren, I'll send notes later this evening. See you in the morning."

"Enjoy Boston, Sue." Lauren gave a small wave.

"Thanks, it was nice to finally meet you."

When they were alone in the elevator, Sue asked, "Are all the women who work for you that tall?"

Adam kissed her again before he answered. "Only the ones who played on the Olympic volleyball team with Lauren."

Sue groaned. She could've sworn Adam wiped a grin off his face, but when he addressed her, he seemed serious.

"This is important. Do you like hot dogs?"

Sue brushed her hair behind her shoulders and grinned. After lunch at an afternoon game at Fenway Park, they'd retrieved Sue's suitcases and walked to Adam's apartment. "So, Mister I'll-get-in-the-dirt-with-the-athletes lives in a big fancy building with a doorman."

Adam ushered her into the elevator. "It's close to work."

"Too good for the subway, huh?"

"Actually, I used to live a few blocks from the office, in the opposite direction. I've always walked to work."

"Was that apartment fancy, too?" Sue asked.

"It was tiny."

"All your sports memorabilia crowded you out?"

Adam smiled. When the elevator opened again, he directed her to his door. "Something like that." He unlocked the door but didn't open it. "Remember when you asked me if I splurged when Sports Mecca started bringing in money?"

"Yeah."

"I bought three things: a car, a TV, and this apartment." Adam held the door open and Sue entered.

"Holy shit." She stood in a large open room with the far wall almost entirely covered by a television.

"I loved the old place, but it was too small for this TV."

"My entire state of Maryland is too small for this TV." Sue walked farther into the apartment and considered the space.

The living room had the massive television on one end and a large leather sectional at the other. The wall between them had two big windows with framed photos of different sporting events and a few mementos hanging between them. The windows had sheer coverings, half rolled up, to reduce the glare on the television. A long galley kitchen with five high-back leather stools along the counter faced the windows.

"I take it this is the go-to place for all the big games."

"Oh yeah." Adam shut the door and came into the room. "It's part of the deal when you buy a television like this."

A narrow hallway between the kitchen and the living room led to a half bath and a room he used as an office. It had all the latest electronics, as well as a flat-screen TV, and photos scattered throughout. A framed photo of her at the steeplechase hung at eye level next to a monitor. Giddy with the discovery, she masked her pleasure at finding it. She wasn't sure she could handle whatever revelations might come if she pointed it out.

The hallway ended at a bigger room with a king-sized bed, a forty-two-inch television hanging on the wall across from it, and a closet a sliver smaller than his enormous bathroom.

"My one thirteen-inch television must've annoyed the hell out of you."

"Nah, we didn't watch any sports." Adam wheeled Sue's suitcases into his closet.

She had another flicker of panic as he closed the closet with her things inside it. In her past relationships, it had been rare for her to bring an overnight bag, let alone allow a man to stow it in his closet for her. She pushed it away, wanting to enjoy him. "I have a great stereo, though. Between the two of us we could build one hell of a home theater."

"I don't stick around just for your miniskirts."

───────────────

Adam took her to dinner at his favorite restaurant. Afterward, they went door-to-door to the bars behind Fenway Park, sampling local bands. She gave him extra points for planning something he knew she'd like.

The next morning, Sue woke when Adam's weight left the bed. Despite the king-size mattress, they'd slept close all night.

"What time is it?" She stretched her arms over her head.

"Six." Adam leaned over and kissed her forehead.

"Coffee, please."

He chuckled. "Stay in bed, babe."

"I don't mind getting up with you." She lifted herself on her elbows and watched him slip on athletic pants and a plain T-shirt.

"I like you in my bed. Stay there."

Sue grinned and tugged the sheet lower, almost baring her nipples.

"Tease." Adam perched on the edge of the mattress, holding a pair of socks.

"It's only teasing if I don't let you touch me." She slid closer to him and skated her fingers down his forearm.

He sighed. "I have to work out. And I have a breakfast meeting. Go back to sleep. Meet me for lunch?"

"I can't. I have lunch with an editor."

Adam pushed his fingers through his hair. "I should've checked your calendar before I booked this meeting."

"It's okay." She pulled him toward her. "You can work out here." She kissed him as she lay back. "Then go to your meeting."

"I could make it a cardio day."

———————————————

Sue went back to sleep after Adam left. When she woke again, she made use of the Sports Mecca gym and went on to her lunch meeting. She and Adam texted throughout the day but stuck with their respective schedules.

She got a call from Tom after her last meeting, as she walked to Adam's office building.

"Everything okay, Tommy?"

"Better than okay. I'd prefer to see your face when I tell you this, but I'm impatient."

Despite Tom saying he had good news, Sue automatically tensed. "What's up?"

"Got a call from the record label."

"Ugh."

"No *ugh*. They're thrilled with *The Tonight Show* appearance, and the fact it's trending on social media."

Sue scoffed. "Like I would let such a kick-ass performance go unnoticed. And don't forget the massive jump in streams and downloads."

Tom snickered. "They know better now. They lifted the album restriction."

"What?" Sue's mouth dropped open.

"You heard me. We still have sales goals for Europe, but now you're a regular contractor. No payback requirement."

"Holy shit." Sue braced herself against a lamppost. "That's...wow."

"I told you if you did your thing it would be fine."

"Shut the fuck up, Tom. I haven't had a good night's sleep since I left home."

Tom laughed. "Congratulations, Sue. You earned it. Celebrate with some sleep."

Sue grinned and shook her head. This victory had been a long time coming. "Thanks, cuz." She ended the call and checked her calendar; Adam was busy for another hour.

She ducked into a copy shop, intending to print a few sample handbills and postcards she'd been working on. She got engrossed in the production and didn't realize it had gotten so late when Adam called close to seven in the evening, looking for her. Sue saved her files and went to him.

A lot of people were in the office when she arrived. It took her a minute to notice most were gathered around televisions, watching different games. If they were working, they looked like they were enjoying it.

Adam met Sue halfway to his office. Again, he kissed her in a way that both thrilled and made her nervous with so many people around.

"Where's all the stuff from the copy shop?"

Sue smiled and stepped back. "Printing in Tom's local shop. I have a few samples, but the rest went to him to forward to Europe."

"You could've done that here. We have the same resources. Plus coffee."

"You would've distracted me." Sue gave him a light kiss on the cheek.

Adam squeezed her to him. "Let's go." He strode to the elevator without giving the office a second glance.

"I hope I didn't ruin your dinner plans."

"Nope. I'm cooking."

When they got to his apartment, Adam took vegetables and other ingredients out of the refrigerator.

Sue sized it all up and selected a bottle from his wine rack. She poured a glass for each of them and leaned against the kitchen counter. "I can cut the veggies. I'm pretty good at that. I have a knack with knives."

Adam raised an eyebrow and she laughed.

"My dad was a line cook in college. He taught me some tricks."

"Ah." Adam opened a drawer and gestured toward a row of cutlery. "What is it with you and cooking? Did your dad only ever teach you how to chop and leave you to fend for yourself?"

Sue selected a knife and inspected the blade. She closed the drawer, satisfied it didn't need sharpening. "Oh, I know how to cook. I'm a great cook. I just hate it."

"You hate cooking?" Adam put a cutting board on the counter near the sink.

"It stresses me out. Making sure you have all the ingredients, the cleaning." Sue gave an exaggerated shiver. "If I had, say, Martha Stewart's kitchen with ingredients measured and laying out for me, and her little cleaning sprites to make the place immaculate when I finished, I'd cook all the time."

"If you had roommates, I bet you could convince them to clean the kitchen." Adam rinsed carrots and lined them up near the cutting board.

"Tried that in college. People talk a good game, but it's a rare thing for them to *actually* clean up." Sue took a sip of wine. "Besides, if I had roommates you wouldn't be able to walk through my place naked."

"Desk sex would probably be out, too."

"Tragic."

Adam chuckled as he put a wok on the stove and lit the burner. "I need to ask you about something."

"I'm not in trouble, am I?" Sue asked playfully as she diced a carrot.

"Not at all." Adam dumped chunks of chicken into the deep pan. "My mom called today about my grandmother."

"How is she? Is physical therapy going well?"

"She's doing great. Taking to the therapy and getting in extra practice every day."

"Good!" Sue rinsed a few stalks of celery and added them to the cutting board.

"My parents have to go back to Colorado this week, and my older sister, Claire, was supposed to fly up tomorrow and stay through the weekend. My younger sister, Jessica, and I were going to split next week."

"Okay." Sue made quick work of the celery. The phrase *was supposed to* had her on alert. "How small do you want this?"

Adam glanced at the cutting board. "That's good. Anyway, Claire's husband is some kind of brilliant engineer, and there's a problem in a hospital that only he can fix."

"He fixes hospitals?"

"He designs the circuitry. Backup power sources, redundancy, things like that. This particular hospital had part of their grid fail. According to Claire, they have no backup power and only Steve can fix it."

"Wow." Sue slid the veggies into the wok. "He's kind of a superhero."

Adam smiled. "Yeah, he kind of is."

"Claire can't make it until the weekend, and I take it your parents can't extend their stay."

"No, they can't."

"You have to go." Sue kept her voice light to hide her disappointment in their week getting cut short.

"Mom's afraid Gram's pushing it. She doesn't want to leave Gram alone and risk another fall."

"You *need* to go." Sue sipped her wine. If the week had to end early, she'd call her contacts in New York. Better to go there than stay in Boston without Adam.

"Come with me." He turned from the stove and caught her eye.

Sue lifted her eyebrows but otherwise kept her face neutral. She didn't want Adam to know how much he'd thrown her. She went from disappointment in his leaving to shock that he wanted her to meet his family. She focused on the practical. "I have to be in New York Sunday."

"We'd go Thursday and come back Saturday. There'd be plenty of time to catch your flight. And I wired her house for internet. You can work while we're there."

Sue considered and took another drink before she answered, making an effort to keep her tone light. "I don't know, Adam. Meeting your grandmother? And your parents and sister? That's a big deal."

"I've met Tom and Gavin. Amy and Robin." Adam focused on the wok and stirred the food. "Man, did those two dissect me."

Sue smiled and shook her head. "They did not."

"It's okay if you don't want to go." Adam stepped toward Sue and pulled her into a hug. "But I like it when you're with me." He kissed her temple and went back to cooking their meal.

Each time he told her he wanted her around, he reeled her in a little bit more. She liked it. She stepped behind him and wrapped her arms around his waist in a tight embrace. "Of course I'll go."

The panic Sue'd been pushing back since she arrived in Boston hit her full force. She tightened her hold on Adam. This wasn't waiting to see where things would go. This was an official relationship.

CHAPTER 18

Adam gave Sue a wide berth Thursday morning. She'd been restless the night before, which he benefitted from, but when he woke, he wondered if Sue had slept at all. He brought a glass of orange juice to her after she showered, then retreated to the closet to get dressed and pack his overnight bag.

He ducked his head into the bathroom, finding her only in her bra and panties, and gave her a thorough once-over before he spoke. "No hurry, babe, but I'm gonna go pull the car around front."

Sue stood with her face close to the mirror as she applied makeup to her eyes. She stood back and blinked rapidly a few times. "Are you taking the bags? Mine is just about packed."

"I can if you want me to."

"Okay." Sue studied the items on the bathroom counter. She swept most of them into a small pouch and walked past him into the closet. Opening her weekender, she rustled the clothes around in it. She dropped the makeup bag on the top, zipped it up, and gave it to him. "All set."

Adam gave into temptation and squeezed her ass as he kissed her cheek. "I'll be back up in a few."

"I'm almost ready."

"Okay." He kissed her again, picked up his duffel and went to the garage.

The apartment and the television were nice, but the garage was the real reason he lived in this building. He wanted a place to park where snowplows wouldn't bury his car. He didn't get to drive it as often as he wanted, and the idea of having to dig it out in the winter held no appeal.

When he got to his space, he stood for a moment and took in the automobile. The sleek lines always made his pulse race. He popped the trunk, stowed the luggage, and pulled out two cloths. He closed the lid and walked all the way around the car, buffing as he went and wiping the rims. After one more glance, he stowed the dusters and got in. The only thing better than admiring his car was driving it. He pushed the ignition button and let the purr of the engine soothe him. Whatever nerves he had about taking Sue to his grandmother's house, the sound of the engine drove them from his mind.

He put the vehicle in gear, pulled out of the parking space, and headed toward the front of the building. Another benefit of his address: the street usually wasn't busy, making it easy to park right in front for a few minutes.

He got out of the car and took one more peek before turning to get Sue. He found her frozen in place next to the doorman, her jaw practically at her knees. Adam couldn't stop his smile.

"I told you I bought a car."

"No kidding. This is the DB9, right?"

Adam bounded up the stairs to the building, took her hand, and pulled her toward the automobile. "Yes."

"This is not a car. This is a work of art." Sue stopped on the curb, her eyes on the elegant machine. "This is the model with the carbon fiber body?"

Adam grinned. "You know about Aston Martins?"

"Yeah." Sue flicked a glance at him and refocused on the car. "All Justin and I talk about on the highway is cars and music. He loves muscle cars. I love *fast* ones."

Adam laughed. He didn't expect Sue to appreciate the DB9 the way he did, but it thrilled him that she saw more than a flashy sports car.

She stepped off the curb and walked around the Aston, even stopping in the middle of the street to take in the view. "I always thought it was a mistake to make them in any color besides silver. But this black." Sue slowly shook her head. "Gorgeous. It looks like a panther." She made eye contact with Adam. "Can I drive it? Please?"

"I don't know." Adam tilted his head. "It's a six speed."

"Duh."

"Have you ever driven a six speed?"

"Yeah." Sue circled the car again, slower. She stopped next to Adam, eyes still on the vehicle. "Paddle shifters?"

"Yep."

"Please let me drive. I promise I won't hurt this beauty."

"We are pretty close to the highway," Adam said.

Sue pulled her gaze from the car to him, her face full of excitement.

Adam shook his head and relented. "Okay."

She kissed him hard on the mouth and darted to the driver's side. She was in the car in a blink. When he got in on the passenger side, she sat still, studying the dash, as he had a few minutes before. When he closed his door, she smiled at him, her eyes shining.

Sue grabbed his arm. "*This* is the most gorgeous car I've ever been in."

"You're the only person I've ever let drive it."

"Not even your mechanic?"

"Driving it on and off the lift doesn't count."

"True. You can't really open her up on the lift." Sue pushed the ignition and moaned as the car came to life.

Adam adjusted himself and blew out a breath. "You're killing me."

Sue gave herself a little shake before she sat back and arranged the mirrors. She took a beat before she put the car in gear and pulled away from the curb.

Adam watched the road closely as he directed her through the city to the interstate.

"How far to the highway?" Sue asked.

"A few more minutes. You want me to drive?" Adam debated whether to have her pull over. He didn't want her to make a mistake because of nerves.

"Hell no." A wicked grin spread across Sue's face. "I need music. Where's my purse?"

Adam lifted it from the passenger side floorboard. "My MP3 player should be right on top."

Adam cautiously opened the small bag. He'd been terrified of purses ever since his sisters started carrying them. He once rifled through Claire's for her car keys only to find a dirty pacifier, unwrapped and sticky mints and a metal nail file that stabbed him. To his great relief, the player sat right at the top as Sue had promised. He plucked it out without injuring himself or even catching a glimpse of anything else lurking inside.

"I have a playlist called *Fast Car*," Sue said. "I need it."

Adam chuckled as he queued up the list and plugged it into the MP3 port. "Ready?"

Sue flexed her grip on the steering wheel and gave him a devilish smile. "Oh yeah."

Adam pressed play, then focused on Sue. As the music pumped out of the speakers, her smile changed from mischievous to happy.

A few minutes later she eased onto the highway on-ramp, took a deep breath, and put her foot down. She shifted gears like glass and gracefully threaded through the other cars that all but stood still around her. She shifted her hips in the seat, flexed her fingers against the steering wheel, and took the car faster and faster, expertly navigating curves and traffic.

Adam had been anxious when he consented to let her drive, and again as they merged onto the highway, but he relaxed as he watched how she handled the car, pushing it above one hundred miles per hour with complete ease. Her eyes were slightly narrowed, her lips held a sly grin, and her cheeks were flushed. She looked excited and satisfied.

The insistent beat of the music from her playlist heightened the sensation and Adam found himself conflicted over enjoying the journey and wishing it would end so he could touch her.

Sue toned it down considerably and obeyed the posted speed limit once they got off the highway. She made it to his grandmother's town in record time.

She swung wide into the driveway and barely had the car in park when Adam hopped out and raced around to open her door. He offered his hand to help her out, then pinned her, crushing her with a kiss.

Sue grinned. "I told you I wouldn't hurt her."

"I will never doubt you again." Adam kissed her again. "Family time." He said the words to refocus his brain, but Sue stiffened against him. He brushed a strand of hair behind her ear and gave her a mostly chaste kiss. "They're gonna love you."

Sue smiled and gave him a quick squeeze. "Okay, let's go."

Adam guided her to the back stairway next to the driveway. He should've taken her to the front door. The house had a sweeping entry, but he never used it. Besides, his grandmother would most likely be sitting on the back deck, where they spent most of their time together.

"Please don't hover. I'm fine, Margaret." Adam glanced up at the sound of his grandmother's voice.

"What are you doing on the stairs, Gram?"

"Hello to you, too, Adam." She stood on the third step from the top. "I have my cane, the railing and your mother. I'm fine."

"It's true, Adam," his mother said. "She's getting along well. She barely needs me."

"You have to give me room to adapt. The last time I saw you, Gram, you had a walker at the rehab center." Adam stopped one stair below her and kissed her cheek.

Gram squeezed his hand. "Adapt fast, young man."

Adam smiled. "Gram, Mom, this is Sue Douglas. Sue, Shirley and Margaret Fletcher."

Sue held out a hand, but Gram kissed her cheek as though she'd always been a part of the family. His mother gave an equally warm welcome.

The older women headed back up the stairs, with Adam and Sue following. When they got to the top, Sue gasped.

"I smelled the salt in the air, but I had no idea how close we were to the water."

Gram smiled. "I like to be close to nature but my husband wouldn't let me live in the middle of the woods. I put up a fight until he built this house."

"I…wow. This is an amazing compromise." Sue walked to the railing.

"It is," Shirley said. "Margaret, let's go turn on the stereo."

Adam held the door for his grandmother and mother as they went inside, then he joined Sue. "Incredible, isn't it?"

"That doesn't even begin to cover it. The neighborhood is elegant driving in, but I had no idea it had all this." Sue leaned over the railing and looked back at Adam. "You grew up here?"

"We had holidays and vacations here. When I moved to Boston for college, it became my weekend home."

"If I didn't know anything about you or your family, I'd think you made the drive up just for this view." Sue faced the ocean again.

"I'd be lying if I didn't admit sometimes that was true." Adam put his arm around her waist, and she leaned against him, her head on his shoulder.

She sighed and wove her fingers between his. "I don't want to ruin this moment, but I need to use the bathroom."

Adam kissed the top of her head. "That last glass of juice, huh?"

"Nerves. I could hold it, but I'd stutter in front of your parents and I'd rather not."

Adam led her into the house through the large yet cozy kitchen and gave her a brief tour of the first floor, leaving her in the small bathroom off the kitchen and joining his mother and grandmother across the hall in the family room.

Gram wanted to show off her mobility and insisted Adam dance with her as his mother watched.

"So, this is where you learned to waltz." Sue joined his mother on the couch.

"Of course. We couldn't send him into the wild with two left feet," Margaret said.

Sue chuckled, but Adam shook his head. "How quickly they forget my soccer career. I was pretty smooth on the field."

"You were." Gram patted Adam's cheek and grinned. "Tell me about the benefit."

"A class act. You would've appreciated the attention to detail," Adam said.

"Did the zoo meet their goal?" Margaret asked.

Sue tapped Margaret's wrist as she answered. "They exceeded it. They'll be able to complete all their open projects, as well as build the proposed habitat."

Gram stopped dancing and faced Sue. "That's wonderful. It's important to take exceptional care of animals when we take them out of their natural environments."

"Adam said you were a zoo vet."

Gram made her way to an armchair with Adam at her side. "Yes. For forty-five years. It was a privilege that kept my mind agile."

"I checked for the key fob when I got here, but apparently you're gonna make me beg." A booming voice preceded his father into the room.

"Sorry, old man. You know the rules, no unsupervised visits." Adam waited until his grandmother was seated comfortably before crossing the room to shake his father's hand. "Dad, this is Sue Douglas. Sue, my father, Russ Fletcher."

Sue stood. "Nice to meet you, Mr. Fletcher."

Russ gave her a half-hug. His eyes crinkled as he smiled. "It's Russ, and the pleasure is all mine, young lady. It's been a while since Adam brought anyone other than his car when he came to visit."

Sue flushed. The pretty color on her cheeks took the sting out of his father announcing that Adam didn't bring women here. He was glad she knew, but he would've preferred a less bombastic way of telling her.

Russ gestured for her to sit again, and he took a seat between his wife and mother. Adam sat on the arm of the couch next to Sue. "When's your flight?"

"Trying to kick me out already?" Russ asked.

Adam grinned and shrugged. Of the family, his father and Claire were the most likely to embarrass him, intentionally or not. He'd managed to have Sue meet them separately, but there was no harm in limiting her exposure, either. He still played the long game. Get her to come back. They could embarrass him some other time.

"We moved our flight to later this evening," his mother said. "This way we'll be here for Shirley's next PT session. We can have an early dinner before we go."

"You can bring me up to speed." Adam smiled at his grandmother. "I'll adjust faster."

"Exactly," Russ boomed. "In the meantime, I'm gonna fire up the grill for dinner. Whaddya say we go to the market for some fresh fish, Adam?"

"Sounds good."

"I'll drive." Russ stood. "Keys."

"No way."

"Look, boy. I have the best insurance rates I've ever had. I'm not even a flight risk. Let me take her for a spin."

"I will happily drive you up the coast, Dad, but there's no way you're getting in the driver's seat."

CHAPTER 19

After Adam's parents left, his grandmother's long-time friend and neighbor, Mrs. Thurston, stopped by with her Mahjong set.

Gram helped spread the tiles across the kitchen table. "Adam, why don't you take Sue for a drive. Show her around."

Sue smiled. "It's okay. We're fine here."

"Please. Neither of you want to watch two old ladies play a game you don't know a thing about."

"It's fine, Gram. I want to stay." Adam set a mug of coffee near each woman.

"Adam, I'm not going to let Shirley away from this game. The stakes are big tonight." Mrs. Thurston gestured toward the carafe Sue set on the table. "And I can refill our coffee while we play."

Adam crossed his arms. The ladies had long been dedicated to their game nights, but they sat and talked at least as much as they played, if not more. The passion was new. "You playing for quarters instead of dimes, Mrs. T?"

Gram waved away his comment. "Go. I will stay right exactly here." She pointed to the chair she sat in.

Adam turned to Sue. She shrugged, leaving the decision to him. He respected his grandmother and her independence, and she'd made great progress since her surgery. But his mother didn't ask him here for fun.

Mrs. Thurston got up and pushed Adam toward the door. "Get out of here; we need old lady time."

Adam glanced back as Gram laughed. Her joy convinced him. She wasn't one to fake being well. Her genuine expression gave him comfort.

"Push Sue out, too. She misses the old lady bracket by a good forty, fifty years."

Sue grinned and scooted out of the way before Mrs. Thurston got to her.

"One hour and we'll be back," Adam said. He knew Gram and Mrs. T would be fine, but he didn't want them to get so comfortable that one of them got hurt.

Gram rolled her eyes. "Sue?"

"Yes?"

"Do me a favor and break my grandson's fancy watch."

Sue laughed as she took Adam's hand and walked with him to the door.

"One hour, Gram," Adam shouted over his shoulder.

Once they were both in the car Sue leaned over and kissed him. "One hour? How much can I see in one hour?"

Adam narrowed his eyes and studied her as he pushed the ignition. Sue taking up for Gram already? That had to be a good sign. He gave her a sideways glance as he turned on the car. She'd even tried to distract him with that kiss. "You're all in collusion."

Adam drove Sue through the town and along the ocean highway, pointing out landmarks as they went. He took her to one of his favorite spots on the beach, away from the houses and public access. He wanted to see her in all the places that meant something to him. They stayed there and talked a while before Adam let her drive back.

When she pulled into the driveway, Adam hopped out of the passenger side before she shut the car off and went to help her out. He was about to kiss her when she interrupted him.

"Adam, Shirley and Mrs. Thurston aren't at the table."

Neither woman could be seen through the kitchen window. Adam swore under his breath and dashed toward the house, keeping Sue's hand in his. He inched open the door to survey the space, hoping he wouldn't startle the women and cause Gram to fall again.

"You said you were gonna stay in your chair all night, Gram." He kept his voice light. He didn't want to surprise the women, and he didn't want them to hear the relief he felt at finding them both upright, slowly walking across the kitchen.

Gram stopped and threw back her shoulders. "I'm going to the bathroom. I can manage. And Abby is right here." She nodded at Mrs. Thurston, who stood beside her.

Mrs. T looked perfectly capable, but he didn't want any more injuries—for anyone. He glanced at Sue, who seemed equally concerned. "Mrs. T, do you want Sue to help Gram?"

"Good Lord, Adam. Of course not. We are *fine*."

The two women continued their shuffle. When they got to the bathroom, Gram stepped away, leaving her friend in the hallway.

Adam leaned against the kitchen island, ready to spring into action, but also trying to be calm lest he annoy all the women in the house. "Do you ladies still play for money?"

"Oh, no. Now we play for Percocet."

"Mrs. T!"

She patted her hair. "It makes the games much more interesting."

Adam went to the table and looked over the tiles. "I don't see any pills."

"Of course not. We're old, not stupid."

The toilet flushed and the faucet ran.

Mrs. Thurston leaned forward. "We play for the gardener."

"What?"

"Louise Teal has a talented gardener, and Shirley managed to convince him to work on her yard once a week for practically nothing. We play for her day."

Adam shook his head. "You play for the gardener?"

"Yes. He's quite good. And" —Mrs. Thurston moved away from the door as Gram opened it and stepped out of the bathroom— "he often works without his shirt during the summer."

Gram bumped Mrs. Thurston's arm. "It's a good thing I have my wits about me now with the weather changing."

"Gram!" Adam scoffed as Sue tried to hide her laughter.

"What? I've got a right to enjoy watching him as much as anyone!"

Adam rubbed his temple. "This is too much."

"Well, Shirley, I'll be back tomorrow to take another crack at him." Mrs. Thurston walked back to the table and packed up the game. She and Gram exchanged a hug, then she patted Adam on the cheek and squeezed Sue's hand before darting out the back door.

"Sue, darling?" Gram carried her coffee mug from the table to the sink. "I hope this isn't asking too much, but could you help me? I'm ready to turn in and sometimes I lose my balance with my socks and shoes."

"Of course."

Confident Gram had asked for help to ease his mind, Adam also hoped she'd asked to have some time alone to get to know Sue more. "I'll get our stuff from the car."

"Kiss me goodnight first. Once I'm changed, I'm going to sleep."

Adam enveloped her in a hug and kissed her cheek. "Good night, Gram."

"Good night, sweetheart."

Adam stood at the bottom of the stairwell and paid attention to the railing as the women went up. When they were safely on the landing, he went to the car and got the luggage.

He dropped their things in the room he slept in when he visited, then searched the house for a docking station or speaker to plug into Sue's MP3 player. He returned with one as she closed the door at the opposite end of the hallway.

She followed him and took her toiletries out of her bag while he hooked everything up.

"There." Adam brushed his hands together.

"What?" Sue called from the attached bathroom.

Adam queued up the "Fast Car" playlist and turned to her.

She tilted her head. "What?" she asked again as the room filled with her music.

"Just something I've wanted to do ever since you drove my car." He stalked to her and kissed her as he pushed her against the wall. He pulled back and held her gaze as he worked his hands up the smooth skin of her legs and under her dress. He held eye contact as he pushed her panties down her legs.

"Here?" she whispered.

"I want you everywhere." Adam bit near her ear and rubbed his fingers against her clit. "It doesn't stop when people are around. It doesn't stop for anything."

She pulled his mouth to hers and kissed him with an intensity that buckled his knees. Her fast shift from family time to focused on him ratcheted up his desire. She matched him kiss for kiss, stoking an even deeper need.

He forced himself to slow as he trailed his lips along her throat, and peeled the small strap of her dress off her shoulder. His fingers under her skirt found a different rhythm, though, keeping time with the music, moving quickly to open her up.

Sue pulled his shirt out of his waistband, making quick work of the buttons. She moaned when she touched his bare skin.

The sound of her voice brought his mouth back to hers. He devoured her as her fingers slipped down his chest and unbuckled his belt. He held her tight against the wall, not letting her get farther than his waist, enjoying the sensation of her touch, as she tried for his zipper, then worked back up his chest and down again as he brought her closer and closer to the edge.

When she trembled, he lifted her up, took a condom out of his pocket, and pushed his pants out of the way. He used his teeth to open the wrapper, rolled the condom on, and pulled her onto him. Sue quieted her moan by mashing her mouth against his shoulder, her teeth teasing his skin. She arched her body against his and kissed the spot she bit, continuing to kiss her way to his mouth.

Adam carried her to the bed, sitting her on the edge as he and pulled her dress up and off, then he pulled her hips to him so he could grind against her as he speared her. He shrugged off the rest of his clothes, anxious to have her bare skin against his. He crawled over her, pushing her farther back on the bed. Needing to touch her, he grabbed and rubbed her skin, his lips following. The heat of her body beneath him electric. He engulfed her mouth in a kiss as she pushed against him and rolled him over.

Sue straddled him and sat up, pushing him back when he reached for her.

"Give me a second," she said, breathless. "I want to try something."

Adam lay back, hands kneading her hips, watching her face until sensation overwhelmed him. He groaned as she repeated a deliciously slow hip roll. Dragging his gaze down her body to watch the movement, he realized she had done that on the dancefloor. His eyes rolled back in his head and he growled.

CHAPTER 20

Sue made it to the kitchen a few minutes before seven with wet hair and a bare face. She started a fresh pot of coffee for Shirley and went outside to take in the view. Leaning over the railing, she marveled at how the deck seemed to hang over the ocean.

"Incredible, isn't it?" Shirley said from the open kitchen door.

Sue jumped. "How'd you get down the stairs?"

Clad in her robe and slippers, Shirley stepped outside. "Adam caught me in the hallway."

Sue's shoulders sagged in relief.

"I can navigate the stairs myself. Even without the cane." Shirley almost sounded like a petulant child declaring she could do something all on her own.

"I know. But I would never forgive myself if you fell while I daydreamed about the ocean."

Shirley joined Sue at the railing. "I'd forgive you. I come out here to daydream all the time."

They exchanged a warm smile. Sue had been nervous about meeting Adam's family, especially Shirley. She'd lost her grandmother years ago, yet it still felt like a fresh wound. Being with Shirley reminded her of Gran, but it didn't spike the dull throb of pain she carried. Maybe her desire to win Shirley's approval distracted her from the loss, maybe the stunning sea view helped, or maybe it was the realization of what Shirley's approval would further confirm. Adam wasn't some guy she passed time with. He meant something to her.

Together, Shirley and Sue set the porch table with bowls of cereal and fruit so they could watch the tide come in.

"I was gonna make omelets this morning." Adam dropped a hand on Sue's shoulder and gave her a chaste kiss.

Shirley angled a cheek toward him, and he kissed her as well. "Thank you, darling, but this hit the spot."

"We have been working on the dinner menu, though," Sue said. "It'll require a quick trip to the grocery store."

Shirley looked at Adam. "She'll need your car."

He scratched his head. "*My* car?"

"Well, she can't drive mine, it's a boat!"

"The Buick is not that big." Adam pulled out a chair and sat.

"It doesn't matter. Give her the keys." Shirley gestured with her spoon.

Sue sat back and grinned as Adam stuttered. She wasn't sure what had him more flummoxed, her planning a meal with his grandmother, or him keeping up the "no one drives my car" charade.

"You're not fooling me, Adam. I saw you get out of the wrong side of your car yesterday."

Adam's eyes widened. "You did?"

"Yes. I was sitting at the kitchen window when you two arrived." Shirley sipped her coffee and smiled. "Now, give her your keys, and soon. My PT comes early today."

Adam watched Shirley for a long moment. "You *cannot* tell Claire or Dad."

"Don't be ridiculous," Shirley said. "We'd never hear the end of it if I told your sister."

Adam sat silently for a long moment, practically staring Shirley down.

Shirley calmly finished her cereal.

Sue followed Shirley's lead and ate quietly, wondering if she'd get in trouble for *actually* being in cahoots this time. She hoped it'd be good trouble.

Finally, Adam slapped the arms of his chair and stood. "Fine." He shook his head and went back in the house.

Sue nudged Shirley's elbow. "Why can't we tell Claire?"

"She talked him into buying that car and he won't let her drive it."

"Why not?"

"She doesn't know how to drive with a shifter."

"Does Russ?"

"Yes, but he has a fancy car, too." Shirley peeled a banana as she spoke. "And he's had to replace the transmission twice and the clutch three times." Shirley took a small bite and waved. "So far."

"Wow."

"How did you manage it?" Shirley asked.

Sue scooped up some cereal from her bowl. "I've never needed a new clutch or transmission."

Adam came back onto the deck with a young woman in athletic pants and a T-shirt.

Shirley's face brightened. "Good morning, Marcy!"

"Good morning." Marcy bent and gave Shirley a small backward hug.

"Would you like some breakfast?" Shirley gestured toward the table.

"No, thank you."

"Marcy, this is Adam's Sue."

"Nice to meet you." Marcy held out a hand.

"Nice to meet you, too." Sue shook it. "Shirley, I'll help you change so you can get started."

"No need. Marcy comes early twice a week to help me with my clothes. I'm almost used to doing it with the cane." Shirley stood as Marcy held the chair. "You go to the market and get what you need for the rump roast."

Sue gave her a wide grin, pleased to do something for Shirley that wasn't directly tied to her recovery. "Absolutely."

Adam didn't speak until Shirley and Marcy were in the house. "Rump roast?"

"Yeah. We were talking about food and trading recipes. I got carried away about my grandmother's roast, and we decided we need to have it for dinner tonight."

"You're gonna cook for me." Adam smirked.

Sue stood and cleared the table. "I'm cooking for *Shirley*. Lucky for you, it'll feed about twenty."

Adam helped bring the food into the kitchen then he pulled Sue into a hug. "She likes you."

"She's wonderful." Sue rubbed her hands up his back, content in his arms and thrilled by his declaration. "She reminds me of my grandmother. We were very close."

They stood together for a minute in the kitchen until Sue heard Marcy and Shirley on the stairs.

She pulled back and put her hand out. "Key fob."

Adam chuckled and gave it to her. "No speeding."

"I would never." Sue gave him a peck on the cheek before she headed for the door.

He swatted her backside and pulled her back for another kiss. "Thank you," he said, still holding her close.

"It's my pleasure." Sue ducked out the door.

■────────────────■

Once they completed a successful—and impressive—PT session, Adam put a rocking chair next to the railing on the deck and set Gram up with a carafe of iced coffee, a book, and a blanket. Then he got out the running to-do list he and his dad kept in the garage.

He needed to keep his mind occupied after all the questions Shirley'd asked about Sue. He suspected she asked both out of curiosity and to give him an opening to talk about his girlfriend. He enjoyed the opportunity but found himself restless once he'd gotten Shirley settled.

He'd finished changing the oil in the Buick when Sue finally pulled up. She climbed out of the driver's seat looking triumphant. Everything fell out of Adam's head, except needing to be near her. He picked up a rag, wiped his hands, and forced himself to walk to her.

"You were gone awhile." He worked to keep his voice casual.

"Shirley gave me extremely scenic directions." Sue opened the trunk and Adam whistled.

"I thought you were getting a rump roast."

"I paid attention when I got breakfast together. I didn't want Claire to have to worry about groceries, so I stocked up on things that looked low."

Adam wrapped his arms around her. "You didn't have to do that."

"I'm enjoying this visit. Claire should enjoy hers, too, without worrying about food."

"That's…that's…" Adam searched for the words. Finally, he kissed her cheek. "I love you."

Sue faced the trunk, loading her arms with grocery sacks. He wasn't an expert in declarations of love, but her turning away didn't seem like a good sign. When she finally turned toward him again, her radiant smile burned away the nerves his confession had brought.

"You're excited I'm cooking. You might want to withhold judgment until you know if I'm as good as I say I am."

Was she testing him? "You could poison us, and it wouldn't change a thing."

Still smiling and with grocery bags hanging from her arms, Sue took a step closer to him and caught his mouth with hers, her kiss rivaling the ones from the night before. Adam pulled her against him, needing her body against his.

Surely, she would say it back. Say something to acknowledge she knew he meant it.

Sue sighed and leaned her head against his for a moment. "Help me bring all this stuff in," she said, her voice hoarse. She stepped out of his embrace and maneuvered around him, carrying the first load inside.

Stunned, he watched her climb the stairs. Did she blow him off? He turned back to the trunk. There had to be at least two hundred dollars of groceries waiting to be carried in. Would she do this for anyone? Was this her way of showing love? Adam loaded his arms with bags and reminded himself he was playing the long game. He'd get her love, and he'd get her to say it, too.

CHAPTER 21

After helping Shirley get ready for bed, Sue found Adam in the den, watching a baseball game. She'd diligently kept herself busy all afternoon by cooking dinner, serving dinner, eating dinner, cleaning up after dinner and playing cards with Shirley, all to avoid facing Adam and the fact that he probably expected her to say she loved him, too.

Did she? The question made her anxious. Love meant it would hurt much more when he got tired of waiting for her and the openings in her crowded life. She wouldn't deny that she liked him, and this week especially had shown her how great they could be together if they figured out their schedules. Her work commitments loomed over her, though. Her business was still new, and she faced hurdles she hadn't expected.

She didn't want to face the idea of losing him when they were having such a great week. Better to keep things fun and let the relationship peter out during the European tour when Adam got tired of having an absentee girlfriend. She gave herself a moment to watch him before she joined him, determined to distract him from her fears.

"Please buy Shirley a footstool." Sue sat on the couch next to him and pulled his arm around her.

"Why?"

"She gets nervous taking off her shoes. If she sits in a chair to do it, she hangs onto the arm of the chair or the cane so hard that it throws her off balance. And she doesn't have the flexibility to pull her foot up to the seat if she's sitting on it."

Adam shifted and turned his gaze toward Sue. "Okay." He kissed her temple. "Thank you."

Sue snuggled into him, unable to focus on the game but afraid to say more. This was the first time they'd been alone since his declaration. He didn't treat her differently, but the weight of her unspoken words pressed on her.

"What else do you help her with?" Adam asked.

"Nothing. Marcy taught her how to manage the rest of her clothes. She even suggested a switch to slip-on shoes, but Shirley worries she'll step out of them."

"Huh." Adam scratched his chin. "If her shoes are the only issue, why won't she let me help her?"

Sue giggled. "She said your dad tried a few nights ago and she had to beat him with her cane because he treated her like an invalid and her bosom is her own business, damn it."

Adam laughed. "Dad tends to shoot first and ask questions later." He tightened his hold on Sue. "I'll pick up a stool tomorrow."

"Make sure it's pretty. Nothing plastic or hospitalish."

"Yes, ma'am."

She watched an outfielder make an easy catch and lob the ball to third base. He liked it when she talked sports. "Did sabermetrics really level the playing field, or are teams still using gut instinct to pick players?"

"Did you guys watch *Moneyball* on the bus?"

Sue rolled her eyes. "I read the book. The guys prefer basketball."

"You read *Moneyball?*"

"Yeah." Sue shrugged. "I told you I like good stories. I should read more Michael Lewis."

"You should read more Michael…" Adam pulled her closer and pressed a hard kiss against her forehead. "I don't know what kind of voodoo miracle put you in my taco place, but damn, I'm grateful."

She pressed a kiss to his chest, also grateful but at a loss for what to say. Everything seemed to bring her precariously close to the "l" word. She wracked her brain for something to give him to make him happy but wound up tormenting herself with her tour schedule. Finally, a stroke of genius. She waited for a commercial before she spoke again. "Are you watching the game for business or pleasure?"

"The Sox are a pleasure no matter what."

"Even when they're losing?" She gave Adam a big grin.

"If you weren't a good cook, I wouldn't let a comment like that slide."

Sue laughed and sat up as she mentally noted this favorite of his. "Sorry, babe. No more ribbing the Red Sox. I promise."

"Thank you." Adam lowered the sound on the television. "I'm not covering the game. Do you want to go out?"

"Nope. I didn't want to talk your ear off if you've gotta remember details for an article."

"I'm all yours. What's up?"

Sue sat sideways on the couch, facing him, and crossed her legs beneath her. "Sports Mecca covers Premier League Soccer."

"Yep. Are you a fan?"

"Hell yes."

"Sports Mecca should be your go-to source for news."

"It has been for a few years." Sue pushed her hair behind her ears.

Adam turned in his seat and faced her. "Why haven't we talked about soccer more?"

"We should talk about it more. You guys always have the whole story."

"Damn straight." He leaned back with a smug grin.

"I check bylines and noticed *you* write a lot of the soccer articles." She hoped she didn't sound like a stalker. She hadn't checked bylines until after a few dates when she had idle time on the bus.

"Is this where you tell me I suck?"

Sue shook her head and laughed. "Never. Your articles are great. Do you write them after watching the games on satellite? Or do you go in person?" She balled her fists in her lap, suddenly nervous.

"A bit of both. The story is usually better when you're there."

"So…" She hunched her shoulders. "Any chance you might be in Europe in July? Like, possibly somewhere in England for the Champions League tournament?"

A smile spread across his face. "That is highly likely."

"Are you up for a rendezvous between taking me to a game or two?"

"Hell yes." Adam gripped her thigh. "What's your schedule?"

"We have a few consecutive days off in July, but I don't remember the exact dates." Normally she'd be able to rattle the dates off in her sleep, but the glint in his eye and his hands on her body distracted her. "It's in my phone. We can figure it out tomorrow."

"Tomorrow? I want to lock you down right now."

Sue's pulse raced. She leaned forward and kissed him. "There are other ways to accomplish that."

* * *

"Where's Gram?" Claire arrived around ten on Saturday morning. As usual, she arrived like a whirlwind and swept Adam up in it.

He turned from the railing going to the second floor. He'd fixed it as soon as he left the hospital after Gram's surgery, but now he reinforced it to soothe his mind. "Walking the neighborhood."

"Adam!" Claire put her fists on her hips. "You let her go for a walk so soon after the surgery?"

"Yeah. She's doing great." Adam sat on one of the lower stair treads. "Marcy says she doesn't have to come so often because Gram is doing so well. She does it because she knows we're rotating in and out and wants to make sure we all know Gram's exercises."

"Seriously?"

"Yeah."

Claire cocked her head. "Still, you're not even trying to keep an eye on her. This is a hilly neighborhood."

"Hardly, and she's with Sue. They both have phones." Adam pulled his phone out of his pocket. "And here's mine."

Claire dropped her arms and squinted. "I thought Marcy was the therapist."

Adam put his phone away after a quick check of the screen. "She is."

"Then who's Sue?"

"Sue's with me." Adam turned back to the railing. He didn't want his sister to see his vulnerability—he loved this woman and wanted Claire to love her, too, but he didn't know if Sue loved *him*. Sue adored Gram, though, and it made him love her even more.

"Is this your date from Savannah?" Claire poked his shoulder.

"Yeah." Adam shook the railing and bent to check the screws, hoping Claire would take the hint and not give him shit about the evening she'd interrupted.

Claire smirked. "Finally sealed the deal, huh?"

Adam rolled his eyes. "We are *not* talking about that."

"Okay. I'll go ask her." Claire bolted out the back door.

Adam followed, shouting to her to leave Sue alone. He stopped short when he got to the deck, hoping Claire would at least hold her tongue in front of their grandmother.

He finished his work on the railing, put the tools away, and washed up, expecting the women to return the entire time. When they didn't, he went after them. He followed the bend in the road until he found them four houses away, huddled together.

At first, he thought something had happened to Gram and jogged toward them. As he got closer, he noticed they were giggling. He slowed to take in the situation. He was about ten feet away when he noticed the gardener.

"You have got to be kidding me."

All three of them jumped and broke into a fresh bout of giggles.

"Here I worried Gram had fallen or something, but no." Adam gestured toward the yard they stood in front of. "You're ogling the gardener."

Shirley pushed her shoulders back. "Sue's visit would not have been complete if we didn't find some way for her to see him."

"And it certainly makes my trip more exciting." Claire wiggled her eyebrows.

"Claire! You're married!" Adam said.

"I'm pretty sure even Steve would concede this man is worth a look." Claire faced the neighbor's yard.

Adam caught Sue trying to hide a snicker and tilted his head toward her. "What about you? Does he qualify as worthy eye candy?"

"You know, I'm starving." Shirley grinned. "Claire, Sue made the most delicious roast last night, and we're going to reheat it for sandwiches today."

"That sounds fantastic." Claire offered Shirley her arm, and the two walked toward the house.

"My grandmother is a cagey old lady," Adam said.

Sue took a few steps and closed the gap between them. She kissed him lightly on the cheek as she pulled him toward Claire and Shirley. "She's wonderful."

"And the gardener?"

"If I was Mrs. Thurston, I would definitely play for him instead of Percocet."

CHAPTER 22

After lunch and the physical therapy session with Shirley and Claire, Sue bid her goodbyes. She held back her emotions when Shirley hugged her and invited her to come back soon. She wanted to, but even with Adam agreeing to meet her in Europe, she knew the odds were low.

She still grilled Adam about Claire as he drove. She and his sister hit it off as though they'd been old friends. When Claire asked for the rump roast recipe, Sue almost scribbled her phone number along the top of the paper before handing it over. So far, his whole family had been amazing. Heaven help her if he ever managed to get her in a room with all of them at the same time.

"Enough about my sister," Adam said when they were about halfway to Boston. "Have you sent your schedule to Lauren yet?"

"No."

"As long as we're sitting here with all this time, let's sync our calendars." Adam pulled his phone from his pocket and gave it to Sue.

"And here I had this fantasy of us sitting at your counter, side by side on our laptops."

Adam laughed. "*That's* your fantasy?"

"No." Sue held both of their phones, navigating hers to the calendar. "But wouldn't it be faster with the computers? We can trade calendars and sync the phones. Then no matter what country I'm in when I lose my phone charger, I'll still know what's up."

"You think you'll lose your phone charger?"

"No, but I like having a backup plan."

Adam squeezed her thigh. "Okay. Why don't you flip through there and tell me which games you want to go to."

"Oh, that sounds like fun." Sue scrolled through his calendar, trying to skip ahead to July. "Man, you travel a lot."

"More in the summer, but yeah."

"When do you get to watch your giant TV?"

Adam laughed. "Often enough. A lot of those trips are only day trips or one night out."

"Do you have a suitcase permanently packed?"

"Two," Adam admitted. "Each has a week's worth of clothes. When I only have a day at home before I go back out, I don't have to worry about re-packing."

When they got to Adam's apartment, he immediately set up his laptop on the kitchen counter. Sue laughed when she realized what he was doing and took out hers as well. They sat side by side, discussing their schedules and figuring out which games they could attend together. Adam leaned against her and read her screen as Sue clicked through her itinerary and checked into her flight to New York.

"What's this?" He pointed at her screen. "Susannah?"

Sue's cheeks heated. "That's my name."

"Why do you go by Sue?"

She clicked through the screens to finish her online check-in and switched to her calendar, getting her name off the screen. "It's faster and I don't have to spell it for people." She waved it away, embarrassed by the ladylike name that had long been an awkward fit. "Only my mother calls me Susannah."

Adam kissed her cheek and stood. "She has good taste."

Trying to will away her blush, Sue focused on her calendar. She counted the days between her departure and when she would see Adam again.

"Forty-three days." She frowned and counted again.

"What?" Adam filled a stock pot with water.

She closed her computer, needing a moment to recover from her instinctual reaction of forty-three days being too damn long to be without him. "Nothing." She hopped off her stool. "Wine?"

"Pick something."

Sue took her time selecting a bottle. She needed a minute to recalibrate so he wouldn't notice her unease. It would bring her back to the "l" conversation, and she still wasn't convinced she was there. She wanted this to last, but she didn't want to force it. She didn't want to say something she didn't believe, and she didn't want him to feel obligated, especially if things went sideways while they were apart.

She felt a stab in her heart. She didn't want to be apart. Shit. She found the corkscrew while Adam took out glasses.

"Are you ready to go back to your rock and roll lifestyle?"

Sue opened the merlot and wrinkled her brow. Of course he would ask her about the thing tormenting her. "Rock and roll lifestyles are *not* all they're cracked up to be."

"No?" Adam poured the wine.

"Uh uh. The sleep is terrible. You hardly get to see the places you go to. The best part is the music, but there's so much other *crap*. Steely Dan may have had the right idea."

"How so?"

Sue returned to her stool. "It probably isn't true, but there's a story that after they wrote and recorded their early albums, they'd stay home and hire other musicians to tour for them. Kind of genius if you like to sleep."

"So, it's not all sex, drugs, and rock and roll."

"If you talk to Chris, hell yes. If you talk to the rest of us, it's flirting, logistics, and rock and roll."

Adam laughed. "Doesn't have the same ring."

"You've seen it. And you know how much sex I have. Drive time aside, without roadies, there's too much to do to leave time for drugs. But I do get to rock out."

"It seems like you've been on a hot streak with the sex lately."

Sue smirked. "It's been a good month."

Adam winked and drank his wine.

"It'll have to hold me over now." Sue rubbed her temples. One more thing to miss while she traveled. Because missing *him* wasn't enough.

Adam raised an eyebrow.

"We're not gonna be on the same continent for a while, let alone the same city."

Adam leaned on the counter between them. "Phone sex?"

Sue laughed. "We'll see." She took a sip of her wine and put her chin in her hand. "Claire told me you've never brought a girlfriend to your grandmother's house." If they were going to talk about her lack of a sex life, it was only fair to talk about his, right? Would he lack?

Adam flushed slightly. "True. What else did she tell you?"

"She said you told her we were in the middle of a kinky good time in Savannah when she called you that night."

Adam straightened and rolled his eyes. "I hope you didn't believe her."

"No, but I also didn't say anything to make her think otherwise." Sue flashed her eyebrows.

"Serves her right." Adam refilled their glasses. "Anything else?"

"Those were the two big revelations."

"That's not too bad."

"No, but I have a question." Sue sipped her wine.

"Shoot."

"How did you manage to go up there all those weekends in college and not bring a girlfriend with you?"

"I just didn't."

"Why?" It seemed to come naturally to him. Meeting the family was weighty, and he treated it as another day. She'd never been comfortable bringing people home, so she didn't.

Adam checked the pot on the stove and adjusted the flame. "I was on the soccer team and going to Gram's was how I unwound. I didn't even bring teammates with me. When I blew out my knee, I went there to figure out what to do next." Adam took salt from a nearby cabinet and sprinkled some in the water. "It wasn't an easy time. Gram's house is a sanctuary. Bringing anyone to it was a big deal." Adam stood in front of Sue, holding her gaze. "Bringing someone there is still a big deal."

"Thank you for inviting me." She struggled to stay outwardly calm. His words meant the world to her, but she didn't know what to give him in return. Protecting herself and her agenda had become so ingrained, she wasn't sure she was capable of lowering her guard. What if she fumbled it? In business, vulnerability was weakness. She'd never learned how to handle it in her personal life, especially since Robin had been the only person in her life who'd never judged her when she'd shown it to him.

"I'm glad you came. You brought extra light to Gram."

"That's sweet, thank you." His compliment was well timed. That she'd been able to bring something to his family fortified her.

Adam walked around the counter and kissed her. "You're welcome, Susannah."

Sue closed her eyes for a moment but smiled. Normally she'd insist on "Sue," but she liked hearing him use her real name. "I have one more thing to ask you."

Adam flattened a hand on the counter. "Go for it."

"I have no business asking, especially since I'm about to go live on a bus with five smelly men for the summer.

But…" Sue stopped to take a beat, ready to make herself vulnerable for him. She gave him a confident smile. "Will you wait for me?"

"What?"

"Wait for me? I like whatever this is, and I was hoping…" Sue struggled to finish. Asking for this had only just occurred to her. Something about his rock and roll lifestyle comment had bothered her. She wanted it clear that while she often woke up in a new city, he was her only lover.

"Yes."

Sue's gaze snapped back to his. "Yeah?" Was it that easy?

"Of course. Are you kidding me?" Adam squeezed her shoulder.

Sue sat back on the stool. "No. I—I wasn't sure if you thought me going away meant things would be more casual." She fidgeted, her cheeks burning. She had no idea how to explain what she meant. Hell, she barely understood it. She was relieved he'd said yes, and yet she still fumbled all over herself. She didn't like feeling so raw. "I'm not casual… with…myself."

"Should I be insulted that you think I am?" Adam asked.

"God, I always put my foot in my mouth." Sue covered her eyes for a moment. He'd been open with her all week and laid everything on the line. She had to fix this awkward conversation. She dropped her hand and tried again. "I'm sorry. I don't think that at all. I'm an idiot."

"No, you're not. You're worth waiting for."

She gave him a relieved smile, slid off her stool and wrapped her arms around him.

"How am I going to let you get on a plane tomorrow and leave me for a month?"

Sue sighed as her mind went back to the forty-three days she'd calculated. "I wish I knew."

The next morning, Sue woke to a flurry of texts from Tom, Amy, and Robin. She confirmed for Tom again that her flight hadn't changed. She told Amy and Robin to hold their questions until she called them. They both sent her messages asking when that would be. She responded with *"entirely too soon."*

For the second time in a month, she found herself in an airport, clinging to Adam and wrestling with her emotions. She finally accepted that she needed to consider what was developing and how she felt about it and him. She'd let a lot of things happen, like meeting Adam's family, things she'd been careful to avoid in past relationships.

After about ten minutes of holding on and sharing a whispered conversation and quiet laughter, Sue's phone buzzed practically nonstop. She sighed and pulled back enough to take the damn thing out of her pocket.

"It's Tom," she said before she answered. "Hey…yeah, it's *still* on time…yes, I'm about to go to my gate. I'll make it, relax. Bye."

"Tom's still freaking out?"

"He wanted me to go to Ann Arbor to fly back to Newark with everyone."

"That's overkill."

Sue sighed again as her phone shook with a fresh round of messages. "Why won't they stop texting?" She put the phone on silent and slipped it back into her pocket. "Give me ten minutes, guys!"

"You have to go." Adam rubbed her arms.

The stab in her heart came back. She didn't want to go. She wanted more time with him to figure out her feelings.

"I'll see you in Manchester."

"Okay." Sue leaned in to kiss him.

He wrapped her in his arms and deepened the kiss. "Be careful. Let me know when you get there."

"I will." Sue pulled out the handle of her carry-on suitcase and smiled.

Adam touched her arm. "I love you, Susannah."

Sue pulled him close with her free arm and kissed him again. "*You* are my favorite."

She knew those words weren't enough, but they were the most honest thing she could offer. She was too raw and confused, scared. But she wanted to leave him with something. And he *was* her favorite. She smiled and headed for the security line, hoping they were far enough apart when she looked back that Adam didn't see the tears pricking at her eyes.

She made it through security and to her gate with about twenty minutes to spare before her flight's boarding time. Rather than respond to the three text messages she had from Amy and the two from Robin, she decided to call them. She'd chastise them properly for interrupting her goodbye with Adam, which provided a tiny distraction from thinking about how much she hated leaving.

"Hey Ames, can you hold on? I want to conference in Robin."

"No need, chickadee," Amy said. "He's right here. I'll put you on speaker."

"Of course he is." Sue rubbed her forehead. "Hey, Robin."

"Hey, Sexy Sue, how's it going?"

"Please don't with that ridiculous nickname," Sue said.

"Why not? It's fun!"

"Please?"

"Are you okay, Sue?" Amy asked.

"I'm great."

"You don't sound great."

"I'm fine."

"Are you being sarcastic or serious?" Robin asked.

"Serious. I had a great week with Adam. He took me to a game at Fenway and to some great clubs and up to Maine to visit his grandmother."

"So why do you sound sort of…sad?" Amy asked.

"I don't want to leave." Sue pinched the bridge of her nose. The emotions exhausted her.

"Wow."

"I know," Sue said.

"I knew it! I knew it! I knew it!" Robin sounded a little too excited.

"Oh, stop! You're not always right," Amy said.

"Thank you, Ames!"

"But I'm right about this," Robin said.

Sue sighed into the phone.

"I am right, aren't I?"

After staying quiet for a minute, Sue finally relented. "He told me he loves me."

Robin bellowed a laugh. "I knew it!"

Sue could tell Robin was doing a victory dance. She grinned at his excitement, though she was grateful Robin couldn't see her face.

"So," Amy drew out the word. "Do you love him?"

"I honestly don't know, Ames." Sue paused, considering why she had asked him to wait for her, and told them the truth. "I don't know. But I want to tattoo my name all over his body."

CHAPTER 23

Newark, NJ

Sue waved at Darryl, happy to see him and relieved her trek from the domestic to the international terminals had come to an end. Thankfully, she didn't have much farther to go to their gate.

Darryl replaced the magazine he'd been reading at the newsstand. "Lookin' good, Suse."

"You're lookin' pretty good yourself, D." Sue offered a low five. While she'd been meeting Adam's family, Darryl had been in Brazil, telling Lena's parents he wanted to propose. "You got their blessing."

"I should make you sweat it out like I did." Darryl took her laptop bag and slung an arm around Sue's shoulders as they continued to their gate, his smile wide. "I'll tell you all about it later."

Justin joined them as they strolled past the coffee shop he'd patronized. "Sexy Sue, how was your week off?"

Sue grabbed his arm. "Justin, I've been dying to talk to you!"

"Yeah?"

"Yes!" After all the hours they'd spent talking about cars, she knew Justin would appreciate this bit of news more than the rest of the guys. "Adam has a DB9."

"The Aston Martin?"

"Yes! Carbon Edition."

"Nice! I wonder what it would be like to drive."

"It's like sex. Scorching hot, intense, mind-bending sex."

Justin stopped, his mouth hanging open. "He let you drive it?"

"Oh yeah." Sue nodded slowly. "Shifts like glass."

"Damn. I can't believe he let you drive it." Justin resumed the walk to their gate.

"Why not?" Darryl asked.

"I won't let my dad drive my Roadrunner, and he helped me rebuild the engine."

"Your dad can't drive stick."

"There's someone in Michigan who can't drive stick?" Sue asked.

Darryl chuckled. "Mr. Arnold may be the only one. At the very least, he's probably the only one over forty."

"The DB9 drives like great sex, huh?" Justin smirked. "Poor Adam."

"Oh, don't worry." Sue gave him a sly smile. "Adam gave me hot, mind-bending sex, too."

Justin gave her a fist bump.

Darryl's eyes widened. "Sue! You've never given us concrete proof of a sex life!"

"I know." She pulled up her shoulders. "But I had to defend the man. He let me drive his gorgeous car really, *really* fast." She dropped her shoulders and sighed.

"Was this amazing sex before or after you drove his car?" Justin asked.

Sue raised her eyebrows, surprised by his boldness.

Justin gazed far in the distance. "Or during? God, that would be incredible."

Sue laughed, grateful he'd kept talking so she wouldn't have to address the question.

Tom sat up from the row of chairs he'd been sprawled across and narrowed his eyes. "What's so funny?"

D didn't miss a beat. "Sue had tales from the security checkpoints at Logan."

"You'd think with the red hair she'd get a pass in Boston, but not so much." Justin shook his head.

"They must be smahht at that airport!" Chris shouted from the next row.

"Smarter than you," Sue answered.

"Ah, we missed you, Sue." Tom stood and hugged her.

"Thanks. Believe it or not, I missed you guys, too."

■———————————————————■

The evening flight to Norway was long and quiet. Sue and Tom finally talked face-to-face about the goals the label had laid out for Europe. The noose of the next album no longer dangled in front of them, but Sue still didn't trust the label. Their goals were mostly sales oriented. Would the execs come after her if she didn't get the band on TV this summer?

She let the guys' restlessness distract her. More than once she switched seats to accommodate movie watching, reading, napping, and even talking. Eventually Sue settled with Darryl into two seats behind the rest of the band.

She leaned back against the window, the armrest pushed up and her knees practically against Darryl's leg, while he sat diagonally with his feet on the floor in front of her seat.

"Lena's parents loved you, right? They had to." Sue'd been waiting since D had left New York to know how his trip had gone. She was especially invested because he'd confided in her first. Even now, only Tom knew where Darryl had been and why. The rest of the guys had assumed he went back to Austin with Lena during their break.

He gave a thumbs up. "I got major points for going to meet them in person."

"Naturally."

"I was super nervous the first day, so who knows what kind of impression I made."

"But you rebounded because you're you" —Sue flashed her palms at him— "and nothing gets you down."

Darryl colored slightly. "I did rebound, and things were great."

"How great?"

"Phenomenally great."

Sue leaned forward. "How long before they gave you their blessing?"

"They had a few agonizingly long phone calls with Lena's sister, Imogen, and her brother-in-law, and took me all over their town and grilled the hell out of me. The night before I left, they had this big family dinner, and her dad said they would be proud to have me as part of their family if that's what Lena wants."

"Darryl! That's amazing!" Sue hugged him.

He ducked his head and looked at her sideways. "There's more. When I got home and told my mom, she cried."

"Good tears or bad?"

"I never knew there was a difference until about two days ago, but they were good tears," Darryl said. "She took the engagement ring my father gave her off of her finger and gave it to me."

Sue gripped his arm. "Are you serious?"

"Check it." Darryl pulled a freshly polished, antique style, diamond ring with small baguette cut stones in a gold setting out of his pocket.

"It's gorgeous." Sue put a hand over her heart.

"Yeah. Dad died when I was seven, and Mom never took off the rings. Until I told her about Lena."

"Whoa."

"I know." Darryl's eyes were wide. "Mom said Lena should have her wedding band and I should wear Dad's."

Sue dabbed at her eyes as he slid the ring back into his pocket. His mother's willingness to give up something so dear to her before she ever even met Lena moved Sue. She hoped D appreciated the deep faith Mrs. Black had in him.

"That's so beautiful."

"It gets better." He crossed his arms. "School ends for her soon, so Lena's joining the tour in Dublin and staying with us through Rome."

"Awesome!"

"Yeah, I can't wait." A huge grin split his face.

"How are you going to propose?"

"I don't know. My impulse is to drop to my knees the second I see her in the airport, but I don't want to freak her out."

Sue's smile took over her face. "I doubt it would freak her out. But I can appreciate if you want to do something with a little more finesse."

"I do." He patted his pocket. "I want her to see what she means to me."

"Does this mean I'm on virtue patrol again?"

Darryl blushed and chuckled. "You don't mind volunteering now that you've gotten some, huh?"

Sue swatted his arm. "That has very little to do with it. And by then it will've been so long, I might be back in the 'if I'm not getting any, neither are you' state of mind."

Darryl shook his head and smiled. "It's up to her. I don't care if she sleeps with me now or on our wedding night as long as she says she'll marry me. I can be patient. Especially if I know she'll be my wife."

His last word struck a chord. "Damn, Darryl. Are we old enough to be husbands and wives already?"

"My parents were nineteen when they got married," Darryl said.

"Mine were twenty-two and twenty-three."

He stretched his arms in front of him. "I guess we're past due."

"It still doesn't feel like we're old enough."

"Marriage isn't about being old. It's about wanting to be linked to someone. How old I feel isn't gonna change because one of the labels I carry does."

Could it be as simple as a label? "That's kinda profound, D. Something I should think about."

"Why? You and Adam getting serious?"

"No." Sue reared back as though the idea could maim her. "Not like you and Lena, anyway. I avoid serious relationships. The two times I tried, they crashed and burned. I figured I wasn't old enough yet."

"Is Adam changing your mind there?"

Maybe? Typically, she used logic and pragmatism to guide her decisions. But lately, she'd been moving by instinct and forcing herself not to freak out. It'd been uncomfortable until Adam called her his girlfriend and told her how much he liked having her around. "I don't know. Maybe."

Darryl knitted his brows together. "Maybe?"

Sue shrugged.

"Explain."

She pursed her lips as she tried to collect her thoughts. "I don't know, D. I mean, even when I was in a so-called serious relationship, I never contemplated or planned a future for the two of us. The last two guys I dated seriously gave me so much grief about it, too. It was always my plans, my career, buying for a house for *me*, not both of us."

"And you're planning a future with Adam?"

"Not planning. At least not past the summer. But maybe willing to consider." Sue picked at her fingernails. She'd been thinking about it a lot; was Adam? Did he have enough patience?

"That's great, Suse." Darryl nudged her knee with his. "It's a long way from Savannah when you were thinking about ending it."

"Yeah." Sue leaned her head against the seat and paused for a minute. "I did something...odd...for me."

"What?"

"Well, two odd things."

Darryl gestured for her to continue.

"First, I asked him to take me to a soccer game in England. I've always wanted to go to a game there and he covers them, so I asked."

"And naturally he agreed."

She grinned. "Naturally."

"That's not weird. What's the other thing?"

Sue drew up into herself, not sure she wanted to admit what she'd done. "The other thing truly is bizarre."

"Well?"

She never should've mentioned this. The mere thought of putting her big ask out there again made her skin crawl. She'd be vulnerable again.

"Don't keep me in suspense."

Sue fisted the hair near her temples and blew out a breath, giving in. She'd said too much, but she knew she could trust D. "I asked him to wait for me."

Darryl's smile crinkled his eyes. "Like, wait for you, not see anyone else?"

"Yes."

"Did he jump at it?"

She nodded, overcome. If he laughed at her, she might die right there.

"Suse." Darryl pushed her shoulder. "You really like him."

Unsure of what to say and so uncomfortable she wanted to crawl out of her skin, she nodded again.

He shifted in the seat and faced front. "Even if you didn't ask him, he would've waited."

"You think?" How did Darryl know? All the men Sue had dated in the past had told her she never gave them enough. She'd taken herself away from Adam for the summer; wasn't that the definition of "not enough?"

"Yeah. He would've been fucking miserable wondering what you were or weren't doing with us and all the other guys who are *always* around." Darryl turned his gaze to Sue. "But he would've waited."

A bolt of nausea gripped her. "Was it stupid to ask?"

"Hell no." Darryl twisted his body toward her again. "Suse, you can take one look at him and know he's not going anywhere."

"You think so?"

"Yeah. But he doesn't know that about you. He's showing up all over the place because he wants to be with you, but he's putting pressure on you by being there, so he waits for you to set the tone."

Sue hugged herself, uncertain. "Did I?"

"Yep."

"Darryl…" Sue pressed her palms against her eyes, then pushed them up her forehead. "I have no fucking clue what I'm doing."

Darryl patted her knee. "We're all making it up as we go."

"Yeah, but am I stringing him along? Is he stringing me along? Am I gonna get dumped in the middle of a soccer match in a foreign country?" Sue's eyes grew as she ranted. She barely contained her bubbling panic. "What the fuck am I doing?"

Darryl covered his mouth, but laughter danced in his eyes. "I wish I had Adam's number. I'd give him some peace."

She punched Darryl in the arm. "What the fuck, D?"

He held up his hands. "I'm not a meddler. But it might be nice for the guy to know how hard you're falling for him."

Sue gave Darryl a look of pure horror. She was in way over her head.

"Shit. You don't even know."

She shook her head so fast her cheeks jiggled. She whisper-yelled, "I wasn't kidding when I told you I don't know what the fuck I'm doing!"

Darryl didn't contain his laughter anymore. "Oh, Suse. I'm sorry. You can't strategize and schedule this one."

"I do not strategize and schedule everything." She faced front in her seat and put her elbows on her knees.

Darryl laughed again but quickly calmed when Sue threw a murderous glare at him. "Okay. Let me try this another way."

Sue narrowed her eyes, waiting for whatever bombshell he'd drop next.

"When Brad and Justin graduated college, the three of us drove to Mexico for fresh tequila."

Sue tilted her head. "That doesn't surprise me."

"When you graduated from college, you bought a townhouse."

"Yeah."

"Why does it throw you that you're in a meaningful relationship when everything else you do has an eye toward significant, permanent things?" Darryl asked.

"It's different. I'm trying to build a life for myself."

"Building a relationship is part of building a life."

Sue rubbed two fingers between her eyebrows. "I don't know how to build a good relationship."

"I bet you didn't know how to buy a townhouse either. But you figured it out."

Sue dropped her head between her shoulders and peered back up at Darryl. "Jesus, D. Next time you decide to drop your PhD in wisdom on me, can you do it someplace where I can actually freak the fuck out?"

CHAPTER 24

Oslo, Norway

Sue's suitcase made its way around the baggage carousel first, and Brad helped her heave it off the moving track. She wheeled it behind the crowd and perched on it while she waited for the guys. Normally she'd be on her feet, ready to help, but when she'd finally fallen asleep on the flight, it had been deep. She didn't wake until the wheels of the plane touched the tarmac. The grogginess stayed with her even after walking through the airport.

"I bet you scared the shit out of Adam with your huge suitcase." Chris smirked. "I'd go into hiding if a woman showed up with that kind of luggage."

Sue shrugged, too tired to care about Chris's bullshit. "He was cool with it. The extra one had him running for the hills, though."

"You have a laptop bag, a carry-on, this suitcase, *and* you had an extra?"

"I'm messing with you. But damn near all the clothing I own is currently in a suitcase." Sue ran a hand through her hair and tugged at a small knot.

Chris grimaced. "Me, too."

"I showed up at his office with this." Sue patted the luggage below her. "My carry on, my laptop bag, and a purse."

"Dude. You went to his office with all that shit? How did he not panic?"

"I sucked up to the receptionist and she let me store it all in her closet. When he first saw me, I just had my purse."

"Good thinking," Chris said.

"It's why I make the big bucks."

"What did he say when he saw all your shit?"

"He took it like a champ and wheeled it all back to his place."

"He's a keeper."

Sue wiggled her eyebrows and pointed to a guitar case circling the conveyor. Chris sprang into action to claim it. As Sue became more awake, she wondered why Chris's teasing didn't have the usual aggressive edge. She chalked it up to jet lag and pulled the list of items they needed to claim out of her laptop bag.

Once they got to the hotel, she tracked the list again as everything was brought to their rooms.

"When does the bus get here?" Sue studied the narrow path left between all the boxes and luggage.

"Tomorrow afternoon. We're sharing it with another band, so I don't know when we'll be able to load our stuff onto it." Tom gestured at all the boxes. "We're sharing a trailer, too. All this will go in there."

"We're traveling with a lot more gear. Any roadies besides you and me?"

"We're sharing a pair with Noble Perversion and another band. It'll be tight, but there's only a few nights where shows overlap. We should be okay."

"It's gonna be interesting managing gear when the roadies are split across three bands," Sue said. Gear management stressed Tom out more than people management, and as much as Sue functioned as a part-time roadie, she spent at least as much time making sure Tom didn't freak out about amplifiers as she did setting up and tearing down stages.

"Yeah, I'm gonna do an initial check tomorrow to make sure everything made it and have an official list."

"Can I help?"

"That'd be great, but it might take all day."

"I don't mind. It'll go faster if you let me help." She knew her help would calm his stress, too. He wouldn't be carrying the inventory burden on his own.

"Okay." Tom flopped on the other bed. "Darryl wants to help, too. Between the three of us we might actually get to see some of this city before we leave."

"That'll be a nice change. How's Noble Perversion?"

"We've never met them, but we like their music and we hear they're cool, so it should be okay. But you'll be the only woman on the bus." Tom lifted up on his elbows.

"I was already the only woman on the bus."

"Yeah, but now it's even more skewed."

Sue swatted the air. "I'll be fine. We're free now. Let's do some sightseeing."

CHAPTER 25

Even with the shower raining on his face, Brad heard the knock on the hotel room door, the door open, and Justin and Sue talking. Moments later, as he twisted his hair to squeeze the shampoo out, a knock landed on the bathroom door.

"I'll be out in sec," he shouted over the water. He rinsed off and grabbed a towel. He wrapped it around his waist and opened the door, only to find himself blocked in. Justin and one of the larger instrument cases crowded the small entryway of their hotel room.

Brad pushed the main door to flatten it against the wall as Justin maneuvered the case out. He automatically flexed when he noticed Sue waiting in the hall. Damn, maybe if he'd slung his towel lower, he'd get a reaction from her. For once, Justin took his sweet time getting the gear through the door. Sue's eyes stayed low enough that Brad was certain they were on his body until the box finally made it into the hall. She leaned down and pushed it toward the elevator.

Justin pushed another box toward the entry and stopped short of the door. "Noble Perversion's show got changed to the first time slot today, so the bus is here now. The trailer's at the festival grounds. We're gonna put all this on the bus, ride over, and move it to the trailer."

"I'll get dressed and help."

"Thanks." Justin took the case out of the room.

Brad took his time getting dressed. He wanted to see if he could get Sue to react to him, and since she ogled his body, being half dressed seemed like a good way to get what he wanted. When Justin and Sue returned, Brad wore pants and shoes. He waited to pull his shirt over his head until after Sue entered the room. He lifted his shirt to scratch his stomach to see if she'd notice. She did. Brad hid his smug grin. Yeah, she'd given him the brush-off in New York, but her staring made it clear that she might be open to him after all. He wasn't going to lose the opportunity. He grabbed one of the boxes and moved toward the door.

He stopped when he got to Sue and gave her a sideways hug. "Morning, Sexy Sue. When we finish this, wanna find some pancakes?"

Sue stepped out of his embrace. "Sure, I'm starved." She moved past him and collected another case.

"An evening with Joe Perry can do that." Justin picked up another large black case.

Sue blushed and smiled. "Joe Perry affects my stomach, but food was the farthest thing from my mind."

Aerosmith was one of the top-billed bands at the festival, and the guys got creative with their jokes about Sue's lust for Joe Perry. The jokes backfired, though. Aerosmith wound up in the lobby at the same time as Words Fail Me, and Sue's show of loyalty earned her an invite to hang out in the classic rockers' suite. Even now, she looked blissful.

Justin grinned. "Poor Adam."

"Adam has nothing to worry about." Sue put the instrument she carried in the hall and held the door open again. "Joe and Billy Perry are desperately in love."

Brad quirked an eyebrow. "*They're* desperately in love?"

"But she's a generous woman." Justin put his box next to Sue's and took the one Brad carried. "She let you drool over her husband all night."

"Such riches are meant to be shared," Sue said.

Brad spent the rest of the time they loaded gear excited about the obvious absence in Sue's comment. Joe and Billy Perry were desperately in love. No mention of her and Adam. Maybe they'd decided to end it after all. If they hadn't, she would've mentioned him, right?

With the memory of Sue drinking him in when he came out of the shower and her general playfulness, Brad sat next to her when they finally stopped to eat, his arm draped over the back of the booth, acting casually affectionate. He paid close attention to her in case she gave him a stop sign. He also kept an eye on the rest of the guys, hoping they wouldn't notice.

Brad swore to Justin before they left Ann Arbor that he'd gotten over Sue. He made a huge effort to make sure

Justin believed the lie. He knew he walked a fine line, but the outcome would be worth it.

242

CHAPTER 26

Vienna, Austria

"Suse, hold this." Chris shoved a Denmark sticker under her nose as Sue tucked her laptop into her bus bunk.

"I thought you were asking women at the shows to do this."

"Yeah, but I got distracted in Copenhagen." Chris leered and waved the glossy paper again.

Sue shuddered but took the sticker. "No more putting these on windows?"

"Nah. I posted our bus window in New York, and it led to an awesome night. But on the festival grounds? No thanks. I don't want muddy chicks all up in our shit. I bone elsewhere."

The idea of climbing on the bus and finding Chris with a random hookup made Sue cringe. She'd seen enough of him and his women when they were traveling stateside, and none of that had been on the bus. The last thing she wanted was to have to coax disappointed or angry women out of her living space. "I am deeply grateful for that, Chris."

He rolled his eyes. "Shut up and pose."

She considered for a moment, then turned to her side and held the sticker against her hip, sandwiched between her hands.

Chris took the picture from a few angles. "You don't want your face on our Instagram?"

"Doesn't my presence piss off the groupies enough?"

Chris snorted. "You're not even a blip on the radar to *my* groupies." He took the sticker and moved past Sue toward the back of the bus.

She shook her head and went in the opposite direction. Of course his groupies didn't care about her. She obviously had no sexual interest in him, and as long as she didn't interrupt their good time, women cruised right past her, often snickering at her lack of glitter and eyeliner. She knew she shouldn't care, her goals were different, but she constantly fought Chris to not be an ass to those women. They didn't need another bombshell story, real or otherwise. The thanks she got included Chris bragging about his condom use and comments like, "You worried about competition?" She had no desire to compete, but she did make the women work for attention from the guys. Every article with photos and every video she got out brought even more women to the shows. Sorry not sorry, ladies.

Sue grew restless on the ride from Denmark to Austria. She paced the bunk area, flipping through book selections on her e-reader, but nothing grabbed her. She went to the small kitchen area of the bus and rifled in the cabinets. Not hungry, she sighed and closed the cabinets, drumming her fingers on them. She wanted to call Adam, but a check of the time and her calendar told her he was in a meeting.

Brad and several of the Noble Perversion guys lounged in the front area of the bus, getting ready to watch a movie. "Mind if I join you guys?"

"Pull up a cushion, lady." The bass player from Noble Perversion patted a spot on the couch between him and Brad.

Sue smiled and took the seat, kicking her feet up on the small table in front of them. Over the past week, the two bands had performed seven shows at three festivals. They'd bonded quickly and managed to work out a system to get each group set up and packed up without breaking or misplacing items, even when they played on different stages.

Settled between the two men, Sue sent Adam a text letting him know she'd be alone in her hotel room in about three hours if he was free to talk, then slid her phone into her back pocket.

* * *

"We're here, Sexy Sue." Brad shook her. "Time to stretch those lovely legs."

Sue jerked and opened her eyes. With Adam on her mind, it took her a moment to reorient herself. Then awareness dawned. Brad had his arm around her, and her head rested on his chest. She bolted upright. "Why were you hanging onto to me?"

Brad grinned. "You fell asleep. You almost fell on the floor."

Sue looked Brad in the eye. "Let me fall."

Brad laughed.

"I'm serious." Sue waited for Brad to stop laughing. "If that happens again, let me fall." Sue went to her bunk, where she grabbed her overnight bag and laptop. She regretted snapping at Brad, but the deep pang of longing for Adam wouldn't let her go. She took out her phone and texted him that she was checking into the hotel, hoping he would take her heavy-handed hint and call her, even though his calendar said he was busy.

Adam texted back almost immediately and called her about twenty minutes later. "I always love your texts, but tonight you got me out of a shitty dinner. Thanks."

"Anytime."

"How's Austria?" Adam's deep voice soothed her more than the hot shower she'd just taken.

As the only woman among eleven men, Sue told Tom she'd pay for her own hotel rooms. She considered it a necessary luxury. She didn't mind being the only woman in the group, but she craved time to decompress, and it gave her an opportunity to talk to Adam in private.

"Rainy. And I hate to say it, but everything blends together." Sue sighed. "I mean, some of the scenery on the highway is nice, but it's still a highway. All the festival grounds are similar. I'll have to come back to actually see the country, not just drive through it." Sue stretched out on the king-sized bed, happy to finally take up as much space as she wanted, remembering the last time she was in a king-sized bed—with Adam.

"I get it. I had layovers in Copenhagen at least a dozen times before I finally saw anything outside of the airport."

"At least Copenhagen has a nice airport."

"It's still an airport," Adam said.

"True."

Adam cleared his throat. "I've been looking at the schedule and realized something."

Sue propped herself up, preparing for bad news. "Good or bad?"

"Good."

She let out a relieved sigh. "I was afraid you were about to say you aren't gonna make it Manchester."

"*Nothing* will keep me from you," Adam said.

Sue smiled into the phone, giddy from his promise.

"We're gonna be in Belgium at the same time."

"Coincidence or good planning?" Sue asked.

"Both. We're negotiating with a Belgian satellite service. I'm flying out for a face-to-face."

"I *love* Belgian satellite services," Sue said.

Adam chuckled. "Can you make time for me?"

"Yes. Are you going to be in Antwerp or Luxembourg?"

"Brussels."

Sue gasped. "In between? What a tease!"

"No way, babe. I have to be in Brussels a few days after you guys hit Antwerp. I'm flying there."

"You are the greatest boyfriend ever. It doesn't even matter what's on the schedule that day. I will find time. Lots of it."

"Damn, I miss you," Adam said.

Sue rolled onto her side and curled up, embarrassed all over again about waking up in Brad's arms. "You have no idea how much I miss you."

"You're not confusing me with Joe Perry, are you?"

She laughed, grateful for Adam's sense of humor. "Meeting him was fun, but it's nothing compared to being with you."

"You sure?"

Humor laced Adam's voice, so she kept her answer playful but honest. "Positive. I've had lots of idle time on the bus to compare experiences. You win, no contest."

CHAPTER 27

Germany

"These boots were the best impulse buy I've ever made. Who knew Germany would be so muddy?" Sue dragged the bottom of each boot against the edge of the concrete pad between the bus and the stage, where Brad, Justin, and Tom were grilling. A tent made their impromptu cookout possible despite the steady rain.

She plopped on the bench next to Tom, who dressed his bratwurst with the random collection of toppings spread across the table. "I swear, that ferret-looking lighting guy with Kinky Bastards is tailing me."

"He's harmless." Tom took a bite out of his creation, then reached for onions.

Sue pushed damp hair behind her ears and took a plate. "How do we wind up constantly sharing a stage with them?"

Justin handed Sue a water bottle from the cooler near his feet. "He has a thing for you. Maybe he rearranges stage assignments when he gets the festival schematics."

"If he had that kind of power, he would also have a masseur on standby for me when I climb out of a light rig." Sue stabbed a bratwurst and dropped it into a bun.

Brad chuckled. "You never should've climbed into the first one. I bet he breaks bulbs on purpose now."

"You know, that wouldn't surprise me." Sue added mustard to her brat and took a bite.

"Want me to say something?" Justin went to the grill and took a few chicken wings off the rack.

"Nah. I'll handle it."

Tom took one of the wings. "Don't worry about it. He knows better."

Sue wrinkled her brow. "What does *that* mean?"

Tom sighed. "Nothing."

Sue twisted to face Tom. "Doesn't sound like nothing. What do you know?"

Tom shook his head. "Can't say."

"Say what?" Justin dropped the plate of chicken in the middle of the table and took a wing for himself, blowing on it before taking a bite.

Sue nudged Tom, lifting her eyebrows as she stared at him.

"Fine." Tom stood and paced behind the table. He stopped and ran a hand through his hair. "He's looking out for you. He said you're out of his league, but he likes being around you. He's trying to embrace being work acquaintances."

Brad grunted and drained a bottle of water.

Sue picked up an orange, stuck her thumbnail into the rind, and aggressively tore off chunks of it. She didn't want the man's attention and she didn't encourage it, but this longing from afar bullshit had to stop. It served no purpose and only reminded her of all the instances where she had to deal with people being stupid. Her dad running off all her dates in high school, Tom and his gamble, Chris and his groupies, lighting guys treating her like a prize instead of a fucking person. "Why do we have to put people in leagues?"

"Have you met yourself?" Brad asked.

Sue glared at Brad. "Stop."

Brad held out his hands. "It's a compliment. Besides, aren't you in Adam's league?"

"This isn't about Adam." Sue threw a piece of orange skin on the table. "How does me doing my job put me in or out of a league?" Sue's finger sunk into the fleshy part of the orange and she growled. "You think he's complimenting me. But he knows fuck all about me. Making me untouchable devalues me and my contributions. And all over his own insecurities. I'm glad he's not touching me, but that doesn't make what he's doing any less shitty. And you letting him get away with it, Tom?" She set an angry glare at her cousin, who of all people should know better. "You're making me an outsider."

Tom perched next to Sue, his back to the table. "How can you feel like an outsider? Especially after all this time?"

Sue glared. "You're turning this into high school all over again."

"Huh?"

"Over-protective dad, over-protective cousin."

"Your dad shut down your entire dating life. I'm keeping creepers from harassing you. Big difference."

"It's not! You're letting some weirdo stalk me." Sue flicked a piece of rind at the table. "You treat me like I'm a child."

"No, I don't." Tom turned on the bench to face forward and pulled the chicken platter toward himself.

"Yeah, you do," Justin said. "Darryl and I look out for her. You pay roadies to tag along."

"Seriously, Tom?" Sue glared.

"Justin, shut up!" Tom slammed a fist on the table. "Yes. I look out for you. We're in foreign countries, of *course* I'm gonna be more careful."

"More careful is walking with me back to the bus. Not *paying* people to make sure I'm never alone."

Tom tried to interrupt, but Sue shook her head.

"Setting up a ragtag security contingent for me may be a nice intention." Sue put a hand over Tom's fist and looked him in the eye before she continued. "But it makes me look incapable." She paused for a moment and went back to her orange. "If we were back in high school, I'd look like a loser."

"You never look like a loser, Sexy Sue," Brad said.

Sue rolled her eyes. "Whatever."

"Come on, Sue," Brad leaned across the table and brushed his hand against hers. "It's not bad that you're in class all your own."

Sue glared. "First, I told you to stop. So fucking stop." Sue put down the orange and flexed her fingers. "Second, you know why I'm in Adam's league? Because we like each other and don't give a shit about the rest. It doesn't have to be complicated." Sue shook her head and picked up the orange, pulling free another piece of rind.

"I was trying to compliment you." Brad nudged her foot under the table.

Sue narrowed her gaze. "You shoulda complimented that chick in high school from *Hairspray*. If you had, maybe you wouldn't be pining after her all these years."

"What?' Brad sat up straight and stared at her.

"Penny Pingleton. From your *Metal Edge* quote."

Brad grinned. "That's a hell of a thing to remember, Sexy Sue."

"No, it isn't."

Tom grimaced. "It is oddly specific."

Sue took in the uncomfortable expressions Tom and Justin wore and the giddy look on Brad's face. "Seriously? Guys, it was the first fucking piece of press I got for you. Of *course* I remember it."

Justin sat next to Brad and shoved him down the bench, away from Sue. "Fair point. And to be clear, Kinky Bastard's equipment manager sure as shit doesn't think you're a loser. Be careful there."

"Thanks, Just." He and Darryl were the only people on the tour who truly treated her as an equal. She tried to never take that for granted.

She finished peeling the orange, challenging herself to get the rest of the skin off in one piece. It went a long way to calm her. She split the fruit in half and pulled a segment off. She took a deep breath before eating the slice. She wanted to get up and do something, but there wasn't much to do. The damn rain wouldn't let up and it put her on edge. She quietly stomped her boots under the table. No one was talking. She'd probably scared them into silence. Sue forced a smile. She looked up and addressed the table.

"Annabelle's meeting us in England."

"She is?" Brad perked up. "She never tells me this shit."

"She worked it out with D." Sue peeled apart another orange segment. "He responded to her text about the schedule first."

Tom grinned. "It'll be fun to have her back on the tour."

"Is she why you brought that shirt?" Sue asked.

"What shirt?" Tom looked genuinely confused.

"The only Oxford shirt you own and somehow managed to make it into your luggage, even though you never wear Oxford shirts." Sue bit into another slice of orange.

"How do you know about that?" Tom asked.

"I saw it when I did our laundry the other day."

"Whatever. You told me to pack grown-up clothes. That's what I had." Tom stood and got a drink from the cooler near Justin.

"Back up." Justin threw a small piece of bread at Sue. "You did Tom's laundry? Not fair."

Sue threw the bread back. "All my jeans had muddy cuffs. I needed one more pair to make a load."

"Yeah, I'm about there, too." He took a slice of orange from Sue. "Next hotel, gimme your pants."

Sue smirked. "You hitting on me, Just?"

"Oh, yeah." He wiggled his eyebrows. "I always wash a girl's pants before I get in 'em."

Sue laughed, some of her tension falling away. "Nice."

"You know, Sue…" Brad brushed her hand with his own again. "Annabelle gave Tom that shirt for his birthday two years ago and he's carted it all over the country."

Tom glared at Brad and checked the grill, flipping a piece of chicken and sucking on his fingers.

"And now it's making it around the world." Sue grinned. "A guy doesn't carry around stuff to be nice. Tom, are you hoping she hits on you next?"

Brad straightened and turned toward Tom.

Tom rolled his eyes. "Please. How do I always manage to get myself into these conversations?"

Sue snickered. "I can't wait to see Annabelle again. I wanna do some fact checking."

"She'll back up everything we've told you." Brad tore a piece of chicken with his teeth.

"I trust what you've all told me. I'm looking to fill in some blanks and get more dirt." Sue batted her eyelashes and gave Brad and Justin a sweet smile.

Tom's eyes widened. "We're in trouble, man."

"You? At least you didn't grow up with her!" Brad spit as he spoke.

"No, but I *did* grow up with Sue. I don't want her and Annabelle trading notes."

Sue gave the guys a devious smile. "I'm sure it'll all work out for the best."

Brad shook his head. "And you wonder why I drink."

"Whatever gets you through, man." Tom clinked his drink against Brad's.

256

CHAPTER 28

Prague, Czech Republic

Brad pulled his hair into a ponytail at the base of his neck, braided it, and tucked the braid into his shirt. He didn't wear hats and it was too warm for a hoodie, but he hated that his hair constantly felt damp.

"Tom has the right idea with his ball cap." Justin stomped into the lounge area, his hair in a low ponytail. "I hate man buns, and I have no idea what else to do."

"Shave your head. I might." Darryl stowed his ball in one of the bench seats. "It beats having glue constantly running down my face." D had recently shaved the sides of his head, giving his spikes a sleeker, more lethal look. The maintenance seemed easier, but the guy still constantly had shit dripping on his face from the rain.

Sue pranced into the lounge, her hair in a sexy as hell librarian bun on top of her head, her face lit with excitement. "You guys ready?" Earlier in the day she'd invited them all to watch a Cowboy Mouth show with her. After taking acres of shit about whether the band had naughty songs, everyone but Chris had agreed to go. The conversation seemed to have lifted their spirits, if only for a few minutes, in the face of endless rain.

"I'm gonna stay here," Tom said. "Both my boots and my sneakers are still wet. It pisses me off to put them on."

Sue raised her eyebrows. "Everyone else?"

Brad grunted and he, Justin, and Darryl followed her off the bus. They waded through mud to get to the stage, and once they were there, Sue drug them farther through the crowd until they were close to the front and right in the center.

Justin complained so much that Brad had no sympathy for him when Sue finally gave him her attention.

"Come on, Just." She had one hand above her eyes shielding against the light rain. "I love this band and I've been looking forward to their show for a while. If you'd rather not deal with the rain, it's cool. But you will miss *all* the songs about oral sex."

He sighed heavily. "I'll deal. I don't want to miss watching you get down to dirty tunes."

"You sure?"

"Yeah." He squeezed water out of his hair and twisted it into a knot at his neck.

"Does she really react to naughty songs?" Darryl asked in a low voice.

Justin shook his head. "I like giving her shit."

A few minutes later, Cowboy Mouth dove headlong into their set. The crowd responded immediately, and as though they weren't slowly sinking into mud.

When one song ended, they shifted right into another fast-paced number with the drummer shouting "Gimme some rhythm!" over and over.

"What the hell kinda drummer needs help?" Justin asked.

Sue pulled Justin's head to hers, pressed a loud, smacking kiss to his forehead, and said, "Shut the fuck up and clap!" She let go of him and raised her arms over her head, joining the other concertgoers in clapping out a rhythm.

Justin turned to Brad, squinting against the rain.

Brad clapped along.

Normally Brad would focus primarily on the stage show, then the audience reaction. But based on the lyrics and the drummer's constant reminders to enjoy the moment, he figured it was appropriate to focus on Sue.

He'd never seen her yell and cheer so much. She didn't dance with her usual grace and polish, she jumped and swayed and moved with the crowd. She'd let her inhibitions go.

Brad had no idea how long he'd been staring at her when she stopped and turned her back to the stage. She laughed and stretched an arm across Justin, pulling his ear close to her mouth.

"Look." Sue gestured toward the crowd behind him.

"Holy shit."

Brad spun around to see what had floored his friend.

When they'd entered the field before the show, Brad thought they were about a third of the way back from the stage. But the sea of people behind them, all dancing and clapping, stretched well past the loose borders of the stage area and even encroached on the periphery of other stages. People had climbed up the scaffolding for the lights, the merchandise booth, and other nearby structures. Aside from Sue, Justin and Brad, every face focused on the stage or the giant screens broadcasting the show.

"Drummer needs some help, does he?" Sue grinned and resumed dancing.

Brad gestured toward the stage. "She's right."

Justin nodded, lifted his hands above his head, and clapped along with the sea of people.

The more Brad got into the music, the more his stress fell away. He didn't care that it still rained, and he could tell his friends didn't care anymore either. Darryl's spikes wilted, and Justin's hair was plastered to his head. All their clothes stuck to them and they had mud splatters up to their knees. Except Sue. The mud splattered up her thighs, almost to her hips, but she looked happy. So happy she could've lit the stage. Cowboy Mouth was contagious.

The band was halfway through a fast rock song when lyrics about kissing inspired Brad. He grabbed Sue even though she jumped with the music and pulled her to him, pressing his lips firmly against hers.

She pulled away, eyes wide.

Brad grinned and reached for her again.

Her face went stony and she gave him a subtle head shake. She moved out of his grasp and danced with Darryl, putting him between her and Brad.

"What the fuck was that?" Justin yelled at Brad.

"Got caught in the moment." Brad offered a sheepish grin.

Justin shoved him, putting himself between Brad and Darryl. "Hands off, man. Way the fuck *off!*"

When the set ended more than two hours after it had begun, Brad didn't want to leave, but he followed the tide of people until he had to veer toward the stage Words Fail Me would play on. "How in the hell do they get everyone to crouch down in the mud and jump up all at the same time?"

"I watched them do it and I still don't know how they made it work," Justin said.

Darryl slung an arm around Sue. "That was better than therapy."

She laughed. "Right?"

"Seriously, Suse, that was fun. Thanks for telling us about it."

"My pleasure." Sue squeezed water out of the edge of her top. "I love bringing new people to Cowboy Mouth shows. It's always a good time."

Tom waited for them in the covered area behind their stage with a stack of fresh towels.

"You're brilliant, Tommy." Sue patted her face and neck dry. She pulled her hair out of the bun, letting it swing around her shoulders before running the towel over it.

Brad peeled his shirt off and took a towel, drying himself and sneaking glances at Sue to see if she noticed. She didn't, and with Justin on high alert, Brad couldn't accidentally on purpose get her attention.

Justin pushed him out of the way and took a towel, making big gestures to dry himself that largely kept Sue out of Brad's line of sight.

"Guys! Did you see the show? Wasn't it awesome?" Chris splashed mud into the area.

"Yeah, we did. How did you?" D had also removed his shirt and sat with a towel draped around his neck.

"Did anyone at this festival *not* see it?" Chris asked. "I had to climb on a merch tent to see the stage. It was awesome."

"Were you on the tent the whole time?" Sue asked.

"Nah, only long enough to see the actual stage for myself. Well, what little of the stage I could see from way back there. It was like a fuckin' revival with all those people."

"Yeah," Justin agreed.

"You trust my band selection now?" Sue asked, her hair wrapped in the towel.

Chris brushed water off his arms. "You get points for this one."

"Good enough." Tom tossed a towel to Chris. "Change into dry clothes. We gotta get our stuff on stage soon."

CHAPTER 29

Sue capped her day on a dancefloor with Carlo. After a muddy week of concerts, he'd rented out a nightclub to throw a party for the bands and support staff who'd closed each night of that week's festival. Words Fail Me, Sue and Tom were the only people on the list who weren't in that category. She and Tom had planned to make the most of the opportunity and network all night, but Sue had never been able to resist the flamenco. She and Carlo danced together for several songs and with others as the dancefloor filled. Being able to move and dance—and not get covered in mud in the process—brought Sue some much needed stress relief. Eventually she danced her way back to the bar where Tom sat with a fresh pint.

"You're always on the sidelines!" Sue said. "You should at least talk to other people."

"I did," Tom answered. "I talked to Barry while you danced with Carlo."

"People you don't already know." Sue crossed her arms. Yes, this party gave them a break, but they had a plan. If Tom wasn't going to enjoy the party, he needed to mingle.

"I talked to that guy." He gestured down the bar toward someone from another band. "And that woman." He nodded toward a curvy brunette with a short skirt who danced on the edge of the dancefloor. "But she's with that guy." He pointed to another band's burly manager, who delivered a drink to her.

"It's a start." Sue gulped a glass of water and set it on the bar. "Come dance with me."

"I can't. I'm wai—"

"Why are you guys standing around?" Brad swooped in, putting one hand on Sue's waist and the other on the bar.

Sue slipped out of his grasp and rolled her eyes at Tom.

Tom knocked Brad's shoulder. "Get outta here, man. I'm waiting for Justin to come back with the guy from Kinky Bastards."

"The lighting guy?" Sue asked with a wary expression. "You know he creeps me out."

Tom shook his head. "Their booking agent. He and Justin used to work together."

"You're gonna meet Ron?" Brad asked. "Yeah, I gotta go. Come on, Sexy Sue." Brad reached for her hand, but she pulled it behind her back.

She hadn't told Tom what had happened at the Cowboy Mouth show. She'd been embarrassed and didn't want to cause tension. Though if she'd told him, she knew

Tom wouldn't be asking this of her. "I need to work the party, too."

Tom leaned forward and lowered his voice. "This guy has connections at bigger venues, but Brad intimidates him. I need him out of here."

"Come on, Sue, I love this song!" Brad tapped his toe and moved closer to the dancefloor, holding his hand out for her.

She pursed her lips and moved to Tom's other side to ensure Brad didn't hear. "Brad's been awfully…familiar lately."

"More familiar than how we all live together?"

Sue rubbed the space between her eyes, trying to decide if this was the time and place to tell Tom about Brad's kiss at Cowboy Mouth.

Tom jutted his chin toward the door. "Please, they're on the way."

Sue wrinkled her nose but gave in. "All right."

Excitement plain on his face, Brad pulled her toward the other dancers.

"You'd better make some magic, Tommy." Sue shouted over her shoulder.

Tom saluted her, an apologetic expression on his face.

Even though everyone danced together during the fast number, Brad stayed close to Sue. She positioned them near a woman who hadn't been subtle about checking him out, then turned her back to dance with other people, hoping the woman would occupy him. But when the music slowed, Brad pulled Sue into his arms.

Holding herself at a reasonable distance, she took in the other couples swaying around them. A fresh pang of longing for Adam hit her. She wanted to call him, but when she'd checked his calendar, he had the whole day blocked. She left him a voicemail before the party, but it wasn't enough. She wanted his voice. Wanted *his* arms around her.

She pulled away from Brad. "Sorry, I need to sit."

"Okay."

Tom stood at the bar with Justin and another man, so Sue headed toward a plush seating area away from them.

"Want me to get you a drink?" Brad asked.

"No, I'm good." Sue sat but leaned forward and put some distance between them when Brad sat next to her and slung his arm along the back of the couch. "Why don't you dance with the woman watching us? She seems to like you."

"Can't leave you high and dry."

Sue lifted her eyebrows. "I don't need a babysitter. Go have fun."

"Off the dancefloor already?" Carlo appeared out of nowhere and gave them each a tall glass of sangria.

"The ballad is a good excuse to rest in a dry place." Sue sipped the sweet drink, regretting that Carlo's presence kept her from shooing Brad away.

"Yes, the rain has been ridiculous." Carlo accepted a glass of sangria from a waiter for himself. "But it makes the Dutch tulips much more aromatic."

Sue fought the urge to roll her eyes, sipping the fruity wine instead. "I'm sure it does."

"You should let me spoil you, Sue."

She shook her head. "Thank you, Carlo, but I thought I was clear. We're not dating. No spoiling. No gifts."

Brad dropped a hand on her shoulder. "She even scolded us for all going in on a bouquet of flowers after Chris showed his ass."

Sue rolled her shoulder to shake Brad's hand off.

Carlo quirked a brow. "No apology gifts?"

"A sincere apology is better." Sue tasted the drink again.

"She's a tough one," Carlo said.

Brad squeezed her shoulder and quickly removed his hand. "She is."

Sue shook her head again. Them talking about her like she wasn't there made all their posturing for her attention even worse. "How's the festival circuit treating you, Carlo?"

"It is driving our wardrobe mistress mad. All our stage clothes are muddy or smell damp. But we've had some amazing shows. Personally, I have no complaints."

"I think it's safe to speak for my band and say the same." Brad tipped his drink toward Carlo. "We could do without the mud, but the shows have been awesome."

"The music is the most important part." Carlo clinked glasses with Brad. "But from a bus? Through the rain? That is no way to experience Europe." Carlo sat next to Sue. "You should travel with me when we play the same festivals. We take the jet instead of highways. We have time to visit places."

Sue stood to free herself from the rock and hard place Carlo and Brad created. "Thank you, Carlo. But I won't leave the band. We've gotten some great press. I have to oversee that, or why be here at all?"

Carlo stood and leaned toward her. "I can come up with several enticing reasons for you to be here." He straightened his posture and chugged half his drink. "I've seen your press. You've done fantastic work, Sue."

She gave him a tight smile. "Thank you." She finished her drink and gave Carlo the glass, the saturated fruit still at the bottom. "I need to find the restroom."

"I know where it is." Brad gulped the rest of his sangria and stood, leading the way.

As soon as they got to the hallway separating the main area from the private rooms, Sue stopped. "Thanks, but I know where I'm going."

"It's okay. I have to go, too."

Sue picked up her pace and strode through the lounge to one of the bathrooms, locking the door. She pulled out her phone to call Adam and got his voicemail again. She texted him.

Miss you.

Even though she'd purposely stalled, Brad paced on the other side of the door when she emerged a few minutes later.

He smiled, his eyes overly bright.

The alarm bells that had been quietly chiming on and off in the back of her mind all day went full blast, all but echoing in her ears. "You didn't have to wait for me." Sue moved toward the exit.

"Hang on." Brad blocked the doorway and directed her toward a couch at the back of the room. "Let's take a few minutes. It's quiet." He sat and tried to pull her down with him.

Sue waited for him to settle on the couch, then sat on the opposite end, her hands in her lap, silently scolding herself for not leaving as soon as he'd moved away from the door.

"Good party, huh?" Brad slid toward the center of the couch.

"Yeah. The sangria was delicious." Sue perched on the edge of her seat.

When Brad leaned toward her, Sue slapped a hand on his chest and pushed him away while tilting as far back as the space allowed.

"What're you doing?"

"I figured we'd take advantage of this rare moment alone." Brad smiled but kept his distance. "I'll slow down."

Sue wrenched herself off the couch and faced him. "Slow down what?"

"Um, just slow down."

She took a few backward steps. She wanted to leave the room but didn't, afraid she might be jumping to conclusions. Instinct told her she'd avoided this conversation for too long.

He stood and closed most of the distance between them, taking her hand in his.

Sue glanced at their joined hand and his face. "Please tell me you've been drinking tonight."

"Only that sangria, why?" Brad stepped closer and brushed a strand of hair over her ear.

"This." Sue let go of him and went toward the far end of the room. Overwhelmed, she found herself speechless. How would she be able to continue to live with Brad—especially in the close quarters of the bus—if she had to fend off advances from him?

"What?" Brad sounded hopeful and again closed the distance between them. He embraced her from behind. The way Adam did.

She jerked away, turned to face him, and backed into a table. She held her hand up in a stop sign. "I don't want you to go slow, Brad. I want you to forget this whole thing. This is not good."

"What do you mean it's not good?" Brad clasped her shoulder. "We've gotten so close the last few weeks. It's nothing *but* good."

She knocked his hand away. "This is a working relationship, a friendship. *Nothing* else."

"Sue." Brad grinned. "There's always been something else between us."

"Yeah. Work."

"Lots of couples meet on the job."

Sue crossed her arms. "You mean like me and Adam?"

Brad leaned a hip against the table she'd backed into. He crossed his arms, mirroring her posture. "Be honest. This is nothing more than a working relationship to you? I see the way you look at me."

"How do I look at you?" Sue narrowed her eyes.

"You check me out. You stare at my body. I watch you do it."

"What?" Sue took another step away, needing the extra space. Had she ogled him? She'd noticed him a few times, but it never occurred to her that she might've stared. And even if she had, so what? "You're attractive. That doesn't mean I want you."

"You didn't answer my question."

Sue gave him a confused look.

"This is nothing more than a working relation-ship to you?"

Sue took a moment to consider before she answered. Whatever she said could taint the rest of the tour. "We all live together. It's different from typical working relationships."

"I knew it."

"Not like that. You guys are my *friends*."

Brad shook his head, pulled her to him, and kissed her.

She pushed against his chest until she broke free. "This is why I can't be myself around you and Chris. You think it's a declaration of love, and Chris thinks I'm trying to ruin his life."

"Forget about Chris. I actually *do* love you." Brad reached for her.

Sue shook her head and walked to the couch but stood in front of it with her back to him, a hand on her head. She willed him to leave the room so she wouldn't have to say things she knew would hurt him.

"Sue, did you hear me?" Brad's voice burst with excite-ment. "I *love* you and I think you love me, too."

She whirled around. He couldn't really believe that. "I heard you."

Brad smiled and moved toward her.

She held up her hand to stop him again. She needed to end this whole thing with the smallest amount of dam-age possible.

He didn't advance further.

"I don't care for you the way you want me to." Sue stayed in her place, overcome with sadness. She set their professional relationship aside for a moment, studying her friend who needed something she didn't have to give.

"You can." Brad went to her and held her face in his hands. "You can." He leaned his forehead against hers. "I know you can."

She gripped his wrists, trying to pull his hands off her as she fought back tears. He pressed his lips against hers and she jerked away. She hit him hard on the shoulder and stalked across the room, then turned and glared at him.

"No!" She balled her fists. "Don't make this harder."

"Adam's not here, you don't have to worry about him. We can figure this out," Brad said.

Sue's sadness flipped to anger. He expected her to cheat? "Why would I date someone—get into a *relationship* with another man—if I was interested in you?"

Brad cocked his head. "I…relationship?"

"Yeah."

Brad smoothed his hair. "He hasn't been around. You haven't mentioned him."

"I talk to him *every day.*"

Brad pressed his lips together. "Adam's a wealthy guy. It's easy to get swept up in the trappings. But he's not here now, things ease off."

"Wow." Sue straightened her posture. "That's pretty fucking insulting."

Brad knitted his eyebrows together.

"I'm a gold digger?"

His shoulders slumped. "Of course not. I'm sorry."

She rubbed her temples. "This isn't about Adam. Even if there was no Adam, there'd be no '*us.*' I work for you. End of story."

"Because of a fucking job."

Sue shook her head, her glare steady. "Because of *me!*"

"But you love me *somehow.* It can grow." Brad's voice held a pleading edge.

Sue shook her head again and crossed her arms, holding herself together.

"Come on, Sue!"

"No!"

"Sue."

"We don't have that kind of connection. We never did."

"Because of Adam." Brad's expression hardened.

"Because of me." She wouldn't betray Adam, but even before she'd met him, she hadn't been interested in Brad. Now Brad had her backed into a corner and all she wanted was to get away from him and call Adam, tell him she'd fallen in love with him and make sure *he* heard those words first, before she shouted them in anger at someone who didn't respect her.

"Damn it, Sue!" Brad shook her out of her thoughts. "Is it because you don't want me? Or because you want Adam more?" Brad stalked across the room and stopped a few feet away from her. "Because I'll keep coming at you until you tell me beyond a doubt that it's him."

"I don't want you. Even before I met Adam, I didn't want you."

Brad narrowed his eyes. "You don't mean it."

"I do." Sue dug her fingernails into her palms. She had to push through and not let her need to keep everyone on an even keel silence her voice or leave Brad with any question as to where she stood. "I'll quit. I'll leave the tour. I'll do anything to prove it to you." Her composure was so tenuous her voice cracked.

"I'll never give up," he said in a low voice.

Panic rose. She'd said everything already. She searched for a new way to say no.

Brad gave her a tender look. "I know you're scared. It's okay. We're in this together."

Sue grimaced. "We...are not...together." She closed her eyes for a moment, mentally bracing herself. She faced him with a steely reserve. "I'm sorry. I led you on. I don't love you. I don't want you. I never have." The words and her gaze were steady and cold. As soon as she finished speaking, she walked out of the room, not able to bear the devastation on Brad's face.

Carlo stopped her as she re-entered the main part of the club. "Here you are." He gave her an enormous smile. "More sangria?"

"No, thank you. I need some air."

"You should let me spoil you." His smile became predatory.

"I appreciate the sentiment, Carlo, but no. I won't take advantage of someone I'm not interested in."

"You're not still with Adam, are you?"

Sue twisted up her face and glared. "Why does it matter? I told you *no*."

Carlo straightened his posture, meeting her challenge. "I don't see him here."

Sue tapped on her chest. "He's here." As she strode past him, Carlo called out to her. She turned enough to look him in the eye. "I said *no*." She picked up her pace, intent on getting out of the damn club.

Tom and Justin stood talking near the door and her heart sunk. What would she tell them? How could she stay on the tour? She couldn't. Her knees went weak.

"You okay, Sue?" Justin offered a hand.

She shook her head, barely acknowledging them. "I need air." She continued toward the door.

"Sue, please." Carlo had almost caught up with her. "I'm sorry."

Sue didn't even glance back when she shouted, "Answer's still no, Carlo."

She made it outside before Tom's voice cut through the noise. She didn't answer, not knowing what to say and deeply sorry that when she finally did come clean, she'd upset her cousin. When Tom grabbed her shoulders, she yelped. She shook her head and kept walking.

"Sue, wait!" he shouted behind her.

"Can't talk!" she said. "I'll call you in a minute." She almost collided with Barry. She did a double take and her brain clicked into gear. "Please help me get away from Carlo."

Barry directed her toward a cab waiting on the curb. He told the driver to take her to a hotel, instructing him to make sure she got inside and got a room. He gave the man a wad of cash and passed Sue a card through the back window. "Call me if you need anything." He banged on the roof of the cab and stepped onto the curb.

Sue sank back into the seat and texted Tom.

Need air. Will call soon.

CHAPTER 30

"What are you sorry for?" Justin stopped Carlo from following Sue out of the club.

Carlo winced. "I hit on her."

"She's seeing Adam."

"Yes, but—"

"But what, Carlo? I heard her say no to you. And this isn't the only time." Justin fought to keep his stance casual. After Brad and his shit earlier, Justin knew he was overreacting, but what he'd seen had him concerned. "Why are you pushing it?"

"Brad was hanging all over her. She obviously wasn't interested. I thought maybe she'd welcome me."

Justin glared at his friend. "Brad hanging on her made it a good time to take a shot?"

"Is she into Brad?"

"No!" He sneered at Carlo, aggravated that his friend cared about the answer. "I trusted you enough to set you up with her because I've never known you to be a vulture. So, what the fuck, man?"

Carlo's expression shifted from defensive to crestfallen. Justin would've felt bad for the guy if Tom hadn't walked back into the club at that moment without Sue, looking wild-eyed.

Justin returned his focus to Carlo. "Where's Brad?"

"Huh?"

"*Where* is Brad?" He gave Carlo a jerk.

"Last I saw he was showing Sue to the bathroom."

Justin left Carlo, intent on finding Brad before Tom did. He knew Sue could handle Carlo hitting on her. That wouldn't rattle her. At least it wouldn't have sent her running out of the party. He needed Brad's side of the story to put it all together.

Brad stood in the back lounge with his hands on his knees as though he'd braced himself to puke.

Justin debated between punching the guy and hiding him from everyone until he figured shit out. Did he protect his band or Sue, who'd become family to him? "What happened?"

Brad kept his head down, his long hair blocking his face.

Moving farther into the room, Justin's patience waned. "Sue bolted out of here."

Brad slowly stood, leaning on a nearby chair. His ashy complexion and the devastation on his face took Justin aback.

"Whoa."

"She destroyed me." Brad shut his eyes and squeezed his forehead.

"What do you mean?"

"I told her I love her and want us to be together." Brad put both of his hands on his head and looked at Justin with wide eyes.

"And she said no."

Brad nodded. "What did I do?"

Tom burst into the room. He stalked toward Brad and punched him.

Brad staggered back but did nothing to retaliate or even defend himself.

Justin pulled Tom away and held him.

"What did you do? WHAT DID YOU DO?"

"I-I'm sorry. I was a jerk and she-she killed me."

"I don't give a *shit* what she did to you!" Tom jerked against Justin, but Justin kept his grip tight. "She won't let me help her!"

"It's not your job to fix everything, Tom!" Justin glared at Brad. "Stay here." He dragged Tom out to the hallway. "You don't even know what happened." Justin kept his voice low, aware of the game rooms full of people nearby. He didn't want to add to the problem by becoming the talk of the party.

Tom opened and clenched his fists. "I got to Carlo right after you. He said they both hit on her."

For someone so level-headed, Tom's need to go scorched-earth impressed Justin. Usually Justin was the one ready to dish out beatings. He refocused; there were loose ends to fix. "Where did Sue go?"

"I don't know." Tom slammed a fist into the wall.

Darryl's head popped out of one of the rooms. He looked wary as he took in the scene and stepped into the hallway. "What's going on?"

Justin rubbed his chin. "Sue took off."

D stepped into the hall. "She probably went back to the bus."

Tom turned toward the room where Brad waited and glared. "After Brad and Carlo fucking harassed her?"

Justin stepped in front of the doorway to the lounge, blocking Tom. "Focus on Sue. Where do you think she went?"

Tom stood blinking, his face bright red. Justin knew the cogs were moving in the man's brain, he just needed the words.

D formed a triangle in the hallway with Justin and Tom. "She went out the front door?"

Tom flinched and glanced at Darryl. "Yeah. Barry put her in a cab."

"Okay." Darryl pulled out his phone. "We talk to Barry."

"Brad first." Tom growled.

"No." Justin crossed his arms, filling more of the doorway. He wanted the next go at Brad, but even more, he needed to know Sue was safe. "Beating up Brad right now won't find Sue. You can talk to Barry or get on the bus."

"She could be lost in a foreign city, you fucker!" Tom shouted toward the lounge.

"She's not lost." Darryl's voice commanded attention. "Barry put her in a cab. We find Barry, we find Sue."

Tom spun and punched the wall again, letting out a frustrated yell. "If Barry doesn't tell us where she is, I'm gonna fucking beat the hell out of him."

"Okay." D grabbed Tom's arm and headed toward the main club area. "Let's get you on the bus. *I'll* talk to Barry."

Justin guarded the lounge door until Darryl and Tom were out of sight. When he went back into the room, Brad sat in an armchair, his head in his hands.

"You need ice?"

Brad shook his head. "You should've let him punch me more. I deserve it. And the physical pain is better than this." Brad made a circling gesture around his head and his chest.

"Physical pain isn't gonna cure any of that."

"I know."

Justin scraped a chair across the floor and settled into it. "You gonna tell me what happened?"

"She radiates joy. I want it."

"And she said no."

"She said she can't." Brad tilted his face up, one hand cupped over his eye. "I pushed and pushed, thinking all I had to do was break through. That she only had excuses holding me back. But there wasn't anything there. It's brutal to hear the only woman you want say she's never wanted you."

Justin silently tapped his foot against the floor. "It couldn't have been easy on her to say it."

"The idea that she's feeling anything like this is not helping."

"Makes you feel like an even bigger asshole, doesn't it?"

Brad nodded.

"Well, she's gone. Let's get you on the bus so Tom can use you as a punching bag. D and I'll figure out where she went."

"You're a good friend." Brad stood, still holding his eye. "I know."

"I'm an asshole."

Justin rose and clapped a hand on Brad's shoulder. "True. But not always a permanent condition."

"I have to tell you something." Pain replaced the sadness on Brad's face. "She threatened to quit."

Justin shook his head. He desperately wanted to punch this asshole. "As long as I've known you, Brad, you've never just messed up. You fuck up to the nth degree."

After checking into the hotel Barry had directed her cab to, Sue slept until eight-thirty the next morning when a porter with a breakfast cart knocked on her door. He told her Barry had sent the meal and a bag for her.

She recognized the proffered backpack as the one she kept ready for their occasional hotel stays. She opened it to find the basic toiletries she kept in it—toothbrush, deodorant, lip balm—and a fresh set of clothes. There were also a few Czech crowns, which she gave to the porter as a tip after he finished setting up the meal.

She didn't have an appetite until the smell hit her. Fresh food. Nothing deep fried or on a stick. A real meal. Her stomach growled even though her heart wanted to crawl back in bed for a week. About halfway through her plate of eggs, she remembered how she'd left Tom, and a new wave of guilt washed over her. She fished her phone out of her purse and powered it on. She called him before the phone loaded all her messages.

"Hey." Tom sounded relieved and guarded at the same time.

"Hi. I am so sorry, Tom."

"It's okay."

Sue ran a hand through her hair and gripped a clump. "No, it isn't. I never should've treated you that way."

"Justin filled me in. Don't worry about it."

Sue's stomach dropped. When she'd gotten into the cab the night before, she knew Tom would learn everything, but she regretted he didn't get it from her. "Brad's with you, isn't he?"

"I'm at breakfast with the other managers."

"Do we still leave at eleven?" Sue asked.

"Yes."

"You guys parked at the hotel in our itinerary?"

A door closed in the background. "I'm alone now. Are you okay?"

"I don't know, Tommy. I'm sad and hurt and embarrassed."

"You have no reason to be embarrassed."

Sue paced the room, noticing the rain had come back. "How's Brad?"

"I don't fucking care."

"Tom."

He groaned. "About the same as you, plus worried and an asshole."

"Worried?"

"Barry wouldn't tell us where he sent you. And Brad thinks you'll quit."

"*I* don't even know where Barry sent me." Sue went to the nightstand for some stationary. "And I *should* quit."

"Don't start with me."

"I crossed a line." Sue slumped onto the bed. "I led Brad on and said horrible things to him. I'm a huge distraction. I need to leave the tour."

"Stop," Tom said. "You're overreacting. We've been all but locked up together for weeks. The raining is never-fucking-ending. Something was bound to happen. We will all get past it."

"I don't know."

"Would you trust me?" Frustration edged Tom's words. "I've been touring for damn near three years with these guys. I know how it works. It'll be weird for a few days, but it'll blow over." He grunted and Sue imagined he pulled at his hair, his typical stress move. "Have you figured out where you are yet?"

"Yeah." Sue read the name of the hotel off the stationary.

"Gimme the address. We'll come get you."

"No," Sue said.

"Fine. I'll find you with our locator app."

"No. Listen, Tom." Sue stalked to the window and tapped on the glass. "It'll become an even bigger deal if the bus comes out here for me. Let me take a cab, and I'll trust you about everything else."

"You sure?"

"Yeah." Sue faced the room, wondering if the app had already put her on the map with the rest of the guys. "I've got my overnight bag. Lemme freshen up. I'll grab a cab and we can pretend like I was never gone in the first place."

"If you're not here in an hour, I'm coming after you."

Sue called Barry next to thank him for the rescue. True to form, he brushed her off, almost coldly, and hung up. She decided she didn't care about his briskness, got dressed, and went to check out. When she asked for her bill, they told her it had been covered in full. She tried to tip them for arranging a car only to be politely refused again. Sue cursed to herself. Despite his cold personality, Barry had a generous side.

To distract herself from worrying about what kind of welcome she would receive, she spent the entire ride to the bus going over the upcoming interview schedule, making notes for Tom. Sue had decided the only reasonable course of action would be to quit. Since leaving would put pressure on Tom, she wanted to prepare him as much as possible.

As the taxi pulled into the parking lot next to the bus, Sue tried to tip the driver, but he refused her money, another service courtesy of Barry. She ran from the cab to the bus, trying not to get too wet in the rain.

Chris jumped when she entered the bus. "I thought I was the last one in. Where'd you come from?"

"Sorry. I guess I am." Sue skirted around him to get to her bunk.

"You okay?"

The way Chris greeted her meant he likely had no idea what had happened the night before. Sue wasn't about to tell him when she didn't know where everyone else was. "Upset stomach."

"Sorry, dude, but you know the rules. No solids on the bus."

"Sure thing." Sue stashed her bag and climbed into her bed, pulling the privacy curtain closed.

A few minutes later there was a knock on the wood framing her bunk. "You okay?" Tom asked.

Sue slid the screen open enough to see Tom crouched, his face level with hers. "Eh. Chris was up front when I got here."

Tom cringed. "I don't think he knows."

"I don't think so either." She winced. "We have to tell him."

"Why?"

"This can't be swept under the rug, Tom."

He fisted a hand in his hair and kept his voice low. "Not on the bus, okay? Not in front of Noble Perversion."

"Okay."

"Get some sleep. D's in his rack. Just and Brad are in the back lounge."

Sue squeezed his arm. "You gave Barry my overnight bag?"

"It was a failed bribe to get him to tell us where he sent you." Tom pat her hand. "Sleep."

Sue almost smiled, realizing she might have to reconsider her opinion of Carlo's prickly handler. She pulled the curtain closed, but shuffling footsteps in the hallway put her on alert. She slid the drape open enough to figure out who'd come into the sleeping area.

"Sue okay?" Chris asked.

"She'll be fine," Tom said.

"What do you mean she'll be fine?"

"She feels like shit now, but she'll be fine," Tom snarled.

"Oh-kay." Chris climbed into the bunk across from Sue's and snapped the shade closed.

CHAPTER 31

Milan, Italy

Sue pushed a handwritten page across the table to Tom.

"I don't need this." He shoved the paper back at her.

"I already emailed it to you and sent you an updated calendar file."

"Then you'll have to undo the calendar update." Tom shoveled a spoonful of truffles into his mouth.

"That's eight hours of work you're casting aside."

"Not my fault you didn't fucking read a book instead." Tom guzzled a glass of wine.

Sue sighed. She wanted to go to Brad and assess the damage, see if they could still work together, but she wouldn't. She didn't trust him not to pursue her again. "Tom."

His fork clattered against his plate. "We're in fucking Milan. Eating the most amazing food to ever cross my lips. Can you please fucking let me enjoy it?"

Sue whispered. "Sorry." She'd been so intent on preparing Tom for her departure that she never considered he might still be reeling. She'd laid out most of what had happened with Brad—she kept the kisses he'd forced on her to herself—but told Tom about Brad's declaration of love – and leapt right to her decision to leave the tour. She hadn't given him time to process all the new information before she shoved a new schematic at him. She needed to stay in motion; Tom needed to sit and think.

Her own meal sat untouched. It smelled delicious. She picked up her fork and poked at the food. She took a bite of the creamy fare and let the butter and cheese take over her senses. She'd been on autopilot when she ordered the city's famed yellow risotto, but once she tasted it, she couldn't stop eating, taking a comfort from the meal she desperately needed. Finally, she tore the crust off a piece of bread and mopped some of the cheese off her plate. When Tom chuckled, she whipped her head up.

"Enjoyed it?"

"Most amazing food to ever cross my lips." She popped the bread in her mouth and gave him a small smile.

"Please don't go."

Sue finished chewing and swallowed before she answered. "We'll let the guys decide."

"Why?" Tom slumped in his chair.

"You hid crucial information to get them to hire me."

Tom crossed his arms. "Do I at least get a vote?"

Sue sipped her wine, tasting it for the first time. Again, the flavor burst through her mouth, the perfect mix of savory and sweet to compliment the risotto she'd inhaled. She held the glass against her chest. "You can flip the coin if we need a tie-breaker."

"That's a shitty deal."

Sue shrugged. "It's the best I'm offering."

"When do you want to do this?"

"Tonight." Sue ordered another glass of wine even though she hadn't finished the one she held. She hoped a little buzz would steel her for the rest of the evening.

Tom sighed, took out his phone, and texted the band to meet.

Thirty minutes later Sue sat at another small table across from Tom, this time in their hotel. Brad faced the window, as far from Sue as the room allowed. Rain tapped against the glass. The rest of the guys were scattered throughout the space, everyone but Chris fidgeting.

"So." Sue cleared her throat. "I'll try to keep this short since we have tomorrow off." She raised her gaze to the light fixture on the ceiling, not wanting to look anyone in the eye. "Last night I realized what a distraction I am on tour. Your budget might be better served if I left and you got an actual crew person."

"Sue," Justin called to her.

She shook her head, not wanting him to try to blow the whole thing off the way Tom had.

"Dude." Chris held out his hands. "You know how to do everything. If we hired someone new *now*, they'd have to learn mid-tour. Our cues would be off for a week. Easy."

Sue's mouth fell open. Of all the people in the room, Chris was the last one she expected to want her to stay.

Darryl barked a laugh. "He's right. We'd have all kinds of glitches if we brought in someone new at this stage."

"You guys want her to stay," Tom said.

"Yes." Justin stomped the floor as though hitting the pedal of his bass drum.

"Good. We're done here." Tom pushed away from the table and stood.

Sue shook her head. "We're not."

"Oh, come on." Tom raked his fingers through his hair.

"We're not done." Sue focused on the one person in the room who had yet to speak. "Brad. Do you want me to leave the tour?"

Brad didn't lift his gaze from the window. "Majority rules."

"I'm not asking the majority. I'm asking you."

Brad shook his head.

Chris glanced between Brad and Sue, then at everyone else in the room. "I'm missing something."

Sue tried to speak, but Justin cut her off.

"It's the fucking rain. We all agree Sue should stay. What's next?"

"Brad has a black eye he won't talk about, Tom looks like he wants to break something, Sue looks like she's about to puke and you two" —Chris wagged a finger between Justin and Darryl— "are unusually quiet. I'm missing something. Who's gonna tell me what it is?"

"I, uh, I caused some trouble last night." Brad turned his head toward the room his gaze on the floor. "I said some things to Sue I shouldn't have and pissed her off." He faced Sue.

She wished for another glass of the delicious wine from dinner to help her stay calm and inwardly beat herself up as he took all the blame for what had passed between them.

"We need you on the tour." Brad buried his fists in his pockets. "You have nothing to worry about. I won't step out of line again."

Sue had no idea what to say; she stared at a spot on the wall over Justin's shoulder.

"How about you apologize?" Tom said.

Sue shot him a sharp look.

Chris's head swiveled to Brad. "Dude. Did you hit on her?" When no one answered, Chris sprung up from his seat on the bed and got in Brad's face. "You *hit* on her? After I asked you not to? After we *all* asked you not to?"

Brad flushed a deep crimson and glanced away from Chris.

"Wait. You all knew?" Sue stood. "How come only Justin said anything?"

Darryl grabbed the back of his neck. "We thought it would blow over."

Sue glared at Justin before shifting her gaze to Tom. "You knew about this?"

He nodded.

"You guys are supposed to tell me if your latest rando got a dick pic, but *this* you keep from me." She glared at Justin and Darryl. "It wasn't nepotism. This is why they didn't want you to hire me, Tom. Aside from Chris, who actually was terrified I would cause a sex drought, this"

—she gestured toward Brad—"is why you didn't want me here, isn't it?"

Darryl and Justin stared at her with stunned expressions.

"How long have you known?" she asked.

"Since Texas," Tom said.

"Texas? Texas!" Sue wanted to shake her cousin. "You all knew about this since Texas?" Sue stalked to Justin, the person she spent the most time with and felt the closest to on the tour aside from Tom. The person who told her not to worry about Brad.

"Justin? Texas?" she asked, one hand on her hip.

He closed his eyes and shook his head. "Missouri."

"Are you fucking kidding me?" Livid, she addressed Darryl. "What about you? How long have you known?"

"Mullet guy in Oklahoma."

"Day one and day four." Sue pointed at Justin and Darryl. "Chris, when did you put it together?"

"Texas."

"Unbelievable. And you all hid it from me." She stalked back to the table and spun around, ready to rip into them again. "None of you trust me to do my job and handle my shit!"

"Shut up, Sue." Chris rubbed his head. "We thought Casanova was smart enough to listen." Despite Brad being at least four inches taller, Chris cowed him. "You're not the only one who thinks she's important, asshole."

Sue stared at Chris as he paced between her and Brad.

He held her gaze for a moment, then faced Brad again. "She believes in this band. She's helping us get there, and you go and fucking, fucking *break* her? Look at her! She wants to quit because of you. What the fuck is wrong with you?"

"I don't know," Brad whispered.

"Apologize to her. *Beg* her to stay."

Brad stood still as a statue, shock etched across his face.

Sue knew that shock. She thought for sure Chris would kick her off the tour. He'd free her from this mess because he'd never wanted her around. Instead, he was her loudest advocate. When had that happened?

"Apologize or I fucking quit." Chris stormed out of the room.

"Oh my God." Lightheaded, Sue went after Chris, but Brad stopped her.

"I have to fix this." He jogged out of the room.

Sue crumpled back into her chair. "This is exactly what I didn't want to happen."

"Brad will take care of it." Justin kneeled in front of her.

Sue tried to get out of the chair. "I shouldn't be here."

Justin boxed her in and shook his head.

Darryl walked over and touched her shoulder. "Relax, Suse. Chris quits at least once a tour."

"I've ruined everything." Sue gripped the arms of the chair.

Justin rolled his eyes. "Stop. You haven't ruined shit." He paced toward the window.

"They're fighting because of me."

"We fight all the fucking time." Justin thumped his foot. "Chris isn't quitting." Another thump. "You haven't broken up the band. This is shitty, but it's not the end of anything."

"Sue, we've been together almost nonstop for six months." Tom leaned against the door. "They'll fight over single versus double-ply at this point."

"It's true." Darryl sat across from her. "We fought over toilet paper last tour."

"This is worse." Sue pressed her fists against her eyes. "I caused this. I'm not even in the band. I can do most of my job from Maryland."

Justin paced back and tapped his index fingers against the table. "They will work it out."

"I'm supposed to be a professional. Making you a bigger band, not creating problems."

"Brad is supposed to be a professional, too," Justin said.

"You haven't done anything wrong, Suse," Darryl said. "I promise you, we will all work this out."

Sue gripped the arms of the chair again, preparing to stand and run to the door. "We're all on top of each other all the time. Some space would make this easier. I can do my job without being on the bus."

"We aren't hiring another crew member. You're stuck with us." Darryl tapped her nearest hand.

Sue stood. Stuck worried about all this tension? Stuck pretending this issue with Brad had never been a big deal? Stuck wondering what else they were keeping from her? No. "Why should I stay? None of you have been honest with me from the beginning. You guys are supposed to be able to tell me anything. Anything! Someone stole your phone and is leaking texts? I need to know. Accidentally fuck someone off a balcony? *I* am your first phone call. But this? Something I can take care of pretty easily, *this* you keep from me. What else don't I know?"

"I'm sorry. It's my fault." Justin thumped a hand on the small table. "I could tell the way Brad talked about you before you joined the tour. I should've told Tom."

Tom grabbed his hair in his fist. "It never occurred to me until Chris figured it out in Texas. I'm stupid."

"No, *I'm* stupid." Sue paced the room. "I didn't listen to my instincts, and none of you were willing to tell me. I seriously should not be here!"

"Sue! Please!" Distress evident in Darryl's voice and on his face. "Please calm down." D didn't speak again until she looked at him. "Suse, none of us said anything because about ten seconds after meeting you in St. Louis, we all knew you were the best person for this job. We didn't want to mess it up."

"It's true." Justin sat in the chair Sue had vacated. "We're the stupid ones. We had no idea how to manage it. That's why we bitched about you scaring away women."

Sue looked at each man in turn. "You weren't comfortable enough with me to say something."

"So you'd quit?" Tom asked.

"Maybe. At least I could've been better prepared to deal with this." Sue perched on the windowsill and leaned her head against the glass. "This hurts."

The room fell silent for a full minute.

Tom crossed to her and pulled her to stand. "I'm sorry." He enveloped her in a hug.

Sue buried her face into his shoulder.

"We were all trying to protect you and massively fucked it up," Justin said.

"Ugh!" Sue pulled away from Tom and paced the room again. "You aren't supposed to do the protecting. I am!" She sat on the edge of Tom's bed and put her head in her hands. "My role is to solve problems, not cause them. It's a problem if you think you have to protect me." She faced them. "I shouldn't be on tour."

Darryl crossed the room and grabbed her arms. "You can't go. Tom can't run the tour and schedule interviews. He has no idea how to prep us, and when he tries to set up Justin's drum kit, the snare always falls off. We need you."

Tom sat next to her. "I don't have the connections you do, Sue. I can't get them the attention you've already gotten."

"You don't have to do anything but maintain the schedule I already put together."

Tom bumped her shoulder. "Your schedule changes damn near every day."

"And the last time Tom set up my drums, a cymbal flipped off the kit." Justin sat on her other side. "Do you know how hard it is to flip a cymbal?"

"I remember that," Darryl said. "Right in the middle of a show, too. Soundchecks took twice as long after that. Please stay. We need you. What can we do to make you stay?"

She walked to the windows. "I don't know. I need to think. And I need it stop fucking raining."

CHAPTER 31

Adam guided the card key into the lock and twisted the knob. He carefully pushed the door open, relieved when a latch or chain inside didn't catch. He picked up his suitcase and slipped into the room. He left his luggage near the door and crept further in, letting his eyes adjust to the dark. His pounding heart sped up when he found Sue's form on the bed. She lay diagonally across it on her stomach, the blankets almost over her head.

He stepped out of his shoes and gingerly crawled over the covers. He was almost even with her head, about to kiss her, when she suddenly flipped over, eyes wide, fists flying.

He grabbed one. "It's me, it's Adam," he whispered. "I'm sorry. I was trying to be gentle about waking you."

Sue stared at him for a moment. "Am I dreaming? You're really here?"

"I'm here, babe."

"How'd you get in?" Sue squeezed his arm.

"I arranged it with Tom." Adam drank in the sight of her as she touched him and studied his face. He wanted to crush her to him, tell her how seeing her in the flesh made all the shitty flights it took to get to Milan—and the layover that got extended twice—worth it. But her blank face left him unsure. Maybe he should've texted her when he'd finally boarded the last plane. He tried to back away, but Sue sat up enough to hug him to her.

"Best wake-up call ever." She said the words right into his ear, then kissed it, his cheek, his lips.

Relieved, he sunk into the bed over her and held her.

"I can't believe you're here."

Adam kissed her neck. "It's good to know Tom can keep a secret."

"I'm surprised he wasn't sleeping outside the door to make sure I didn't leave." Sue pushed the covers away. "Get into bed." She pulled him closer with one arm while she tried to move the blanket over him with the other.

Adam gasped. "You're naked." Her skin shimmered in the dark room, teasing and tempting, her nipples perking up.

"I guess I managed a surprise, too." She tugged at Adam's shirt and went for his belt as he yanked the shirt over his head.

"Babe." Unable to resist, Adam leaned down and darted his tongue across her peaked nipples. "You have to be careful in hotels. Naked, no latch on the door—it's not safe."

Sue made shushing noises against his lips. "It was a one-off. I was worn out when I got here."

Adam brushed his fingers across her stomach and burrowed his nose against her neck. "God, I missed you."

"I missed you, too." Holding him tight, Sue murmured the words against his skin.

"I know." Adam devoured her mouth. "I got your texts."

"Why didn't you respond?"

Adam kissed her chin and neck as his hands continued to roam over her body. "I knew I'd blow the surprise."

"This is the best surprise." Sue's fingers played down his back and cupped his ass, brushing away his pants. "Take these off already."

Adam flipped onto his back and pushed his pants and underwear off. He leaned over and kissed Sue before sliding to the edge of the bed.

She grabbed his biceps. "Where are you going?"

"Condoms are in my bag."

Sue relaxed her grip and dragged her hand along his arm. "I didn't even pack any." She tightened her grip around his wrist. "Come here."

Adam lay back on the bed, angled away from her. He felt like a teenager, electrified with want and ready to explode.

Sue rolled to her side and slid closer, kissing him as she brushed her fingers through his hair. She threw a leg over his hip and pulled them together. "I went to the doctor the morning I flew into Boston."

Confused, Adam kept one hand on her thigh, the other arm curled under her. "Okay."

"I got birth control. And my tests are all clear." Sue paused for a moment. "Not that they wouldn't be. But it's nice to have it official."

It took a moment for what she said to register. He rolled on top of her and breathed in her scent from her neck up to her ear. "Is it?" He enjoyed her shiver as he rubbed himself against her.

It took a moment for what she said to register. He rolled on top of her and breathed in her scent from her neck up to her ear. "Is it?" He savored her shiver as he rubbed himself against her.

"Yes," she whispered.

"I'm clear, too. You know I've been waiting for you."

Sue wrapped her legs around his waist. "There's only you, Adam."

He kissed her, stealing time to let his emotions calm. "You keep making this night better and better."

"I wished you would be here so many times." She tightened her arms around him, then held his face so they made eye contact. "I don't want anything between us."

Speechless, Adam softly pressed his mouth to hers, reveling in her as he slid his tongue past her lips.

Sue tilted her hips, moaning as she rocked against him.

Adam broke their kiss and gripped her hand, moving her arm over her head and pressing his body against hers from his chest to his hips as he positioned himself.

She shifted, forcing him to look at her face, and tightened the leg she had around him. "Now."

She sighed when he entered her.

He fought to keep control, overwhelmed by having her this way, feeling all of her, knowing she'd waited for him.

She rolled them over and clung to him, kissing his face, his neck, and down to his chest before she sat up.

She was a vision, all dazzling skin and wild hair, throbbing around him. How had he gone weeks without her? He sat up and held her against him. "I missed you so much it hurt."

Sue gripped him with her whole body. "I need you," she whispered.

Adam bucked his hips and pulled her face to his. "Tell me you're mine."

Her head fell back as Adam's lips skimmed her neck and along her shoulder. She ground her hips against him, drawing him even deeper. She put her forehead against his. "Adam. I'm yours."

Hearing his name as she gave him what he wanted stoked his lust. He claimed her mouth again, dragging her down and pinning her to the bed.

She wrapped herself around him, lighting up nerves from his shoulders to his knees.

He drove into her again and again, holding her gaze. She met each of his thrusts, her fingers digging into his skin, forcing his body tighter and tighter against hers. Without air between them, she was making him part of her.

"Come with me, Adam." She bit his lip, then caught his gaze again. "Come with me now."

Her body worked the orgasm from him and stretched it out so long that nothing existed but her.

When he finally floated back to reality, he couldn't let her go. He rolled onto his side, holding her against him, wondering if he was really shaking or if it was in his head. He didn't care. He'd been emptied as she walked away from him at the airport three weeks ago.

Sue hugged him as tightly as he did her. She nuzzled his neck and chest. "I still can't believe you're here. I'll be devastated if I wake up and this is all a dream."

"It's not a dream, babe. Anywhere you go, I'll follow."

<hr>

Sue woke again a few hours later, still in Adam's arms, sun streaming through the window. She sighed and snuggled closer to him. She waited for the sadness and worry from the last few days to swamp her again, but nothing eclipsed her happiness. She quietly thanked whatever impulse had driven Adam to surprise her. When the edges of hunger gnawed, Sue peppered Adam's face with kisses until he stirred. Then she focused on his mouth, hoping to convey how thrilled his presence made her.

"Talk about a great wake-up call," Adam said.

Sue smiled and stretched beneath him, wrapping her arms around him again. "Oh, I can do better."

Adam smiled and nipped at her earlobe.

"You brought the sun with you."

"Did I?"

"Yeah. It started raining after our second show." Sue glanced at the window. "Even when it would let up for an hour or two, there was never any sun. I needed the sun."

"I'm glad it followed me." Adam propped himself on an elbow and studied her face, rubbing his thumb along her cheek. "Are you okay?"

"Yeah." Sue smiled.

"You don't look like yourself."

"You haven't seen me in a while."

"Nineteen excruciating days." Adam kissed her forehead. "But until I left Boston, we talked every day. You've been tense. Is everything okay?"

"I'm much better now with you here." Sue caught him in another kiss.

"Tell me what's wrong."

Sue sat up a little, still clinging to Adam. She knew she had to tell him what had happened, but she didn't want to get into it yet. She wanted to enjoy being with him again before she revisited all the bullshit. "We've been fighting. We've been forced together because of the rain and I thought things were easing up but everything kind of erupted over the last two days."

"Touring isn't for the faint of heart."

Sue traced designs on his chest with her fingertip. "No, it isn't. And I think I might leave it."

"Why?"

"I shouldn't be fighting with them. I'm supposed to get press and exposure. I can do that from home. I don't need to complicate things on the bus."

"You've fought with them one way or another all along." Adam caged her in his arms.

"Fighting over doing interviews is one thing. Fighting over everything else is another. I'm supposed to be part of the solution, and all I'm doing is making problems."

"What you're going through is normal. You've been forced together more than any of you expected. You rely on each other since you aren't all multi-lingual, and there's a ton of stuff to keep track of." Adam pushed a hank of hair over Sue's ear. "Plus, you're all high energy people. When you can't get to a gym or scream on stage or do whatever to burn off steam, fighting is kind of natural."

"That's...huh. I didn't think about that."

"It's true."

"Still, I can stop some of the fighting by removing myself from it. I'm going to tell Tom that I'll stay until he can get a new crew person to replace me."

"That's not fair," Adam said.

"What do you mean?" Sue sat up all the way, forcing Adam to move back. Not only had he defended the shit show of the last few days, now he wanted her to stick with it? She was flummoxed.

"The rest of them can't bail. Tom can't manage the band from Ann Arbor. They all have to get through it. It's not fair for you to quit. Especially since you do more than coordinate interviews."

"Huh." Sue considered his point.

"You know I'm right." Adam grinned.

Sue raised her eyebrows. "You don't even know what the fights were about."

"Doesn't matter. They can't quit. Neither should you."

Sue wrinkled her nose. It sounded great, but as soon as she told him what had actually happened, she suspected his opinion would change.

"I can help. I rented a Bugatti. I'll drive you to Switzerland." Adam leaned close, kissing her shoulder. "I can run interference for you for four whole days."

Sue kissed him hard and slid back into the bed. She'd enjoy the morning, then tell him the details of the fight.

When he finished raging, she'd arrange her flight back to the States. Maybe she'd fly to Boston for a few days before going back to Hagerstown. "You're lucky I missed you."

"Yeah?"

"Yeah. Normally, I wouldn't give in so easily."

CHAPTER 33

"What's the plan for today?" Sue stood in the bathroom in her bra and panties, putting on her makeup while Adam showered.

"Spend the day with you."

Sue smiled even though he couldn't see her. "You flew halfway around the world to surprise me and you didn't have a plan for what you wanted to do when you got here?"

Adam pulled the shower curtain open enough to stick his head out. "We already did what I wanted to do." He arched an eyebrow. "And we can do it again any time."

Sue chuckled. "Can we do it outside? I missed the sun almost as much as I missed you."

"Do the Italians have laws about exposure?"

Sue laughed again.

"Doesn't matter," Adam said. "Challenge, accepted."

"Should we leave bail money with Tom just in case?" Sue leaned toward the mirror as she put on eyeliner.

"Good idea. In the meantime, why don't you tell me about the fighting."

Sue's stomach dropped. She'd meant it when she told Adam she didn't want anything between them. But she hadn't figured out how to explain the fight. Especially when she should've seen it coming. "Are you sure you want to hear about it?"

"Yep." Adam cut off the water and opened the curtain.

Sue gave him a towel. "We should be focused on fun."

Adam scrubbed the towel over his body. "It'll gnaw at you. Tell me. Get it out of your system."

Sue sighed. "It was about me."

"I figured." Adam wrapped the towel around his waist and stepped out of the shower. "And?"

Sue brushed blush across her cheeks, trying to decide the best way to relay the information.

Adam lowered the toilet lid and sat, watching her.

Sue put down her makeup and faced him. "Brad kissed me."

Adam's eyes darkened.

"Twice." A twinge of panic hit her as Adam's expression got even angrier. "I'm not sure the first time counts. And Justin yelled at him. But the second time—"

"Both times count."

Sue nodded, blinking back tears as her stomach roiled.

"Tell me about the kisses. Both of them," Adam said through gnashed teeth.

"I didn't kiss him back. Either time."

"Good." Adam rolled his shoulders. "Tell me more."

Sue sat on the edge of the bathtub and told him everything, from Brad's kiss at the Cowboy Mouth show all the way through Barry putting her in a cab. As she told the story, she saw the signs she'd missed—or ignored. And she thought about the signs she'd put out that had also been ignored. Anger built, but she swallowed it, worried about Adam. He'd been mostly silent as she spoke. Occasionally he asked questions, but mostly he listened. His silence made her nervous.

Sue stopped talking long enough to take a breath. She put a shaky hand on his arm. "Are you okay?"

He nodded, grinding out a "yeah" without looking at her.

"Adam." She waited until he made eye contact. "I made sure I was clear with Brad. Now I'm going to be clear with you." Sue sat on his lap and forced him to keep his eyes on hers. "I have never been interested in Brad. Even if we'd met outside of a professional context."

"Carlo hit on you, too."

"I went on one date with Carlo and knew twenty minutes in there wouldn't be another. You're it for me, Adam. Only you."

He pulled her into a hug.

Sue let herself relax into his arms. "Our relationship is important to me. I'm protecting it."

Adam held Sue tighter against him and pressed his lips to her forehead. "Thank you," he whispered. He hugged her for another moment. "What happened next?"

"Justin said Tom punched Brad after I left."

"He did?" Adam sat back enough to catch Sue's eye.

"Brad has a black eye."

"Damn. Nice, Tom." Adam rubbed Sue's back. "I never thought he'd hit his friend."

"Tom, Gavin, and me, we always go to the mattresses for each other."

Adam cocked his head. "Is that why you want to quit? You think you're putting Tom in a tight spot?"

"No. I don't want to fight." Sue balled her fists. She didn't want to fight. But she'd been so worried about whether and how she'd disrupted the band's dynamic she hadn't considered her own feelings. Now emotions swirled through her. She plucked at the one that had her the angriest. "And I'm pissed that Brad second-guessed you and me."

Adam covered her fists with his hand. "Sue, you won't let me kiss you in front of them."

"Because I'm trying to be professional at work." She stood and glared.

He held up his hands. "I understand."

She went to the sink and fiddled with the makeup on the counter. "Anyway, we had a band meeting last night. I said I should leave the tour, and *Chris* was the first person to say I should stay."

"No shit."

"Right?" Sue uncapped a lipstick. "He was the only one who wasn't around when I left the party." She rubbed the color over her lips and smacked them together. "He put it all together in the meeting and got pissed and threatened to quit the band if Brad didn't apologize and beg me to stay."

"Whoa." Adam stood behind Sue and rubbed her shoulders.

"I know. I have whiplash."

"So Brad apologized."Sue furrowed her brow. "No. He chased after Chris."

"Huh.""The whole thing is a clusterfuck." Sue twisted open a tube of mascara.

Adam kissed her shoulder and left her at the sink.

Sue drummed her fingertips against the counter, giving herself a moment to feel her anger. Why hadn't Brad apologized? Promises to behave came easily; he even took the lion's share of the blame. But no apology. Even D and Justin offered them up. Sue's frustration simmered.

Adam got her attention when he flung his suitcase onto the dresser. He pressed his fists against the furniture before yanking the luggage open.

Sue's stomach dropped again. "I'm sorry, Adam."

He turned to her, eyes wide. "You have nothing to apologize for."

"You're upset." Sue walked toward him, stopping a few steps short, unsure of how to act.

"Not with you." Adam smoothed his palms down her arms and wove their fingers together. "But I'm not surprised by Brad. Impressed it took this long, but not surprised." Adam squeezed her hands and went back to the case on the dresser, all but ripping clothes out. "He's fucking pathetic for waiting until he got you away from me."

Sue got another burst of nerves. "Adam, you can't do anything about this."

He banged a fist on the top of the dresser. "You're funny, Sue."

"I'm serious. This is my career. I can't have my boyfriend roughing up my clients."

"Sue—"

"Adam, please." She got between him and the dresser and wrapped herself around him, pressing her face into his neck. "I missed you. All I want to do is spend the next four days with you. Don't let this ruin it."

He deflated. "You're killing me, babe."

"Please."

He hugged her back, rubbing his knuckles along her spine. "I won't say anything."

"Thank you." She lifted up on her toes, suddenly aware of her breasts in her thin bra rubbing against his chest. She pulled him into a heated kiss.

He groaned and patted her ass. "Wear clothes next time." His voice was a husky whisper.

"Huh?"

"If you ever have to tell me something like this again, please be fully clothed. Hell, wear a parka." Adam slid his fingers below the elastic of her panties. "It's fucking confusing listening to all that when I can see your nipples through your bra."

Overwhelmed with relief and a little humor, she whispered, "Is that why you stopped looking at me?"

"Sorry."

She nipped at his neck. "God, I thought you were mad at me. I was waiting for you to explode."

"I'm not mad at you. A little pissed at this powerless feeling. But not mad."

Sue pressed her forehead against his shoulder. "I'm sorry I made you powerless."

"It's not you. I'll figure it out." Adam pulled her chin up and squeezed her ass. "You gonna put clothes on or can I undress you now?"

Sue tugged the towel off his narrow hips.

CHAPTER 34

"If I didn't know better, Tom, I'd think you were campaigning for me to stay last night so you wouldn't have to explain my empty hotel room to Adam." Sue joined Tom on the deck behind the hotel, dropping into the empty lounge chair next to him.

He smiled as he sipped a coffee. "Yeah, that would've been awkward."

"Thank you for helping with the surprise."

"It was his idea. All I did was leave the extra key at the desk."

Sue nudged his arm. "You still helped and I'm grateful."

"Was it weird, considering what all the fighting has been about?"

"After I got over the disbelief that he's here, I was just happy. So no, no weirdness."

"Good."

"And—" Sue paused for effect. "You'll be happy to know he all but convinced me to stay on tour."

"Yeah?"

"Yeah."

Tom nodded. "Adam does good work."

"I still want all the guys on board." Sue crossed her arms, keeping her newly found aggravation at bay. "And things are gonna be different with Brad. If that's an issue, all bets are off."

"You know we're all on your side."

"I don't want sides." Sue leaned back in the chair and tilted her head up, soaking in the sun. "And there's the fight between Chris and Brad. I'm not gonna create more tension there."

"That's settled," Tom said.

"You talked to Chris?"

"No, but the guys said Brad and Chris didn't get back to their rooms until practically sunrise. That usually means they hashed it all out."

"Did they beat the shit out of each other?" Sue asked.

"Even if they did, it wouldn't have been more than a few punches. They're lazy."

Sue chuckled. "I should go find them and make it official." She walked into the lobby of the hotel and spotted Adam at the coffee bar. She wrapped an arm around his waist and kissed him below his ear. "I have to go talk to Chris for a minute, do you mind?"

"Of course not. You don't have to ask."

"Five minutes." She kissed him again. When she stepped away, Adam pulled her back.

"I like that you wear this when we're together." He rubbed his finger down the length of the chain, stopping at the sunburst pendant he'd given her in New Orleans.

"I wear it every day."

A smile crawled across Adam's face. "You have no idea how much I love you."

Emotion swelled, but she bit it back. She knew as soon as she told Adam how she felt, she'd have no interest in dealing with the band. That needed to be settled if she wanted to truly enjoy her time with him. She didn't resist kissing him, though. "I have an idea."

Sue headed for the elevator bank. She'd barely pressed the buttons to go up when an elevator slid open and Chris walked out.

"Hey! I was on my way to see you." Sue gave him a once-over, checking for swollen knuckles and bruises. "Are you okay?"

"Yeah. Why were you coming for me?" Chris narrowed his eyes. "Not to quit, right?"

"I won't stay if you and Brad are gonna fight."

"Sue." Chris gripped her shoulder. "Brad and I are gonna fight. That's how we are. Brad's the assy big brother, I'm the assy little brother. We piss each other off. We may even fight over you again. But probably because of an interview, not him being a dick."

"I have to *let* you fight it out?"

"Yeah." Chris strode toward the lobby, stopped for a moment, and came back. "Tom was right to hire you. You're making waves for us and we all trust you. I trust you. Crew bullshit aside, we need you. Please stay."

She stood still for a good ten seconds with no idea how to respond. She shook her head a little and squinted. "Chris? Chris Lorenzo?"

"Yeah, yeah, I deserved that." Chris flushed and looked away.

"No, really." Sue put her hand on his forehead. "Are you feeling all right?"

He brushed her away and gave what seemed like a genuine, though shy smile. "I'm an asshole, I know. But I'm an asshole who's willing to admit when he's wrong. Once in a while."

Sue crossed her arms. "That is more humility than I want from you ever again."

Chris barked a laugh. "Good. I'm all out."

Sue leaned forward and hugged him. "Thank you."

"You staying?"

"One more hurdle to clear."

"You'll clear it."

Sue pulled back. Suddenly overwhelmed with emotion, she focused her attention on getting the elevator back. "Tom's outside."

"Cool." When the doors opened, Chris nudged her forward.

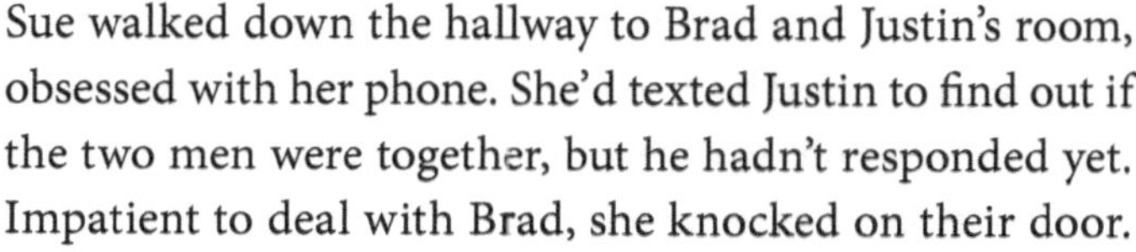

Sue walked down the hallway to Brad and Justin's room, obsessed with her phone. She'd texted Justin to find out if the two men were together, but he hadn't responded yet. Impatient to deal with Brad, she knocked on their door.

It sounded like someone had fallen out of bed or knocked over furniture before Brad answered.

"Hey." He squinted, sleep still evident on his face, his straight hair mussed.

"Hi. Is Justin in there?"

"He's in the shower. You want to come in and wait?" Brad opened the door wider and stepped to the side.

"No. I came to talk to you. But I can do that from here." She didn't move an inch.

"You can come in."

"No." Sue did her best not to fidget. "This is good."

"Okay." Brad leaned against the open door.

"Chris says you guys worked it out."

"Um, yeah." Brad crossed his arms. "We did."

"You sure?"

"Yeah. He's still a little angry with me, but we'll be okay."

"Are you angry with him?" she asked.

"No."

"I'm with Adam." The words came from left field, but Sue knew she needed to say them. She wanted to be crystal clear before agreeing to stay on the tour.

"I know." Color rose in his cheeks, and Brad raked a hand through his hair.

"That's not changing."

Brad glanced down. "I know."

"You don't touch me anymore." Sue took a step back. "At all."

"Okay."

"We're coworkers. *Nothing* else."

He lifted his gaze toward the hallway. "Understood."

"You sure?"

Brad looked her in the eye. "I'm sure."

"I'll stay as long as we can all work together." She tugged on the strap of her purse. "If any lines get crossed, I'm out."

"There'll be no more line crossing from me. I know exactly where I stand. With everybody."

"Okay." She took another step away.

"Thank you for staying."

She straightened her posture. "Just doing my job."

"We would've let you out of it."

"I know."

He held out a hand to shake. "Thank you."

Sue looked at him as though he'd grown an extra head, and he withdrew it.

"Right."

"Okay." She paused for a moment. "Justin's in the shower?"

"Yeah."

"Bang on the door. I have a question for him."

Brad held the room door open with his foot and banged on the bathroom door.

"Yeah?" Justin called out.

Sue gestured for Brad to move out of the way. Once he'd backed up enough, she shouted through the bathroom door. "Hey, Just, will you teach me to drum?"

"That's what I've been trying to do on the bus!" The shower went off. "No, I mean, like, drum for real. On your kit."

Justin opened the bathroom door a crack. "You wanna be a drummer?"

Sue nodded.

"Hell yeah, I'll teach you." He pushed his fist through the crack.

She knocked knuckles with him. "Thanks."

"Everything okay?"

"Yeah. I'm staying."

Justin's smile lit up his face. "Awesome."

"Adam's here, so I should go. Have fun on your day off."

"Adam's here?" Brad's voice cracked.

Sue forgot Brad stood nearby and whipped her head toward him. "He got in overnight. Happy coincidence."

"You two have fun," Justin said.

"Thanks." Sue backed out of the room. "Have a good day." She took off to catch the elevator.

CHAPTER 35

When Sue stepped off the elevator and gave him a diamond bright smile, Adam's ideas for the day evaporated. He'd planned to put her in the exotic car he'd rented and drive all over the countryside, but now he didn't want to drive. He'd have to keep his eyes focused on the road when he wanted to watch her.

"How much of this city do you want to see?"

"As long as I get you and the sunshine, I don't care."

Adam took her hand and led her outside. They walked the streets until he found a small market where he put together a sack of fruit with a bottle of wine and a silk blanket.

Sue squeezed his palm a few minutes later when he led her into a park tucked away near the center of the city. "This is beautiful."

"It's a good place for sunshine."

She pulled him into her arms. "Sunshine and you. Perfect." She kissed him, then took in the scenery. "I don't know if I want to walk through the park first or sit in the sun."

Adam squeezed her ass. "I have an idea."

Sue batted his hand away and pulled him toward a pond at the center of the park. "Did you leave bail money with Tom?"

Adam laughed. "No. I didn't want him punching me, too."

"It might've shocked him enough not to hit you."

"I don't know, Sue." Adam shook his head. "Based on what I've seen with this tour, I'm not sure there's much that could truly shock him."

She squinted at him. "Now that I'm thinking about it, you've been around for all the fireworks. It's mostly pretty dull."

Adam pulled her away from the pond, toward a sunny patch of grass. He laid the blanket out, using the bag of food to anchor a corner, and pulled Sue down to sit. "There's never a dull moment with you."

She leaned back on her elbows and rolled her head back, basking in the sun. "You're good at this."

"What?" He leaned over her to take out the small bottle of wine. He took a moment to appreciate her body beneath him. He loved how she let him move over and around her. She never tried to get out of his way; she molded to him, as though she didn't want to be away from him either.

"Finding perfect spots to occupy together. You did this in New Orleans, too. And Maine."

Adam smiled and opened the wine. "Ah, I forgot glasses."

"Doesn't matter." Sue pulled him to her and kissed him.

Adam didn't know how long they lay in the park. He didn't care. Sue stayed in his arms, sometimes talking, sometimes watching other people. She sighed when the sun eventually shaded over.

"I am perfectly content to never move another muscle." Adam tightened his arm around her waist. "But if you want more sunshine, we'll have to find another spot." He rubbed her hip.

She smiled, rolled on her back, and stretched. "I bet there's a little more to this city than the park."

Adam dropped his head against her chest for a moment, then kissed her and stood. He held a hand out to help her up.

She stepped off the blanket and picked up two corners. He picked up the opposite end and folded the blanket toward her, taking the opportunity to kiss her again.

He enjoyed the view as she leaned over to pick up the empty wine bottle and sack. "We can walk a loop around the city. Stop if anything jumps out at us."

"Okay." She wove her fingers between his.

When they got to the Duomo, Sue stopped, her head tipped back and mouth open. "The cathedrals at home are huge, but wow. This dwarfs them."

Adam tilted his head back to take in the full height of the building. "I bet there are days when it looks like those spires reach right into heaven."

"I wonder if people feel like they're in heaven when they get married here."

"Let's find out." Adam pulled her toward the cathedral. His heart skipped a beat at his own words, but they were out. He wanted to see them through.

"Adam."

"What?"

Sue stood still, her arm outstretched, hand squeezing his. "You can't be serious."

"Why not?"

A parade of expressions crossed her face. She blew out a breath. "I can't go in there. My arms aren't covered."

Adam grinned and held up the blanket from the park. He shook it out and draped it over her shoulders. "Let's go." His palm on the small of her back, he gently pushed her toward the cathedral.

"Adam." Sue dug in her heels and shook her head. "Adam!"

He stopped and faced her, his arm still around her waist.

"Adam. As much as I love you, I can't get married without my parents here. And you haven't even met them yet."

"Wait." Adam wrapped his other arm around Sue and pulled her against him. He needed her to anchor him after she'd blown his mind, and he had to be sure of what she'd said. If she'd said what he thought, he would never let her go. "You love me?"

"Yes." She angled her head down.

Adam crouched enough to catch her gaze, hoping his manic smile didn't scare her. She didn't look scared, though. She looked sure.

"A lot. I love you a lot, Adam."

He crushed his mouth to hers, holding her even tighter. "You have no idea how good it is to hear that."

Sue laughed. "Yeah, I do."

"Why are you shaking?"

Sue's body stiffened in his arms. She closed her eyes and took a beat before she locked her gaze with his. "I've never told a man I love him before. Not like this."

Adam whispered. "Never?"

Sue shook her head. "My dad. My brother. Robin. Never like this."

Adam kissed her softly, reverently. He rubbed his hands along her back, pressing his forehead against hers. "Can I fly your parents in? We can all have dinner, tour the cathedral, get married. It'll be a nice day."

Sue laughed and squeezed him. "You're too much."

"I want to get this locked down."

Sue gave him a quick kiss. "You have me locked down." She hugged him again. "And now I'm starving. Feed me, please."

Adam kept one arm around her waist as they resumed their walk. She hadn't said no. Not exactly. She said she couldn't get married without her parents. That was a problem easily solved.

"I really would fly them in, you know. My parents, too."

Sue smiled at him. "I love you even if you couldn't."

He could push, get a real answer out of her. But after how he'd found her, ready to quit her dream job because she'd been jerked around by people who supposedly cared for her, he decided to keep it light. Not only had she confessed her love, he was the only one to hear those words from her. That alone had him walking on air.

"I should spend the rest of the day saying things to make you respond that way."

Sue lifted her eyebrows. "Maybe I shouldn't say it so much. You might take it for granted."

"Never." Adam pulled her close again and kissed her temple. "I love you." He kissed her cheek, her neck, her forehead, and her lips, saying "I love you" after each one. "Are you tired of hearing it yet?"

"No."

He kissed her palm. "I love you."

Sue smiled. "I know."

"Such a tease."

Sue lay his hand flat over her chest. "Can you feel that?"

"What?"

"My heart beating I love you, I love you, I love you."

Adrenaline swamped him. "You're killing me."

CHAPTER 36

Sue drew a hand over her smooth leg and put her razor down. She'd shaved already? She checked the other leg and found it smooth as well. She tilted her head back into the stream of warm water. Had she washed her hair? She worked her fingers through it, massaging her scalp as she went. She had to shake her nerves and focus. The day before, Adam had given her exactly what she needed—time to not worry about the fight or how things would go with the band after. She wanted to spend another day with him, not go back to work, but knowing he'd be waiting made facing the band seem less daunting.

She had something else on her mind, too. Not only had she told Adam she loved him, she'd also told him she didn't want anything between them. That meant she had to tell him about the secret she and Tom were keeping from the band. What would he think of her when she told him? It was a hard knock against her integrity, and telling anyone, even Adam, put Tom at risk. The problem was as daunting to her as all the tension with the band.

Adam walked with her to the office building where the interviews would be held. As they parted ways, Sue remembered the point he'd made about her not letting him kiss her in front of the guys. She didn't think anyone had arrived yet, but a quick check of the time told her they could at any moment. It was the perfect time for her to practice being affectionate at work.

"Hey," she called Adam as he walked away.

"Yeah?"

She stepped out of the building and closed the gap between them. She hugged Adam and kissed him. "Have a good day. I love you."

"I love you, too." Adam patted her ass before he walked away. He glanced back and grinned.

"Suse!" Chris crossed the street, his arms out. "What are you doing out here? We have interviews to do."

"Right." She waited for Chris to get to her and walked into the building with him. "The first and last interviews will be more general, but the second one will be all about the album."

"I can nap through the first one. Excellent."

"No, you can't!"

Chris found the room with their poster on a stand near the door. "Whatever, Sue." He went in and helped himself to an espresso.

She glared at him, but inwardly she relaxed. Chris acting the way he always had turned out to be exactly what she needed.

Tom burst into the room next. "You couldn't text me back that you were already here? I've been looking for you, Chris! And where's everyone else?"

"Dude. Have you seen the way Italians drive? I'd be taking my life in my hands if I tried to text while I walked here."

"Sue!" Justin entered the room, pointing his phone at her. "We need to discuss this photo."

Tom held up hands. "Where's Brad and Darryl?"

"Right behind me, relax." Justin flopped on the couch next to Sue and put his phone in front of her face. "The Veyron?"

Sue gave him a closed-mouth smile to temper her glee. "The super sport."

"All the production models are sold out!"

"It's a loaner. Adam knows a guy."

"Shit." Justin shook his head and zoomed in on the photo. "You could've at least stood next to it to show the whole grill."

Darryl and Brad arrived while Justin asked more questions about the car. They fixed themselves drinks before settling into the couches and chairs set in a circle. Brad took the seat farthest from Sue.

After sailing through the first two interviews, they all relaxed during the break before the third reporter arrived.

Chris stood at the open door, watching the people who moved through the building. "Man, Italian women make the best scenery."

"Real nice, Chris." Tom shook his head.

A wolf whistle filled the room.

"Dude!" Tom threw a small spoon at Chris.

"Ow!" Chris rubbed his arm. "It wasn't me!"

Someone whistled again.

Darryl snickered.

"Come on, guys." Sue put her latte cup down. "I don't want to have to figure out how insulting Europeans find whistling."

Another whistle came.

"It's your phone!" Chris pointed at the coffee table in front of Sue.

"No, it isn't." Sue checked the device. The message indicator blinked. She picked it up and unlocked the screen to find three texts from Adam.

> **S: Did you change the message tone on my phone?**
> **A: Yeah. You like it?**

"Holy shit, it *is* your phone!" Tom leaned toward Sue.

Heat rushed to Sue's cheeks. She covered her eyes for a beat before she answered him.

> **S: I thought Chris was whistling at women.**
> **A: Ha! Not this time.**

"Oh my God." Sue's cheeks burned. She refused to look up, especially when Justin and Darryl laughed. The phone lit up in her hand as Better Than Ezra's lead singer belted out lyrics about knowing she loved him.

"Oh my God." Sue answered the phone before it sang at her again. "Subtle like a sledgehammer, Adam."

A coffee cup clattered against the table in front of the couch. When Sue glanced up, she caught Brad's back as he strode out of the room.

Adam laughed. "I was celebrating. It's not every day that your dream girl tells you she loves you."

Sue dropped her head into her hand to give herself space to focus on Adam. "You. Are unbelievable."

"Maybe. But I don't care because you love me."

Sue smiled in spite of herself. "Yeah, I do."

"Did you read any of my texts, or were you too busy trying to get Chris to shut up?"

"The latter."

"Do you want to tour the Duomo? I can get us tickets for a tour tonight."

"Just us?"

"It's not too late to book a flight for your parents."

Sue shook her head even though he couldn't see her. "Stop."

Adam laughed again. "Sorry, I couldn't resist. It's a standard tour. Docent, tourists, no surprises from me."

"I would like that."

"Done."

Sue sat back in her seat and finally glanced around the room. Darryl sat across from her with an ear-to-ear grin. She stifled a laugh. "We have one more interview. I'm putting my phone on silent like I usually do, so you don't screw it up for us."

"Okay. Meet you there in forty minutes?"

"Yeah."

When the call ended, Sue immediately silenced the phone and dropped it on the table.

"That was awesome." Darryl stood and refilled his drink. "I'm doing that to Lena's phone when she gets here."

CHAPTER 37

Bern, Switzerland

"You know, even world-famous rock stars usually aren't brought to the tour in a Bugatti." Rich, Noble Perversion's tour manager, stopped next to Sue's bunk as she stowed her bag.

"You said you needed me here fast."

"If this is the kind of attention you give your clients, I'm glad I'm signing up."

"You're a smart man." She took out her laptop, ready to focus on business, but reconsidered. Adam had made some important points when she told him about Brad. He deserved more from her. She straightened her shoulders. "Lucky for you, my boyfriend likes fast cars. And driving fast through the Alps is fun."

"Boyfriend? Here I had you pegged as a free agent."

"Nope." Sue pasted a smile on her face to cover her guilt. Adam never left any doubt that he had a girlfriend. She needed to do the same. "Doing the long-distance thing while we're on tour. He's watching an early show while we do this, and he'll be around again when we get to Belgium."

"The guy from Kinky Bastards'll be devastated." Rich hooked a thumb in his belt loop.

Sue rolled her eyes. "He'll get over it. Where are we taking this call?"

Rich guided her toward the back lounge, where Tom waited, cell phone in the center of the table, tablet and legal pad at the ready.

Sue sat across from him and gestured for Rich to sit as well. "Funds are released for the tour, right?"

"Yeah. But if this goes well, I wanna talk long term. Our current PR guy barely dials it in. The boys don't mind doing their own grams and tweets and shit, but none of us have the time or the deep connections to court serious press. And we need to move more units on this circuit."

Sue opened her laptop and a fresh document. "I can help with all of that. Let's get the execs on the phone and map out a plan."

Tom dialed the record company, and they spent the next forty minutes hammering out a deal to split most of Sue's travel fees between both bands and get her additional payment for handling Noble Perversion. Eventually, Rich shifted the conversation from immediate needs to slightly longer planning.

"We're set for the rest of the summer, but we have studio time booked the day after the last festival gig. They're already trying out new tunes on stage. I know the priority is promoting festival dates, but I also want buzz for what's up-and-coming."

"You pinning the next album on this broad, too?" the exec asked.

"The broad is still right here and has a name," Sue said. She caught Tom's eyes across the table. They reflected pure panic. "You have all the provisions you need. Stop jerking around and enjoy the results I'm about to deliver."

Rich sat back and whistled. "Don't tangle with Ms. Sue Douglas!"

"You don't deliver, Ms. Douglas," the exec threatened through speakerphone, "you won't get away with that kind of attitude."

"As supportive as your team is, you're lucky I don't have more attitude." Sue clicked on a new email. "This document came over fast."

"We want it executed this afternoon."

Rich leaned forward, draping himself over the table. "The band ain't here. You need them to sign, it may not be done until after the show tonight."

"This is short term," the exec said. "Your sig is enough."

Sue put the document side by side with her notes and made sure each point matched. And there was no bullshit about her performance being tied to either band's next album. She looked at Tom. "I'm good. You?"

Tom caught her eye. He looked steadier, but still rattled. "Yeah."

Sue clicked through the document in all the places where initials and signatures were required. When she finished, she addressed Tom. "Done?"

He grunted and passed his tablet to Rich. "You can pull up your email and sign, too."

"Thanks, man." He took the offered device and tapped through until he had his copy in front of him.

While Rich read the document, Sue took the opportunity to silently communicate with Tom. She mimed taking deep breaths, prompting Tom to actually take them. She knew it wouldn't calm him after the exec had hinted at the album provision Tom had kept from Words Fail Me, but she needed him to stay calm long enough to finish this meeting. They could figure out how to handle the threat later. Right now, they had a good deal in front of them. They needed to execute.

"Does he know?" Tom mouthed to her.

Sue gave a subtle head shake. After listening to Rich negotiate, she was confident he had no idea what the exec had been referencing. If he had, he would've said something.

Tom pressed the heels of his hands against his temples. "You sure?"

Sue nodded and mouthed, "Relax. I got you."

Rich dropped the tablet on the table. "Signed, sealed, and delivered, suit. What next?"

"Go sell some music." The exec's line went dead.

"All right!" Rich held his hand out to shake. "I am looking forward to doing business with you."

Sue took his hand. "Likewise. This is gonna be fun."

"Thomas." Rich stretched his hand across the table. "Thank you for a fair deal. You coulda pushed way more on us than you did. I appreciate your integrity."

Tom looked like a deer in headlights as he shook Rich's hand.

Sue pressed her lips together, forcing herself not to react. Aside from this one huge lie, Tom did have integrity. The lie had become a heavy weight around both their necks. They needed to come clean and put it behind them. But not in front of Rich. Sue closed her laptop and nudged her new business partner.

"Should we celebrate?"

"Yeah! We at least need a toast." Rich went to the mini fridge and pulled out three beer bottles. "All we got in here."

Sue took one of the bottles and twisted off the top. "To getting the music out."

Tom clinked his bottle to hers. "To you saving our asses."

Rich laughed. "I like that. Getting the music out and saving asses. Let's do it!"

Bremen, Germany

Sue arrived backstage as Justin and Chris rolled the drum kit out of the trailer.

"Grab my axes." Chris grunted as he and Justin lifted the kit a few feet to get from the trailer to the ramp without rolling it through mud.

Sue got Chris's basses and followed them onto the stage.

Once on stage, Sue unfurled a cord, tossing one end toward Chris as she plugged it into an amp. She moved to the next coiled wire, prepared to whip one end out toward Darryl, only Darryl wasn't setting up his keyboards. Sue took a moment to look around.

"Where is everyone? This is all-hands-on-deck time."

Justin went to the keyboards and held his hands out, ready to catch cables. "Lena called, so D gets a pass this time." He caught the first cord and waited for the next. "Someone from the label called Tom about our recording schedule when we get home."

"Brad?" Sue asked.

Chris placed a microphone stand in the center of the stage. "I'd love to be a dick and say he's hiding from you, but that's not true. Not this time, anyway."

"So what's he doing?"

"He's recording a track with Kinky Bastards." Chris opened the microphone case and slotted one into the stand, then gestured for Sue to toss him a cord.

"Why?"

He moved on to the microphone stand near his bass. "Apparently he can play some magic scale they need for their single, so he's recording it for them."

Sue grunted and moved on to the next pile of wires. She mentally scolded herself for not responding with words. Maybe she needed to break out a pair of heels again to remind herself she didn't have to become one of the guys even though she lived with eleven of them. "I hope he teaches them how to play it, too. I don't want to spend any more time around their crew."

Both men laughed, Justin giving her a high five as he set up the microphones around his kit.

"What's with this '80s knot, Sexy Sue?" Justin tugged on her shirt as he made another pass with more equipment.

"It's torn." Sue untied the knot and showed them a tear running from her ribs through the edge of her shirt. "Even if I tuck it in, it's obvious, so I tied it."

"Why didn't you put on a different shirt? You wake up in a strange place this morning?" Chris snickered at his own joke.

"Your tour bus is definitely a strange place." Sue shook her head. "All my T-shirts have random tears in them. This one was the easiest to hide. I had to get off the bus to talk to your label."

"You need the recording schedule, too?" Justin asked.

"No. You guys got invited to play another zoo benefit."

"We going back to New Orleans?"

Sue shook her head. "Detroit."

"Nice! Sort of a hometown gig." Justin pulled the stool out from behind the drums. "Wanna have a lesson right now?"

"Sure." Sue finished with the amplifiers and joined Justin. He passed her sticks as she sank onto the stool.

"Let's do something basic while we test the amps." Justin explained what he wanted Sue to play, then stepped back while she tried it. "Good, but you're going too fast. Try slowing it down." He clapped out a beat. "Nice. Keep doing that. We're gonna talk to you and you have to maintain the beat."

"Okay." Sue nodded and lost the beat. "Damn it." She restarted, picking up the rhythm quickly. "Okay, let's do this."

"Why do you want to learn drums, anyway?" Chris asked.

"I need an outlet."

Chris gave her a befuddled look. "For what?"

"Dealing with you." Sue hit the bass drum pedal.

"Nice!" Justin laughed and bobbed his head to the beat.

Chris scrubbed his head. "Don't encourage her, man."

"Adam pointed out that I'm not getting real workouts, and with all the rain, there hasn't been a lot of opportunity for me to be active. He suggested I find a hobby."

"And you chose drumming?"

"Yeah." Sue shrugged. "I figured there's so much to do behind the kit that my brain might let go of some stuff so I can focus."

"If Justin had anything in his brain, I bet that would work for him, too."

"Dude." Justin snapped one of the cords across the stage and plugged it into an amplifier. "I can build a better brain to replace yours."

Chris rolled his eyes. "It's been a while since you busted out your engineer brag. But you're still here playing music with me. What a fucking genius."

Sue giggled. "Mozart was pretty smart."

Chris snapped his head up. "You know what you should teach her?"

Justin glanced at Chris.

"*Money Maker*. With all that—" Chris flailed his arms around his head and body. "In the opening."

Justin pointed at Chris. "You're right. She'd love that."

"What's *Money Maker*?"

Justin walked behind Sue and put his hand out for the sticks. "Black Keys. You'll know it when you hear it."

Sue went to the front of the drum kit as Justin settled at the stool. He tapped out a short count while Chris strapped on Brad's guitar. They both tore into the song at the same time. While Justin's movements behind the drums were far more controlled than what Chris had acted out, the power from each of Justin's hits could've pushed Sue off the stage.

Excitement traveled through her like electricity. "Fuck yeah!"

Chris laughed while Justin continued to beat out the rhythm. "I told you."

"I love this song! And damn, if those drums were people, they'd be bruised! Go Justin!" Sue bounced on her toes, counting out the beat as she watched him play.

Somewhere in the middle of the song, Darryl appeared and joined in on the keyboards, adding another layer. When they finished the song, the guys launched into one of their own.

"Sue!" Tom called out to her from the sound booth. "Get on bass so I can get a level."

Sue spun toward the front of the stage and spoke into one of the mics. "I don't know how to play bass."

"Talk her through a chord, Chris."

Chris pointed his chin at one of his basses. "Put it on, Suse. If you're gonna play drums, you should learn bass, too. We're the pulse of the band."

Sue lifted her eyebrows but approached Chris's set up. The man bitched when she went anywhere near his stuff, but not only did he ask her to carry his instruments on stage, now he encouraged her to play them. She had no idea how to process the turn of events.

"Song's almost over, dude!" Chris barked at her.

Sue picked up the bass and slung the strap over her shoulder. "Pick?"

Chris shook his head. "Don't need one for this." He explained where Sue should put her fingers, watching until she had it right. He nodded at Justin and Darryl, and the three of them shifted into another song, with Sue strumming a simple bass line.

Even though she wasn't breaking any new ground with the chord she played, Sue dialed into the energy coursing through them. As the song approached its peak, another wave of momentum hit and she grinned. "Shit. I totally get why you guys do this."

———◼————————————————◼———

Randers, Denmark

"I *knew* it!" Sue swung into the doorway separating the lounge from the sleeping quarters of the bus. She bore down on Darryl, who squatted in the aisle between bunks, a box cutter in one hand, one of her T-shirts on the floor in front of him.

"Jesus, Suse. Anyone ever teach you not to sneak up on a man with a knife?" Darryl closed the blade and slid it in his pocket. "Whaddya think?" He picked up the T-shirt and put his hand in the neck and flared the area around it where he'd made slits about an inch long, almost like a necklace.

"If this was an Iron Butterfly tour, it would be perfect. But Darryl, that was my last fucking T-shirt!"

"Finally!" Darryl grinned and tossed the shirt on her bunk.

"What do you mean, finally?"

"I'm running out of ideas that are annoying but still wearable."

Sue crossed her arms. "You're kidding me, right?"

"Hell no. We all only have so much packed. How you managed eighteen T-shirts is beyond me."

"It's mostly because you keep cutting them!"

Darryl laughed. "How'd you finally figure it out?"

"I had my suspicions, but Chris's expression when I explained one of the tears to Justin confirmed it."

"That fucker. I didn't even tell him what I was doing. He must've seen me."

"Yeah, 'cuz you're such a ninja, D."

Darryl smirked. "I got away with it this long."

"Damn it. Now I have to figure something out before Lena gets here."

"Only five more days." Darryl wiggled his eyebrows.

"Yeah, and in five days Echo Chamber goes to New Zealand, so I lose my secret closet." Sue held the newly cut shirt in front of her and shook her head.

"That's what you've been doing? Stowing all your clothes on Robin's bus?"

"Yeah, it made sense on the nights I crash there, but when my clothes started getting eaten up—" Sue glared at Darryl. "It seemed safer to move my stuff there, especially my non-road crew clothes."

"You don't have to worry about your street clothes. I'm strictly a tour shirt vandal."

Sue tossed the shirt on her bunk. "Why?"

"Suse. You can't only wear our shirts anymore. You're working for Noble Perversion now, too. They deserve more representation."

Sue did a double take. "What?"

"You heard me. You have like two Noble Perversion shirts and a raft of WFM rags. I love that you wear our shirts, but let's not piss off our bus mates and your new clients. Time to mix it up."

"Darryl. You mangled my clothes to show your support for me working with another band?"

"Yup."

"Shit."

Darryl cocked his head. "What?"

"That's a nice reason to pull a prank. Now I have to be extra creative."

Darryl grinned. "Bring your A game."

CHAPTER 38

Paris, France

Sue gripped her phone as the taxi she road in sped across the city. She was late and doing too many things at once when the one thing she'd intended to do was spend time with Adam. She sent up thanks for his patience and a plea that he didn't lose it with her now.

She refocused her attention on the voice in her ear rattling out dates, and honed in on the one that would work for her. "They're available for a full day to do on-camera interviews on the 30th, but they have shows the day before and after," Sue said. "If you can't shoot on the 30th you have to work around their shows." She checked for the nth time that she'd opened the schedule for Noble Perversion, not Words Fail Me. She usually moved fast on her feet, but with so much on her mind, she'd prefer to be somewhere quiet with her computer, not speeding through Paris in a cab, upset that she was running late. The opportunity for Noble Perversion was important, though, so she pressed on.

The production assistant on the other end of the line confirmed the dates Sue wanted and asked for time the day before the interview to shadow the band for B roll. She hastily agreed and added it all to the right calendar.

"Thanks, Ms. Douglas. You never know, this interview could help get Noted Pervs to *Top of the Pops*."

Sue grinded her teeth at the incorrect band name but decided not to make a correction when one more red light would officially push her into a surly mood. "I'm sure their music can get them there, but I'll take any extra push you want to give us."

"Perfect, we'll see you in a few days." The line went dead, and Sue finally sat back.

She took a few deep breaths, then looked around, paying attention to the streets as the driver took her closer and closer to the party where Adam waited.

It'd been petty, but Sue had decided that attending Carlo's latest party with Adam as her date was necessary. She hadn't even told Adam what he'd be walking into, figuring she would've been there first and he'd rise to the occasion anyway. He was great like that. Instead, she was late, and her French was barely transactional, let alone functional, so she couldn't even beg the cabbie to drive faster. She sat quietly and flicked through the messages on her phone.

Adam had texted when he'd arrived and then sent a photo a few minutes later. The lavish party included women dressed like Vegas show girls mixing in the crowd. His next text included a photo of Chris looking like a kid in a candy store and the caption *Chris says this place looks like the Moulin Rouge and Las Vegas fucked and made the sexiest party of all time.* Sue laughed, and envisioned all the party photos Chris might post to Instagram with various amounts of drool on his face. A few minutes later, Adam texted, "there's a camera crew."

Sue hadn't known Carlo planned to film the party and it made her even more anxious. He was usually clear about details like that. She noted it as one more thing about him to be aware of, especially when it involved her boyfriend and her clients.

Finally, the cab pulled to the curb. Sue leaned forward to pay, adding a generous tip and offering her best "merci" before she dashed inside. When she made it to the door the host asked for her name, then handed her a release. Caceres was making a music video. She skimmed the language, took a photo with her phone, then scribbled her name at the bottom of the paper. "Has everyone inside signed one of these?"

"Not yet, miss. The production team was told a later time than the guests. We're working on it."

Sue didn't like the subterfuge, but was relieved this was under Caceres' control, not the media. She trusted Barry.

She joined the party with wide eyes, trying to take in all the activity. If she didn't know better, she would've thought she'd walked into a dance routine in the middle of *Dirty*

Dancing or *Moulin Rouge*, complete with swirling lights and vibrant, though skimpy, costumes. When she didn't see Adam, she consulted the photos he'd sent. They were taken near a bar. She found the wall with bottles lining it and moved toward it.

It took a few minutes to thread her way through the bodies in the room, but eventually, the space opened, and she saw Adam. He looked amazing. His hair was pushed off his face, he wore jeans that hugged his thighs just right and his button-down shirt was open at the throat, giving a tiny hint at his firm chest. He stood with Chris, Carlo, and a woman wearing an elaborate headdress and not much else. Her nipples and groin were covered in sparkles that glittered under the lights. The woman stepped away from Carlo and took Adam's hand. She did a few simple, but exaggerated dance moves, then shimmied against him. To his credit, Adam looked like he wanted to trade places with Chris for once.

Fucking Carlo. Sue rushed Adam, leaping into his arms and taking him in a fierce kiss.

He held her tight, squeezing her ass as he kissed her back. For a moment, Sue enjoyed feeling him hold her and smelling his grass scent as they kissed, everything else fading away. She hugged him and let him nuzzle into her neck, finally relaxing. She heard a wolf whistle and opened her eyes to Chris cheering her on and the glittery woman pursing her lips.

Sue squeezed Adam tighter. "Mine."

He growled against her neck. "Let's get out of here."

She spun in his arms and led him out of the party, never glancing back.

CHAPTER 39

Edinburgh, Scotland

"How much longer, Suse?" Darryl whispered while Brad waxed poetic to a Scottish reporter about songwriting.

She shushed him and whispered. "Ten minutes."

"I didn't mean to let Brad hog the spotlight." The reporter smiled at Darryl. "You had some interesting insights into how you prepare music for your fans. Do you have more to add, Darryl?"

"I'm sorry, I'm antsy. You've got Brad on a roll. Go on."

Brad held up his hands. "I'm done, D. You take it."

"The one time you got nothing left to say." Darryl shook his head.

"What?"

The journalist glanced between Brad and Darryl, letting the silence hang between them.

Sue got his attention and took control of the conversation. "You still have a few minutes. Do you have any more questions?"

"You guys have been touring almost nonstop for a year now. What's the worst part of it?"

Without hesitation, Darryl and Brad responded at the same time. "Rain."

"We just came through about a month of rain on the festival circuit. There was no sun." Darryl elaborated. "Only rain. And mud."

"Heavy skies. Brutal," Brad added.

Sue flicked her gaze away from Brad when his eyes landed on hers. The heavy skies *had* been brutal, and neither of them had discussed anything that happened under them after the morning in Milan. Sue had set her boundaries and they hadn't discussed much of anything since. The wistful look Brad gave her as he answered the question made her wonder if he had something to say.

After a few weeks of avoiding him as much as possible, she'd come to accept they might never have an easy comradery again. Professionally, it was the best way forward, but the person who shared a bus with eleven men didn't like being uncomfortable with any of them. Still, she held firm. She had her career to consider. And Adam. She wasn't about to let anything jeopardize her relationship with him.

"Best part of the tour?"

"There's a lot of upsides, man." Brad flopped back in his chair and scratched his neck. "We get to play every day.

We meet amazing people. We have the best fans. We get to see the world."

"That's a lot of benefits. A little rain couldn't put a damper on so much."

Sue, Darryl, and Brad all laughed. They sounded hysterical, but Sue let it go.

"You have no idea, man." Darryl shook his head. "But it doesn't matter. Touring has brought us a lot of great experiences. And this week we get to share them with people we love."

"Oh yeah?" The reporter leaned forward in his chair.

"My sister is joining us in Dublin. But" —Brad patted out a drum roll on his thigh—"Darryl's girlfriend is due to arrive in Glasgow any minute now."

Darryl gripped his legs. "I'm about to jump out of my skin. I can't wait to see her."

The reporter gave Darryl a wide smile. "How long has it been?"

"Thirty-fucking-three days." Darryl grabbed Sue's phone. "And if this is local time, her plane is about to land."

"Well, don't let me keep you!" The reporter stood and offered his hand.

Sue also stood and shook it, the guys following suit. She walked the reporter to the door, discussing publication dates and offering photos.

The man had barely cleared out of the pub when Darryl shouted "Yes!"

Sue turned toward him. "She's here?"

"Fucking finally! Later!" Darryl skidded past Sue out the door and jogged down the street shouting for a cab.

Sue laughed at Darryl's exit. "Do you think he'll run past the car waiting for him?"

Darryl did miss the car, but the driver hopped out and waved. D doubled back and threw himself into the backseat, talking and gesturing wildly the entire time. Sue laughed so hard tears pricked her eyes. She quieted when she realized Brad stood in the doorway next to her, and trained her gaze on the street.

"Thirty-fucking-three days since he saw Lena."

Sue slid her hands into her pockets. "Yeah."

"How many days passed between Boston and Milan?"

"Nineteen." She'd tracked the days closer than she did her period. Now she had two more days until she'd see Adam again.

Brad nodded. "I should've paid better attention. I only saw what I wanted to."

Sue rubbed her temple, not sure what to say.

Brad cleared his throat. "Okay. Later."

As he left the pub, Sue went back to where they'd sat for the interview. She pushed in chairs and gathered empty glasses and napkins, stacking them in a pile. Not only was that the first non-business conversation she and Brad had had since Milan, it'd been the first time they'd been alone, too.

Sue gave herself a few seconds to acknowledge that she missed the friendship they'd shared when they first started working together. She refocused. Even though they had only been alone a minute or so, Brad had respected her boundaries. It was a tiny step forward.

CHAPTER 40

Sheffield, England

Annabelle shuffled off the bus and plopped down at the picnic table next to Sue. "Whatcha working on?"

Sue lifted her eyebrows and gave Annabelle a once-over. "I figured you'd sleep longer today."

The only outward sign that Annabelle might've been a little groggy after arriving the day before was the messy bun she'd pulled her long black hair into. Otherwise, the woman was fully dressed and drank from a chilled bottle of water, not a giant mug of coffee the way her brother often did.

"It's afternoon at home. I'll get good sleep tonight and be on track. I do okay traveling east. Going back home'll be a bitch."

Sue grunted, all too familiar with jet lag. Although with her current lifestyle she had a more difficult time shifting from being mostly nocturnal to keeping more traditional hours.

"So." Annabelle sipped her water. "Whatcha doing? Can I help?"

"I'm going over the article from the interview Brad and Darryl did a few days ago." Sue moved the computer so Annabelle could read the screen. After finally meeting in New York, the women had kept in touch. Eventually, Sue had offered Annabelle a job. She wanted more time with Adam, and working with two bands on tour, the radio station, and another band at home, she needed help. Annabelle jumped at the offer, resulting in Emily insisting on live signatures on the contract to mark the occasion of "employee number one." Sue thought it all silly until she had the document in her hands. It actually had been exciting to hold the papers. "You don't have to do this, though. I wasn't planning to rope you in until tomorrow."

Annabelle pulled the computer toward her. "I don't mind jumping in."

"It would help to hear it."

"Sit back and listen, boss lady."

Annabelle read out a full page before Justin joined them.

"Morning Bells, Sexy Sue." He kissed his palm and touched it to Annabelle's head.

"Hey, Just. Everyone waking up?" Sue asked.

"Chris is moving around, but D's out cold in the lounge. Brad's still snoring. Curtains were drawn on Darryl's rack, so Lena's probably asleep, too."

Justin let himself into the trailer and Annabelle resumed reading.

"Wait. Read back those last two lines for me, please." Sue stood and paced behind Annabelle. She nodded when Annabelle finished reading. "Okay, keep going."

Justin rolled his drum kit out of the trailer. "You guys mind if I play around? I have a beat stuck in my head."

"Go for it."

Justin made a few tweaks to the kit before he sat and quietly tapped out a rhythm.

Sue paced between him and Annabelle, pausing once in a while to study how he played. As she stood in front of Justin, Sue held up a hand. "Stop! Annabelle, stop. You're good, Just." She spun and went back to Annabelle. "The last three questions were wrong. It was subtle at first, but it got worse with each question." Sue sat next to the woman and showed her where to pull up the recordings of the interview. "Let's listen back."

They listened to the recording for a minute before Annabelle paused it. "That's the first place you stopped me."

"Yep."

"It's wrong." Annabelle faced Sue. "*Belfry* removed their contractions and made shows singular instead of plural."

"Yep."

"How did you remember that?"

Sue shrugged. "I live with these guys. I know how they talk."

"Why did you let the error go?"

"The change was minor and didn't manipulate the intent of the statement. But now I won't let it go since they made bigger changes." Sue gestured toward the computer. "Hit play again."

Tom stepped off the bus and joined them as the recording resumed. "Is that the interview from a few days ago with *Belfry?*"

"Yeah," Sue said.

"They're changing what the guys said." Annabelle paused the recording and read back what the magazine sent. "Wow, that's bad."

"It is," Sue agreed. "I'm canceling their interview with Noble Perversion and sending word back to the label not to let other artists near them. I should tell Jack and Robin, too."

Tom sat at the table across from Annabelle and held out a fist. She bumped him back. "Aren't they new? This isn't the best way to get known."

"They are, and they aren't getting any more of my bands." She pulled the computer toward herself and typed an email. "I don't even care how the article ends. They aren't running this." She hit send on the message and sat back.

"Let's listen for the rest of the mistakes." Annabelle took over the computer and resumed reading the doctored transcript aloud.

Sue stood and paced again. "Wrong!"

Justin hit his drum a little harder in response.

Annabelle played the recording.

Tom squinted at Sue. "Damn. He said lyric and they printed lyrics. It's almost not a mistake. They could explain it away."

Sue put her hands on her hips. "That's their M.O. They start with things that could be typos or translation errors.

Then they change something big. Keep going, Annabelle. We'll find the next one."

Annabelle picked up where she'd left off.

Brad stumbled off the bus, working to keep his over-sized mug upright.

"Wrong!" Sue crossed her arms and glared at the computer.

Brad slumped onto the bench next to Annabelle. "What did I do now?"

Sue sighed. "Not you. The transcript. It claims you said you'd like to collaborate with Caceres. But you didn't say that."

"We already did. I'd love to do it again, though." Brad knocked his shoulder against Annabelle's, then folded his arms on the table and put his head on them.

"I know. Annabelle, the recording."

When the audio got to the part where Brad discussed collaboration with Caceres, he stuck his thumb in the air. "Good catch," he mumbled into his arms.

Justin gave Sue a rim shot, making her smile in his direction. "I'm not done yet."

Annabelle continue to read the transcript, with Justin playing a menacing Jaws-like beat, giving Sue a hit on the bass drum each time she caught an error. Despite being aggravated by the deeply flawed article, everyone waiting for her to catch an error and commenting on the severity of each one turned her fact-checking mission into a game.

"You better run for the hills, Suse!" Chris jumped off the bus.

Sue shook her head. "I don't run from anything."

"You should consider it." Chris plopped down on the other side of Annabelle and drained the rest of her water. "D's awake and it isn't pretty."

Sue pulled a hand over her face to cover her grin. When she knew she could keep a straight face, she said, "I have no idea what you're talking about."

"Sure." Chris drew out the word.

"What *are* you talking about?" Tom asked.

Chris smirked. "Give it a minute. You'll see."

Sue's phone vibrated across the table. Tom scooped it up and tossed it to her. Sue stepped away from the group when she read Lena's text.

Do you know where the hair clippers are?

Sue tapped out the answer and hit send. She took another moment to school her features before facing the group. Tom, Annabelle, and Justin stared at her.

"What?" Sue asked. "You can keep reading Annabelle."

Chris laughed into his fist.

Brad lifted his head and glanced around. "What's about to happen?"

"Nothing." Sue crossed her arms. "Keep reading, Annabelle."

Annabelle went back to the transcript, and Justin resumed his menacing drumbeat. Sue called out another error, but Darryl burst out of the bus before Annabelle played the audio.

"Susan Whatever Your Middle Name is Douglas!" He stomped toward her as every head in the courtyard swiveled in his direction. "This would've been cool if you didn't make it look like fluorescent puke!"

Sue choked back a laugh. "I know. That's why I mixed the veggie pieces in there. I couldn't let you play it off like you had badass spider webs in your hair. And my name isn't Susan."

"It's Susannah." Tom stood and circled Darryl.

Chris shook his head. "I never would've pegged you for a Susannah."

"Right?" Sue shrugged. "My mom likes it."

Darryl waved his arms. "Can we please focus on the fucking mess on my head?" He'd been talking about shaving his head ever since he met Lena. In anticipation of her joining the tour, he'd shaved the sides, leaving vicious-looking punk rock spikes shooting straight up. He sometimes sprayed them different colors, but he regularly voiced concerns about possibly stabbing Lena with his hair. He'd taken to sleeping in the lounge with his hair pointed off the side of a couch, which had stabbed everyone except Lena.

Lena stood by the picnic table, holding hair clippers. "I can't chip it out."

"What *is* that?" Tom poked at Darryl's spikes. They were solid and more immovable than usual. Thick strings resembling bright yellow cement connected them with chunks of peas, corn, and carrots.

Sue grinned. "Remember the slime your mom used to make for us when we were kids?"

"Shit." Tom put his hands on his hips. "That stuff gets rock hard if you don't seal it up."

Sue gestured to Darryl. "Yep."

"Oh, good work, Sue." Annabelle offered a high five. "This is why you're the boss."

Brad and Chris laughed while Justin beat out a jaunty tune.

"Darryl." Lena held up the clippers. "It'll grow back."

"Fuckin' aye, Suse."

Sue grinned. "You kept saying you were gonna shave it when it wouldn't stop raining. Now you're worried you'll stab Lena." She held out her hands. "I did you a favor."

Darryl narrowed his eyes. "Shit."

Sue pulled a folding chair out of the open trailer and set it up next to the table. "You told me to bring my A game."

Darryl shook his head and sat. "Go for it, Lena."

Lena kissed his temple, turned on the clippers, and started shaving at the back of his head, working her way forward.

Brad clapped and whistled while Chris and Tom cheered. Justin sped up his drum solo.

"D." Annabelle stretched past Chris and caught Darryl's eye. "This is better than the time your sister put glue in your underwear."

"Yeah, well, Renee let the glue sit too long. By the time I went to put them on, all the pairs were stuck together."

Everyone laughed, then Chris tossed out a story, followed by Brad. Lena methodically worked her way around Darryl's head, slowly lifting off the crown of hair and paste as she went. Darryl mostly stayed quiet, laughing from time to time but not adding to the conversation.

Sue danced in front of the drum kit. "What song is this, Just?"

"Don't know yet. The rhythm was in my head, and I had to hear it for real." Justin sped up the beat until he got to a specific combination and played it twice.

Brad bopped his head along and strung together random words in a terrible impromptu rap. Chris booed him loudly while Tom and Justin laughed.

Lena stood behind Darryl, the spikes gone, brushing her hands across his neck and shoulders.

Darryl smoothed a palm over his newly bald head. He grabbed her hand, pulling Lena to stand in front of him. "These are my people." He gripped her hands. "I love them, but they're all fucking nutty."

Lena laughed. "They're fantastic."

"This is my life."

Lena smiled as she looked at their group.

"It's loud and insane and I love it. But I need to change it."

Lena tilted her head. "Change what? You said you love this."

Darryl slid off the chair and landed on his knees in front of Lena.

Sue gestured for Justin to look toward Darryl. When he did, he stopped drumming.

"I can't do this without you anymore. You make it a million times better." D let go of Lena's hands and fished in his pocket.

Justin played a quiet drum roll.

Darryl pulled his hand out of his pocket but kept it in a fist. "Lena. I was happy before I met you, but I don't know how. You make everything…more."

Lena visibly shook and sunk to her knees.

Darryl held up his mother's engagement ring. "I went to Brazil."

Lena gasped and covered her mouth.

"No shit," Chris whispered.

"And told your parents you make me a better man and asked for their blessing to propose." Darryl wiped a tear from Lena's face. "They gave it to me. Lena, please, please, please take this ring and be my wife. *Ser minha esposa.*"

Tears rolled down Lena's cheeks. *"Sim, sim, sim!"*

Darryl laughed and crushed her in a hug.

"Wait, what did she say?" Tom shouted.

Darryl turned toward the group, Lena still in his arms. "She said yes! *Sim* is yes!"

Sue cheered with her friends, thrilled and excited to see all the love for Darryl and Lena.

"I get another girl on tour!" Sue clapped.

Annabelle laughed and wiped away her own tears before shouting "Congratulations! My new sister!"

Lena's hands trembled as Darryl finally slid the ring on her finger. "Don't ever take that off."

Lena sniffled. "I won't." She glanced at the ring and hugged Darryl. "You really went to Brazil?"

"Yeah. From New York. I put you on a plane to Texas, then ran clear across the airport."

"Oh *meu Gog*, Darryl." Lena kissed him. "I love you."

"Eu te amo."

"You're even learning the accent!"

"Jesus, Lena." Chris went to her and lifted her off the ground, squeezing her into a hug. "You should hear this fucker on the bus." He held her at arm's length. "He downloaded some app and has been shouting at us in Portuguese ever since we left Austin. It's fucking annoying. But you're worth it."

"Holy shit!" Annabelle pointed at Chris. "You were nice to a girl!"

Chris sneered. "Fuck you, Bells."

"And he's back!" Justin gave Chris a rim shot.

Chris strutted toward the table. "I'm nice to all kinds of girls."

"But only for about fifteen minutes." Brad stood and shook Darryl's hand. "Congrats, man." He kissed Lena's cheek. "Welcome to the madness."

CHAPTER 41

Manchester, England

Adam watched Sue's ass move under her short shorts. He'd seen and explored every inch of her naked body, but something about those shorts made it difficult to take his eyes off her. It had been difficult for the team captain he'd been interviewing, too. Adam handled that fuckery when he clicked off his recorder mid-interview. He had no idea if Sue noticed, but the midfielder sure as shit did. And more importantly, the man made a point to focus on Adam.

"Shouldn't we be in the press box?" Sue asked as she made her way to the first row of the stadium.

"It's better out here." Adam pointed down the row to their seats. "We could be in the pen with the photographers, but you'd lose some of the excitement from the fans."

Sue tossed a smile over her shoulder. "Good man, remembering how I love that energy."

Adam smirked and let her get a few more paces ahead of him so he could take her in. It didn't matter how often he saw her or how long they were apart. He didn't forget a thing about her.

When Sue finally sat, Adam exhaled. He took a long look at her legs, then settled in next to her, dropping a hand on her knee as she sent a text message and pocketed her phone.

"Are you gonna tell me what to watch for?"

"Do I need to?" Adam happily answered each question she lobbed at him about any game he took her to, but he knew she could probably teach him a thing or two about soccer.

A grin spread across her face. "I like listening to you talk sports. It's way better than the usual commentary. It's kind of a lesson in psychology and strategy."

Adam raised an eyebrow. This woman did not need lessons in psychology or strategy. "Remind me to play poker with you next time I need my ass handed to me."

Sue laughed. "You think I'd beat you?"

"You're a master of strategy, and it's fucking hot to watch in action."

Sue raised her eyebrows and sat back. "Noted."

Adam squeezed her knee. "I saw Darryl at the festival grounds. Why'd he finally shave his head?"

Sue grabbed Adam's hand, turned her whole body in her chair and faced him, her eyes dancing. "My prank."

Adam's eyes widened. "I don't know whether to be impressed or scared."

"Impressed."

Adam laughed. "You're proud of yourself."

"Oh yeah." Sue's smile brightened enough to light the stadium. "The prank was so successful, it netted D a fiancée."

"They're engaged? Already?"Sue nodded.

"Go, Darryl." Adam draped his arm along the back of Sue's seat. "Did she freak out?"

Sue shook her head. "She didn't even hesitate. I think he surprised her, especially when he told her he went to Brazil to ask for her parents' blessing. But her answer was immediate."

"Darryl went to Brazil?"

"Yeah. When we were in Boston."

Adam squeezed Sue's shoulder. "Hardcore."

"He knew it was important to her."

She said the words so simply, Adam needed to know more. "Is that important to you?"

"I want my parents there if I get married. But I'm twenty-five, I'm too old and independent for a man to seek out my father's blessing."

"My dad says it doesn't matter how old Claire and Jessica get, they're still his little girls."

Sue smiled. "I can see that about Russ."

Adam remembered his spur-of-the-moment proposal outside of the Duomo. It had only been the two of them and she'd insisted she couldn't get married without her parents.

"Is that what you want? A proposal in front of everyone in your life? A public gesture?"

Sue shook her head. "No. Just you."

Adam let his smile steal his face.

Sue flushed. "Most guys would freak at a slip like that."

Adam pulled her toward him. "I liked it. But was it a slip?"

Sue's color deepened. "I'm happy for them. I'm not secretly planning or hoping for anything."

Adam leaned in. "I have all kinds of hopes and plans."

Sue's eyes went wide, and she obviously struggled with what to say.

He kissed her. He liked her flustered. It wasn't often he—or anyone—threw her off.

"I don't want you to feel pressured." Sue fiddled with the pass hanging from her neck. "I'm not ready for any of that."

Adam tilted his head. Did she want to take pressure off him, or was she truly not ready for a stronger commitment? He was ready for it all with her. "What if I think D has the right idea?"

Sue smirked. "And if Darryl jumped off a bridge, would you?"

"I would if you did. I'll follow you anywhere."

Sue straightened, suddenly sober. "You don't have to. I know you're following me around Europe to give me a break from the tour. I appreciate it. But you don't have to."

Adam pulled her chin toward him. "I'm following you around Europe because I can't stand being away from you. You were gone for nineteen days, and I was crawling the walls." Adam kissed her lightly. "Hell, *before* Europe I was losing it." He slid his hand behind her neck and angled Sue for a deeper kiss.

"I missed you, too," she whispered the words against his mouth.

He pressed another kiss to her lips, not caring that he was on the job or they might be too affectionate in public. He didn't get moments like this with her often.

"Oy! Fletcher!"

Adam groaned as Sue pulled away from him.

A ruddy man with a Chelsea tattoo on his forearm threw himself into a seat behind them and kicked Adam's chair. "Stop eating that poor woman and tell me what the manager tipped to you. Old bastard won't even crack a smile for me, let alone talk." The man leaned forward and offered Sue his hand. "Ryan McGinnty, *Isle Sports*. And you are?"

"Sue Douglas."

Ryan shifted in his seat, digging through his pockets. "'Ere you go, Sue. A stick a gum in case Fletcher still tastes of his greasy English breakfast."

Sue laughed and shook her head. "He's good." She dropped a hand onto Adam's leg and squeezed.

"You sure? He likes his bangers."

"Stop hitting on her, McGinnty."Ryan smirked. "Heh. I heard Philips almost lost an appendage for leering."

Adam flashed his eyebrows. "You could, too."

"Boys." Sue shook her head. "Be nice."

"Rest assured, darling, this is as nice as Fletcher an' me get."

Sue shook her head again and glanced at her phone. "I guess Emily forgot Annabelle's on the job today."

"Call her," Adam said. "We've got about twenty minutes before the stadium gets too loud."

Sue faced the field and dialed.

"Philips in good form today? Aside from his wandering eyes?" McGinnty asked.

Adam chuckled. "Yeah. He looks strong."

Adam's phone went off as Sue said, "Wait. What?" The color drained from her face.

He checked his Caller ID, surprised by the name on the screen. "Hey, Tom."

The man didn't even offer a greeting. "Is Sue with you? Emily's trying to reach her."

"She's right here telling Emily that Annabelle's working today."

"Emily's not calling for work. Sue's roof is on fire."

Adam touched Sue's shoulder and she turned to him, wide-eyed and shaking, her phone still to her ear. "What?"

"Sue's house is on fire," Tom said. "Right now."

"Fuck." Adam stood and pulled Sue up with him. "I'm putting her on a plane." Adam ended the call and dialed his assistant, Lauren. He pulled Sue to him. "It's gonna be okay."

Sue continued to shake, but her voice remained steady as she asked Emily if their legal arrangements gave Emily access to the police and fire department.

Adam guided her out of the row and up the stadium stairs. As soon as Lauren answered, he barked orders at her. "There's an emergency at home. I need tickets for me and Sue on the next flight out of Manchester. We need to get back to her place."

"Dulles or BWI?"

"Whichever we can get to faster."

"Got it, call you back in five."

Adam led Sue out to the front of the stadium and hailed a cab.

Sue grabbed his arm, her phone still in her hand. "The roof is on fire."

Adam's heart clenched at the fear plainly visible on her face. Her color was still ashen. "I know, but it's okay. No one's home."

"The unit on the other end of the row lost the whole second floor."

"The fire department is there. They'll stop it."

Sue shivered. "What if it's moving fast?"

"Don't, Sue." Adam pulled her into a hug, holding her tight. "Don't guess. It'll fluster you. It won't be long before we know exactly what happened."

As soon as a cab pulled up, he put Sue in the back and gave the driver a wad of cash. "We have an emergency. I need you to get us to the airport as soon as possible. If the police flag you, keep going. I'll pay for it all."

Adam climbed into the cab and pulled Sue against him. "I know you need something to do. Call Tom. Tell him we're going to the airport."

Sue dialed Tom, still shaking. "Tom. Adam's taking me to the airport. Is Annabelle with you?"

CHAPTER 42

Sue gripped the strap of Adam's sling bag as she ran through BWI to the arrivals exit, where Emily waited for her.

They'd only been able to get one seat on the flight. Before she got on it, Adam took his passport out of the bag and slipped it over her head.

"There's a phone charger in here, and my tablet is at 100%. You can use it to talk to Emily and Annabelle." He took a beat. "Or, you know, read a book or something."

Antsy about all the quick decisions they were making, Sue hesitated. "What about your interview?"

"Everything is backed up to the cloud and a server at the office." Adam squeezed her shoulders. "I can get to it."

She tried to smile but couldn't. "Thank you."

"It's going to be okay."

Sue nodded. "I love you."

Adam wrapped her in a tight hug. "I love you, too."

What she wouldn't give to have him running through the airport next to her now. The idea of facing her fire-damaged home without him overwhelmed her.

She finally made it to the baggage claim area and practically hopped in place, searching for the spot where Emily said she'd be waiting. She heard her name and spun, finally noticing Emily near giant sliding doors. Sue jogged over and gave her a half hug as she tried to push her friend to the parking lot.

"Are you parked on the curb?"

"No." Emily shook her head and gripped Sue's arms. "We can't go yet. You're not the only one I'm picking up."

Could Adam have made it here so quickly? The next flight had left four hours after the one she'd taken. Did he find another way?

"There." Emily waved again. "Over here!"

Sue found herself wrapped in her mother's arms.

"Susannah, Tom called us. We jumped on the first flight here."

Sue gripped her mother and glanced around for her dad. She gave him a small smile and reached out a hand.

He grasped it. "We're here for you, kiddo."

Sue walked to the car, flanked by her parents. Having them there was a comfort, but they were asking all the same questions Sue had asked Emily through Skype during the transatlantic flight. There were still no answers. The fire department hadn't let anyone into the building because it needed to cool and they had to determine the safety of the structure. Sue didn't want to snap at anyone, so as soon as Emily unlocked the doors, she slid into the front, snapped on her seatbelt, and curled into herself. She sat quietly, only speaking when someone spoke directly to her. Not speculating about the damage and what it all meant was difficult. Emily hadn't even taken photos of the brick exterior. She said she didn't want to mislead anyone about the state of the property. Sue had to wait through the hour-long drive from the airport, and she still might not be able to do anything more than stand outside of the building. She went through interview schedules in her head to distract herself.

When Emily finally parked the car about a block from the building, Sue jumped out and jogged down the street. She stopped long enough to take in the scorch marks that crept over the peak of the roof like long fingers. She braced herself and stepped toward the police tape across her small front yard. An officer stopped her but let her continue when she showed ID.

She gasped when she got to what remained of her front door. It had been cleaved in two. Wood splintered from a gash in the frame. The heavy carved doors that made the first floor a separate apartment hadn't fared as well. Sue knew how difficult it was to see the lock and knobs in the dark. This door lay in pieces.

"They had to make sure no one was inside." Emily's voice at Sue's back jarred her, but the comment made sense.

Sue went up the stairs. Water dripped from above and patches of blue sky peeked through the back.

Most of the roof at the far corner, where her townhouse joined with another, was missing. Scorch marks covered the walls and smudged the remaining ceiling. The chandelier that once hung in the center of the room rested on the floor, evidently knocked down by the streams of water used to douse the fire. Shattered crystal pieces lay around it. Sue walked gingerly toward the French doors at the back. The floor seemed sound, but the policeman had warned her to watch her step. Glass was strewn across the floor, and the doors were close to where the gaping hole in her roof ended.

Sue stopped at the doorway, taking in all the damage, and choked back a sob. Her deck was mostly burned, along with the plants she'd labored over.

Her mother came to stand next to her and rubbed her back. "I'm so sorry, darling."

Sue put her head on her mother's shoulder, her eyes squeezed shut. She knew the damage could've been much worse. So far, what she saw could be repaired or replaced, but she'd labored over this house and put all the money her grandmother had left to her in it. How would she fix it when she still had at least two months on the road? Plus, she was still training Annabelle and needed help with the radio station. How could she operate her business and afford to fix her home? She needed a moment to slow her spinning thoughts before she assessed the rest of the damage. Finally, she straightened and put her hands on her hips. She needed a plan. "Emily, can we put a tarp up now? Do we have to wait on anything?"

"We have to clear it with the fire department. Last night they said it was too hot to tarp."

"Has the insurance company been here yet? Can we start cleaning?"

"They took exterior photos but have to come back for interior. I texted your agent when we left the airport. She should be here any minute."

"Okay." Sue dug through the bag for her phone and activated it.

"Calling Adam?" Emily asked.

Sue shook her head. "Taking my own pictures."

She badly wanted to call Adam, but she put it off. She knew it'd been stupid to hope he'd taken the next flight. He had things to do. A business to run. He didn't need to be here, even though Sue desperately wanted it. She texted him when she landed and silenced the phone, focused on getting to Emily and the townhouse. It would break her if she called him and he answered. It would mean he wasn't on his way. She couldn't handle that as she stood in her smoldering townhouse.

She went outside to capture images of the broken door, carefully walking through the boggy grass to get photos of the roof and her charred garden. Her mother and Emily followed.

"Those plants can't all be gone." Her mother marched toward the garden. She stepped over the vines that had fallen from the deck above and squatted next to one of the beds. "We'll find the green parts and nurse them."

"I'll help you, Linda." Emily pushed up her sleeves and crouched next to Sue's mother, raking her fingers through the flower bed.

Sue wiped tears from her cheeks and went inside, back to the second floor. She loved her mother's spirit to move forward, but Sue couldn't focus on fixing yet. She needed the whole picture first.

As she took photos, she studied the damage. Some came from the fire, some from smoke, and a lot from water. She took photos of every wall and every part of the floor, even if it appeared untouched.

Sue's dad stayed by her side, taking notes on a tablet. Finally, she turned to face the John Singer Sargent reproduction he'd given her.

"This didn't do too bad." He walked toward the art, taking it in. "Those smoke marks along the top and side add a little something."

Sue snorted and kicked away some of the chandelier glass at her feet. "It'll take a few days before we know if the water warped the frame." She didn't want to get her hopes up that it had survived the fire when she wasn't an expert on smoke or water damage

The print was one of her most cherished gifts. She'd wanted a small copy, but when her father visited the townhouse for the first time and saw the upstairs loft, he'd ordered the full-sized version—almost eight feet tall and eleven and half feet wide. The painting stunned Sue at any size, but the full-size let her imagine being part of the scene. She loved that her father knew her well enough to know the joy it brought her.

"I'd say let's lay it out on the side yard, anchor the corners, but the grass is too wet."

Sue rubbed her temples. "Maybe tomorrow?"

"Okay." He gestured for her to go downstairs.

Sue mentally braced herself. She lived downstairs. All her things were there. Could she handle the damage she would find? She steeled herself as she took the first step. It didn't matter. It was her home, and it needed her attention.

"Sue!" Adam stepped into the townhouse and visibly exhaled. Like Sue, he still wore the same clothes he'd had on at the game the day before.

Something released in her, and she sat in the middle of the staircase. She dropped her head into her hands and let go a torrent of tears.

Adam pounded up the stairs and put his arms around her as her dad rubbed her back.

"It's okay, you're okay, it's okay," Adam whispered.

Sue shook her head. "All the plants are gone."

"I'm so sorry, babe."

After a few more heaving sobs, Sue took a deep breath. With one hand shielding her eyes, she shifted toward her father. "Dad, do you have a tissue or something?"

"Of course." The man rifled through his pockets and produced a handkerchief.

Sue dried her eyes and wiped her face. "Okay. I'm okay."

Adam moved to kiss her, but she stood quickly and squeezed his hand.

"Dad." Sue sniffled and tried again. "Dad, this is Adam. Adam, my dad."

"Glenn Douglas." He held out his hand and Adam shook it.

"Adam Fletcher. Nice to meet you, Mr. Douglas."

Sue studied her father as he scrutinized Adam. She silently prayed her dad would go easy on the man she loved. "Let's get off the stairs so I can take pictures of them." She marched forward, unwilling to look at either man. It was all too much, and if she got any hint that her father didn't like Adam or planned to torture him in some way, Sue knew she'd lose the tenuous grip she had on her emotions. She needed this one thing to be okay in middle of her damaged home.

"Call me Glenn," Sue's father said as they all moved down the stairs.

"Thank you, sir."

Sue fidgeted with her clothes as she waited for them, then took a few pictures.

A knock at the doorframe made her jump.

"Sorry, I didn't mean to startle you." Sue's insurance agent crossed the threshold and introduced herself to Glenn and Adam.

Sue made another rapid adjustment, focusing on the instructions the agent recited. She made sure the woman spoke freely in front of her parents, Adam, and Emily, knowing the four of them would have questions she wasn't clearheaded enough to ask.

As they finished the tour of the interior, noting the first-floor damage was mostly water and smoke related, the agent handed Sue a legal-sized paper. "This is a list of approved vendors in the area. If you call this roofer"—she pointed to a name at the top of the list— "he'll come out today and put up tarps for you. He can also prepare a quote and start work as soon as the structure is cleared and ready, if you approve it. He'll bill the company. All you have to do is give him permission. He's the best in the area."

"What about a front door?" Adam asked.

"Great question," Glenn said.

The agent nodded. "I don't know if the roofer has someone who can handle it on short notice, but if you want to do it—"

"Emily, may I borrow your car?" Glenn jumped in.

Sue watched with watery eyes as Emily gave Glenn her car keys and told him where to find the nearest home repair store. These four people were her biggest supporters, and gratitude for them overwhelmed her. "Thanks, Dad," she croaked.

Glenn kissed Sue's cheek, then took Linda's hand. "We'll be back soon."

After her parents left, the agent continued to explain the process. When she finally finished going over everything, Sue called the recommended roofer and gave him directions to the house.

"While we wait for the roofer, why don't we get your clothes out." Emily said. "You didn't bring any luggage, and you might want to wear something different tomorrow."

Adam wrapped an arm around Sue, holding her close. "I brought your suitcase from the hotel."

Sue leaned her head on his chest. "Thank you."

Emily coughed. "Should we get the stuff out of your closet and take it to the dry cleaner for smoke?"

Sue liked having something to do. They went to her bedroom and piled the things from her closet on her bed.

"Babe, do you have a drill?" Adam called from the front room.

"There's a toolbox under the sink." Sue went into the kitchen, where Adam dug through her toolbox. "But the power tools are in the laundry." She went into the small room and took a few cases off lower shelves. As she stood, Adam pulled her into a tight hug. "You okay?"

Sue shook her head. "I don't know. I am, but I'm not. Maybe I'm in shock."

Adam pushed her hair back and framed her face with his hands. "Whatever you need, I'll do it."

Sue pressed her lips together, trying not to cry again. He'd already done what she needed. She burrowed into his chest. "I can't believe you took the next flight."

"Where you go, I go."

Sue swallowed a sob and curled her hand around his shoulder, pulling him even closer to her. "Thank you," she whispered.

Adam squeezed her and pressed his lips to her forehead. He held her for another minute, then took one of the cases. "I want to get the doorway cleared out so we're ready when Glenn gets back."

"Thank you."

Adam kissed her again and went to the entry.

She returned to her bedroom and picked up some of the dry-cleaning bags Emily had taken from the closet.

"You should take all your personal stuff—clothes, soaps, whatever—to my place tonight."

Sue tried to smile. "Thanks for taking me in."

Emily took another armful of dry-cleaning bags and followed Sue outside. "Shit. I forgot your dad has my car. And your car's parked at my place."

Adam stepped out of the house and popped the trunk on his rental. "Load it up."

Another wave of relief hit Sue and she smiled, blowing him a kiss before following Emily and laying the clothes in the trunk over the suitcases Adam had brought back from England. Sue noted even her messenger bag with her laptop was there.

Emily caught her eye and grinned. "He's a keeper."

For what seemed like the millionth time in twenty-four hours, Sue fought back tears.

CHAPTER 43

Adam kept his voice gentle as they finished dinner and Sue asked him to take her back to her townhouse. "What can we do there? There's no electricity, and the sun is setting."

Sue kept her focus on her plate. "I feel like I have to be there." They had done all they could before leaving the house, including installing an ugly steel door at the threshold, but even though the insurance agent explained that the process might be slow, Sue still felt compelled to be in the middle of the townhouse.

Emily traced her finger around the rim of her glass. "I still know someone in the electrician's guild."

Sue's head snapped up and she frowned. "Not worth it, Emily. He's an ex for a reason."

"I can rein him in."

Sue shook her head. "Thank you for offering, but no. I need to go over all the insurance paperwork anyway."

"You want some help, kiddo?" Glenn shut the check holder and positioned it near the edge of the table. "I've completed a claim or two in my day."

"Thanks, Dad." Sue smoothed her eyebrows and shook her head. "I should read them on my own, though. I'll let you know if I have questions."

Linda reached across the table and patted Sue's hand. "You're not alone in this, Susannah."

"I know." Sue met her mother's gaze. "Thank you."

As they walked to the cars, Glenn offered to drop Sue and Emily at Emily's apartment. "You can check into the hotel sooner and get some sleep, Adam."

"Oh." Adam glanced at Sue, not sure how to handle her dad's offer. Did he simply want more time with her? Did he harbor old-fashioned attitudes about his unmarried daughter sharing her bed? Did he think they were only friends? That last one stung. Emily spoke up before Adam had fully formed his thoughts.

"Adam has to come back with us. His stuff is at my place."

"That's right, from the showers." Linda nudged her husband toward Sue's car. "Come on, honey. You need sleep, too. We'll see the kids in the morning." She gave Adam a small smile as she got in the car.

Adam unlocked his rental and held the door for Sue. She'd missed the whole conversation, her focus on her phone. "Robin wants pictures. Should I send them to him?"

"If you want. It might help him to see the damage isn't too bad."

Sue nodded and got in the car, back in her own world.

Emily caught his eye. "She'll come around."

"Soon, I hope."

"Can you drop me at my office? I need to check on some stuff."

"Yeah." Adam walked around the car and got in, staying silent as Emily directed him to her office and gave him directions back to the apartment before she got out of the car.

Sue barely registered that Emily wasn't with them anymore. Instead, she texted furiously with Robin. When they got to the apartment, she sat on the floor in front of Emily's coffee table and dug into the insurance packet.

Adam sat on the couch with his tablet, keeping an eye on her as he went through his email.

Almost an hour passed before she finally groaned. "This is overwhelming." She pushed her laptop across the table and flipped over the papers in front of her.

"What can I do?"

"You're doing it." Sue leaned her head on his knee. "You're here. That's exactly what I need."

Adam dropped to the floor next to her and held her until she pulled away.

"I can't figure out how I'm going to manage the repair work and the tour. Annabelle can fill in for a lot, but not everything. This is officially a two-person job. Lena's helping with the interviews right now, but she's only there for another week. And it's too expensive to fly back and forth weekly."

"I know Emily's busy, but she can check the progress for you. She can give you a little more time between trips." Adam rubbed her back as he spoke.

"It's asking too much." Sue shook her head. "She already does a ton for me. Most of it for free. I can't ask for more." Sue leaned back on the couch.

"I can stop in, too. I have to go to Atlanta soon for a project. I can spend a few days here on my way back to Europe." He almost said, "on my way back to you," but stopped himself. The distance she'd put between them hurt. He hoped it was stress and not signs of a problem.

"Adam, I'm floored you would do that. But you've already done so much. I can't keep taking you away from your life."

Adam turned to face her head on. "Sue, you *are* my life."

Her eyes widened, but Adam couldn't read her expression. Finally, she hugged him tightly. "I love you," she whispered.

"I love you, too." He hoped she took comfort in his arms. When she'd reached for him, it had soothed some of his anxiety. Until he felt her mentally shift away, and a few moments later, physically move away.

"I could probably get Gavin to stay there for a bit before he goes back to school. Maybe he can come out for the last week of the European stuff."

Adam squeezed her shoulder. "There's another option I hope you'll consider."

Sue raised her eyebrows.

"Sell the townhouse. One of your neighbors might be interested."

"And ask Emily to be roommates again? I don't think she'll go for that long term."

Adam made his voice nonchalant, not wanting to give away how much he wanted her to agree to his next statement. "Live with me after the tour."

Sue blinked. "You want me to live with you?"

"Yeah." He touched her leg and smiled.

Her eyes narrowed. "What would I bring to the table?"

Adam laughed. "Yourself."

"No, I mean, you bought your apartment. What do I bring to the equation? Even if I sell my place, it won't yield enough money to be an equal partner."

"Are you serious?" Adam wrinkled his brow.

"Yes."

Adam held her hands. "I'm not worried about us being financially equal. I want us together. Besides, Boston is a good city for you. Some of the magazines you work with are based there. The music scene is great, and it's a commuter flight to New York. Boston can help you grow your business."

"Would you be willing to sell your place and buy something else together?"

"What's wrong with my place?"

"Nothing. I just can't let you pay my way." Sue leaned forward and drummed her fingers on the coffee table. "Which reminds me, I need to call Lauren about that flight and give her my credit card to cover the charge."

"You're kidding, right?"

"No." Sue stood and stretched. "You took a huge weight off me by getting me home, but I can't ask you to pay for it. Your flight, either. Let me pay for them."

"I don't care about the flights."

"Adam."

"Sue, stop. You have enough to deal with." He gestured to the papers spread across Emily's coffee table.

"I need stuff to deal with. Give me more to deal with." Sue paced Emily's small living room. "I need things to focus on so I don't go out of my mind obsessing about all the what ifs with this fire."

"Come here." Adam tried to hold her.

"I can't right now. I'm sorry. I can't."

———————————————

Adam leaned against the bedroom doorjamb as Sue paced the room, her phone glued to her ear. He tried to offer her a glass of juice, but she barely noticed him. After she blew off his invitation to live together, Sue had clung to him when they went to bed. Twice throughout the night she got up, but when morning came, he woke tangled in her. He made it a personal goal to take care of some of the issues with her house today so he could revisit the idea of her moving to Boston without her being cold and analytical. Solve some big problems, get her feeling better, then talk. That was his plan. Until Robin called. Repeatedly. He kept calling until Sue finally answered.

"Stop badgering me. I'm fine!" she shouted into the phone, making no effort to hide her frustration. "I *knew* I shouldn't have sent you the photos."

Adam put down the juice and got dressed. He watched Sue continue to pace and wondered whether he should intervene or if it would aggravate them both more.

The doorbell rang and Adam signaled he would answer it.

"Hi Linda, Glenn, come in." He held the door for Sue's parents.

"Good morning. We brought coffee." Linda smiled and gestured toward Glenn, who carried a travel tray with five cups. Sue got her sunshine-bright smile from her mother. Seeing it soothed him a little, even though the smile didn't come directly from Sue.

"Thank you. Sue's on the phone with Robin. Emily's already at work. She'll meet up with us when she breaks for lunch."

Glenn set the drinks on the coffee table and sat. "I figured today we'd get a truck and a storage locker and move her things out of the townhouse to get ready for the remediation."

"That sounds good. Sue called two more roofers. They'll be at the townhouse in about an hour. And her adjacent neighbor called to coordinate the work."

"I'm so glad the neighbors are cooperative. I was worried." Linda gave Adam one of the coffees and sat next to Glenn.

Sue stomped out of the bedroom, eyes blazing, and shoved her phone at Adam. "Robin wants to talk to you."

Adam raised his eyebrows and took the phone, not missing the look that passed between Linda and Glenn.

"He's Robin-approved." Linda smiled at Glenn as she took the lid off one of the coffees and blew on the drink.

Sue's eyes narrowed, and she pushed Adam into the kitchen.

"Hey, Robin." Adam gestured for Sue to leave the room.

"Hey, I'm glad you're there. Has Sue slept at all?"

"Hang on." Adam put the phone against his shoulder. "He wants to talk to *me*. A minute please?"

Sue glared, but after a moment she left the room.

Adam put the phone back to his ear. "No. And probably not on the flight here either."

"Shit." Robin sighed. "Her parents are there, aren't they?"

"Yep."

"I thought I heard Linda in the background. Have you met them before?"

"Nope."

Sue stomped into the kitchen, got milk and sugar, and stomped back toward the living room.

"Hell of a way to meet the family. You're a trooper."

Adam chuckled. "That'll be the easiest part of this week."

Robin gave him a hearty laugh. "You're smart."

Sue came back and got a spoon, then stood, watching Adam. When he moved the phone to his shoulder, she glared and left again.

"What's up, Robin?"

"I need the truth. She sent me pictures and she's making it sound like it's no big deal. But her fucking house caught fire. That's a big damn deal."

Adam took a moment to form an accurate but careful answer. "The second floor is in bad shape. The first floor seems to only have water damage in a few areas, but the whole place reeks of smoke. Today we're gonna clear her stuff from the first floor and see how bad the damage is."

"Is it habitable?"

"Technically. We're staying at Emily's. Sue needed a new front door and they tarped the roof. She needs some basic repairs up there before an inspector clears it."

"Should I fly out?"

"Aren't you in the middle of a tour?" Adam pushed around the magnets on the refrigerator.

"So?"

"You guys are the headliners."

"And? I can get someone to play a few shows for me. She's more important."

Adam rubbed his forehead. "She is. And she'll go ballistic on both of us if you fly out here before you actually have a few days off."

"I can handle it."

Adam leaned his elbows on the kitchen counter. "What should we do for her?"

"Beats the shit outta me." Robin groaned. "Is she shutting down?" His voice shifted from the business tone he'd been using to sounding truly concerned. "She hasn't slept. Her parents are there. I know this isn't how she wanted you to meet them. How many times has she called or texted Tom and Annabelle?"

Not wanting to be heard in the living room, Adam gave Robin a low laugh. "You're gonna love this. Tom blocked Sue's number from Annabelle's phone."

"Oh shit!"

"Annabelle doesn't know how to undo it, so Sue's been texting her from my phone. I bet she's doing it now. Tom keeps telling her to stop worrying about them and focus on her house."

"And focusing on the house is freaking her the fuck out."

"You got it."

"You ask her to move in with you yet?"

"Yeah." Adam's voice hardened as he recalled the conversation. "That went over like a lead balloon."

"Adam, listen."

"What." He regretted the impatience in his voice, but there was freedom in finally being able to express it.

"This isn't about you."

"I know, but—"

Robin cut him off. "This goes so much deeper than what you know. And I'm not saying this to be an asshole. Trust me. Sue never introduces guys to her parents. We've never dated, but I knew her three years before she introduced me. And she made sure Amy was there. Sue can juggle ninety-nine problems at work. But in her personal life? She sucks."

"No shit, Robin."

"Sorry, man. She loves her parents, and she's freaking out because it'll break her heart if they don't like you. And she's not gonna say as much because she doesn't want to insult you or let you see the insecurity."

"That makes no sense. They seem like nice people."

"Glenn and Linda are the salt of the earth. But her dad is like fucking Kim Jong Il when it comes to men and his little girl."

"I haven't seen that at all."

"He's mellowed since college, but he gave me all kinds of shit for years. And I've never tried to get in his daughter's pants."

"Huh."

"Don't tell her, but Amy is on the way. Gimme your number so I can forward it to her in case she needs a lift from the airport."

Adam and Robin talked for a few more minutes before Adam brought the phone back to Sue. She immediately left the room while she shouted at Robin.

"Everything okay?" Linda asked.

"We think she hasn't slept in two days."

"Ah, shit." Glenn slapped his leg. "This is gonna be rough."

Linda stood. "Why don't you guys go get the truck and let me take care of Susannah for a bit."

Glenn looked toward Adam. "Whaddya say? Wanna head out?"

"Let's do it." Adam picked up his keys and phone from the coffee table. "Linda, let Sue drive. She needs it." Adam checked his texts. "She's been using my phone to talk with Annabelle. I'll forward her any messages I get."

Linda gave Adam a bright smile. "I can see why Robin likes you."

CHAPTER 44

"Ames, I love you, but you shouldn't be here." Sue gave her friend a half hug, even as she scolded her.

"Be grateful it's only me. Robin wanted to come, too."

"Robin's in the middle of a tour!"

"That's what I said!" Amy opened one of the pizza boxes she'd brought with her. She lifted out a slice and took in the aroma. She nudged the box toward Sue. "But he said he'd get someone to fill in for him, and if Jack wanted to fire him over it, so be it."

"Jack threatened to fire him?" Sue bit into a slice of pizza.

"It wasn't a real threat. He was trying to get Robin to stop ranting."

"Adam!" Sue called out.

"Yeah?" Adam and Glenn were in the side yard. They seemed to have bonded over installing the new door for her and had since undertaken a raft of small projects, including managing all the radio station interns Axel sent over. They had the interns help load up Sue's belongings and unload them at the storage unit. When the men returned, they'd taken her El Jaleo print outside to check the frame.

"Amy brought pizza, and I have a question!"

Adam and Glenn appeared at the back door, stomping their feet from the yard before they entered the kitchen.

"Hey, Adam, Mr. Douglas!" Amy dropped her slice of pizza in the box and embraced Glenn.

"Hi, Amy." Glenn patted her back. "You're awfully alert for someone who flew all night."

Amy offered a slice of pizza. "I slept on the plane."

Adam went to the sink and rinsed his hands. "What's up, babe?"

"Did Robin mention anything about flying out here?"

"Yeah. I told him he'd be risking his life if he did."

"Good job." Sue hid her grin by taking another bite of pizza.

"Is he coming out?"

Amy shook her head. "No, but if Sue isn't back on tour by the time Echo Chamber hits their break, he will."

Sue rolled her eyes. "Look at this place. I have all the help I can handle and then some." The radio interns had left after unloading her things at the storage unit, but a crew worked on the second floor, removing the wet drywall and assessing the floor damage. Sue's books and the music and art from the second floor had all been taken to a smoke and water specialist to see if they could be salvaged. She only had to finish packing her kitchen, a task she could've accomplished in an hour.

Amy grabbed a bottle of water from the case she'd brought with her. "Robin's worried. Let the man make a plan. You certainly do."

Having lost her appetite, Sue put down her slice of pizza and wiped her hands on a napkin. "I appreciate you all being here. But I need to do some of this myself. It's my house. I have to make the decisions."

Glenn crossed the kitchen and touched Sue's arm. "No one is trying to take that from you. But you don't have to face it alone."

Sue took in everyone in the room. "Dad. You and Mom left vacation in Sedona. Adam, you have a business to run and articles to write. Amy, you should be with Jack. Robin needs to stay on his fucking tour, and Emily is missing too much work over my drama." Sue grabbed fists of her hair and paced the kitchen. "Everyone has a life. Go do your lives!"

Adam crossed his arms. "I'm staying."

Sue's stomach flipped. He looked angry. She hadn't forgotten what he said the night before, that she was his life. He'd become her life, too. Still, she'd said the wrong thing, again, and she didn't know how to fix it. She wrapped her arms around herself. "I'm sorry."

Amy put her water bottle down. "You're forgetting this is what people do for those they love."

"Thanks, Ames. I need more guilt now."

"Stop it, Sue." Glenn said in a low voice. "You're getting dangerously close to saying something you'll regret. Eat some pizza or go break something, but stop talking."

Her father was right. She needed to get control of herself. "Axel asked me to stop by the station. Can someone please give me a set of car keys so I can go?"

"I can take you," Adam said.

"Thank you." Sue dropped her arms from her self-imposed hug. "But I need to go alone. Dad's right. I'm about three seconds from being a complete asshole to everyone I've ever loved."

Glenn pulled Sue's car keys from his pocket and gave them to her.

"Thank you. I have my phone if anyone needs me." Her phone vibrated in her pocket as she walked out of the house, but she waited until she stopped at a traffic light before she took it out and read the message.

A: I love you.

She pulled the car to the side of the road and finally let go of the iron grip she had on her emotions. She let out thick, heaving sobs and banged on the dashboard. After a few minutes, she calmed down. She rifled through the compartments until she found napkins and dried her face. A quick check in the rearview mirror made her groan. Her eyes were swollen and her skin splotchy. She sighed and drove to a convenience store, where she washed her face with cold water in the bathroom. She bought a bottled water and some lip balm. She pressed the bottle to her face as she drove, hoping the cold would help reduce the swelling enough that she wouldn't get many questions.

When she finally parked at the radio station, she gave herself a little pep talk before going inside. "Don't be an asshole. Don't. Be. An asshole."

CHAPTER 45

Sue stood outside the laundromat, desperate for any kind of breeze. The building's air conditioning didn't work, making the air inside stifling.

Adam pulled up and parked on the far side of her car. Sue smiled when he headed toward her. She thanked her lucky stars he was still in town. After her breakdown a few days before, everyone had left. Except Adam. They didn't leave right away, but by last night, Amy was on a flight back to Jack, and Sue's parents had resumed their vacation in Arizona. Robin had promised not to leave Echo Chamber's tour unless she explicitly asked him to, but he also made her promise to check in with him daily. She begrudgingly accepted, until Adam reminded her that she talked to Robin daily anyway.

That left Sue with Adam and Emily. Emily mostly stuck to her normal work schedule. Adam gave Sue room to communicate with Annabelle, do some work with Axel at the radio station, and talk to her insurance agent and the contractors about her house. He also encouraged her to talk to a realtor. Which she did, alone.

As Adam walked toward her, emotion built in Sue. She wanted to hold him close. She'd spent days mostly avoiding contact from everyone, shell-shocked from the fire and its aftermath and nervous as the center of attention. Now they were alone, and she wanted to give him her undivided attention.

"Why aren't you doing laundry at Emily's?" Adam gave her a chaste kiss on the lips.

"I'm washing my comforter and the futon cover and the stuff that needed big machines. I brought our clothes, too. Get everything done at once." Sue put her hand on the back of his neck and kissed him again.

He responded by gripping her waist, getting closer to her. "Why are you out here?"

Sue barely moved her lips away from his when she said, "It's hot in there." She kissed him again, pulling him flush against her.

"It's hot out here." Adam pushed her against the wall and slid his hand up her leg and into her shorts as he kissed her. "No underwear?"

Sue shook her head and tilted herself against his fingers. "Washing them."

Adam kissed her again as he slid a finger inside and pressed his hips against hers.

Sue gasped. "I want you."

"How soon until the laundry is done?"

"I don't know." She found her car keys in her pocket and hit the unlock button. She pushed Adam toward the car, kissing him as they went. She opened the door to the backseat and got in, pulling him with her. He slammed the door behind them and climbed over her.

Even though they shared a bed every night, this was different. Sue had finally found space to let go of all the things she'd been worried about and focused on Adam and the sensations he stirred in her body. He quickly brought her to a frenzy, and she opened his pants, stroking him.

He hissed and tugged at her shorts.

Sue lifted her hips enough for him to yank her shorts down, then positioned him to slide into her. They both groaned when he did. It was fast, but exactly what Sue needed. When they finished, Sue held Adam close until their breathing slowed.

He shook his head and looked around.

"What?"

"I can't believe we got away with that." He pulled her shorts and his pants into place before sitting up.

"We were due for a break." Sue smiled and sat up. She leaned forward and kissed Adam's cheek.

He gave her a half smile and finished zipping and buttoning his jeans. He raked his fingers through his hair and stared out the window. "Let's get the stuff and go."

"Sure." Sue leaned over him and grabbed the door handle, purposefully rubbing her breasts against him. She sat back when he didn't acknowledge her. "What?"

"Nothing."

"Adam." Sue nudged his leg with her own.

Adam shook his head and faced her. "You'll barely touch me when your parents are around, but you'll fuck me in the back of your car in broad daylight."

"I…what?"

"I asked you to live with me and you're worried about money. Not thinking about us, thinking about money. What the hell, Sue?"

"I'm sorry."

"Are you?"

Sue drew back. "Yes. What's that supposed to mean?"

"I can't talk about this now. Let's get the stuff and go back to Emily's."

Dazed, Sue opened the door on her side of the car and went into the laundromat. She didn't know what had come over Adam, and she had no idea how to address what he'd said.

They silently emptied the dryers she indicated into her laundry baskets and each carried one to her car, loading them into the trunk.

"You're following me to Emily's?"

"Of course."

Sue climbed into her car, turned over the engine, and waited for Adam to do the same.

■———————————————————————■

Sue dropped her laundry basket on Emily's coffee table and took the one Adam carried. She plucked the first thing off the top and started folding, lining up clothes and linens along the arm of the couch as she folded.

Adam paced the small living room. "I'm going to Atlanta in the morning. I have a few days of meetings there next week. It's better if I go early. I've been working on this project piecemeal, and a few days of focus will be good leading into the meetings."

"Okay." Sue snapped a towel and folded it.

"After the meetings, I can go back to Europe and cover more of the Premier League, or I can go wherever you are. The choice is yours."

"No, Adam, the choice is yours. It's your company. You know where you're needed."

Adam blew hair off his face. "I know exactly where I'm needed at work. But I don't know where I'm needed with you. Or even *if* I'm needed."

Sue stopped folding clothes and looked at him. Between what he said and his frank expression, her stomach rolled. How could he not know? "I need you."

"Do you? Because I keep telling you I'll do what you need, go where you want me. And you keep *not* telling me."

"I needed you here."

Adam shook his head. "Needed."

"The big stuff is handled. And you just told me you're leaving tomorrow."

"Okay." Adam took an item from the laundry basket.

"You don't have to do this. It's mostly my stuff, anyway."

"It's fine. I *want* to do it."

"I know I've been difficult this week. I'm sorry."

Adam dropped the towel he folded on Sue's pile and picked up another. "You had a lot to deal with."

"You being here made it a lot easier for me."

"I'm glad."

Sue touched his arm and caught his eye before she spoke. "Are you really going to let me decide your next move after Atlanta?"

"Yes!"

Sue flinched. "You don't have to. I mean, I hope I'll be heading back to the tour, but I don't know yet."

"Don't, don't, don't. That's all I ever hear from you."

Sue furrowed her brow.

"I don't have to be with you in Europe, I don't have to be there when things fall apart for you, I don't have to help you fucking fold laundry. You keep saying *don't* to me. I'm tired of it."

"And you keep telling me you'll do whatever I want, but you never tell me what *you* want. Stop laying whatever all this is on me."

"You want to know what I want?"

"Yes!"

"YOU." Adam snapped the towel he held. "I want to be with you whenever I can. I want to live with you, I want to travel with you, I want to watch you succeed, and I want to be there when things are rough. I want a life with you, and I don't get what *you* don't understand about that. Christ, Sue, I asked you to marry me in Milan. And you take it all in stride until the shit hits the fan and you treat me like I'm just some guy. I am *not* some guy. I love you. I want you."

Overcome, Sue responded with the first thing that came to her mind. "Your proposal...we were playing in Italy."

Adam crowded Sue but didn't touch her. "Were you playing when you told me you love me?"

"No."

Adam took the laundry out of her hands and threaded their fingers together. "Sue, if you'd said yes, I would've walked into the Duomo and done whatever they said to marry you right then and there."

"What?" she whispered, shocked.

Adam wrapped his arms around her and kissed her. "I want to be with you. It doesn't matter how we make it happen. Let's just make it happen. I'll do anything for you. I'll sell my apartment and move here. We can get something new in Boston. We can start fresh in a totally different city. I don't care. All I want is a life with you."

"Adam, I can't ask you to upend your life for me."

"Why not?"

Sue hugged him again, then stepped out of his arms. "I can't do the same for you. I have to go where my clients are. If I stop, I can't even support myself. Sure, I can go back to the radio station, but it's here."

"I'll come here."

"I want to give you everything, but I don't have it yet."

"I wish I knew who made you think you aren't everything. Because you are."

Sue reached for Adam, but he wouldn't let her hold him. He gripped her hands instead. "Now you know what I want. While I'm in Atlanta, figure out what you want. And know this—whatever it is, I'll give it to you."

CHAPTER 46

S: Is your calendar current?

A: Yes

S: What's the physical therapy appointment for Shirley? Isn't she done?

A: Yes. She wants to do water aerobics. The appointment is to give her the all clear

S: That's fantastic. I hope it goes well

A: Same. I'll let her know you said as much

S: I'm rejoining the tour in 2 days

A: Do you need me to stop by your house when I leave Atlanta?

S: No, but thanks. Roof is done. It'll be a few days before the drywall guys can come out

A: I can fly through Baltimore before I go to Spain for the Real Madrid games

*S: I think it'll be okay. The realtor I'm talking
to offered to keep tabs on the place
A: You willing to sell?
S: For the right offer
A: What if I made an offer
S: If your offer is to meet me in Budapest next
week, I'm all over it
A: Nice evasion. Make sure you pick up some
fresh garlic when you're in Rome
A: I love you
S: I love you*

■————————————————————————————————■

Sue slipped into Axel's office and slumped into his desk chair, rubbing her temples. It'd been a long day, and when she hadn't been training her new hires, she'd spent much of it trying to talk to Adam. Texting came easier than actual talking, but most of their conversations were stilted at best and at worst, awkward and tense. It was all her fault. After he laid out what he wanted, Adam had backed down and let her set the tone, which was worse than if he'd demanded an answer. She felt like she was dancing around everything when all she wanted was for him to continue to be her safe place. She knew if she asked him to do that, he would, but Adam deserved more from her, and she wanted to give it to him. She struggled with the idea that if she agreed to live with him, essentially letting him solve her housing issues, she would be taking advantage of him, not coming to him whole.

Being back at the radio station turned out to be exactly what she needed to keep her occupied between dealing with her townhouse and talking with Annabelle whenever the woman could call her. The challenges at the station gave her a new perspective on her strategies for Words Fail Me and Noble Perversion, as well as fresh ideas for Bloody Maggots. Getting back to work again after a few days of intense focus on her house—and her heart— refreshed her.

"You all right, Sue?" Axel leaned in the doorway and offered her his coffee cup.

She waved away the drink. "Nothing some vodka and a few hours of sleep won't cure."

Axel walked in and took a seat in one of the visitor chairs. "Interns slowing you down?"

"They're not too bad. And my new hires are gonna whip them into shape."

"You know I'll hire them directly."

Sue shook her head. "I want them on my payroll. I can put them on projects for me when things are slow here and ramp them up for the book in the spring." Hiring people had been a calculated risk. The station had salary money in their budget, but Sue wanted more control. Despite still figuring out how the fire would impact her finances, her focus remained on growing her business. For now, she'd bill the radio station for their time and prepare them to move into other positions with her. She worried she wouldn't be able to support the heavier payroll if insurance didn't cover all the repairs her home needed, but she reminded herself she could still sell the property—even if she didn't know where she'd be living.

"Here's the million-dollar question." Axel leaned forward and rested his elbows on his knees. "Do you think they're gonna run off with a band like the last two chicks I hired?"

Sue laughed. "You're telling people I ran off with a band?"

"Didn't you, though?" Axel crossed his arms and sat back. "Actually, that didn't occur to me until your replacement did it. I hope the girl's okay. I never met someone so…"

"Dick hungry?"

Axel guffawed. "I love that you don't pull any punches."

Sue covered her smile. "I heard she had a big appetite, but I thought she liked DJs. I had no idea she'd go for a rocker, especially considering hardly any come through here."

Axel chuckled. "Seriously though, did you write an awful threat into their contracts?"

"No. I'm not worried about them running off."

"You sure? Rockers are getting more and more built. One of them could bolt."

Sue smiled. "They're not going to run off with a band because I'm going to keep them busy. And even if by some strange quirk of fate they did run off, it would have to be an exceptional band."

"Why's that?"

"Nora and Stacey are a couple." Sue leaned forward and positioned an elbow carefully among the clutter on Axel's desk. She rested her cheek on her fist. "And they seem pretty solid."

Axel raised his eyebrows. "A couple, huh? Very creative."

"It's a coincidence. They're type-A personalities who get shit done. I know some of their references personally. They have a great track record. They're smart, reliable, and they have my blessing to cock punch any joker around here who asks them to make out in front of him."

Axel raised his eyebrows. "Are you sure you want to go back on tour? You could be station manager with your eyes closed. You could even take on Philly and Baltimore and barely crack a sweat."

Sue smiled. "I'm sure. But thank you. Your confidence means a lot to me."

"Anytime you want a job, you call me."

Sue nodded. "Will do."

"How much longer are you gonna grace our halls?"

"I fly out the day after tomorrow."

"Gonna come to the event tomorrow night? Or let Nora and Stacey handle it?"

"Both. I want to watch them work the event up close and personal."

"You gonna fire them if they fuck up?"

"They won't fuck up. But if they do and I fire them, I'm still getting on that flight."

"You gonna pick up the new boyfriend on the way?"

Sue stood and put her laptop in her bag. "Don't know. He's got some business in Atlanta." Sue rounded the desk and gave Axel a kiss on the cheek. "Thanks for letting me use your office this week."

"Anything you want, Sue."

She closed her eyes at the words, so similar to what Adam had said to her. Anything she wanted.

CHAPTER 47

Rome, Italy

As the plane circled the airport and touched down, Sue remembered the last time she'd visited Italy. She'd arrived in crisis but left whole and with Adam.

She wanted him. She wanted everything he did. She had a lot of decisions to make about her townhouse and she wanted to discuss it all with Adam, but if they didn't agree, would she wind up alone again? She finally understood the coming changes didn't only affect her. But they were changes to things she'd done with only herself in mind. How did she think broader without losing herself? Her independence? If they made these choices together, would she have anything left to give him?

Sue had kept these fears from Adam, and she hated it. Even more, she hated that she thought he might try to push her one way or another. The whole time she'd known him, he'd only ever pushed for them to be together.

Adam asking her to live with him wasn't a bad idea or impulsive, though Sue had tried to frame it that way. They'd already moved in together by way of hotel rooms. She'd watched it happen and didn't stop it or even acknowledge it. She liked it. She'd been too comfortable not thinking about the conversation she knew they would've had when the tour ended. The fire had simply sped everything up. Again, she reminded herself that Adam deserved more from her, and she had to figure out how to give it to him or risk losing him. In the past she'd been fine with letting relationships go; now she wanted to hang on, but she had no idea how.

She walked through the airport slowly, almost in a fog. Annabelle's smiling face brought her back to the moment.

"Hey!" Sue pulled her bag off the luggage carousel and hugged Annabelle. "I would've taken a cab to the festival grounds."

"I know." Annabelle took Sue's laptop bag and slung it over her shoulder. "But we all agreed you deserved a better welcome back than a cab."

"Aw, you guys!" Sue gave Annabelle a theatrical punch in the shoulder as the woman led her to the vehicle borrowed from the tour.

"You should know" —Annabelle opened the back door to the van and loaded Sue's bags— "Brad's kind of on the outs with everyone."

Sue snapped her attention to Annabelle. "Why?"

"We found out exactly what happened at that party."

Not sure how to react, Sue climbed into the passenger side and closed the door behind her. The night in Prague might as well have happened in another lifetime, yet Annabelle mentioning it put Sue right back in the middle of it.

Annabelle got in the driver's side and faced Sue. "Why didn't you tell anyone Brad assaulted you?"

Sue widened her eyes and pressed her lips together, gathering her thoughts. Because there were too many people to tell? Because it had been traumatic enough without reliving it? Because she was embarrassed? "I didn't realize it until I told Adam."

"Are you okay?" Annabelle looked genuinely concerned for Sue's wellbeing.

Sue gave her friend a small smile. "Yes."

"I'm a little shocked Adam didn't kick his ass." Annabelle's faith in Adam stung. It served as one more reminder of how much he gave and how ungrateful Sue had been.

Sue wrapped her arms around herself. "I asked him to leave it alone."

"Sue!"

She held out her hands. "It was a business decision. What happens when it gets around that my boyfriend roughs up my clients?"

Annabelle jammed the keys in the ignition. "You tell them the guy had it fucking coming!"

"He's your brother."

"Yeah. And I love him, but I have no problem pointing out when he's wrong. If someone did to me what Brad did to you, my brother would be first in line to rearrange their face."

"That's partly why it took me so long to figure it out."

"What is?" Annabelle pulled on her seatbelt and turned on the ignition.

"He protected me from creepy guys around the tour. I never thought…" Sue shook her head and sighed. "I never thought he would be one of those guys."

"Neither did he. He's mortified."

Sue put on her seatbelt as Annabelle pulled out of the parking lot. "How did it get out?"

"They were working on new songs, and Chris said the lyrics on one of them sounded rapey. Brad got defensive, so Chris read them out loud. The more they all agreed and pointed stuff out, the more Brad freaked."

"No."

"Yeah. Chris saying even *he* knew not to touch a woman unless she said yes finally put Brad over the edge."

Sue rubbed her temples. "Holy shit." She shifted in her seat toward Annabelle. "Is that when you all went radio silent for a few days? And Tom texted that I didn't have to come back?"

"Yeah. Tom feels guilty he made you stay when you had good reason to go."

"What a clusterfuck."

Annabelle laughed. "Yeah. Touring with these dickfaces usually is. But even I have to admit, this is a whole new level."

"How's everyone now?"

"Brad is mostly in self-imposed exile, probably writing maudlin poetry and burning it so Chris can't find it and make fun of him. Tom is angry. Justin feels betrayed by Brad and thinks he failed you."

"Whoa, whoa, whoa. There were failures all around. This isn't on him."

"You know Just."

"I wanted to put this all behind me, and now look at all the shit I have to untangle." Sue banged a fist against the door.

Annabelle glanced at Sue with a small smile. "They're grown men, Sue. Let them untangle their own shit. Besides, they don't want you to know they're fighting. That's why they went dark." Annabelle huffed. "It's the one thing they all agree on."

"Wait." Sue pinched the bridge of her nose, trying to contain her temper. They didn't want her to know. Again. Sue spent an evening in Milan hammering home the fact that if they couldn't be forthright with her, she should leave, and here they were, hiding more shit. Assholes. "They don't want me to know they're fighting. And the fight is over something that involves me?" Sue's voice rose as she spoke. "What the fuck?"

"They think they're protecting you."

"What in the ever-loving fuck?" Sue slammed her fist against her leg. "We're back to square fucking one! This whole thing happened because no one fucking told me the score, and now they're doing it *again?*" Sue choked back a scream. Where had she gone wrong? "What do I have to do to get this through their thick fucking heads?"

"In their defense, it was mostly Tom keeping it from you. He wanted to give you space to deal with your house."

Sue fisted her hands in her hair. "Tom should know better than everyone! I cover his ass with the label, I cover his ass in front of Rich, I cover every fucking nervous breakdown he has. The one fucking thing I ask him to do is communicate with me, and he shuts me out!"

"What do you mean you cover his ass with the label and Rich? Rich isn't in our band." Annabelle pulled the van to a stop at a traffic light and nudged Sue's leg. "What are you covering for?"

Sue slowly uncoiled her fingers from her hair. Of all the things to almost spill, she had to mention Tom and the record label. Shit. She shook her head, silently scolding herself. "They were assholes when we negotiated the deal with Noble Perversion. Tom was losing it, and I covered for him. You know he likes to keep that shit hidden."

Annabelle narrowed her eyes. "It had to be a shitty negotiation for him to get bad."

Sue waved it away. "We were talking finances with another band. It made him uncomfortable."

"That doesn't seem like the kind of thing to shake Tom."

Sue closed her eyes and dropped her head against the seat back. "Well, it did. And I covered for him and he repaid me by—"

"Giving you space to settle your personal business," Annabelle said. "He's not so deluded to think you wouldn't catch on when you got back."

"Yeah, well, hopefully I finally learned my lesson about living in denial."

"We all know you're too smart to make the same mistake twice."

"Am I, though?" Sue drummed her fingers against her leg. "Maybe I'm repeating the same patterns everywhere."

"I don't have perspective there, but it seems like after all the shit that's been thrown at you this tour, it would be pretty hard to keep up patterns."

Sue let the silence hang for a few minutes as she considered the mess waiting for her. "What about Chris and Darryl?"

"D's disappointed but dealing. Chris is stoked it's not his fuck up this time."

Sue laughed. "I'm sure if he gives it a minute, the tables'll turn."

"Right?"

"How about you? Are you okay? Do you want to leave?" Sue pushed her hair over her ears. "You don't have to stay to protect me."

Annabelle steered into the line of traffic entering the festival grounds and gave Sue a warm smile. "You don't have to worry about anyone but you." She held up a finger when Sue tried to protest. "I am disappointed in my brother and sad and worried for you. I don't want to leave, and I don't want you to be uncomfortable. We have goals for the rest of this tour, and I want us to crush them. And I suspect you need a break from your townhouse."

"Preach."

"When you need a break from the guys, tell me. I'll make space for you." Annabelle put the van in gear and moved forward with traffic. "And when you want to crack their heads, I'll help."

"It's okay to side with your brother," Sue said.

"Not when he's wrong."

Sue let Annabelle's words sink in. She'd been impressed with the much-teased sibling before, but the woman's integrity floored her. She was lucky to have Annabelle beside her in business, and as a friend. She sat in silence for a few more minutes before deciding to leave the drama behind. "How's Noble Perversion? They had three interviews while I was gone."

Annabelle grinned. "They're great. Rich is thrilled because one of the interviews got picked up and got them some radio attention."

"Nice work!" Sue beamed.

Annabelle grinned and drove through the festival gates. "You're okay?"

"Yeah." Sue thumbed through her phone, debating with herself about texting Adam. What would she say? She got here, she missed him, please don't give up on her? Afraid to be so blunt, she didn't send anything and locked her phone.

"Are you sure? You could've taken a few extra days. We can do this on the phone."

Sue shook her head. "I do better when I'm busy. I got things at home to a point where there isn't much to do but wait. I hate waiting. I need to get back into the thick of things."

CHAPTER 48

Budapest

Sue rubbed her eyes and closed her laptop, leaning her head on her arms. When she wasn't coordinating interviews, helping with the gear, or booking the next round of interviews, she slept. She slept a lot. Far more than she had before. She was still tired.

"Suse!" Chris shook her shoulder. "Some guy who smells like feta cheese is asking for you. He said he's supposed to take pictures of us tonight, but it's not on my schedule."

Sue looked up with a wry smile. "Not on your schedule?"

"Yeah. Bells yelled at me for being a slacker and put an app on my phone. Now I get alerts and shit about where I'm supposed to be. She even added a daily 'wash your dick' reminder." Chris rolled his eyes.

Sue snickered. "I should give her a raise." She stretched her arms over her head. "A guy is gonna take pictures during the show. I hope the show's on your schedule."

"Ha ha," Chris deadpanned. "You and Bells together is a bad idea. You encourage each other."

"We rock the girl power."Chris shivered. "Whatever."

"Before I forget, I got a text from Skylar. She said she tried to message you, but it failed."

Chris snapped to attention, then opened the refrigerator and dug around. "What'd she say?"

"To tell you thanks for the help, and the tests came back negative. You got her in touch with the father?"

"Hell no. The father's a piece of shit. I fronted her some money. The negative test results are good. I'll call her later."

"Can I ask what the test was for?"

Chris straightened but still looked in the refrigerator. "They thought the baby she's carrying might have Cystic Fibrosis."

"Whoa."

"Go give feta cheese guy his pass."

Sue stood and made her way to the front of the bus. "Remind me to have Annabelle put cultural sensitivity training in your schedule."

"What?" Chris slammed the refrigerator closed and gave Sue his attention. "We're not in Greece anymore. And that's what he smells like."

Sue stopped in the doorway. "One of your comments is gonna get us banned somewhere, and I'll have to come up with some kind of extra special PR magic to fix it. Even that might not work."

"Yeah, because PR magic is difficult for you." Chris shook his head. "You've already fixed some weird shit. You'll be fine."

Stunned by Chris's kind words, even with the side of sarcasm, Sue accepted the compliment. The rest of the guys might be walking on eggshells, but the person who'd had the most doubt handed her a ringing endorsement. It might've been her biggest professional win yet.

Sue checked her pocket for the extra press pass before heading to the backstage area. She stopped just inside the gates when her phone vibrated. Figuring the photographer was looking for his pass, Sue sighed, but her heart skipped a beat when she saw the message.

A: Gram got cleared for water aerobics. :) She and Mrs. T start next week

S: Yay! Can the gardener go with them?

A: He has to break his hip first

S: They'll have a reason to dote on him

A: Good point. Will refer him to Boston friends

S: Can I see you in Marseille?

A: Yes. No game that day though

S: I know. I miss you. I'll meet you at the Old Port

A: I can pick you up

S: I want to come to you

A: I'll be waiting

CHAPTER 49

Marseille, France

"Adam." Sue whispered his name in his ear as she wrapped her arms around him from behind.

His body leaned into hers before he turned and engulfed her in a hug.

"God, I missed you." She squeezed her arms tighter around him.

The ten days between Atlanta and the Old Port had felt like a lifetime.

Adam kissed her and held her close again. "I missed you, too."

Sue relaxed in his arms. Being with was him a much-needed balm. "This is my favorite place."

"Marseille? You've been here before?"

"No." Sue ran her hands up and down his arms, elated to finally touch him again. "Here." She kissed his chest. "Here."

Adam pressed his forehead to hers and sighed. "What's on the agenda today?" He pulled away enough to catch her eye. His expression was tentative, as though he held back his true reaction.

When Adam had joined her in Milan, she'd told him she didn't want anything between them. She'd meant it, but she'd let things stack up. If she had any chance of keeping this relationship, she needed to clear the air. She had no idea where to begin. Sue shook her head. "I don't know. I just missed you."

He studied her a moment, his face still wary. "Okay. We'll play it by ear." He guided her along the street, one arm still around her.

"I got you something." Sue handed him a small box.

"Gifts? You need more dates before you can give me gifts."

Sue gave a soft laugh. "I want all your dates."

Adam's expression brightened. "They're yours."

She put an arm around his waist, squeezing him against her. Knowing he still wanted her gave her a moment of security, even though she had things to tell him that might change his mind. "Open it."

Adam flipped open the lid with one hand, then let go of her to take one of the cufflinks from the box. They were square with handcrafted mother-of-pearl inlaid diagonal stripes.

"When I saw them, I thought of the tone-on-tone chevron vest you wear with your tuxedo. I asked the jeweler if he had that pattern, and he said it would have to be bigger. Didn't seem like your style, though."

"You're right. Thank you." Adam kissed her gently. "I'm surprised you remember that."

Sue ran her hand from his shoulder to his wrist, enjoying that she could touch him, needing it after they'd spent so much time apart. "I remember everything about you."

Finally, his face was open and unguarded. It did more to calm her than anything that had happened since the moment he'd appeared in her burned townhouse a few weeks before. She sunk into his arms, happy to have a moment together before she unleashed what she'd been holding back.

Adam rubbed his knuckles along her spine, his touch loosening her nerves even further. "I'm going to have to take you to another black-tie event soon."

"Not too soon. The studs aren't ready yet. He's sending them to your place. Though if you wear a Windsor, it'll be fine."

"I'll wear whatever you want."

She giggled and stepped back. A child running down the lane had bumped them and reminded her they were on a busy walkway.

Adam nudged her forward, weaving his fingers with hers.

"How was Atlanta?" she asked.

"Pretty good. I got so much done, I may wind up with most of September free."

"Nice! The mystery project is all wrapped up?"

"The mystery project is ready to launch." Adam smiled.

"Congratulations." Sue leaned up to give him a peck on the cheek.

He turned his head and took her lips. "Thank you."

"Tell me all about it."

"Sure, but first, how's your place?"

"Kind of a mess."

"What do you mean?" Adam stopped and faced her. "Last time we talked, they were done with the fire stuff and rebuilding everything."

Sue tugged his hand and resumed their walk. "When I remodeled, it was with the intention of having two spaces so I could sell or rent part of it."

"I remember."

"I never filed the paperwork to reclassify the unit from one to two." Sue ran her free hand through her hair, embarrassed to admit her oversight. "I was happy the core of the remodel was done. I wasn't ready to make any moves, so I didn't even ask Emily what the first step might be."

Adam squeezed her hand. "I can appreciate taking time to enjoy the peace and quiet."

"It was a bad move."

"Your insurance claims were denied?"

"Not the main ones. The roof is fixed, the floors, the windows, drywall, even the balcony."

"But?"

Sue sighed. "They aren't putting back the kitchenette upstairs or the double doors on the first floor."

"That's not too bad. We can get new doors."

Sue took a moment before she responded. She appreciated his willingness to do this with her, but she made a mistake and she had to fix it. She had a lot to fix. "It'll be expensive."

"I know you want to do this on your own, but if you need help—"

"See, this is where it gets hairy." Sue looked around and pointed at a bench. "Let's sit, and I'll explain."

"What's hairy about it? Did you find out the property is a historic site or something?"

Sue sat and waited for him to join her. "Nothing like that."

Adam stared at her.

Sue rubbed her forehead. "I did a lot of stuff while you were in Atlanta."

"Usually that'd pique my interest, but you look like you're in pain."

Sue grabbed his hand and pulled it into her lap. "This is about money and business. Not us. You may not like the decisions I made, and it might hurt us. But I told you our relationship is important to me, and I protect it. I always mean to protect it."

"Okay." He studied her again, his eyes softening after a moment. "Tell me everything,"

Sue looked out at the boats, gathering her nerves. "I can afford to make it two spaces again and file the paperwork and even make upstairs an official apartment. I think I can do it all and still keep Annabelle, Nora, and Stacy on my payroll. Though if I can't, Axel said he has the budget to take Nora and Stacy. I'll hustle my ass off to keep Annabelle."

"That's excellent." Adam wrapped an arm around her shoulders. "It's not easy to save money when you're on the road all the time."

Sue leaned into him, taking comfort in his arms while she could. "I can afford it because I saved most of the money Words Fail Me has paid me, in case Tom got fired."

Adam furrowed his brow. "Why would Tom get fired?"

Sue pointed at herself.

"Because of what happened with Brad?"

"No." Sue looked to the sky, then sat sideways to face Adam. "No one but Tom, Emily, and Amy know what I'm about to tell you, and it *has* to stay that way. For Tom's sake."

"I would never betray your confidence."

Sue gave a wobbly laugh. "I know. But Tom doesn't know I'm telling you this. It stays between us."

"Of course." Adam squeezed her hands.

"There was a clause in my contract. If I didn't achieve certain goals the record label set, the band had to pay back my salary. If they couldn't, they'd forfeit their next album."

"That doesn't sound like something you'd agree to. Why is it in the contract?" His voice was gentle when he asked. His face didn't hold judgement, but curiosity.

"Tom told me they'd agreed."

"But they didn't."

Sue choked back a sob. "They don't even know. He hid it from them. He said he had the money to pay out the contract. We had inheritances from our grandmother. He says he never spent his." Her eyes welled with tears, but she kept talking, faster now to make sure she got it all out before she lost her nerve. "But if he paid back my salary, he'd be destitute, and if the guys found out, he could get fired. Who would hire him after that?"

"So, you saved all the money to give it back."

Sue nodded and pressed her fingers against her eyes to keep the tears at bay. She hated telling Adam this terrible thing about an important person in her life. Even more, she feared that he would see her differently, would think her weak and unworthy of him.

"Babe." Adam pulled her into his arms. "Of course you did. And then your house caught fire and you left the tour, and now everyone's asses are on the line."

She clung to him, not sure why he was supportive of her living a massive lie, but grateful for his comfort. "I fulfilled the requirements when they got on *The Tonight Show*. I got the video to go viral, and their sales went through the roof."

Adam laughed and rubbed long circles down her back. "Why are you crying? You came out on top."

"Because I let my cousin do this awful thing, and I've been covering for him ever since." Sue sat up to look him in the eye. If he was going to judge her, he needed to do it now and put her out of her misery. She decided to lay it all on the line. "Adam, I've been living with this lie, and I don't know how to get out of it without destroying Tom's career. I hate lying. I hate that I hid it from you. I hate that I'm hiding it from the band. I *hate* it. It's almost come out a few times. How much longer will it stay a secret?"

Adam's expression softened. "I don't know, babe."

"I've been keeping it from you all this time. I'm sorry."

"It wasn't only your secret to tell."

"That's not the reaction I was expecting," Sue said.

"What were you expecting?"

"Anger." Sue looked toward the water. "Judgement."

"If I'm judging anyone, it's Tom. I'm surprised he'd take such a big risk without letting the band know what was on the line. Did they have to sign your contract?"

"Brad did as the representative member."

Adam grunted. "Not surprised."

"It wasn't like that." Sue bristled at the accusation.

"No, but if he'd bothered to read the contract instead of chasing you, maybe you wouldn't be beating yourself up right now."

Adam was right. Brad had a history of turning a blind eye to important details, but it didn't absolve her. "I should've made sure he read it."

"No. Tom's the manager. They hand off a lot of these decisions to him. It's shitty he didn't tell them this, but not unusual."

"You don't think I'm doing something wrong by keeping his secret?"

"You didn't lie in the first place. And you held up your end of the contract."

"I was unethical." Sue pressed on, waiting for the judgement she was sure Adam held. She judged herself every day that she kept this secret.

Adam took an agonizing moment before he spoke again. "If Chris asked you about this clause, would you lie?"

"No."

"Then you're fine. Tom is the one who has to face the fire."

"Tom has a lot of integrity. This was...out of character for him. I know he trusts me, but I still don't understand why he was willing to do it." Sue drug the back of her hand across her nose and pushed her hair over her ears. Tom had risked his reputation for her, and what for? What if she hadn't been able to get Words Fail Me on *The Tonight Show?* Or she hadn't been able to bury the smear job about Chris from *Sound Spectrum?* She'd made this work through sheer determination and a few strokes of luck. So many things could've gone wrong and put Tom out on his ass and it would've been her fault.

"He believes in you. Kinda weird he wasn't willing to have the fight in the first place, though."

Sue narrowed her eyes. Adam had a point. She always thought she and Tom fought for each other, and while having the money set aside showed he clearly had the band's back, he hadn't done much fighting for *her.* Why? She stayed true to their relationship while Tom seemed to take the path of least resistance. He must've had some doubts in her ability. Why else would he bury the clause? She'd have to consider it later. She put it aside and braced herself for the next round of revelations. She looked Adam in the eye. "It's about to get worse."

"Doubtful."

"This is why I can't move in with you. All my money is tied up. If I leave the townhouse as-is, I won't get my investment back. If I spend the money to make it two units, I wind up cash poor. If I fuck up my business, I wind up poor poor."

"Sue."

"Don't '*Sue*' me. We're partners. I can't put the financial burden on you."

"It's not a burden."

"Not for you. It's important to me to be able to support myself."

"I understand. What you're missing is partners share the burden, but they also carry different parts of it. Let me carry the money for now."

"Adam, it could be years before I can contribute equally. I don't want to saddle you with anything."

"You don't."

"I make you follow me all over the world and I spend your money, and now I'm supposed to just let you support me like a wh—"

"Do not. Finish. That. Sentence." Adam clenched his jaw, and the muscles near his neck throbbed.

She shrunk back.

"Do you really think so little of yourself? Of me? That our relationship is a...transaction to me?"

"No," Sue whispered.

"Then why'd you say it?"

"Because I want to give you everything."

"You just gave me your biggest secret. You give me your time. You give me love. How is that not everything?" Adam slid away from her, balling his hands into fists. "Because I can't pay the fucking mortgage with it? Guess what? I don't have a mortgage." He stood and paced away from her, weaving through the people walking along the path.

She followed, desperate to keep him close, to try to explain herself so he wouldn't be upset and would stay. She tripped on her feet when he turned to face her.

He grabbed her, preventing her fall, and forced her to make eye contact with him. "I don't want to live with you because I'm rescuing you, or to have sex on demand, or any reason other than the best moments of my life include you. Even when you have me so pissed I want to spit nails."

Her mouth dropped open, but a quick inventory of her own life brought her to the same conclusion. They hadn't known each other long, but each victory she'd shared with him had been sweeter, and the hardships more bearable. "I'm sorry."

"You have nothing to be sorry for. Unless you're sorry we're together."

Sue gasped, his words stabbing her heart. "Never."

Adam pulled her into a hug.

She clung to him, distraught not only that he doubted her feelings, but that she had given him reason to. "I love you, Adam."

He held her for another moment, tightened his hold, then let her go. He put an arm around her shoulders and resumed their walk. "Why do you love me?"

"Because you're kind and smart. You make me laugh and I feel safe with you," she said without hesitation. She snaked her arm around his waist and got closer to him as they walked, looking up for his reaction.

"How much does all that cost?"

Sue recoiled.

"Pretty fucking disgusting, huh?"

It wasn't what Adam said that hurt, but that she'd driven him to say it.

He pulled her into his arms. "I'm sorry," he whispered over and over into her hair.

Her face buried in his chest, she finally let the tears flow. "It's not you, it's me."

After a few minutes he wiped the tears from her face and kissed her forehead. "Come on, let's go watch some music."

"What?" His request threw her off kilter.

"We need some air from this conversation, and music is your zen space. Let's go do that."

As he looked for the train going to the festival town, Sue questioned him again. "This is taking you way out of the way for your game tomorrow. We can find something in Marseille."

"I'll be fine."

"Adam."

He bought the tickets and faced her. "I need music. Let's go."

She got on the train with him. When they arrived at the festival, she got him through security and took him to the stage where a band she knew he liked was mid-set. When it ended, they sought out food and sat together in a quiet backstage area. Adam talked about the show they'd watched, but the way he spoke was unusual for him.

"You didn't get to a zen state, did you?" she asked.

Adam shook his head. "Did you?"

"No," she whispered.

Adam put down his food and caught her eyes. "You don't want this, do you?"

If she hadn't been sitting when he said those words, she would have fallen. The damage she'd done was unfathomable. "Adam, all I want is you."

"Then have me."

She wanted to have him forever. "I don't know how to do that. Show me."

Adam wrapped himself around her and held her as people moved in and out of the area, the space coming into use as a show on another stage ended.

Finally, he kissed her gently. "I love you."

"I love you," she answered.

"I have to go."

Sue looked at his watch. "It's almost three hours until the next train."

"I know." He gently let her go and gathered the remains of their food, stacking it all together and not looking at her.

"I'll come with you and wait."

"No." His firm voice startled her.

"Why?"

"Sue, I'm desperate. If I don't go now, I will spend the rest of the night persuading you to give me what I want. That's not fair to either of us."

"What do you want?"

"A home with you. No strings attached. Just you." Adam kissed her again. "I love you."

CHAPTER 50

Madrid, Spain

"Holy shit," Sue breathed as she read an email from Emily. She tilted her phone sideways and pushed her fingers across the screen to enlarge the words.

"What's up?" Tom dropped into the chair next to her and splayed his legs.

"I can't read this contract on my phone. Do you have your tablet?" Sue glanced around, barely taking in the huge cafeteria-style room she sat in, her eyebrows furrowed.

Tom gave her his folio.

She flipped it open to find a legal pad full of notes on one side and his iPad on the other. "Still writing everything by hand first, Tommy?"

"It's how I remember shit. It's science. Remember?"

Sue crinkled her eyes. "Yeah. If only Chris would accept that." She brought the iPad to life, opened a browser and logged into her email. "That's…fuck." Sue passed Tom the folio. "Here. I can't be reading it right."

"What is it?"

"An offer on my place."

Tom let out a low whistle. "Is this what you paid for it?"

"It's a little more than I paid." Sue widened her eyes and shook her head. Not only would she get her investment back, the extra money would give her the cushion she needed to secure the moves she'd made in her business.

"No shit." Tom grinned. "They want to close in ten days. Can they do that?""It's a cash offer." Sue fisted her hair. "Holy shit, a cash offer!"

Tom's grin grew. "We'll be stateside in plenty of time to get your stuff out. I'll help you."

"My stuff's already out." Sue jumped up and paced. After her day with Adam, she'd pulled the trigger and asked Emily to file permits to change the dwelling and bring in contractors to do the necessary work. She'd been deter-mined to restore the property to its most valuable point. "Holy shit, Tom. What do I do? I have crews scheduled to work in there. What do I do?"

Tom read through the contract. "They want the place as-is. Cancel it all. Pay the cancellation fees. Will the over-age cover it?"

"Oh my God." Sue took her seat again, staring at her cousin. "I'll be homeless."

"Accept the offer. You can stay with me until you find a new place." Tom pushed a hand through his hair. "Ann

Arbor is closer to Cleveland than Hagerstown is. You can bounce between us and Bloody Maggots."

"What?" Sue was genuinely confused. "How do you know that?"

"I used to date a woman in Cleveland. It's three hours. You can day trip it. Why do you live in Hagerstown, anyway? It's shit for music."

"You move up faster at a small radio station."

"Better contacts, though."

"I did pretty good getting contacts in Hagerstown." Tom nodded. "Do you accept?"

Sue took the iPad and read the offer two more times. The details were simple; she only had to say yes or no. She pulled out her phone and texted Emily.

> **S: This offer is legit?**

Emily's response was almost immediate.

> **E: Yep. It's a family held company that's been working the Pittsburgh-Baltimore corridor for 30 yrs**
> **S: I should take it**
> **E: Yes**

Sue sat, gave Tom all the devices, buried her head in her hands, and cried. She'd known this time would come, and she still wasn't ready for it. She should've listed the townhouse when she first joined the tour. She'd known it then, but she liked the idea of having a place to come back to. Now, with all the offers she'd gotten from friends and family since the fire, she knew she had more places than she'd ever considered. The clarity made her grateful for the people in her life. And if she was being totally honest, she felt bitchy for taking them all for granted.

The townhouse was always supposed to be an investment, not a long-term residence. If she let it go now, it would give her some freedom. One question remained. What would she do with the freedom? She sobbed even more.

"Whoa." Tom lurched back in his seat. "What's this about?"

Between sobs, Sue said, "I accept."

Tom laughed and patted her back. "Congratulations!"

Sue cried harder and Tom laughed harder.

"Bells sent us back so Brad could finish the interview solo." Darryl walked into the room, followed by Justin. "Uh, guys? Everything okay in here?"

"Yeah." Tom patted Sue's back again. "She's happy."

Sue wiped her face. "Incredibly happy." And terrified, but they didn't need to know that. Sobs overtook her again, and she covered her eyes.

"Those are happy tears?" Justin asked.

"Don't ask me," Darryl said. "I'm new to the concept."

"Tom, does she cry like this whenever she's happy?" Justin asked.

"I don't know. I mean, I've seen her happy cry before, but this is…I don't know. An epic happy cry?"

Sue looked up, her sobbing under control but the flow of tears still steady. "I don't know."

With a gleam in his eye, Darryl said, "Do you think she cried like this the first time Adam showed her his dick?"

Sue let out a surprised squeak and wiped her face. "What?"

Justin mirrored his friend's expression. "Like, oh-my-God-that-dick-is-so-amazing-I'm-crying-with-joy?"

"Yes!" Darryl bounced on his toes. "How awesome would that be?"

"I can tell you, my friend." Justin put a hand on Darryl's shoulder. "It happens to me all the time."

D crossed his arms. "I can see that about you."

Sue pursed her lips, fighting the urge to laugh at their act.

"Women cry when I get naked, too." Tom shrugged. "I figured I'm so pale it burned their eyes. Now I know."

"You guys are the worst." Sue wiped her eyes with the sleeve of her shirt.

"Dick power," Darryl said.

Tom adjusted himself. "Yep."

"Oh my God! Stop!" Sue held out her hands and sniffled. "I don't want to know!"

"We've intimidated her." Justin shook his head. "Dick power is a responsibility we shouldn't take lightly, gentlemen."

"Gimme the iPad, Tom." Sue wiped her face again, finally able to regain control. "I have to sell my house and call Emily. I need a break from dicks."

Portugal

"Amy Ragnar! Where are you?" Sue shook a plastic barrel as she entered Jack and Amy's luxury bus. "I have cheese balls and I'm ready to grovel!"

"Did I hear cheese balls?" Amy popped her head out of the bedroom at the back.

"You did. I figured they would make my apology easier to swallow." Sue held the barrel out to her friend.

Amy accepted it, sat on a small, leather couch, and unscrewed the lid. "Apology for what?"

"You crossed an ocean to help me and I was an ungrateful bitch." Sue buried her hands in her pockets. She tried to mentally push away her self-consciousness. "I am so, so sorry."

"I should've asked before I flew out." Amy popped some cheese balls into her mouth and patted the couch next to her.

"No. You were amazing, and I was awful. I'm sorry."

"Stop saying sorry. We're good." Amy tipped the barrel toward Sue. "We've always been good."

Sue gave her friend a genuine smile and took a handful of the snack. "How's it been? Are you writing?"

"Turns out I'm pretty good at travel adventures." Amy grinned. "Good at writing them, that is. Jack would have to tell you if I'm good at experiencing them." Amy pulled her phone out of her pocket. "Robin's on his way. He has the passes for tonight's party. You guys are coming, right?"

"Wouldn't miss it."

"Robin wants to prank Words Fail Me since it's their last show on the circuit."

"No," Sue said. "Noble Perversion should prank them, not Robin!"

Amy scooped out more cheese balls. "It's Robin. Threaten to cut up your leather pants and he'll stop."

Sue blanched. She'd never hurt those pants.

"Ames! Why didn't you answer my text? I need you to get me Sue's pass!" Robin's voice echoed through the bus before he boarded it. When he did and his eyes landed on Sue, he grinned. "And now I know why." Robin plucked Sue off the couch and spun her around in a hug. "Glad you made it back in one piece, Sex-ay."

Sue squeezed her friend. "Thanks. Me, too."

Robin put Sue down but kept his hands on her shoulders. "Are you moving back into the townhouse? I need to make you another sculpture."

"One phallus per townhouse is plenty, Robin." Amy threw a cheese ball at Robin's head.

Robin snorted. "Maybe for a convent."

Sue snickered and sat. "Those are nuns I'd like to meet."

Robin nodded at the barrel. "Bring them some balls. They'll love it. Seriously, though." Robin ruffled her hair. "Where are you going tomorrow?"

"The more important question is why do you need my pass?"

Robin took a handful of cheese balls and mashed them into his mouth. He didn't finish chewing before he spoke. "To kidnap you for our show and after party, obviously."

Sue raised her eyebrows. "And?"

Robin narrowed his eyes at Amy. "You told her."

"What is she gonna tell me, Robin, that I wouldn't already be able to figure out after ten years with you?"

"You've been with *me* almost ten years, but Amy's been with you way longer. You two probably did some weird mind meld Venn shit before you even got on the bus and you're covering her ass."

Amy shook the snack barrel. "We didn't mind meld this morning. We haven't in a while."

"Nope. Not since New Orleans. And booze and abs were involved.""And Nomads. Yum." Amy popped a cheese ball into her mouth.

"Shut the fuck up. You both have men." Robin took the barrel from Amy and balanced it on his head. "Now help me with my plans today or no more balls!"

"Height is an unfair advantage, Robin!" Amy climbed onto the couch and tried to grab the food, but Robin moved away from her, perfectly balanced.

"I have to use every advantage I have with you two."

"Gimme back my balls!" Amy climbed on Robin's back as he lifted the barrel out of her reach with his long arms.

Robin grinned and dangled the barrel over Sue's head. "You're gonna be covered in balls if you don't give me your pass, woman."

"No! She'll crush my balls to spite you!" Still on Robin's back, Amy waved one of her arms toward the food.

"I would never crush your balls, Amy. Even if Robin did taint them." She crossed her arms and squinted at Robin. "I might crush yours, though."

"Never!" Robin positioned Amy over the couch and nudged her off his back. He gave her the barrel. "Go ahead, put some balls in your mouth."

Sue snickered, then shrieked when Robin picked her up and tossed her over his shoulder.

"I will find your pass!" He patted all over her body until he found the small placard tucked into the back of her shirt. "Got it!" He traced it back up to the lanyard around her neck and pulled it out of her shirt as he put her down.

"Robin! I need that!"

"I know, relax." Robin rifled in a box under the couch Amy sat on and pulled out a pair of men's underwear. He clipped the briefs to Sue's lanyard behind her pass and draped the whole thing around her neck.

"What is this? Why are you putting your underwear on my pass?"

Robin laughed. "It's not my underwear. It's yours. Now you have something to hold your balls." He took some from Amy and shoved them in the underwear, snickering as some fell through the leg holes.

"You're insane." Sue pulled the pass away from herself and looked at the Jockey shorts. "You printed your party invitation on underwear? Where your junk is supposed to go?"

"Hell yes." Robin grinned. "And the bouncers won't let you in unless you have the all-access pass *and* the nut huggers."

"Do those grandpa underpants count as nut huggers?" Amy stood and inspected the underwear dangling from Sue's lanyard. "I thought speedos were nut huggers."

"Yeah. I'm broadening the definition for today." Robin crouched down and pulled a pair of bright yellow bikini briefs out of the box. "These are for Adam." He tossed them at Sue, narrowly missing her head.

Sue recovered the briefs and tossed them back to Robin. "He's not here. Save them for that German porn star you like. He's roaming the grounds."

Robin stood and put his hands on his hips. "Where is he?"

"Last I heard, Zenza was at the meet-and-greet tent waiting for Caceres." Sue smirked as she wondered whether Carlo would recognize the actor and how he would react if he did.

"No." Robin threw a cheese ball at Sue's forehead. "Where's Adam?"

Amy leaned forward. "I would yell at you for wasting my balls, but I want to know where Adam is, too."

"He's in Boston. He's doing a big thing with the Red Sox."

"Bullshit." Robin threw another cheese ball.

"Stop hitting me with your balls!" Sue recovered some of them from the floor and threw them back at Robin. She didn't know how to explain that Adam was upset with her and she didn't know how to fix it.

"Sue, Adam's been around all summer and rearranged everything to help you with the fire." Amy stood and leaned against Robin. "Why isn't he here now?"

Sue held out her hands. "He rearranged everything for me. Now he has to make up for it. He may be the boss, but he still has shit to do."

Robin and Amy stared at Sue.

"What?"

Robin scratched his head. "Are you sure?"

"Yes."

"He didn't leave when you kicked everyone out, did he?" Amy asked.

"No! Of course not!" Even though Sue didn't want to talk about the weird place she and Adam had gotten to, she also didn't want her friends doubting that he was anything but supportive. "We talked about it before we left Hagerstown. He's about to launch a big project."

"Really?" Robin asked.

"Yes. We were together in Marseille the other day."

Robin scooped up some cheese balls. "Okay. I know you fight through your problems. I was gonna go rip him a new one if he ran away."

Sue crossed her arms. "He didn't run away." She peered out the window, mentally biting her tongue so she wouldn't admit she'd pushed Adam away.

"But you're not happy that he's in Boston," Amy said. "What's up?"

Sue shook her head. "Nothing."

"Tell us or I'm calling him," Robin said.

"He wouldn't tell you, Robin."

Amy hopped to her feet. "Something *is* up!"

"Shit." Sue squeezed her forehead. "I'm off my game."

"Tell us," Robin said. "We can help."

Sue rolled her eyes. "Fine." She put her hands on her hips to brace herself. "He's upset because I told him I couldn't afford to move in with him."

Amy looked at Robin.

Robin scratched his head.

"I know, I know. It's stupid," Sue said. "He got me to understand."

"Why is he still upset?" Amy asked. "You're moving in with him, right?"

Sue winced. "I haven't said yes yet."

"Jesus, Sue, how can such a smart woman be so fucking stupid?" Robin asked.

Robin's words stung, yet she needed to know why he'd said them. "I thought you'd say stubborn."

"No. You were stupid." Robin mirrored her posture. "Is he just a cock and a bank account to you?"

"Oh my God! No!" Sue reared back and gripped her arms. "How could you say that?"

"Because you basically told him all you had to offer was your snatch, which is complete fucking bullshit—"

"I know!" Sue shouted.

"So the other option is you only keep Adam around for sex."

Sue sank into the couch and buried her face in her hands. "Oh God, no."

Amy sat next to Sue and nudged her. "If you don't want the same things Adam does, it's okay. But don't push him away over money. You, of all people, can *always* make more money."

Sue blinked rapidly to fight back tears. How had she missed this? No wonder Adam thought she didn't want him. All this time she'd been focused on how to be a partner to him and completely missed that in his eyes, she'd devalued him. Why did Adam even continue to talk to her?

"I don't know how to fix this," Sue whispered.

"You need to talk to him," Amy said.

"Soon." Robin sat on Sue's other side.

Sue looked at each of her friends in turn, still clueless about her next move but grateful they were there for her even when she was so fucking stupid. "Thanks, guys."

Robin leaned in as if to hug Sue and shoved cheese balls in the neck of her shirt. "Chicks like balls on their tits, right?"

"Seriously, Robin?" Amy asked. "Right now?"

Sue wanted to glare at Robin but laughed instead, grateful he was giving her room to process. "Depends on the chick."

Robin pulled Sue into a tight hug.

"Ugh, you're crushing my balls!"

Robin held Sue against him. "You were right, Ames, she is a ball crusher!"

"Robin!" Sue tried to push him away.

"Shut up and enjoy it, Sue." Robin pushed Sue toward Amy and took the box from under the couch. "I gotta go get the invitations to your band."

"I can take them. Won't be the first time I walked across festival grounds carrying underwear."

Robin laughed. "I bet. You hang out. I got this."

CHAPTER 51

Atlanta, GA

Sue, Annabelle, Tom, and the members of Words Fail Me grunted when the plane touched down. The landing wasn't particularly rough, but they all nursed hangovers from Robin's party. In fact, Sue wasn't sure she'd been entirely sober when she got on the plane in Portugal. Thankfully, Tom forced sports drinks into them all before the flight. Chris threw up in an airport bathroom right before they boarded, but they all managed to hold it together as they crossed the Atlantic.

Between the sun streaming through the windows and the noise people made as they prepared to get off the plane, Sue and her companions kept a low profile with sunglasses and earbuds all around.

Sue momentarily lost her balance when the jetway leading back to the terminal wobbled.

Tom moaned behind her. "I don't think I'm gonna make it."

Sue looked back as her cousin turn a shade of green she hadn't seen on him before. She put a hand on her stomach. "No sympathy puking today." She rifled in her backpack, and pulled out Robin's underwear party invitation, and shook her head, then held it as pain surged.

Annabelle pushed Sue to the side of the walkway and helped her dig through her carry-on as people passed them. Sue came up with the plastic bag she used for her toiletries. She emptied it into Annabelle's hands and gave the bag to Tom.

"Thanks." He belched and covered his mouth.

Sue grimaced as she and Annabelle shoved her makeup and deodorant back into her overstuffed pack.

"Let's see how close to the bathroom we can get you." Chris gripped Tom's elbow and steered him through the jetway.

"Will they make it?" Sue asked Justin.

"Dunno. I'm impressed it took him this long to finally feel nauseous."

Brad stalked along the jetway, head down, one hand gripping the backpack over his shoulders and the other rubbing his temple. "D, shut the fuck up. Let me have some coffee first."

"Too fucking bad you were asleep when the flight attendant hooked me up!" Darryl practically bounced past Brad. "You guys think they need you holding up the walls of this tunnel?" he asked Justin and Sue. "Come on, we still have to get through Customs."

Sue corrected her posture and followed Darryl. Annabelle, Justin and Brad were behind her.

After they cleared Customs, Darryl checked the flight schedules on a nearby monitor, then addressed Sue. "Get yourself a candy bar. And some water. Lots of water before the next flight."

"Aye aye, captain." Sue saluted.

"I've never seen you full-on drunk, Suse. I wanna make sure you're okay."

Sue pushed her sunglasses up her head and gave him a tired smile. "I'm good. Thanks, D."

"Are you sure? I don't want to fly to Austin with you in bad shape."

"I'm getting better every minute. Go. Tell Lena hi for me."

Darryl nodded. "Bells, wanna walk with me to my next gate?"

"I need to walk like I need another shot of tequila." Annabelle sighed. "But yeah. I'll go with you. It's that or risk sympathy puking when Tom turns up all pasty and gross."

Darryl hugged Sue. "Thank you for knocking it out of the park on this tour."

Sue patted his back. "Darryl—"

"And thank you for Lena. It isn't enough. But thank you." He squeezed Sue and stepped back. "Don't puke on the next plane, chuckleheads!"

"Fuck you, too, D!" Brad shouted at his friend's back.

Justin smacked Brad in the chest with the back of his hand. "People can hear you, man."

Brad shrugged. "Safe home, D!"

"Later, Darryl." Justin grinned. "Hug Lena for me."

Darryl waved and flashed a thumbs up as he continued down the terminal, Annabelle shuffling beside him.

"I'm gonna buy some overpriced coffee. You guys want some?" Brad asked.

"Can you get me orange juice?" Sue dug through her pockets and produced boarding passes, her driver's license, and her passport. "Shit." She pulled her backpack around.

Brad held up a hand. "I can swing airport OJ."

"Thanks."

"Want a shot of vodka in it?" Brad grinned.

Sue made a sick face. "No vodka. Not for a while."

"What about you, Just?"

"Coffee." Justin held his hands far apart. "A super big coffee."

"You got it." Brad headed toward the coffee sign.

"At least our gate is nearby." Sue gestured at the screen announcing the on-time status of their flight to Ann Arbor.

"Small miracles." Justin gestured for Sue to walk ahead of him. "My faculties are returning and we're alone, so you have to tell me—how exactly did Robin manage to hang half a dozen pairs of underwear across our stage and in the middle of the show?"

Sue chuckled. "I swear I don't know. The last time I saw him before the party he said he was on his way to deliver them. That was a good hour before the show. He pinned mine to my pass. I figured he'd do that to you guys."

"That guy has some kind of magic."

Sue made her eyes big. "I know, right? I'm still trying to figure out how much it cost him to have party invitations printed on the codpieces of two hundred pairs of underwear."

"Magic." Justin dropped his carry-on bag onto a chair and slumped into the one next to it.

Sue sat in the next free seat and put her pack on the floor in front of her, resting her feet on it.

"You can tell me to shut the fuck up if you want, but I figure after all those hours in your car, I've earned the right to be a little nosey."

Sue leaned her head against the back of her seat. "You've been through my entire music collection, Just. There are no secrets between us."

"Sweet." Justin mirrored her posture. "Why are you flying to Ann Arbor with us instead of going to Boston?"

"Ugh." Sue rubbed her temples. "I hope you're into foreplay when you get laid, because holy rough start."

Justin grunted. "It's only a matter of time before they all find us. And I can keep a secret."

Sue sighed. "I know you can." She pulled her feet off her bag and sat forward, rubbing her eyes. She glanced back at Justin. "I fucked up."

Justin sat up and frowned.

"I'm such a jerk." Sue twisted in her seat to face him. "He saved me. Adam got me back to Maryland when I was so shocked, I couldn't find my own ass with both hands. Then he followed me. I'd convinced myself he wouldn't because of work and me being stupid. He was like a sexy white knight breaking through police tape and fire hoses and lingering smoke. And I fumbled it. Big time."

Justin squeezed her shoulder. "It couldn't have been that bad."

Sue barked a laugh. "Right." She drew out the word. "Tom called my parents. They left their vacation to help me. Their flight landed a few minutes after mine. Instead of being happy they were there, I was disappointed they weren't Adam. I was ashamed. What kind of asshole is like 'oh, hey, Mom and Dad, thanks for leaving your vacation to take care of me, but you're not who I want right now?'" She buried her head in her hands.

"Sue." Justin shook her arm. "That's a reasonable reaction from anyone in a healthy relationship."

She laughed. "Yes, because I know *all* about healthy relationships."

"Suse."

She shook her head. "It gets worse. I didn't know everyone was running to my side. And I was so fucking stupid. Instead of introducing him to my parents as my boyfriend and finding a quiet moment to tell him he's better than anything I've ever wanted in a man, I barely touched him until my parents left, and then I fucked him in the backseat of my car."

Justin sat in stunned silence for a moment. "You what?"

"I know. It was all my idea. I dragged him to the car, pulled him into the backseat, and fucked him hard and fast."

Justin gaped. "That is the greatest and the worst thing I've ever heard."

Sue didn't hide her confusion.

Justin sat up straight. "What car guy—hell, what *guy*—doesn't want the person he's hot for to pull him into the backseat and do dirty things to him? It's Grade A spank bank material." Justin kissed his fingers. "But damn, Sue. You didn't tell your parents you're dating? He loves you. If you don't love him, you have to tell him."

Sue shook her head. "I do love him. I love him more than anyone."

Brad tapped Sue's shoulder with a bottle of juice. "So why are you here with us?"

She froze for a second before she took the bottle. She looked up at Brad, worried over what she would find.

He passed Justin a large cup of coffee. "Well?"

Sue gave herself another moment to recover from both Brad's silent arrival and his curious expression before she decided to answer honestly. "I don't know how to be with someone. I always wind up making them leave."

Brad dropped his backpack next to Sue's and sat across from her, slumping in the seat. "I find that hard to believe."

"It's true." Sue unscrewed the lid from the juice bottle. "Either we stopped communicating or they flat out left me. The last one was the worst."

"What happened?" Justin asked.

"I bought the townhouse." Sue sipped her drink. "I was so focused on buying a house and doing it by myself. He toured properties with me a few times and made suggestions. I didn't even acknowledge them. He wanted to move in together, and I avoided any conversation about it. I was selfish and cold. He was a nice guy. He treated me well. But I didn't care enough. He even said the words 'you don't care about me enough.' He was right." Sue bowed her head and pushed her fingers between her eyes, letting sadness roll through her. She finally cared enough, and she had no idea how to show it. Regret and grief almost overwhelmed her. She wasn't a cruel person, and yet it seemed to be her default setting in her romantic relationships.

Brad nudged her foot with his own until Sue looked at him. "You think you don't love Adam enough?"

Sue shrugged.

"Suse, you light up the room wherever you go. But when Adam shows up? You're off the charts. You aren't capable of having a conversation with him without being right by his side. Most of the time you have to touch him to talk. You answer his texts before he's done typing them."

Stunned, Sue said, "You said you hadn't paid attention."

"Hindsight." Brad took a long drink. "You never ask us for help with anything. Even when you got stuck a hundred feet in the air on a light rig, you figured it out. But you hired Annabelle so you could spend more time with Adam."

"I needed her help for more than that," Sue said.

Justin barked a laugh. "If we've learned anything about you over the last few months, it's that you would've found a way to make it work without Bells."

Brad nodded. "But Adam made you want to have a life." He sipped his coffee. "I was a supreme asshole. And when I stepped *way* out of line, you stood up for yourself. But you stood up for Adam, too." Brad tilted his head. "You think that isn't enough?"

Sue stared at the bottle, picking at the label as she lifted and dropped one shoulder. "What if it isn't?"

"There is nothing about you that isn't enough."

"Brad," Justin warned.

Sue glanced up at the tone in Justin's voice.

Brad held up his hands. "I'm not speaking as the selfish, deluded douche who almost fucked up the whole tour. I'm saying this as a friend, I hope. The guy who left you over your place? He might've been nice, but if *he* had cared enough for *you*, you would've given each other what you both needed, and you guys might still be together. You and Adam care enough about each other. If you didn't, you wouldn't have spent the last few weeks in a fog of misery."

Sue looked back and forth between her friends, speechless. She closed her eyes to fight off tears.

"From where I'm standing," Brad said, "the only thing left is to go to him. I'd love to say Adam's a stupid bastard, but he isn't. He loves you. If you go to him now, he'll never let you go."

Sue sat back in her chair and peered at Justin, who nodded. She drank more juice and turned her attention back to Brad, her eyes narrowed. She sat in silence until one of the flight status boards caught her eye. She drank the rest of her juice and screwed the lid back on, then picked up her backpack as she stood. "Tell Tom I'll text him later." Sue settled her bag on her shoulders.

Justin's eyes lit. "You're going?"

She moved toward the walkway. "On the next fucking flight."

Justin fist pumped. "Yeah!"

Brad grinned and sipped his coffee.

Sue doubled back and tugged on a strand of his hair. "Thank you." Sue smiled at him, then hauled ass to the nearest reservations desk with an agent.

CHAPTER 51

Boston, MA

Sue rinsed her face and studied herself in the mirror as she dried off. After alternating coffee and sports drinks between Atlanta and Boston, her hangover was mostly gone, but she looked like she hadn't slept in days. She suspected she smelled like booze but hoped the fresh layer of deodorant helped mask it. She spread the contents of her backpack on the bathroom counter until she found blush and concealer. She put on the makeup, swiped on lip balm, and repacked her bag. She wanted to shower, but she'd waited long enough to see Adam. She left the restroom and made a beeline for his office, ignoring the curious glances she got from the open work area.

"Hey, Lauren!" Sue gave Adam's assistant a bright smile.

"Hi!" Lauren returned her smile. "I have you in Ann Arbor today."

"I know, and I know he's in a meeting right now. I want to surprise him."

Lauren's smile warmed. "He'll love it. Let me get him."

Sue held up a hand. "Please don't. I can wait. I kind of have this fantasy of reliving the last time he found me in his office." It was a handy excuse, but in truth she was afraid he didn't want to see her or would send her away.

"It might be a while. This meeting is scheduled for another ninety minutes."

"That's fine. I can catch up on email." Sue shifted her pack on her shoulder, hoping she wouldn't have to do more to convince Lauren to let her have her way.

Lauren pursed her lips. "You sure?"

"Yeah."

Lauren gestured toward Adam's office. "Make yourself comfortable. Can I get you anything?"

"No, thanks." Sue smiled and darted into Adam's office before Lauren noticed her caffeine and nerve-induced jitters. She considered the couch or one of the guest chairs, but decided she wanted to see him coming down the hall toward her. She settled in at his desk, took out her laptop, and plowed through her emails.

Ninety minutes later she'd answered all her messages and scheduled a few meetings with Bloody Maggots, Noble Perversion, and Axel. With work in a good place and a flight booked for her closing in Hagerstown, Sue packed up her stuff and waited. Work had settled her mind, though her leg still shook under the desk. Twenty minutes went by before her nerves threatened to overwhelm her. She picked up a sports paper and read it cover to cover. Every letter to the editor, every article, every photo caption, and ad.

Her stomach rumbled, finally ready for food after all the re-hydrating she'd done. Sue checked her watch, thinking a walk might settle her again, but despite only having eaten in-flight snacks, she wasn't willing to leave without Adam. Robin had told her to talk to Adam "soon." It had already been more than a day since he gave her the advice. Even though she'd texted Adam a few times, their schedules had never meshed before she got on the long international flight to come home. Now the need to talk burned in her. Maybe she should have Lauren summon him after all? She slumped in the chair and spun it around to take in the view from the floor-to-ceiling windows behind Adam's desk while she decided on her next move.

■——————————————————————————■

"Sue."

She woke with a start and immediately covered her mouth, worried she'd been drooling. Adam knelt in front of her, his hands on her thighs.

She wiped at her mouth, then smiled. "Hi."

Adam squeezed her legs. "Hi. I didn't mean to scare you."

"You didn't scare me." Sue leaned forward and gave him a small kiss. "I missed you."

Adam pulled her closer to him. "I missed you, too. How long have you been here? Lauren should've gotten me."

Sue kneaded his shoulders. "I asked her not to." She rubbed her hands down his biceps and squeezed, trying not to show her nerves. "I sold my house. I'm sorry I didn't tell you sooner."

"When did you sell it?"

"Two days ago. Maybe three." Sue squinted. "My time zones are still off."

"Congratulations!" He sounded enthusiastic, but his expression held none of the emotion.

Sue shook her head. "I didn't mean to sell it. I mean, I would've told you before I listed it."

Adam tilted his head but didn't speak.

"I wasn't trying to be sneaky. I was talking with a realtor about options. She called me with an offer. We didn't even have a listing contract in place before she had an offer."

"That's a motivated buyer."

"Yeah. But it's not why I came here."

"You never need a reason to come here." Adam stood and pulled Sue into an embrace.

"But I have one." Sue pushed Adam back enough to look at him. "I made you doubt my love for you. I was cruel and wrong. I'm sorry."

"You weren't cruel," Adam whispered.

"I was. I was scared and let it make me so stupid. I told my parents everything. If you're up for it, they want us to go to Connecticut over the weekend so Dad can torture you. You can meet Tom's parents, too. It'll be awkward but my mom is a fantastic cook."

Adam laughed. "I'd like that."

"I didn't plan to sell the townhouse."

"I know."

"And I didn't sell it because I need the money."

"Why did you?"

"I don't need it anymore." Sue paced behind Adam's desk, shaking out her body as she walked. She jumped from one thing to another, but there was so much she needed him to know. "The realtor Emily recommended knows everyone from Dover to Myrtle Beach. As soon as I gave her my address, she had a list of options for leases, re-zoning, it was intense. She called me in the middle of an interview with an offer."

Adam leaned against the desk. "Is it a good offer?"

"It's enough to give me a small nest egg." Sue stopped pacing in front of Adam. "We close next week."

"That's fast."

"Yeah, but I'm good with it. All I have to do is show up, sign the papers, and walk away with some money." She'd cried herself to sleep over this sale. Not because it was happening, but because she was afraid once she told Adam about it, she'd be without him, too.

"That'll be fun."

Sue smiled, nervous about her next step. "Maybe. Tom offered me his spare room. And Robin wants me to move in with him in LA. Amy said I can take over her guest house."

"Lot of options." Adam hugged her. "LA could be a good city for you."

"I don't want to be on the West Coast right now."

"Where do you want to be?" Adam whispered against her temple.

Sue tightened her grip around him. "Here."

"In Boston?"

Sue squeezed him again. "*Here.*"

Adam untangled himself from her and stepped away, running a hand through his hair.

Sue slumped into his chair and rubbed her eyes, defeated. She'd waited too long; she'd pushed him away, and now he was pushing her away, too.

Adam dropped his sling bag on the desk and rifled through it. He gave her a slim card. "This is for the garage. I keep mine in my car, but you might want to keep it in your purse." He held up a keyring and separated the keys. "This one is for the mail. This one's the apartment." He pointed a small fob at her. "This is for the office. The main door and the elevator." The whole keyring dangled from a larger fob. He put it in her palm. "This is for my car."

"What?" Sue closed her fingers around the keys.

"Do you need me to go over them again?"

She shook her head.

"Good. We're moving the TV in the bedroom to the wall on your side of the bed. Your El Jaleo print is going on the wall in front of the bed. That wall needs a big print."

Sue tilted her head. "You want my art in your bedroom?"

Adam yanked Sue out of the chair and pulled her close. "No. I want *you* and your art in *our* bedroom."

Sue's stomach flipped as she hugged him. "I want a life with you, Adam."

"Jesus," Adam said on a breath. "That ranks right up there with 'I love you.'"

"I do love you. More than anyone."

Adam squeezed her tighter against him. "Thank you," he whispered.

"All those things you said you'd do for me?"

"Yeah?"

"Do them *with* me."

"Partners in crime."

Sue grinned and played with the hair at the back of his neck. "Come with me to the closing next week."

"We'll get your stuff while we're there."

Sue kissed him. "And Darryl's wedding in Brazil."

"Done." Adam stroked a hand up her back.

"And all those football games you were talking about in September."

Adam raised an eyebrow. "Yeah?"

Sue nodded. "Where you go, I go."

He took her mouth with his and groaned.

"These keys were in the bag when I took the flight from Manchester." Sue whispered.

"I put them together after you charmed the hell out of Gram."

Sue gave a contented sigh. "I never should've said no to you in Milan."

Adam kissed her again. "I didn't hear no. I heard not yet."

"Such a smart man." Sue curled a leg around him when she kissed him.

Adam grabbed her ass, then stopped, moving his hands back to her waist. "Sorry, you don't like making out in front of all the windows."

"It's your office. You can do what you want."

Adam laughed. "Yeah, I can." He kissed her again.

"Wanna go home?"
"Hell yes."

The End

Thank you for reading. I hope you enjoyed Sue and Adam's story.

ACKNOWLEDGEMENTS

Just like the book before it, *Have Love Will Travel*, had a tsunami of people behind it, encouraging me. If I forgot anyone in these acknowledgements, I am deeply sorry. I promise it is unintentional.

They say you write with the door closed and edit with the door open. If it hadn't been for my amazing writing and critique partners, especially the Canton Writing Circle and the Lowcountry Romance Writers, I might never have gotten the door open more than a crack. My beta readers give me so much of their time and care and have made these books better. Alyssa, Brigid, Colleen and Sita, thank you so much, your insights are invaluable to me.

Patricia and Angela, I really need to get you two in a room together. Your tough love and senses of humor pulled me through my own frustrations. Not only did you guys make me a better writer, you made the shape of this story better. I promise to delete double takes and not to write so many puke scenes in the future.

Suzanna, your cover designs are always incredible, as are you for dealing with me and my rambling emails when I'm not entirely sure about what I want. You get me and I appreciate that more than I can express.

The Shark Sprinters and the Sharks Writing All the Words are still my stealth cheerleaders. I love hanging out in our groups and spreading the positive vibes I find in there. You guys are amazing.

I have the world's greatest ride or die. First: Matthew, Amy, and Mandy who would bail me out, no questions asked and maybe even bring some chocolate, and hot guys/booze along for the ride. Darren and Sarah – Lightyear Forever! You guys propped me up when my energy was flagging toward the end. Mom, Dad and my sibs, honestly, sorry for all the cursing, but you shouldn't be surprised. And thank you for the encouragement. Crawfedos still rule.

My husband let me run band names by him, put up with me mumbling passages of the book to myself, and let me sneak away whenever I said I needed to, to make this all happen. He's a trooper and after all these years he still laughs at (most of) my jokes. Thanks, babe. I love you.

ABOUT THE AUTHOR

ELAINE REED

Elaine lives in South Carolina's Low Country. When she isn't writing, she can be found exploring Charleston, taking in live music and searching for shark teeth on the beach with her family.

www.elaine-writes.com

Sign up for her newsletter: https://www.elaine-writes.com/newsletter/

Instagram https://www.instagram.com/writeelaine/

If this book made you feel something, whether love or hate, please consider leaving a review on Amazon, Goodreads, your blog, or other book site. Share your thoughts on Facebook and Twitter. If you believe the book has value and is worth sharing, would you take a few seconds to let your friends know about it? If it they like it, they'll be grateful to you. As will I.

ALSO BY ELAINE REED

The Girl U Want

Sue Douglas has no time for men. At least not any more men. She scored her dream job as a publicist for an up-and-coming rock band, but they're putting her through her paces:

The bass player despises her.

The lead singer lusts for her.

The band manager dumped a career-ending secret on her.

The band's record company is determined to see her fail.

And if she even stumbles, she could lose everything.

In the middle of it all, she meets *the* man. The one she wants in her schedule. He sees the mayhem of her life but refuses to let her go. He says he'll only take her spare time, but there's no time on a tour that will make or break her as a publicist.

Have Love Will Travel

Sue Douglas has no time for crap. At least not any more crap. She's trying to turn her dream job as a publicist into her dream career, but it's more complicated than it looks:

Her bass player attracts trouble like it's his job.

Her lead singer is too flirty.

Their record company is throwing shade her way.

But then, there's Adam.

Through it all, he's there. Willing to take whatever pieces of time she can give him. But his love softens her, and in her world where power is access, softness is a weakness. Now Sue has one very big puzzle to solve: how to cherish the soft without losing all she's worked for.

Take a Chance on Me

This win-win is starting to feel like a lose-lose.

For the past two years, Justin Arnold has been on tour with his band, Words Fail Me.

Vaughn Williams is the woman Justin sees whenever he's home. She'd like to say that she hasn't thought about him once while he was gone, but that would be a lie.

They're only supposed to be friends with benefits. Except now that Justin's sticking around to finish his next album, he's becoming a regular fixture in her life.

That used to work for Vaughn.

But she's not sure her heart can take it. Not when she knows that he'll go on tour soon and leave her behind. Again.

She should tell him she can't do this anymore, but she's never been able to tell him no.

When Justin's offered the lead role on a reality dating show, Vaughn is sure it'll be a win-win for them. He'll get to have his fun and she'll get to try to move on.

No one was supposed to get hurt.

But the more they're apart, the more Vaughn can't help but feel that she's made a terrible mistake.

Even though nothing has changed, Vaughn wonders whether not seeing Justin for a few months is better than never having him again.

Novellas

Champagne Supernova

Autumn Powell believes the right pair of shoes can change her life, and she's determined to start the New Year on the right foot. Unfortunately, the pair she's wearing isn't hers.

Chester Quartermain has a great eye for detail, and the woman before him is a masterpiece. Too bad she's wearing his stolen shoe design.

Getting her out of them might have to be his New Year's Resolution.

Caught Up in You

Emily Davis is about to have her first face-to-face meeting with the man she's been video chatting with for four years. He's a rockstar, an artist, a fantasy who lives rent-free in Emily's head. And he's her roommate's best friend.She's not sure whether she'll jump on him the moment she sees him or run away. Either way, she's been pining too long. She's ready to see whether their chemistry on the phone can translate to real life.

A Drummer Boy for Christmas

What would you do if a gorgeous man with a huge tray of free food from the best Chinese restaurant in town walked into your bar?

Vaughn Williams starts by buying him a drink. She wants more excuses to talk to him, but it's Christmas night and her family's bar has become a refuge for the community.

Justin seeks her out in quiet moments. He's charming and *hot* with a clear interest in her. One Vaughn's tempted to pursue even though she's busy slinging drinks and keeping her uncle from giving away all the top shelf liquor.

Kegs need to be changed, and the freezer door is stuck. Vaughn can't spare a bartender to help her, but maybe Justin can give her a hand or two.

www.ingramcontent.com/pod-product-compliance
Lightning Source LLC
Chambersburg PA
CBHW021219060726
47590CB00005B/1556